CHAIN OF
COMMAND

D0681606

Baen Books by Frank Chadwick

How Dark the World Becomes
Come the Revolution
The Forever Engine
Chain of Command

★ CHAIN OF ★ COMMAND

★★★

FRANK CHADWICK

CHAIN OF COMMAND

A Baen Books Original

Baen Publishing Enterprises
P.O. Box 1403
Riverdale, NY 10471
www.baen.com

ISBN: 978-1-4814-8297-4

Cover art by Kurt Miller

First Baen printing, October 2017

Distributed by Simon & Schuster
1230 Avenue of the Americas
New York, NY 10020

Printed in the United States of America

10 9 8 7 6 5 4 3 2 1

For Beth

ACKNOWLEDGEMENTS

Thanks first of all to my many friends and colleagues who read the work and offered both insightful criticism and generous support, especially Nancy Blake, Rich Bliss, Linda Coleman, Craig Cutbirth, Tom Harris, Bev Herzog, Glenn Kidd, Jim Nevling, Bart Palamaro, and of course Jake and Beth Strangeway. I remain enormously indebted to my three writing/critique groups. How essential they are to my creative process was particularly brought home by this project. The book which emerged from rewriting after their critiques and always thoughtful suggestions is immeasurably superior to the earlier version. I know, a lot of folks say that, but it's really true here. Without meaning to slight anyone else, I want to single out Elaine Palencia and John Palen who consistently see what I miss and seem to know where I want to (or ought to) take a character before I do.

Above all, I am most indebted to Tony Daniels and Toni Weisskopf at Baen Books who put their collective editorial finger on exactly what was wrong with the original manuscript of this book. That insight not only produced a superior book, it made me rethink how I was writing.

A word about science: aside from the interstellar jump drive itself, most of the differences between our universe and the fictional one of Stars and Hard Vacuum stem from engineering advances, not breakthroughs in theoretical physics. That notwithstanding, this novel at its heart is more space opera than hard science fiction, but I've never felt that authors of space opera needed to check their brains—or their hearts—at the door. Nor should their readers be expected to. In keeping the physics within what I consider the bounds of willing suspension of disbelief, I am indebted to Rich Bliss, Jim Lenz, and Jim Nevling as well as several enormously useful books by Ken Burnside of Ad Astra Games. That said, none of this should be considered an endorsement of the physics of the book by any of them.

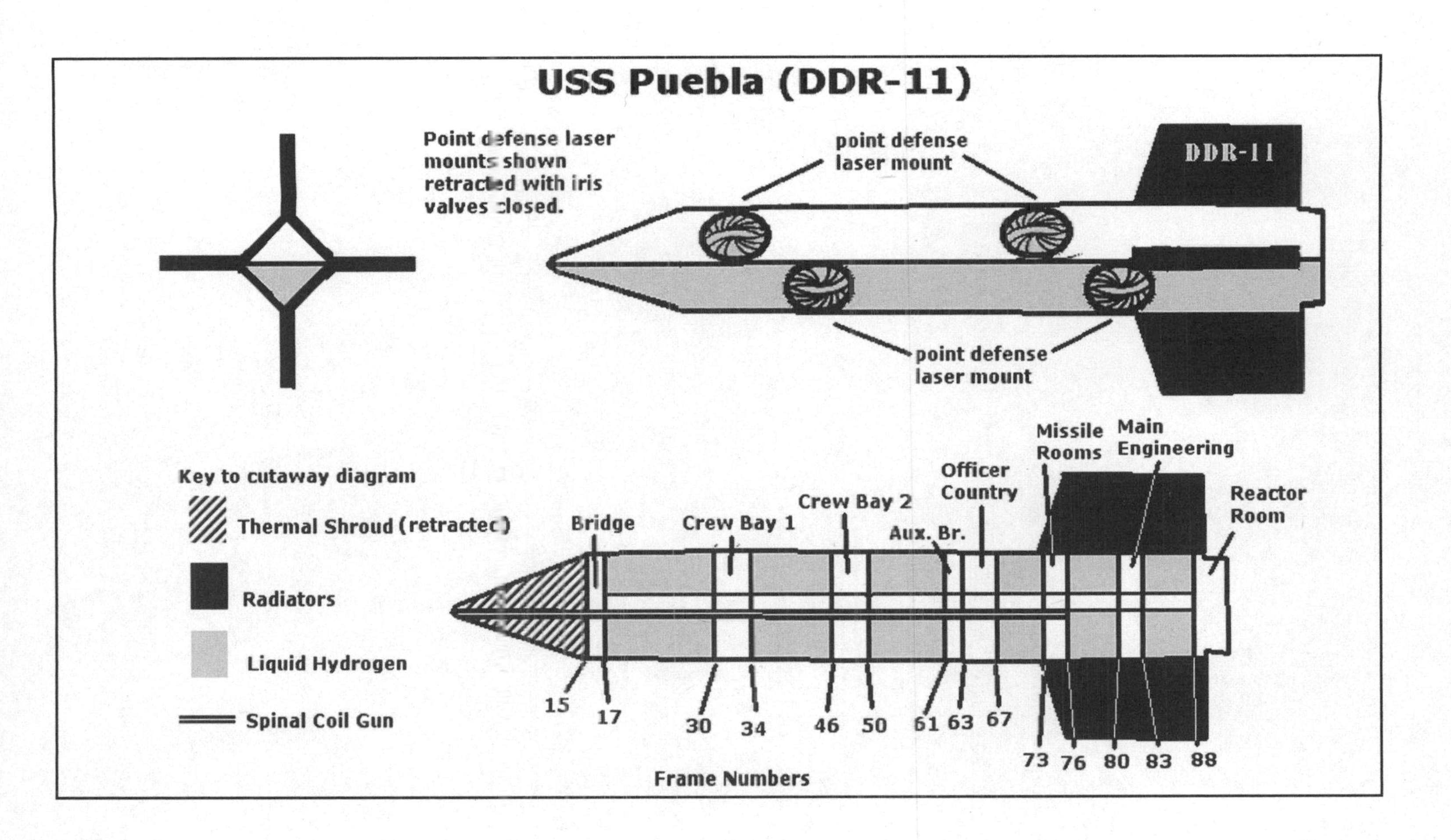
USS Puebla (DDR-11)
Point defense laser mounts shown retracted with iris valves closed.
point defense laser mount
DDR-11
point defense laser mount
Key to cutaway diagram
Thermal Shroud (retracted)
Radiators
Liquid Hydrogen
Spinal Coil Gun
Bridge
Crew Bay 1
Crew Bay 2
Aux. Br.
Officer Country
Missile Rooms
Main Engineering
Reactor Room
15
17
30
34
46
50
61
63
67
73
76
80
83
88
Frame Numbers

CHAIN OF
COMMAND

But war's a game which, were their subjects wise,
kings would not play at. Nations would do well
T'extort their truncheons from the puny hands
Of heroes, whose infirm and baby minds
Are gratified with mischief, and who spoil,
Because men suffer it, their toy the world.

William Cowper, *The Task*, 1785

CHAPTER ONE

15 November 2133

(thirty-six days from K'tok orbit)

Seventeen days before the course of sentient history changed irrevocably, Lieutenant Sam Bitka stood at attention in the office of Lieutenant Commander Delmar Huhn, executive officer and second-in-command of the destroyer USS *Puebla.*

"Why are you being so *stupid*?" Huhn demanded.

Sam thought about that. It wasn't a bad question; it just didn't go far enough.

Tension had been growing between Human and Varoki colonists on the planet K'tok, so the US Navy's Second Destroyer Squadron—including Sam and his shipmates—had been sent "as a precaution." When they emerged from jump space earlier that day, the Varoki heavy cruisers in the K'tok system had immediately gone into low-emission mode. Now everyone found themselves trembling on the brink of what might turn into the first all-out interstellar war in the history of all six known sentient species.

And the only thing Lieutenant Commander Huhn had on his mind was a sexual encounter between two petty officers in Sam's tactical department. Why was *everyone* being so stupid? But Sam didn't say that.

"Um, stupid, sir?"

"You call this *disciplining* these two? Why, it's not even a slap on the wrist."

"I informed petty officers Menzies and Delacroix that their

fraternization constituted an infraction of Navy regulations concerning conduct injurious to order. Any repetition would result in more serious disciplinary action which would show in their permanent records. As per your orders, I altered their watch and duty assignments so they would neither work together nor have significant overlapping off-duty time."

"And what'd they say to that?"

"That they intend to marry upon completion of the deployment, sir."

Huhn's mouth twisted at that and he looked as if he wanted to spit. "Marry! Navy won't let a married couple ship out together. They'll get different assignments and replace all this enforced intimacy with enforced separation. That's why these shipboard romances never last, that's for damn sure. Did you tell them that?"

"As part of my counseling I acquainted them with the relevant statistics, sir."

"And what'd they tell you?"

"That they were not statistics."

Huhn looked at Sam and softly tapped the Annapolis class ring on his left hand against the surface of his desk, the ring that was a constant reminder of the gulf which separated the academy professionals—like Huhn—from Naval ROTC amateurs—like Sam.

Lieutenant Commander Delmar Huhn was slightly older than Sam, in his mid-thirties, but he looked younger when he smiled and older when he scowled—which was more often the case. Between his height of five-six, spindly arms, and the start of a middle-age paunch, the executive officer was not physically impressive, but he somehow managed an intimidating presence despite that. He shaved his head and, because his sparse eyebrows were a light blond nearly matching his skin tone, he had a pale, hairless look which Sam found vaguely unsettling.

"I can see this doesn't sit well with you, Lieutenant Bitka. Your heart's not in it. What's the problem?"

"No problem, sir."

"Sure there is. I can see plain as the nose on your face."

He leaned back in his desk chair and switched to simply fingering his ring, moving it back and forth with the tip of this thumb. "I know the way we do things in the Navy takes some getting used to, especially for you reservists. They pull you out of nice civilian jobs back home in the United States of North America and stick you out here with a bunch of hard-charging warriors. Let me know what you're thinking. You have permission to speak freely. In fact, that's an order."

As if to emphasize this new familiarity, he smiled—a broad smile as full of small off-white teeth as it was of professed warmth.

In his seven years in the civilian corporate sector Sam had several times been told by superiors to speak freely, but they had never meant it, any more than Lieutenant Commander Huhn meant it now. But this was different. This was the Navy, and an order from a superior officer here carried the weight of law, or at least so Sam told himself.

"Come on, Bitka, spit it out."

Sam's heart beat faster and he took a breath.

"Well, sir . . . I think this is exactly the sort of chicken shit that makes people hate the Navy."

For a moment Huhn froze. Sam expected his superior's face to redden, but instead it lost color—a bad sign. Huhn slowly leaned forward and placed his hands on his desk, palms down and fingers spread.

"Chicken shit? You think maintaining proper order on deployment is *chicken shit*?"

"No, sir. But there are two sexual liaisons going on among commissioned officers of *Puebla's* wardroom, including your protégé Lieutenant Goldjune, and every man and woman on this boat below the rank of ensign knows it."

"How do they know it?" Huhn demanded.

"A destroyer's a small boat, sir. Hard for anything to go on and nobody notice. You want to make a point? Come down hard on the officers. The enlisted personnel will get the message loud and clear."

Huhn slowly stood and leaned forward, the knuckles of his tightly balled fists resting on the desk top.

"Larry Goldjune is one of the most promising young officers I've ever served with. You wouldn't understand this, Mister Bitka, but the Navy's in his blood. His father Jake is a rear admiral in BuShips and his uncle Cedrick is in line to be the next chief of naval operations. If you think I'm going to blemish Larry's career with a reprimand for something like this, you don't know the United States Navy."

Sam was pretty sure he did know the United States Navy, but he did not say that, either.

"Have it your way, sir. But if you make me come down on my enlisted personnel for doing what you're winking at among officers, they will despise us, and they will be absolutely right."

"I-I'm the goddamned executive officer of this boat! You can't *talk* to me like that!"

"Am I to assume then, sir, that your direct order to speak freely has been rescinded?"

Huhn glared at him for several long seconds before shaking his head in disgust.

"Get out of my sight!"

"Aye, aye, sir."

Out in the corridor Sam paused and with trembling hands checked his biomonitor, to see if he was in danger of a stroke, or perhaps a heart attack. To his surprise they registered almost normal. Well, he had only been following orders.

The broad and warmly lit corridor rose up and away from him to either side, and even though he was used to the optical illusion created by the rotating habitat wheel of the carrier USS *Hornet*, today it took on an unpleasant significance. No matter which way he turned, sooner or later he would end up back here. For a moment he felt dizzy, but he knew that was simply the coriolis effect of the habitat wheel's rotation. Its hundred-meter radius was not enough to keep his inner ear from noticing his feet moving slightly faster than his head.

He took the four steps over to the opposite wall and stood at the broad "window." It wasn't a window, of course. It was simply a smart wall keyed to show the view aft.

The carrier USS *Hornet* stretched over half a kilometer astern from the habitat wheels, terminating in the intricate lattice-like crossings and re-crossings of the interstellar jump drive generator, softly glowing and sparkling against the pitch black of deep space. Between the habitat wheels and the engineering spaces aft, a dozen black vessels clung to the carrier's gray hull in three rows, like sticks of dynamite around the torso of a suicide bomber. One of those was his destroyer, USS *Puebla*. He waited until the rotation of the wheel brought it into view. Apart from the blocky low-contrast gray hull number, DDR-11, it was indistinguishable from the others.

Each one a hundred-forty-meter-long dart, the DDRs were austere, angular, and slab-sided to reduce radar reflection, built for battle and little else. The lack of an interstellar jump drive in the destroyers, and the subsequent need for a large ship to carry them from star to star, officially reduced them to the status of "boats," as opposed to starships, but they were dangerous boats.

They weren't large enough to have their own habitat wheels, so in transit the crews lived in *Hornet*. Even with exercise, crews in prolonged zero gee began suffering from bone density loss and muscle atrophy within six months, but more serious were the effects of intracranial hypertension which began showing up in half that time, sometimes less. One thing a century and a half of space travel had made clear: gravity wasn't a luxury.

The sight aft was spectacular and chilling at the same time. Sam found it hard to accept this massive ship and its deadly cargo—so cold and inhuman in appearance—as a work of man. He had stood here and looked often, and had gotten used to this strange mix of emotions, in part because he knew he did not have to make a lasting peace with it. He was a reservist, activated for a three-year hitch due to the current emergency. In a little less than two years all this would just be a strange memory, raw material for stories told at cocktail parties, and even now, looking out at the disturbingly beautiful jump drive and the deadly destroyer riders, he knew he would be unable to recapture this strange unsettled feeling later. He would remember that he had felt such a thing, he would remember the words he had used to describe it to himself, but the actual feeling would elude him.

Sam stood closer to the smart wall to let a squad of twelve Marines in PT gear jog past in formation. Trust the jarheads to be getting ready for a possible fight when everyone else had other things on their minds. As he stood there watching them move away and up the outside of the wheel's curve, the smart posters on the wall chatted quietly to him about post-enlistment education and employment, and about destination resorts for his next liberty which were guaranteed to be romantic, exciting, picturesque, and restful—all somehow at the same time.

"I sure hope you guys are right," he said to the posters,

Several hundred thousand kilometers from where USS *Hornet* and its twelve destroyer riders continued their long approach toward K'tok, the uBakai heavy cruiser KBk Five One Seven coasted behind the cover of its thermal shroud on a converging course. Unlike Humans, no Varoki navy gave its warships names—a practice widely disdained as foolish and sentimental. Ships were simply inanimate pieces of machinery, and to think otherwise was evidence of clouded judgment.

In the cruiser's fleet tactical center—low-ceilinged, crowded, and dimly lit except for the glow of the tactical displays—the access hatch hissed open and Vice-Captain Takaar Nuvaash, Speaker For the Enemy, what the Humans called a *military intelligence officer*, entered his admiral's comparatively spacious office. The admiral continued working, absorbed by the smart display on his desktop. Nuvaash examined him again, searching for some additional clue to the man who carried all their fates in his pocket.

Admiral Tyjaa e-Lapeela was of no more than average height for a Varoki, although a Human would still have to look up at him. His hairless iridescent skin gleamed in the lamplight and his broad, leaf-like ears for the moment rested back against his head, but not tightly so. Part of the skin on the left side of his face was discolored, remnant of a burn he had sustained during the failed military coup a year earlier. Most senior officers associated with the coup—those who had survived—had been retired or imprisoned. Nuvaash did not know how e-Lapeela had avoided a similar fate. As the admiral read from the screen, Nuvaash noticed the tips of his ears tremble slightly in relish.

The admiral nodded to himself as he finished reading the report and looked up at Nuvaash. He reached out his hand, palm up, and curled his fingers—long even for a Varoki—in summons.

"Come closer, Nuvaash. I have read your threat assessment. It is quite thoughtful. The inclusion of recent Human warship traffic near the outer gas giant of their primary is an imaginative gauge of their ability to reinforce their forward fleet elements on short notice."

"Thank you, Admiral. I live to serve."

"Of course, as do I." e-Lapeela leaned back and gestured to the chair across the desk. "Please, sit. I see you have served as a liaison officer to several Human fleets. I once did as well. Did you know I also began my career as a Speaker for the Enemy?"

"Your public service record mentioned that, Admiral."

"And as a conscientious Speaker, you learned what you could about your new fleet commander. I expected nothing less." The admiral fell silent for a moment and shifted slightly in his chair. Nuvaash sensed that the conversational preliminaries were complete.

"Nuvaash, we are about to embark upon an undertaking of enormous danger, but also of historic significance. You understand that. You have read the plan for First Action."

Yes, Nuvaash had read the plan for First Action—a euphemism for the surprise opening shot in the first interstellar war in *Cottohazz* history. What he could not understand was *why?* Why now? Why here at K'tok? Why risk tearing asunder the entire fabric of the *Cottohazz,* the stellar commonwealth which the Varoki had labored so long to assemble and maintain? What could be worth all of that?

The admiral nodded, as if knowing the unspoken question.

"You know our history, but take a moment to consider its grand sweep. Three hundred years ago we Varoki learned the secret of the jump drive and began exploring the stars. Every sentient race we found, we added to our *Cottohazz* as equals. We are not conquerors, Nuvaash. All that we have retained for ourselves is the secret of the jump drive, although we license it to the others. Our laws, and other tangible measures, protect its secret, but within those limitations it is theirs to use."

Nuvaash knew all of that, of course, but he sensed e-Lapeela was laying the groundwork for something else. The 'other tangible measures' he had mentioned were the deadly anti-tamper devices which effectively kept anyone but the manufacturers from examining the interior of the sealed jump drive components, a so-far effective way of preventing reverse-engineering.

"The other four races we contacted have been content with the arrangement," the admiral continued. "The Humans, though . . ." The admiral paused and shook his head. "You know them. They are like children who never grow out of their questioning phase. 'What is this? How does that work? Why can't I see that? Why can't we manufacture this ourselves? Why? Why? *Why?*'"

Nuvaash knew it was so. He had experienced it many times but did not find it as annoying as did the admiral. Still, he nodded in sympathetic agreement.

"But mostly," the admiral continued, "they want to know the secret of the jump drive—our most closely guarded secret, something which only a handful of Varoki even know."

"But others have wanted to know as well, Admiral. We have always prevented it."

"Yes, we always have. The intellectual property covenants make scientific research along those lines already explored economically fruitless, as the Varoki houses which own the core knowledge own any discovery based on it. Every member state agrees to this as a condition of access to the jump drive itself. But the Humans persist.

"When Human research firms began making dangerous progress, Varoki trading houses bought them up and redirected the research, as we have done elsewhere, but the Humans persist. Now there are private Human charitable foundations dedicated to pure scientific research—with no hope of commercial gain. Their curiosity is inexhaustible and relentless."

Nuvaash knew that as well. He had never found it anything but interesting and sometimes admirable. Now he began to understand the potential threat it posed.

"But even if they discover the underlying science, commercially it will still belong to the Varoki trading houses," he said.

"Not if the Humans withdraw from the *Cottohazz*," the admiral answered. "Once they discover the secret on their own, what is to keep them? And if they withdraw, what is to keep the other races with us? The stable and peaceful star-spanning civilization we have built will unravel and the Humans—aggressive, violent, and impulsive—will end up our rivals, and in all likelihood eventually our masters."

Nuvaash felt his skin flush with fear as he listened to the admiral, fear of the future the admiral prophesied but also a more immediate one—fear of where the idea that war was the only road to peace might take them.

"It must not come to that, Nuvaash. It *will* not come to that.

"This war, which starts here in the K'tok system, will not end here. It will end with Human fleets swept from space, Human cities in ruins, and the Human spirit broken forever. But before it can end, it must begin."

An hour later Sam Bitka sat over coffee in *Puebla*'s "away" wardroom in *Hornet's* habitat wheel, with Lieutenant Julia

Washington—"Jules" to her friends—and Lieutenant Moe Rice. Moe, the largest and most heavily muscled member of *Puebla*'s crew, a former offensive lineman from Texas A&M, made Jules's diminutive figure look out of scale next to him. They were his two best friends on *Puebla*, in Jules's case maybe even more than that.

"Oh, Sam," she said. "Commander Huhn can ruin your career. How could you be so *stupid*?"

"Boy, howdy," Moe added.

Sam laughed. "I think it must be a gift."

Jules sipped her coffee, but her green-flecked brown eyes stayed on him. She had good eyes in a good face, clear-featured and softened by her thick curly black hair cut short, but not the buzz cuts popular with a lot of starship crews, something called a pixie cut. Her *café con crema* complexion—classic American hybrid—contrasted sharply with the white of her officer's shipsuit. Moe was much darker, the only black Jewish cowboy Sam had ever known

"He can't hurt my career back at DP," Sam said. "Oh, you mean here. Well, the thing I figured out today is I'm bulletproof. See, I don't really have a Navy career to worry about. Do my job and stay out of prison for two more years and I'm out of here. Nobody back in The World is ever going to read the fine print in my fitness reports."

That *was* something he'd realized. He really was bullet-proof, as least as far as Del Huhn was concerned. Sam had a good career, just starting to turn into a *damned* good career, waiting for him back home. It took him seven years with DP—Dynamic Paradigms, LLC—to work his way up through middle management, but he had just finished the company's Emerging Leaders program, the first step to executive service. Activation of his reserve commission had interrupted that, but only for three years. His corporate mentor had assured him it would look very good on his resume when he came back. It would set him apart. To rise, you needed to stand out from the herd.

"In the meantime," Sam added, "I'm just not going to worry about Del Huhn any more, that's all. Besides, I got him so pissed off at me I think he forgot about Menzies and Delacroix, which is good. Those two he *could* hurt."

"We call that drawing fire," Jules said, "and you know how well that usually works out in the tactical exercises—for the draw-er."

"Bulletproof, remember?"

"Can you reason with him, Moe?" Jules said.

"Reason?" Moe said and shook his head. "I'll tell you what, if stupid ever goes to ninety bucks a barrel, I want the drillin' rights on Sam's head."

"Very funny," Sam said. "I'll tell you something else I figured out today. Jules, I've been riding you guys in the tactical department like a whip-wielding overseer—updating squadron contingency planning and SOPs, running drills, memorizing Varoki naval manuals and ship energy signatures. And now I'm wondering why."

"Because you're *Puebla's* Tac Boss, and it's your job," she answered. "And I think you're right."

Sam shook his head. "I'm just a dumb reservist. Look at the regulars, the Annapolis grads—other than you, I mean. Goldjune's looking for an open slot on the admiral's staff and Captain Rehnquist is getting his resume together to retire into a cushy job with a DC defense lobbying firm."

"Nest featherers," Moe said, his voice heavy with disdain.

Sam shrugged.

"Yeah, there's a lot of that going around. And ever since Jules rebuffed his amorous advances Del Huhn just wants to be Bedcheck Charlie. Every regular officer on this boat *above* the rank of lieutenant junior grade has their head full of everything except getting ready for a war.

"So what do they know that I don't? The odds-on favorite answer is: damned near everything."

"Ain't wrong there," Moe agreed.

Jules sipped her coffee and thought about that for a while before answering.

"So, fewer drills?"

She didn't look happy about the prospect. Sam knew Jules took pride in the 'missile monkeys,' in her weapons division, took pride in their efficiency and professionalism, but also in the sense of *esprit* she'd fostered in them. There wasn't a sharper, more square-away division on *Puebla*, and every one knew it—especially her missile monkeys.

"I got the word right before I talked to Huhn: we decouple from *Hornet* in three days. Our destroyer division's taking point, right out front, the 'position of honor,' somebody called it."

Moe snorted at that but Jules straightened slightly in her chair and her eyes brightened.

"So, yeah, drills are cancelled until we're separated. Between now and then we'll have our hands full just getting the crew moved over and settled in, and making sure all the systems are nominal. Tactical department's got a nice edge and we'll start running cold drills out there to keep it, once we're on station. But I'll tell you something, near as I can tell I'm the only department head taking this whole imminent war thing seriously. I guess that makes me either the smartest guy in the Navy or the dumbest."

"Pretty sure I know the answer to that one," Moe said.

Jules glanced at Moe and then back at Sam, and she smiled, showing even white teeth with one crooked incisor which he suddenly and inexplicably found very sexy.

CHAPTER TWO

2 December 2133
(seventeen days later) ***(nineteen days from K'tok orbit)***

Later, Sam would decide it had been a mistake to accelerate, but later still he would realize the captain had made the best call he could based on what he knew at the time. Captains sometimes just don't know enough to know what the right call is, but they have to make one anyway.

But that all came later.

Sam woke to bedlam—harsh, repetitive, mechanical bleating, deafeningly loud, which made no sense and nearly drowned out the voice trying to be heard. His body responded before his mind did, hands tearing open the zero-gee restraints on his sleeping cubby, feet kicking free first. His right arm became tangled in the restraint netting as his brain separated the sounds and made sense of them: the regular gongs of the call to general quarters, the whooping siren of the hull breach alarm, and the klaxon warning of imminent acceleration. He had never heard all three at the same time.

"General Quarters. General Quarters. All hands to battle stations," the calm but insistent recorded female voice said over the boat's intercom. "Hull breach. Hull breach. All hands rig for low pressure. Warning. Warning. All hands prepare for acceleration. General Quarters. General Quarters," the voice continued in its synthetic loop.

Suddenly there was gravity, enough to turn the rear wall of the stateroom into floor and drop Sam's feet against it. That would be the first pair of MPD thrusters. He untangled his right arm as the second and third pairs kicked in, upping the gravity to a half gee.

He yanked the helmet from the locker beside his sleeping cubby, now a narrow bunk bay set into the wall and parallel to the deck, and he sealed the collar of the white shipsuit—short for ship environment suit—he'd slept in. He prepared to catch himself when the acceleration stopped, but it didn't, so he pulled open the stateroom hatch and sprinted down the trunk corridor to the hatch to the boat's spine and the access tube leading forward. "Sprinted" was a misnomer; he used the low-gravity fast shuffle, the only way to cover ground quickly at a half gee without his head slamming into the overhead. He ducked past half a dozen crew on their way to their own battle stations. The acceleration cut out as he approached one of the main bulkheads and he sailed the rest of the way, colliding with two ratings and sliding past them.

"Mr. Bitka!" one of them called out. "What's up?"

"Get to your battle station, Cummings. Your section leader will tell you."

If he knew, Sam thought. He hadn't kept exact count but he guessed the acceleration burn had lasted at least forty seconds, perhaps more, and the thought made him sweat. At full thrust the *Puebla's* low-signature MPD thrusters had less than two minutes worth of juice in the energy storage system. Whatever was going on, it was bad. The General Quarters and Hull Breach alarms continued to sound but at least the acceleration klaxon had fallen silent. With his free hand he snagged the handhold above the bulkhead hatch as he nearly collided with it. The sudden stop at an awkward angle wrenched his back but he launched himself through the hatch, into the spinal transit tube, and forward toward the bridge.

The tube itself was square and three meters across, but was also interrupted by half-bulkheads jutting out from the sides, closing off the port half or starboard half of the tube, alternating back and forth every three meters for the length of the boat. It made travel through the tube tedious in zero gee, but it also kept the tube from becoming a hundred-meter-deep shaft of death when the boat accelerated.

Within twenty or thirty meters he encountered a mass of men and women, mostly in blue enlisted personnel shipsuits but with a couple in the khaki of chief petty officers.

"Make way," Sam called.

The crew closest to him looked back, saw his white shipsuit, and one of them shouted, "Officer. Make way!"

Each half-bulkhead also included an extendable hatch which could completely close the shaft, sealing it in the event of a hull breach. Sam moved forward and several hands helped pull him to the extended and sealed bulkhead hatch, with flashing red lights around its perimeter: low atmospheric pressure on the other side. As he watched the lights changed to solid red: vacuum.

Surgically embedded commlinks included a limited visual menu controlled with eye pressure. Sam squinted up the boat's directory and pinged Damage Control.

Damage Control. Go, a harassed-sounding female voice answered inside his head.

"Lieutenant Bitka aft of frame fifty-five with a sealed hatch and a vacuum warning forward," he reported.

Wait one, she said and for a few seconds the connection went mute. Then the brusque voice returned. *A-gang on the way. Do not open the hatch until they arrive. Acknowledge.*

"Bitka acknowledged," he answered and cut the connection. His commlink vibrated softly almost at once. He opened the command channel and the captain's voice filled his head.

Mister Bitka, this is Captain Rehnquist. I understand there's a block at frame fifty-five.

"Yes sir. I'm here with about a dozen other crew trying to get forward to our primary battle stations."

Understood. We have maneuvering watch personnel here to cover the bridge stations, and Lieutenant Washington will ride the TAC One chair. Send the crew aft to their secondary stations. You go to the auxiliary bridge and help Lieutenant Commander Huhn.

"Aye, aye, sir."

So Jules would ride the TAC One chair in the bridge. Whatever was happening, she could handle it as well as Sam could. He passed the captain's order on to the nearby crew and made his own way aft to the auxiliary bridge.

Puebla's auxiliary bridge was only half-manned by the time Sam got there. It was a smaller, cramped version of the main bridge. A smart wall comprised the forward bulkhead, able to display any combination of sensor and instrument readings. The nine crew stations were built into the bulkhead three meters back.

The dorsal row consisted of the TAC One chair to the right, Communications to the left, and the command chair in the center, with Huhn buckling himself in. The broader second tier consisted of two more TAC chairs on the right with Petty Officer Third Elise Delacroix at Tactical Three, the hatch giving access to the central communication trunk in the center, and the two maneuvering station chairs on the left, with Ensign Barb Lee at the helm. The bottom row, usually called "the pits," held another empty Tac chair to the right side of the access trunk tunnel and engineering petty officer second Rachel Karlstein at boat systems station to the left.

"What are you doing here, Bitka?" Huhn snapped.

"Captain's orders, sir. Blockage at frame fifty-five, so people are reshuffling their stations. Jules is sitting TAC One up front." Sam pulled the folding workstation over his midsection and locked it in place after strapping himself into the chair. He plugged the life support umbilical from his shipsuit into the work station socket, slid the helmet cover down over his face, and checked to make sure his suit was sealed and had positive air flow, in case they lost pressure in this compartment as well. All his internal system telltales showed green and he slid his helmet cover back up.

"Damage report," Huhn demanded, now ignoring Sam.

"Umm . . . multiple hull breaches forward and amidships," Karlstein answered, her eyes flickering across the different data feeds and flashing red indicator lights at her workstation. "We've lost atmosphere on decks one, four, five, and nine, as well as parts of number one crew bay. All of the compromised spaces are sealed and pumped down to vacuum. No casualties reported yet. We're losing hydrogen from tanks eleven, twelve and fourteen through seventeen, and have some O2 contamination, but it's under control."

"How bad's the hydrogen loss?" Huhn asked.

"Not critical. Cumulative loss rate looks like about twenty liters per minute and dropping," she said. "Automatic self-sealing is working. The thermal shroud is compromised as well."

"Christ, we're a sitting duck without that shroud!" Huhn said. "Bitka, where are your other people?"

Sam looked up from his operations display, which was blank except for the faint thermal signatures of the other eleven destroyers in the squadron and the one larger signature of USS *Hornet*, the squadron carrier.

"There's Ramirez," he said, as Petty Officer Second Ron Ramirez glided through the hatch and toward Tactical Four. Neither of the two weapons specialists had shown up yet. Sam punched the manning roster up on his display.

"Sir, Smith and Chief Patel are probably coming from the forward crew bay and if it's sealed they'll have to cycle through the lock," Sam answered. "Ramirez, we don't have any sensors active so move weaponry to your board for now. Guns up. Delacroix can handle the passive sensors,

"Aye, aye, sir. Guns up."

"Sir, do we know what hit us?" Sam asked Huhn.

Huhn didn't answer for a moment, probably listening on his embedded commlink to the bridge command channel. Then he shook his head. "Negative. No energy spike, no radiation, no thermal plume anywhere nearby. Just impact shock, holes, and interior spalling, so something small and solid—a bunch of somethings."

Sam scanned back through the recorded integrated operational displays to a minute before the impact and saw nothing.

Petty Officer First Kramer, their communications specialist, glided through the hatch and toward her station. She looked shaken.

"Where the hell you been?" Huhn barked.

"Sorry, sir. We lost pressure. I had to wait a cycle to get through the crew bay airlock."

"Didn't you tell them you needed to get to a critical battle station?"

"The casualties had priority, sir."

"Casualties? *What* casualties? I thought you said there weren't any, Karlberg," Huhn said, his voice angrier.

"It's Karlstein , sir," she answered, "and none reported so far."

Huhn turned back to his own display. "What the hell's the medtech doing?"

Probably tending the wounded, Sam thought. Of course, anyone admitted to sick bay would be scanned into the system already, but until the medtech made an assessment there wouldn't be a report.

Nobody on board *Puebla* had ever been under fire in a space battle before, including the captain and exec, but Sam had still expected to look to the regular officers as models of how he should behave. Sam wasn't sure Huhn was giving all that good an example so far.

"One KIA," Karlstein said, her voice flat. Sam's vision became more focused, the colors on his monitors a little more vivid, and for a moment he tasted metal.

Puebla's complement was only fourteen officers and eighty-one enlisted personnel. Now one of them was *dead*? Which one? After five months he knew all of them by sight, all but a few in the engineering department by name. He shook his head. He'd find out later; for now he had to focus on the job.

Unbidden, an image of Jules came to him. At least the bridge was okay. He'd have liked to say something to her, although he couldn't think what he'd actually say if he had the chance. "Hey, you okay?" That sounded stupid even to him.

She'd be doing fine. Since he met her she'd been eager to prove herself, even more so once her promotion from ensign to lieutenant junior grade came through six weeks earlier. Sam had a more cautious approach to demanding situations, not that that mattered now; whatever sort of trouble this was, it had found them.

The boat shuddered and the feed indicator on Sam's tactical display flickered from "slave" to "direct."

"Multiple hits forward!" Karlstein called out, her voice rising in excitement. "Deck two now depressurizing. Hydrogen loss rate up to fifty-four—no, *sixty-one* liters per minute."

"Sir, I've lost the bridge feed on my ops display," Sam said. "I've still got a feed but it's direct from the sensors now and updated locally."

"Same here, sir," Ensign Lee reported from the Maneuvering One station, followed by a chorus from the others.

"Yeah, I lost the commlink to the command channel," Huhn said. "Kramer, get those internals back up."

"Sir?" Kramer asked.

"I'm on it, sir," Karlstein said before Huhn had a chance to answer.

Petty Officer Delacroix in the Tactical Two seat below Sam turned her head back and raised her dark eyebrows. Sam frowned at her and shook his head, which drove the petty officer's attention back to her screens, but her unasked question was obvious. What was Huhn thinking? Kramer's station was for boat-to-external communications and vice versa. All the internals ran through Karlstein 's Boat Systems board. The exec knew that.

Sam put that out of his mind. His job was the tactical situation, and right now it was out of their control and getting worse. They had to do something to regain some initiative, and quickly.

"Sir, something's hitting us and I still got nothing on thermals or HRVS optics," Sam said. "I want to go active with radar."

"*Active?* Are you *insane?* Everyone in five hundred light seconds will see us."

"I think they already know we're here. This feels like those pellet cluster things the uBakai were supposedly deploying. Intel called it 'buckshot.' You remember the briefing on them? If the launch vessel isn't close enough to pick up, we should at least be able to detect incoming pellets."

"Permission denied, and it's the captain's call anyway. Karlstein , any luck on the command channel?"

"Negative, sir. Looks like whatever hit up there cut the data and comm feeds. I've alerted Engineering and they have a damage-control party headed there now."

It might have cut the hard feeds, Sam thought, *but everyone's embedded commlinks up there should still be working. Why weren't they?*

"*Cha-cha* has gone active with a drone!" Delacroix reported from the Tactical Three seat beside him, and Sam saw it on his own screen as well. USS *Oaxaca*, the command vessel for their four-boat destroyer division, nicknamed *Cha-cha*, had just launched a sensor drone and turned on its active radar.

"Multiple radar echoes," Delacroix continued, "small projectiles incoming, bearing zero degrees relative. Range nine thousand kilometers and closing fast. *Very* fast."

The projectiles were coming on the exact opposite heading. All the captain's burn had accomplished was to add about two hundred meters per second to their collision velocity. Sam checked the calculated closing rate: 97,000 kilometers per hour. *Jesus Christ, that was twenty-seven kilometers a second!* They'd better get out of the way quick. He set a course intersect timer.

"Three hundred thirty seconds to impact," he said.

Ensign Lee at Maneuvering One began working the current and

projected courses. "Best evasion track is ninety degrees relative and flat. Permission to align the boat for burn."

"Negative! It's the captain's call," Huhn answered.

Ensign Lee, the only reservist line officer other than Sam, turned and looked at Huhn and then at Sam, her eyes questioning. Her face was round and fine-featured, chin recessed, mouth small, eyes always open wide, and her nose was incongruously large and wedge-shaped, which gave her the look of a slightly startled bird, even more so just then. She was right, though. Sam was sitting TAC One. It was his job to speak up.

"Sir, you're in command until we've got comms to the bridge. We need to get the hell out of that cloud's way."

"Kramer, get me the division commander," Huhn said. That would be Captain Bonaventure aboard USS *Oaxaca*.

"Incoming text from *Cha-Cha* now, sir," Kramer answered from the Comm Station "Message reads: All red stingers, evade. Seventy-eight degrees relative, angle on the bow ninety, forty-second MPD full burn. Expedite. Signed Red Stinger Six Actual. End message."

"Aligning the boat," Ensign Lee said immediately, punching the acceleration warning klaxon. Huhn visibly started in his command station as it sounded. Sam saw him open his mouth to speak but then hesitate and close it again. For just a moment Sam was sure he had been about to order Lee to belay the alignment. Then Sam felt the sideways acceleration as Lee turned the boat's orientation with the attitude control thrusters. After a dozen or more seconds he felt the acceleration switch direction, begin slowing them to the new orientation. Sam played with the range adjustment and resolution on his tactical display just to keep his hands busy, waiting for the boat to finally settle on its new track, feeling the precious seconds bleed away.

"Boat aligned," Lee finally announced. "Full burn."

Again Sam noticed she didn't ask for permission. He felt himself pushed back into his acceleration rig from the first thruster pair, then rapidly climbing to a half gee once all six thrusters kicked in, roaring out 8,500 tons of thrust for forty seconds.

"Two hundred five seconds to impact," Sam said when the thrusters fell silent and they were weightless again. A plot of the course change due to the burn showed they'd have displaced forty kilometers laterally from their former position by the time the cloud got to them. Forty kilometers wasn't much in deep space, where they usually measured distance in light seconds, each of which was about three hundred thousand kilometers.

If the intel briefing had been right, the pellets in the cloud were small, maybe not much bigger than sand, and the search radar couldn't track individual particles that size, just the collective reflection of a whole bunch of them. That made it hard to tell how wide the cloud was and exactly how far they were from its leading edge. The shipboard tactical system had made some assumptions about likely dispersion and had predicted they'd avoid the likely danger zone, but assumptions weren't facts.

How had a cloud that small, relatively speaking—actually three of them in succession—happened to hit them in all this big black vacuum, and on an exact reciprocal course? Whoever lived through this had better give that some hard thought.

"One hundred sixty seconds to impact."

They sat in silence, feeling the burden of time's glacial passage, waiting to empirically discover their fates. As they did so, Chief Petty Officer Abhay Patel glided through the hatch and wordlessly strapped into the Tactical Two chair. Sam nodded to him.

Maybe they should have burned longer, but for *Puebla* that would have meant emptying their energy storage system. They'd have had to use the direct fusion thruster to get back on course. Everyone in the star system would see that. Maybe everyone already knew where they were. Maybe they all should have just used the direct fusion thrusters and poured on two gees of acceleration for the full two minutes they had until impact. Maybe.

One thing occurred to Sam: if the pellet cloud hit them now, it would hit them broadside, and that would do a lot more damage. Huhn didn't look as if he was thinking things through very well, and it was Sam's job as Tac One to remind him.

"Commander Huhn, I recommend we reorient the boat nose-on to the angle of attack. The forward micrometeor shield will give us some protection."

Huhn jerked a bit in his acceleration rig and looked at Sam, eyes wide.

"Sir, shall I order Ensign Lee to reorient the boat?" Sam asked.

Huhn stared at him blankly. His eyes blinked.

"Yes, sir," Sam said. "Ensign Lee, reorient the boat to our previous heading."

"Aye, aye, sir," she said and sounded the boat-wide acceleration klaxon.

"One hundred to impact," Sam said as he felt the *Puebla* begin to turn.

Why wasn't Jules or anyone else on the bridge answering their commlinks?

She and Sam had hit it off almost as soon as he came on board. They were officers and both understood their responsibilities—she probably better than he—so they hadn't crossed any lines, hadn't broken any rules. Maybe they should have.

The radar image of the pellet cloud disappeared when it crossed the 1700 kilometer range band and snuffed out *ChaCha's* drone and its active radar. Sam's screen went back to displaying just the passive thermal images of the nearby friendlies.

"Sixty seconds to impact."

It was funny. His taste in women usually tended toward the buxom, but Jules was thin, wiry even. But people aren't just types, are they? You think you know what you want, where your life is going, and then someone comes out of nowhere and just surprises the hell out of you. She had this amazing smile.

"Twenty seconds to impact."

"Damage control party has reached the bridge," Karlstein reported, her voice strained. "Multiple casualties."

Sam breathed in slowly.

"Impact in five, four, three . . ."

CHAPTER THREE

2 December 2133
(two hours later) *(nineteen days from K'tok orbit)*

"She's over there, Mister Bitka," the medtech told him, "with the others. Ensign Waring and Chief Nguyen, too."

Sam turned and saw the seven gray body bags floating softly in zero gee, nuzzling against each other as if for comfort. They were tethered to a fitting at the aft end of the wardroom, which had become a temporary casualty dressing station. The air had been vacuumed and filtered now, but two hours earlier it must have been like hell in here. The circular stains on the bulkheads and walls bore mute testimony to globules of blood having floated in the air like a child's soap bubbles.

"Sir," the medic said, "if it means anything, she never felt a thing. There was a lot of high speed fragmentation when they took that hit, most of it on the starboard side of the bridge. I know it's none of my business, but . . . well, if I were you, I wouldn't look inside. Remember her how she was last time you saw her. I mean . . . there was a *lot* of fragmentation."

Sam had already seen Captain Rehnquist, still alive but missing his right leg below the knee, right arm at the shoulder, and his lower jaw, nose, right cheek, and eye. Rehnquist had already gone into a cold sleep capsule to wait until they could get him to a hospital and start reconstructive surgery. Sam looked away from the bags and shuddered, then nodded. He wanted to thank the medic but no words came, so he just patted him on the back.

The medtech went back to his patients and Sam floated to the gray composite bags, found the one with the tag reading "Washington, Lieutenant Julia K, Tactical Department" and closed his eyes.

"Hey, Jules," he said very softly, "How did this happen? It doesn't mak sense. Little over a year ago I was back on Earth in civies, happy as a clam. Now here I am. Here you are.

"One year. That was a pretty quick change from weekend spaceman to head of a department, but I wasn't worried. I had you backing me up. Now peoples' lives depend on me making the right call, on my own, and I wonder how ready for all this I really am. Maybe everyone's wondering that, huh?"

His embedded commlink vibrated. He opened the circuit and heard the voice of Senior Chief Petty Officer Constancia Navarro, the Chief of the Boat, COB for short.

Lieutenant Bitka, all department heads are to report to the executive officer's cabin.

"On my way, COB," he replied. Sam touched Jules's bag one last time. "Goodbye, friend. God, I'll miss you." He pushed off toward the hatch, grateful for someone having ordered him to do something, anything.

He paused in the main access trunk to let another damage control party hurry past going forward, where most of the damage had been suffered. The XO's quarters were just aft of the wardroom and when Sam got there the stateroom already held three other officers besides Lieutenant Commander Huhn.

Sam had never been inside Huhn's stateroom and as he glanced around he was struck by its sterile, institutional feel. Most of that was due to the smart walls being turned off, showing nothing but bare gray composite panels. What sorts of pictures or background did Huhn normally display on his walls? Or was this it? Maybe so.

He nodded to the others as he glided in the hatch and grabbed a padded handhold to anchor himself next to Lieutenant Moe Rice, the supply officer and the only other reservist in the room. Rice looked at Sam with eyes wider than normal and nodded a sad greeting. Jules had been his friend as well.

Lieutenants Marina Filipenko and Rose Hennessey floated side-by-side against the opposite wall. Most of the others had zero-gee drink bulbs, but Filipenko had a "bat-rat", a battle ration in a self-heating bag. She took a bite, pausing first to sniff the bag's dispenser valve. Sam had noticed that habit of hers before: she always sniffed each bite of food before eating it.

She was short and slender, but Sam knew from working out with her that her leg muscles were like steel springs—a legacy of growing up in the 1.1 gees of Bronstein's World, the only Human extrasolar colony. Now she looked at him with that eyes-a-little-too-wide expression which always made him uncomfortable. Not that she singled him out—she looked at everyone that way, as if trying to see past their skin and into their souls, trying to solve the mystery of their existence with one good, long stare.

Hennessey, the chief engineer, was a regular officer, but her degree was from MIT instead of Annapolis, and her solid build, ruddy complexion, and buzz-cut reddish-blonde hair, contrasted with Filipenko's slighter physique and paler palette.

Huhn was in his sleep cubby with the covers wrapped around him. He looked like a cocooned caterpillar to Sam. What kind of way was that to conduct a meeting? Sam looked quickly back at Moe Rice and raised his eyebrows slightly in question. Moe shrugged.

"I see Lieutenant Bitka has finally joined us," Huhn said. "Good of you, considering there's a goddamned war on."

"Yes, sir, I heard the war announcement an hour ago. I came here as soon as I received word of the meeting."

"Oh, no hurry," he answered, his voice heavy with sarcasm. "At least no one higher up the chain of command seems to think there's any hurry. Do you know when the uBakai turned over their declaration of war to our consulate on K'tok?"

He looked around at the faces of the other officers—glared at them, his rage barely contained.

"Seven damned hours ago! Some bureaucratic screwup. We didn't get the formal word until fifty-seven minutes ago, although an hour before that we got the message loud and clear, didn't we? That's for damn sure! My God, we're in the shit."

"What'd they go and start a fight for?" Moe Rice asked, looking from face to face in genuine bewilderment.

"Who knows why leatherheads do anything?" Huhn said.

"K'tok," Filipenko said, eyes unfocused, as if she were talking to herself, her fork hesitating half way to her mouth. "That's the brass ring everybody wants."

"Let's not argue over why," Hennessey said. "They did it. That's what counts. So what comes next?"

Huhn hunched his shoulders and pulled the covers tightly around him.

"I'm taking command of the boat, effective immediately. Captain is officially off the duty roster. Hell, he's an icicle down in the med bay. The bad news is we took a lot of damage. Worse news is *Hornet* couldn't get out of the way of the particle cloud and the *really* bad news is she was turned broadside trying to evade when she got hit."

He paused and glanced at Sam for a moment and then looked away. Was that a veiled thanks for Sam getting them turned into the pellets or a veiled apology for freezing up himself?

"Our anti-collision nose armor stopped most of the stuff that hit us, but *Hornet's* crippled and the squadron commander was killed. *Hornet* barely has internal power. Their A-gang is working to get emergency maneuvering and life support up, but even if they do, she's out of commission for the foreseeable future. Her jump drive's shot, too, so she's not going home soon, which means we aren't either."

"Damn! What do we use as a backup carrier?" Moe Rice asked.

Huhn's mouth twisted into an ugly scowl. "I guess they'll tell us when they figure it out themselves, okay? We've got our own problems to worry about, starting with holes in the personnel roster and . . . well, we've got to get organized. *Re*organized, I guess. Filipenko, what's Lieutenant Goldjune's status?"

Filipenko looked up sharply as if her mind had been elsewhere. Her white shipsuit was stained—with grease, Sam had first thought, but now that he looked more closely he recognized the stains as dried blood. When they'd taken the hit she had been on the bridge in the communications chair, to the captain's left, and that was probably his blood on her uniform. It was a miracle she hadn't been killed or injured. She wrapped her arms across the front of her torso, hugging her shoulders, and shivered, then cleared her throat.

"The medtech tells me he will be alright. He was on the bridge, was wounded by fragments in the shoulder, and passed out from oxygen starvation when his suit failed, but they got to him quickly enough. I saw him and . . . the others." She shuddered again. "He was lucky. The medtechs already have him bandaged and stabilized but they want to keep an eye on him for a few more hours."

Sam understood her revulsion. His own brief glimpse of their mutilated captain would inhabit his nightmares for some time. Goldjune had been lucky his chair was on the port side of the bridge; no one on the starboard side—all of them people from Sam's tactical department— had survived

"Thank God!" Huhn said, shaking his head. "We'd really be in the shit without Goldjune. I . . ." Huhn stopped and cleared his throat, then continued in a reedy voice. "I don't know how I'd run the boat without him."

Sam looked at Huhn and tried to match the figure in front of him with the officer who, a little more than two weeks earlier, had described himself as a "hard-charging warrior."

Huhn shook himself once, the way a dog shakes off water, took two long deep breaths, and looked up.

"What shape's the boat in, Hennessey?"

Rose Hennessey put a pair of viewer glasses on and gave them a short and to-the-point summary of the damage *Puebla* had suffered and how far her damage control teams had gotten in repairing the worst of it. They had atmospheric integrity and all fuel leaks had been patched. The thermal shroud was operational again at about 95% efficiency. That struck Sam as a hell of a lot accomplished in only two hours. Beyond that, the drives and life support were operational, although their High Resolution Visual Spectrum—HRVS—optics were still down along with their active radar.

Hennessey pushed the viewer glasses back up on her head. "Problem is I only got eight EVA-qualified A-gangers, and they can only get so much done on the outside of the hull at one time. I'd like to get back to them as soon as possible."

Huhn looked away and frowned. "You got snipes can turn a wrench. I need you here, figuring out what we do next. But I'll keep it as short as I can. Rice, what's the final casualty count?"

Moe listed the holes the uBakai buckshot had torn in their boat's roster: two officers and five others dead; one officer—the captain—and three others critically injured and in cold sleep; one officer and twelve others injured but expected to return to duty soon. It was a big bite out of a total crew of ninety-five, but the biggest bite had been out of Sam's tactical department.

As if thinking the same thing, Huhn's gaze settled on Sam

"Bitka, I don't know how you're going to manage the tactical department without Lieutenant Washington. She was a hell of an officer. You lost your senior chief, too, didn't you? And Waring?"

Sam looked away and swallowed before answering.

"Yes, sir. Chief Nguyen was killed on the bridge along with Lieutenant Washington, Ensign Waring, and one of my sensor techs. But our weaponry is up, except for one point defense laser mount. I'd like to get the power ring recharged as soon as possible so we've got plenty of juice for the spinal coil gun and lasers, but TAC's up and running otherwise."

The power ring was the boat's Superconducting Magnetic Energy Storage System, or SMESS, wrapped around the boat's waist like a corset, buried under armor and coolant lines.

Huhn stared at him for a few seconds. "Well, can you handle the department without your best people? No officers, no senior chief—do you know what you're doing?"

Once Sam might have felt a surge of anger or resentment at that, but he looked at Huhn's scowling face, wrapped in his ridiculous blanket, and he felt nothing: no anger, no resentment, no contempt—nothing. He tried to remember what it had felt like to be intimidated by Huhn, but he could not. He felt detached, withdrawn from everything going on in the room, as if it was happening to someone else. His body was here but his mind—part of it, at any rate—was in the wardroom staring at a floating gray body bag.

"My two division chiefs are rock-solid sir. Chief Burns is ready to move up to Bull Tac, and he's got a good machinist first behind him in weapons division to move up to chief." Sam decided not to mention his candidate for promotion to chief was Joyce Menzies, one of the two petty officers Huhn had argued with him over earlier. "I've got a good set of acey-deucies to fill in behind them. We'll manage, sir."

Bull Tac was the unofficial title of the senior chief petty officer in the tactical department, the position Chief Nguyen had held. Acey-deucies were the petty officers first and second class, the men and women who did most of the real work in the boat.

"I hope to God you're right," Huhn said. "We're going to need your department up to speed where they're sending us, which is right straight into hell. There's a combined task force following us in, about six days behind us. It was meant as a show of force, to keep the Varoki from pulling something like this, but it's too late for that. Now they're the counterattack force, and we're riding point for them, all the way down to low orbit around K'Tok. When I said we were in the shit, I meant it. This is definitely Charge of the Light Brigade stuff "

Hennessey and Filipenko exchanged a worried look, but again Sam wasn't sure if they were more worried about the new mission or Huhn.

"I think somebody better warn the follow-on force to expect the same attack we got hit with," Sam said.

"Noted," Huhn answered and looked away—which was Navy-speak for *Who cares what you think?*

"I'm serious," Sam said. "We need to get a tight beam message to the main task force right away or they're going to get whacked."

"They came in later than we did so they're in a different intercept corridor," Huhn said.

"Doesn't matter."

They all looked at him and Huhn opened his mouth to cut him off but Sam pushed on. "This attack was launched along an exactly reciprocating course track. That's nearly impossible. There is only one way this attack could be executed."

"Oh? So please educate us all, *Mister* Bitka," Huhn said.

"Yes, sir. Buckshot is just inert pellets, so once it's launched there's no way to alter its vector. That means the launch vessel has to already be on the correct course. The only practical way to do that would be to leave orbit around K'tok and accelerate into the reciprocal course, but to do that they would have to already know our position and incoming course. That means the vessel had to leave K'tok orbit after we came out of J-space and began our glide. I bet there's a departure report somewhere in the intel feeds for the last two weeks "

"You mean they had us detected all along?" Filipenko said.

"Impossible!" Huhn spat.

"Not if they knew where to point their hi-res optics," Sam said. "If they have a couple optics platforms out in the asteroid belt we don't know about, all they have to do is point them at the right spot, look from a couple different angles, and wait for us to occlude a star."

"But how would they know where and when to look?" Huhn

demanded. "Do you have any idea how enormous the volume of space above and below the plane of the ecliptic is?"

"Yes, sir, I do. But according to our standard operating procedure, we always enter this star system from above the plane—galactic north—always at the same distance from the orbital plane, and we always do it so that our residual momentum from the final sprint at Bronstein's World carries us on a zero-burn intercept with K'tok. And we always do it with the same residual momentum so we don't have to recalculate the intercept problem."

"Wait one," Rose Hennessey said. "You want to unwrap that a little for the benefit of a poor engineer who doesn't know beans about astrogation?"

"Boy, howdy," Moe agreed.

Sam looked at their blank faces. Even Filipenko, who was supposed to have some background in astrogation, frowned in thought.

"Sure. The galaxy is a flat spinning disc of stars. There's no real north or south, up or down, but for purposes of reference, if you're looking at it from a distance and it looks as if its spinning counterclockwise, you're 'up', or galactic north of it. If it's spinning clockwise, you're galactic south. Got it? Okay.

"Same with a star system. Over 99% of the matter that makes up a star and its planets, asteroids, all that stuff is concentrated in a very flat disc. The planet orbits, the asteroids, all of them are in that disc, called the plain of the ecliptic. Only stuff that wandered in and got captured later, like some comets, move outside of it.

"When we jump from star to star, we pop out of J-space into real space. If we come out and some part of the ship is in the same space occupied by, say, a rock the size of a baseball, you get what's called an 'annihilation event.'"

"That sounds bad," Moe said.

"Sounds bad, is bad. So we like to do it above or below the star's plane of the ecliptic, because there's hardly anything floating around there.

"When you make a jump you retain whatever momentum you had from before. So we jump here from Bronstein's World, which has a plane of the ecliptic aligned almost the same as K'Tok's: both of them angled between thirty and forty degrees off the galactic disc. Before we jump, we accelerate down, stellar *south*, away from the Bronstein's

World plain of the ecliptic, but we calculate the jump to come out *north* of K'tok's plane."

"Okay, so our momentum is carrying us down toward the plane and the planets," Moe said.

"Right. We know where K'Tok is in its orbit at any given time so the astrogator calculates the jump to come out exactly where our residual momentum will carry us on an intercept course with K'Tok."

"Of course," Huhn admitted, finally speaking. "That way we don't have to expose ourselves with a mid-course correction burn. All we do is decelerate into orbit once we get there."

"Yes, sir. But here's the thing: at any one time there's only one place we can emerge from J-Space with that vector and make that intercept. It's a moving exit point, because K'tok is moving in its orbit, but it's pig-simple to calculate where it is. Maybe they aren't idiots. Maybe they noticed that. And so maybe that's where they point their optics."

Rosie Hennessey ran her hands back through her buzz-cut hair and looked at Huhn. "Shit, sir, sounds to me like he's on to something."

"Okay, okay, so you're on to something, Bitka. What does that get us?"

"If they saw us, they'll use the same method to spot the follow-on force and may have buckshot on the way to them, so they need to be warned.

"But we also know when *Chacha's* probe went active there was no ship on that course within normal detection range of our radar. Unless they've got some new super-stealth ship out there—and there's nothing in the intel briefings to suggest it—they did a low-signature course correction *after* they launched the ordnance, and they got way the hell away by the time we started getting hit, which means they did it a long time ago."

"Get to the point," Huhn snapped.

"They had to have fired that buckshot *days* before the incident on K'tok they say started the war.This was a carefully-planned surprise attack."

For a moment the only sound in the compartment was the hiss of the ventilators.

Moe put his hand to his temple and squinted, a habit he had when getting an incoming message on his embedded commlink. He nodded a few times absently, then his eyes opened a bit wider.

"Roger that," he said and turned to the others. "That was Yeoman Fischer. We sent the casualty report up to squadron and just got the modified chain of command. Commander Huhn, you're skipper, of course."

Moe turned to Sam. "Looks like *you're* second in command, Bub."

"*What?*" Huhn said. "No, that's got to be a mistake! They must have drawn it up not knowing Larry's returning to duty status."

"No, sir," Moe said. "Seems like Bitka has almost a year's seniority in grade over Goldjune."

"Were you on active duty when you got your promotion to full lieutenant?" Huhn demanded.

Sam shook his head.

"Don't matter, sir," Moe said. "Effective date is effective date." He turned to Sam, his right hand out. "Congratulations, XO."

CHAPTER FOUR

2 December 2133

(ten minutes later) *(nineteen days from K'tok orbit)*

"Thanks for staying after," Huhn said, pulling his blanket more tightly around his shoulders and avoiding eye contact with Sam. "I know we haven't exactly been on the same page a whole lot, but we're deep in the shit now, and we need to work together. You know what I mean?"

"Work together. Yes, sir," Sam said, trying to concentrate on Huhn's words instead of the image of gray body bags.

Huhn frowned at him and then looked away.

With the others gone, Sam now saw a part of the smart wall near Huhn's cabin workstation which was live, showing a rotation of family pictures. Most of them looked posed. They featured three people: Huhn, usually in uniform and with a variety of different hair lengths and colors; a woman ranging from her mid-twenties to late-thirties in different pictures, but always with the same tentative smile; and a boy ranging from six or seven up to late teens. The younger version of the boy looked bored, the older one defiant.

"You've got a good tactical head on you, Bitka," Huhn said. Sam looked up from the pictures with a start, but Huhn's attention was on the blank gray expanse of the opposite wall. "You've shown that much. That was quick thinking during the attack, recommending we realign the boat. I had to think about it a little before agreeing, but you were right." Huhn glanced at Sam again, perhaps gauging his reaction to this rewriting of history.

"Thank you, sir."

Huhn fidgeted with his blanket for a moment, as if unsure how to proceed.

"Okay. Like they say, water under the bridge, right? Okay. So . . . XO, huh? Quite a feather in your cap. Something to brag about to the folks back home, that's for damn sure. It's a big job, and a thankless one—take that from me. No one appreciates the XO, but you'll learn that as you go. You'll have to keep the tactical department too for now. Short-handed."

"Yes, sir. Not a problem."

"I'll help you out with this job, show you the ropes. But you need to help me out too. I'm new to being captain, you know."

Something was happening here but Sam was too numb to understand quite what it was or what to do in response. His brain—the analytical part anyway—was still sharp, but the emotional part remained punch-drunk, useless. He knew he should say something.

"Yes, sir."

"Okay. Well . . . we'll take this up again later. Now you better get started on drafting the new watch list and general quarters assignments. Oh, and since you're still Tac Boss, you're also the boat's intel officer. We need to let the crew know what's going on. You know, big picture stuff, keep it simple, but put together a summary and broadcast it over the all-crew channel. So . . . well, dismissed."

Sam glided out and closed the hatch, then spent a moment holding a stanchion on the bulkhead, thinking through the conversation. Once Huhn got over his surprise having Sam as his XO he had at least been polite, had sounded as if he wanted to get along, work together. Sam wasn't sure the two of them could manage that, but then he shrugged. What choice did they have?

First things first.

"All hands, this is Lieutenant Bitka the executive officer speaking. Captain Huhn directed me to tell you about our current situation and our mission. As you all probably know, as of 0937 Zulu today, the United States of North America, along with our allies—the West European Union, the Republic of India, and the Federal Republic of Nigeria—have been at war with the Varoki Commonwealth of Bakaa. The biggest thing we know is they shot at us first.

"Something to remember is we're not fighting every single Varoki out there. Like us, the Varoki don't have one central government. They've got almost thirty sovereign nations, and we're only at war with one of them: the Commonwealth of Bakaa. They're called the uBakai in their language.

"You've probably heard USS *Hornet* was badly damaged by the sneak attack. The other destroyers of the squadron took damage and suffered casualties too. We don't know the extent yet, but for the moment it appears that all twelve destroyers are operational. Our own damage is repairable and does not threaten our survival or that of the boat. Our losses were heavy, though—seven dead and seventeen injured. The good news is, all but four of our injured have already returned to duty or will shortly.

"We're here in this system for one reason only—to protect Human colonists on the planet K'tok. Why is K'tok such a big deal? Because of all the ecosystems any of the Six Races have discovered in the last couple hundred years, K'tok's is the only one that has proteins compatible with Humans. That means it's the only place other than Earth where we can eat the fruit and vegetables and meat without it killing us. People can grow food in the ground, not just in hydroponic tanks.

"The Varoki settled a corner of the world before anyone knew it was compatible with us, but when they found out, they tried to cover it up. That all came out a couple years ago and there's been a flow of Human settlers there ever since. The local Varoki—the uBakai—started getting rough and so our government sent us to keep everyone honest. Instead they pulled a sneak attack on us.

"There's a big combined task force following us, ships from all four Human allied navies. They're headed for K'tok, and so for now our mission is to provide the forward screen for that task force. That's exactly what they built our destroyers for, and what we've trained for.

"In twenty minutes we'll secure from general quarters and go to Readiness Condition Two. That will give half of you a chance to grab some chow and rest. They you'll spell your shipmates.

"We're in a shooting war. We didn't want it, but we've got it, and there's a lot of combat power backing us up. I was proud of the way everyone I saw performed during the attack, and I'm sure the captain feels the same way. Carry on."

★ ★ ★

Two hours later Sam was supervising a repair party, welding permanent patches over the holes in the interior of the central transit tube where uBakai "buckshot" had punched through. The all-boat commlink alert sounded.

"All hands, bury the dead," he heard Lieutenant Marina Filipenko, the officer of the deck, announce.

He waved his work party to a halt and they all anchored their feet to stanchions and came to attention. Captain Huhn's voice came on next. He must have been aft in Engineering, where the large maintenance airlock would allow all seven of their dead to be buried together, as was customary. The captain read off their names and said something about each of them, although he sounded as if he read summaries from the service folders.

Sam's mind wandered, as it always did during ceremonies. He tried to look serious and attentive, mindful of how important ceremonies were to other people and unwilling to hurt or offend them. The truth was he never really understood—whether it was a birthday, wedding, graduation, or funeral—why people believed those particular five or ten or thirty minutes were more meaningful than the five or ten or thirty minutes which came before or after. They always felt the same to him and that made him feel slightly awkward, as if he were missing something important.

Not that all moments in his life were the same. Some took his breath away, some would stay with him forever. His first sight of the seven gray body bags was one of those moments. But the important moments almost always came upon him by surprise, and never as the result of planning, never because time had been set aside for them in his schedule.

As for this ceremony, he felt as if everything important which could happen to Jules and the others already had.

"Honor guard, hand salute," Captain Huhn ordered.

"Mariner Striker Louise DeMarco, Chief Petty Officer George Nguyen, Machinist Mate Second Class Vincent Pulaski, Quartermaster Second Class Ernest Schwartz, Sensor Technician Third Class DeRon Velazquez, Ensign Robert Waring, Lieutenant Junior Grade Julia Washington.

"We therefore commit their remains to space, to rejoin the universe from which we all came, and to which we all surely will return."

There was a pause of several seconds, presumably as the outer door of the airlock was opened and the bodies released, and then Captain Huhn spoke again.

"All hands, resume duty."

"Okay," Sam quietly told his work party, and they all returned to the job of repairing their boat, but without the banter which had filled the transit tube before.

Vice-Captain Takaar Nuvaash, Speaker for the Enemy, sat in the fleet tactical center of KBk Five One Seven and studied the sensor readings from the thirteen Human ships. All communications between them were by tight beam and so interception of actual messages was out of the question, but he could at least see evidence of the volume of signal traffic by their changing emission states. What they said was unknowable, but it was clear they were all saying *something*, which meant none of the vessels had been disabled. He was not sure how he felt about that.

Why were they at war? What was the point? What was its strategic purpose? What did his government hope to gain by it? Admiral e-Lapeela clearly supported the attack. He must know the objective, the stakes, the plan for prosecuting the war after the opening salvos were fired. What else did he know?

Nuvaash glanced at the admiral who sat in the console to his right. Three months earlier, when the admiral had assumed command of the First Striking Fleet, Nuvaash had made several unobtrusive attempts to draw a response from him which would indicate membership in one of the shadow brotherhoods, the secret societies which cut across boundaries of class and nationality and which riddled Varoki society. Nuvaash knew the secret challenges of nearly a dozen such organizations, and he knew how to insert them casually into conversation, in ways that might provoke a reaction. He always arranged it so he could ignore a positive response and carry on as if the challenge was a coincidence, the significance of its answering countersign unrecognized. In e-Lapeela's case, however, that was an unnecessary precaution. The admiral had responded to none of the challenges, and so Nuvaash had no more understanding of his commander's true loyalties now than he had before he had heard his name.

"Admiral, it will be easier for me to assess whether the attack has produced the desired effect if I knew what effect was desired."

The admiral chuckled and tilted his head to the side, the Varoki equivalent of a shrug.

"Nominally, we aim to end the criminal colonization of K'tok by Humans. Since the re-integration referendum, all of K'tok is legally uBakai soil."

Nominally, e-Lapeela had said, so there was a larger objective in sight than simply the planet K'tok.

"The biocompatibility issue complicates—" Nuvaash began but e-Lapeela cut him off with a gesture.

"It does not complicate the *legality* of the situation, Speaker. That much is simple. K'tok was discovered by Varoki survey vessels one hundred thirty-four years ago, colonized by Varoki settlers sent by the uZmataanki and our own uBakai governments a decade later, became a sovereign and independent member state of the *Cottohazz* two years ago, and voluntarily became a confederated territory of the Commonwealth of Bakaa eleven months past. Legally, Humans have no claim on any part of the world."

"Legally," Nuvaash said, and e-Lapeela nodded.

"You are right. Legality matters little to Humans. Every world in the *Cottohazz* where there are Humans, they are involved in crime. Some places they have even taken over the other criminals and *organized* them. Can you imagine? But you have experience with them, so you do not need to imagine. That is why I retained you in your post as Speaker when I took command here. I could have brought my own specialist, but you know Humans. You understand them.

"So speak for the enemy. How will they respond to our First Action initiative?"

"Rage," Nuvaash answered immediately. "Like us, Humans have a cultural aversion to wars begun by treachery, particularly the main Human nations involved in the colonization effort of K'tok. An unprovoked surprise attack such as this will produce righteous rage in these governments and their people. This will complicate our task."

"How? Humans are savages and they will fight savagely. Will they be docile if we begin the war politely?"

"Of course not, Admiral. But if they feel wronged, they will fight longer. Their governments will be less likely to come to terms. We will pay a higher price in warriors and ships. In both categories these four Human nations combined outnumber the uBakai Star Navy. But most importantly, in their rage they will strive to find a way to revisit on us not merely the physical damage of the attack, but also its psychological toll. They will attempt to strike back harder than they were struck."

Admiral e-Lapeela nodded and smiled.

"They will not simply react to our attack," he said softly."They will *over*-react. I believe you are correct, Nuvaash. I certainly hope so. All of our plans rest on that.

"Humans have been a problem since they were admitted to the *Cottohazz* seventy years ago. At long last, we are going to solve that problem."

Nuvaash shuddered, and he could not tell if fear or excitement made up the greater part of the feeling.

CHAPTER FIVE

3 December 2133
(one day later) ***(eighteen days from K'tok orbit)***

Sam paused at the hatchway and surveyed the men and women gathered in the wardroom. Apart from the captain, the only officers not present were lieutenants Marina Filipenko, who was Officer Of the Deck (OOD) on this watch, and Carlos Sung, the Duty Engineering Officer (DEO). He saw a microcosm of the boat's society and hierarchy, both formal and informal, all absorbed in conversation. Sam pushed off and glided across the room, over their heads, toward the far wall.

"Ah, the XO!" Moe Rice called out with a smile. "Can the cap'n be far behind? What's the latest word from the task force?"

Sam thought the jovial mood seemed a little forced, the smiles around the table a little brittle, but twenty-four hours into an interstellar war that made perfect sense.

"Since Newton's First Law of Motion hasn't been repealed locally, the task force is still coming," Sam answered as he floated past them. He stopped himself at the bank of automated food and drink dispensers and punched in the code for black coffee. The zero-gee drink bulb popped out almost immediately.

"Any more word on the attack?" Rose Hennessey the senior engineer asked, and most of the soft conversation stopped. Sam collected his warm drink bulb from the dispenser and turned to look at them.

Captain Rehnquist had programmed the smart walls of the

wardroom to duplicate the look of the wardroom on USS *Olympia*, Admiral Dewey's flagship at the Battle of Manila Bay over two centuries earlier. The deck had looked as if it were covered with teak planking, while the walls had sported mahogany wainscoting and brass-rimmed circular portholes which showed the exterior star field instead of the broad expanse of the Pacific Ocean—all of it an illusion, of course, and all of it turned off when the room had been used as a casualty dressing station. Sam noted that Huhn had not turned it back on, and so the walls and deck were now all simply neutral gray, like the new captain's cabin. At least the blood had been scrubbed from the walls.

"I imagine you've already pumped the communications people of all the information they're willing to share," Sam said. "I can give you this bit of news. I just received word the entire crew will receive the pay augmentations for both hazardous duty and duty in a combat zone, retroactive to yesterday's date. Beyond that you'll have to wait for what the captain has to say."

Hennessey looked away with a worried expression. Everyone probably figured Sam knew and was just playing hard to get, but he had no idea what the tight beam messages Filipenko had patched through to Huhn from Task Force One said, as the captain hadn't shared them with him. The XO was as much in the dark as anyone—a strange way to run a boat in wartime, Sam thought.

"Whatever it is, we'll be ready for it," Larry Goldjune said. His left arm rested in a black medical restraint, the only visible relic of the attack. The triangle of black across his white shipsuit, like a ceremonial sash, seemed to add substance and credibility to his words. "You all know the only time an Earth ship has ever been in a space battle was three years ago, right here in the K'tok system, when USS *Kennedy* got caught in the middle of a fight between the uBakai and the uZmatanki. *Kennedy* took out two Varoki cruisers and then held the whole goddamned system until her relief showed up. The leatherheads have an edge on us in technology, but they're not much good in a fight."

Sam hoped Goldjune was right. That's certainly what had been drilled into all of them in their training and indoctrination, probably in all fleet training for the last three years, ever since the First K'tok Campaign—in which the Earth fleet forces had never been technically at war with anyone and USS *Kennedy* had acted solely as a local peacekeeper for the *Cottohazz.* The others at the table certainly seemed to take some heart from Larry's speech and began talking again.

Goldjune ran the operations department—astrogation and communication—and he was the sort of officer others talked about as a "future chief of naval operations." His family connections—two admirals—didn't hurt. Although Sam didn't have much use for him on a personal level, he had to admit that Larry was a competent Ops Boss. He was handsome in a strong-jawed, blond, Aryan sort of way, the effect slightly mitigated by the ten or fifteen extra kilos he carried on his frame.

The central feature of the wardroom was the long table affixed to the deck—now the aft bulkhead. When the boat was under acceleration it served as a standard table, but in zero gee, as now, its supports were extended so its surface rested closer to the center of the compartment, and the zero-gee brackets fixed to its underside were extended to hold the food and drink containers of the officers dining along its length.

The captain's place at the head of the table was empty, but along the table to the captain's right floated the officers of the operations and tactical departments—the line officers: astrogation, communication, and combat specialists who formed the actual chain of command of the boat. Normally the executive officer sat to the captain's immediate right but Sam saw that Larry Goldjune had taken that position. He turned and looked at Sam, his expression challenging. Goldjune's normally round and fleshy face had been made even more so by two weeks of zero gravity and now his eyes seemed particularly recessed and hostile.

Sam used a handhold to launch and glided over to the table.

"Good to see you up and looking fit, Lieutenant," Sam said. "You know, I don't much care where folks sit but it's sort of traditional for the XO to sit here, in case the captain has something he wants to go over with him."

"Cap'n *asked* me to sit beside him," Goldjune drawled with a look of triumph in his eyes.

"Well then we're fine," Sam said. He pushed off from the dispenser wall and took a place further down the table, on the far side of Ensign Barb Lee, head of the maneuvering division. He anchored his drink bulb in the food holder and clipped his tether lanyard to the table's restraint ring to keep from floating away. A glance at Goldjune gave him the feeling he had just avoided some sort of trap intended to make him look foolish. He felt his face flush, but not from embarrassment. They were at war. People were dead—*Jules was dead*. What was the point in these stupid head games?

Rose Hennessey sat to the left of the captain's place, then three of her officers and then Moe Rice, *Puebla's* supply officer. That side of the table was informally called *support-side* because the supply and engineering officers who sat there were technical specialists not in the chain of command. There had been a time, a century earlier, when engineering officers were also line officers, but that was before fusion reactors had become standard shipboard issue. Now they were expected to concentrate more on their specialty. Rose Hennessey had over a year of seniority on Sam, but she couldn't step up into a line or command slot—like the executive officer job—except in an extreme emergency. So far this didn't qualify as that. Sam figured they'd have to get down to no line officers left, except maybe Ensign Lee, before Rose Hennessey stepped up to command.

Line officers to the captain's right took precedence over support branch officers to his left. Engineering and Operations sat closer to the head of the table than did Supply and Tactical, showing another subhierarchy. And then there were the regular officers versus the reservists. They only had eleven officers remaining of their original fourteen, eight of them floated at the table waiting for the captain to join them, and they were as thoroughly sifted and labeled and divided by rank, job, specialty, and service status as exhibits in a museum.

Sam had always accepted this hierarchy, never questioned it. He was just one of the cogs, focused on doing his job and making his boss happy—usually. Now it was different. Now he was executive officer and his job was to make all these cogs mesh into one efficient machine. The carefully regimented hierarchy was supposed to make it easier to understand the extent and limits of every other officer's authority and responsibility. It was supposed to make it easier for everyone to work together, but Sam wondered.

"Good evening, Ladies and Gentlemen," Captain Huhn said as he coasted through the hatchway to the wardroom and then kicked off the compartment wall toward the table. "As you were. No standing on ceremony here. Let's enjoy our supper, but cover some business while we're eating, okay? Go ahead and order. I hear the curried chicken's good tonight."

Sam couldn't imagine why the machine-reconstituted and cooked curried soy-chicken would be different tonight than it was any other night but he ordered it to be agreeable, punching the order into the smart table surface. Huhn seemed awfully cheerful one day into the war, nothing like on the auxiliary bridge or in his cabin. Maybe he'd recovered his balance, his self-confidence.

The mess attendant handed Sam his dinner tray with the sealed food packages held to it by fibre pads. Sam peeled back the cover of the entrée container, unclipped the fork from the tray, and started eating curried chicken. Not bad, but nothing special. Food eaten in zero gee never tasted all that great. For one thing, the aroma never rose from the food, so unless he brought it right up to his nose he couldn't smell it, and that cut a lot of the enjoyment. Even when he did lift it up, Sam couldn't smell it all that well. Along with everyone else after the first couple days in zero gee, the fluid accumulation in his head meant a permanent stuffy nose.

"Well, it's customary for a new captain to call a wardroom meeting like this to get acquainted," Huhn said once the orders were in and the mess attendant began bringing out the food and beverage containers. "But we already know each other, don't we? What's really changed everything is this war. Some of us saw it coming, and Captain Rehnquist and I were among them. Nobody upstairs would listen to us, of course. Staff officers have a hard time listening to the people who can see what's what, and so here we are."

That was surprising. As far as Sam could tell, Captain Rehnquist and Delmar Huhn had been singularly unconcerned about looming hostilities. It was possible they had logged warnings to their superiors and had not said anything to the crew to avoid worrying them. Anything was possible, he supposed.

"Well, that's all water under the bridge," Huhn went on. "The important thing is we're in a war and we have a job to do. The task force coming behind us has seven heavy cruisers from four different navies: the WestEuros, India, Nigeria, and us. Transports, too, carrying three cohorts of troops—two of them Mike Troopers, and one conventional infantry. The grunts were going to land and reinforce the local security forces in the Human colony while the Mikes would be an orbital reserve and quick reaction force. Now the plan is to drop the whole expeditionary brigade right on T'tokl-Heem, the Varoki colonial capital, and grab the needle. The brass thinks that should be enough to force them back to the bargaining table."

"They gotta be kidding!" Rose Hennessey said and Huhn looked over at her, eyes suddenly wide with surprise.

"What do you mean?" he asked.

She shook her head, her cheeks and neck turning a splotchy red, either embarrassment or anger, Sam couldn't tell which. "Jesus, grab the *needle?* An elevator from planet surface to orbit is just about the most delicate and complicated piece of engineering anyone in known space has ever built, and it costs a fortune. One wrong move, one stray shot, and we're gonna have a hell of a mess on our hands."

"You mean *they* will," Larry Goldjune said from across the table. "*They* started this fight, they attacked *us* by surprise, killed our shipmates. If we break their needle, I say too goddamned bad. Fuck 'em."

Several officers nodded and growled their agreement.

"But our people gotta live down there too, Goldjune," Hennessey said. "Hell, they broke the needle on Nishtaaka twelve, thirteen years ago and *still* haven't got it working right."

"Okay, okay," Huhn said. "Settle down, you two. I'm inclined to agree with Larry on this one, but let's not worry about that stuff until they tell us to pin stars on our collars. Alright? Okay."

Huhn was right, this was way above their pay grades, but Hennessey had a point, too. Whatever commercial viability a world had was tied to it having a functioning needle. Boosting payloads to orbit by rocket was absurdly expensive, not remotely economical. Star drives were fine for exploring the galaxy and all that, but the reality of interplanetary and interstellar commerce was that almost all the cost of moving something from one planet to another—regardless of which star it orbited—was paid once you got it into low orbit. A needle cut the cost per kilo of lifting cargo and people to orbit by two orders of magnitude.

Sam had read about needles his whole life, and lived with the images of them, but the first one he actually saw was the Central Pacific Needle, shortly before he rode it to orbit his second summer of NROTC training. It shone bright gold in the Pacific sunlight, and stretched up into the haze, an impossibly long, impossibly thin column, plated in gold only molecules thick to prevent oxygen erosion of the carbon nanotubes that formed the core of the structure.

It was really a bundle of nanotubes, a big vertical cable in permanent Synchronous Planetary Orbit—SPO—over one spot in the equator, but reaching past the SPO orbit track and tethered to a massive captive asteroid, far enough out it moved at escape velocity and would depart orbit if it weren't for the mass of the Needle holding it back; the centrifugal force of the asteroid trying to escape orbit held the Needle up and balanced the centripetal force of gravity trying to pull the whole thing down. It all made sense mathematically, but that never changed the chill Sam felt whenever he stepped into the passenger compartment of the elevator and realized *he was already in orbit*, even though he was still at sea level. The whole structure and everything on it was in orbit.

But needles were huge investments: difficult to build and almost impossible to restore to their original condition once they suffered major damage. Fighting anywhere near one *was* a hell of a gamble.

Huhn was talking again and Sam shook the vision of a shattered needle from his mind to listen.

"Now, because of the damage we took," Huhn went on, "they are modifying our job. The task force has accelerated and is overtaking us. The other eight boats in the squadron will accelerate as well and form the forward screen, but our four-boat division will hold back to escort *Hornet*, at least until they can get power up. Then we'll be the task force reserve.

"I know this is probably a disappointment to everyone. I'm sure all of us want to be in on the first strike back at these people, to avenge our shipmates and because . . . well, just because, that's why. But in the Navy we follow orders, no matter how unpleasant they may be, and we do it without bellyaching."

As Sam looked around the table, a few officers showed looks of genuine disappointment but Delmar Huhn wasn't one of them.

CHAPTER SIX

4 December 2133
(one day later) ***(seventeen days from K'tok orbit)***

"Coupling, arm, servo-mechanical, one-point-seven-four-meter, type alpha seven dash seven one," Sam read.

"Um . . . right here," Ensign Robinette answered and pointed to the twisted piece of metal, one of several hundred items floating tethered in long swaying lines in the storage bay.

Sam clicked the "verified" box by the part on his data pad. "Gain conduit, electro-thermal, twelve-kiloamp."

"Over here. Ow!"

Sam looked up and saw Robinette sucking the tip his right index finger.

"Sharp edge. Cut myself," the ensign explained.

Sam clicked the correct box.

"Plasma flux regulator, serial whiskey romeo one niner four niner."

"Yeah, here it is."

"Okay, Robinette, what the hell is a plasma flux regulator?"

The young engineering ensign looked up from his own data pad.

"Um, it says here it's part of the Magneto-PlasmaDynamic thruster's magnetic containment system, sir. I think it keeps the plasma jet from touching the ignition walls, so the exhaust nozzle doesn't heat up. That's why the MPD thruster is low signature."

Sam thought it was a little strange an engineering officer had to look that up, but Robinette was pretty young and new to the job—he was the only officer on *Puebla* who had arrived after Sam and Moe

Rice had transferred over from USS *Theodore Roosevelt.* Being skinny made him look younger than his years, and his thin, weedy moustache younger still. His large ears stuck almost straight out from his head, like jug handles. If Robinette hadn't been an officer and gentleman by act of Congress, Sam was pretty sure his nickname among the crew would be *The Jughead.* Maybe it was and they were just careful not to let it slip near anyone in a white shipsuit.

"What's your specialty, Robinette?"

"Oh. Well, electronic warfare, I guess," he said and looked back down at his data pad. Sam was pretty sure he was blushing, but had no idea why asking about his specialty would be embarrassing.

"I thought we didn't take any damage to the drives."

Robinette's head rose and he looked relieved at the change of subject. "No, sir, but one of the slugs went through a storage bay and damaged some of our replacement components."

Sam nodded and stretched his neck. They had been at this component damage survey for nearly an hour and hadn't made as much progress as they needed to. Engineering work parties were pulling damaged components and replacing them at a heroic rate, but every damaged item would have to be replaced, and that meant every single one had to be surveyed and inventoried by engineering, and then verified by the executive officer—Sam—before a requisition could be sent on to squadron support on USS *Hornet.* The fact that *Hornet* was in worse shape than *Puebla* and was in no position to get them the replacement parts at any time in the foreseeable future was—as Captain Huhn had pointed out to Sam earlier—not germane.

What bothered him most was the utter stupidity of the entire arrangement. There was no good reason for storing and stockpiling parts when the fabricators on *Puebla* and every other ship in the fleet could manufacture any part required. All they needed, other than the fabricators themselves, were electricity, the correct raw materials, and the part generation software. The software was the sticking point, and for a change it wasn't Navy bureaucracy standing in the way. The suppliers wouldn't release the proprietary software codes, so Navy ships (and boats) like *Puebla* had to haul around parts bays that looked like old-time hardware stores. Absurd.

Yes, having the parts on hand meant they could make urgent repairs more quickly. Yes, that was a possible advantage in battle. But the parts were vulnerable to damage themselves, as this plasma flux regulator thing showed, and if now the main one broke, then what?

His imbedded commlink vibrated and he heard the accompanying ID tone of the captain's own commlink. *Great. Now what?*

"Yes, sir."

How's that damage survey coming?

"Finishing up the first part of it with Ensign Robinette from engineering now, sir."

Well get it squared away. I'm looking at your revised watch-standing list. Some of this just won't fly. I'm making a list of modifications

"Modifications. Yes, sir."

I also need tomorrow's plan of the day ASAP. I want to check the schedule of drills.

"Plan of the day. I'll do it as soon as Robinette and I finish the damage survey."

Okay, but don't dawdle over it. One more thing. I decided I'm going to have Filipenko take over the tactical department from you. You've got your hands full with all the administrative stuff.

Sam didn't answer for a moment.

"Filipenko? The communications officer? Sir, I don't recall that Lieutenant Filipenko has any background in either sensors or weaponry."

It's covered in the line officer basic course we all took post-academy, and she's a fast study.

"Yes, sir, but . . . if you want to move someone into that position, why not Lieutenant Goldjune? He did a deployment as leading sensor officer on USS *Reagan*."

I need Larry in Ops. Filipenko can handle TAC.

And then Huhn cut the connection. So much, apparently, for their brief honeymoon as captain and XO.

"Trouble, sir?" Robinette asked.

Sam was still unused to ensigns calling him "sir," even though he had two pay grades and about ten years on Robinette.

"Captain's just giving me a hard time, that's all. We don't always see eye-to-eye. Look, I'm going to go out on a limb here and just check all the rest of these parts as verified."

"Is that kosher, sir?"

"Based on my assessment of the efficiency of the engineering department and the chief engineer, I feel confident the list as submitted is a complete and accurate report of our damage situation—at least so far. I'll append an explanatory note to that effect. These peacetime procedures don't really take into account the kind of situation we're facing here, so they'll understand upstairs."

Robinette looked doubtful.

"Or they won't," Sam added with a shrug, "in which case they can fire me and send me home. You'll probably have another couple hundred parts to survey by the next watch change."

"Yes, sir. I bet we will."

"Okay, Ensign, get back to it and tell the repair parties I appreciate the job they're doing. Oh, and uh . . . if you should run into him, no need to let the captain know how we're expediting the survey, okay?"

Robinette glided out the storage bay hatch and Sam turned back to his data pad and the reports queued up for his attention. The first one was from Moe Rice: an inventory of destroyed consumables—mostly rations. They had lost one of the water recycling units and several atmosphere scrubbers, but Moe had appended an estimate of how long they could safely put off repairs.

Sam also had a list of next-of-kins waiting for holograms. That was the captain's job but he had delegated it to Sam. What was he going to say to Jules's folks?

Thankfully, he brought up the blank form for the Plan of the Day instead and began filling in the entries.

"Mister Bitka, have a minute?"

Sam looked up and saw the broad face and thick shoulders of Senior Chief Petty Officer Constancia Navarro, the Chief of the Boat, hovering in the storage bay's hatchway. As the senior noncommissioned officer on *Puebla*, Navarro occupied a special, almost exalted, place in the boat's hierarchy. In theory, every officer outranked her. In practice she had the ear of the captain and XO in ways few if any of the officers did. No junior officer, with the possible exception of the least experienced and most stupid of newly minted ensigns, would think to give her an order. Sam had spoken with her before and she had always been respectful, but she had never taken much notice of him beyond that, so her appearance took him off guard.

"Absolutely, COB, come on in."

Her features showed her American Indian lineage without much evidence of either Spanish or Anglo genes. She was only a few years older than he but already had fifteen years in uniform, and gray streaks softened the stark black of her short, coarse hair.

"Thank you, sir." She locked her feet through a handhold on one wall, looked around the cluttered storage bay and nodded. "Quite a job to have to tackle without much warning."

Sam almost said he could handle it but stopped himself. Navarro was here for a reason but he wasn't sure what it was.

"This is my first deployment out of the Solar System," Sam said instead, "my first introduction to shipboard administration—and my first war. Any advice you have would be very welcome."

Navarro continued to look around the bay, nodding slightly to herself, perhaps collecting her thoughts. She cleared her throat.

"I've seen some pretty good execs in my time," she said, "and some . . . not so good. To be good, you have to understand that for most of the crew, you speak for the captain. So you need to understand the captain."

"Easier said than done," Sam said and he smiled, but Navarro didn't return the smile. She didn't look offended, just thoughtful to the point of preoccupation. She nodded slightly, in acknowledgement of the truth of what Sam said, if not exactly in agreement with it.

"The way the Navy uses the word captain," Navarro continued, ". . . well, it's funny, isn't it? Captain's a rank, O-6, but no matter what their rank, whoever's senior line officer on a vessel, they're the captain."

"Sure," Sam said, "the job, not the rank."

"That's right, sir," Navarro said and nodded for emphasis. "The job. A ship captain is . . . well, as far as the crew's concerned a ship's captain *is* the navy. Admirals can tell captains where to take their ships, and what to do with them once they get there, but not how to run them. Captains are monarchs on their own ships, absolute dictators."

"Subject to Navy regulations," Sam added.

"Yes sir, subject to Navy regulations. But with that one limit, captains are always right. They're infallible, and it's official—you know, like the pope."

Sam chuckled. "In theory, anyway."

"Yes, sir, in theory. But people going into war, they got to believe in something, even if it's just a theory, and on a ship that something is the captain."

Sam began wondering how long Navarro had been outside the open storage bay hatch, how much of his conversation with Ensign Robinette she had overheard.

"Chief, what if it turns out the captain is, well . . . *fallible*?"

Navarro looked him in the eye for the first time.

"Sir, here's the dirty little secret: they're *all* fallible. There's not a man or woman in uniform who can live up to that job and never stumble along the way. Some more than others. That's why we have execs."

"To keep them from stumbling?" Sam said. "That's going to be a good trick. He won't listen to a thing I say, Chief. You know that."

She kept looking him in the eyes. "Yes, sir, that's true. So all you can do is back him up, no matter what he does. Anything he does, according to you, is the smartest thing you've ever seen. Anyone disagrees, you bark 'em down. *No matter what he does.*"

Sam felt his cheeks flush, thinking again about what he had said to Robinette. He hadn't said anything disloyal, had he? Not exactly. But he'd hinted. He'd tried to get the ensign to keep information back from the captain just to make his own job easier.

"Chief, how much of my conversation with Ensign Robinette did you hear?"

Navarro squinted at a ventilation duct somewhere above Sam's head.

"Sir, the Exec and the Chief of the Boat need to have a close working relationship founded on mutual trust. So it's important for you to know that I would never deliberately eavesdrop on a conversation of yours."

Sam almost said that was no answer, but he stopped himself. Instead he said, "Fair enough. Go on."

"Well, sir, here's the hard part. You can't just go through the motions. When the captain does something stupid, something petty, something the crew will hate, you have to defend it so convincingly the crew will think it must have been your idea, and *you* talked the captain into doing it. Do you understand what I'm saying?"

Up until now it had sounded difficult and unpleasant, but all in the line of duty. But this last bit made him feel momentarily dizzy. Sam liked most of the officers and crew, and he knew most of them at least didn't *dislike* him. He wanted to keep it that way. He wanted to do his job and have people like him for it, respect him for it. But this . . .

"So you're saying I have to look like such a flaming asshole the captain will look good by comparison?"

"That's not exactly what I had in mind, sir. But that is one way of looking at it."

Sam always thought people who lived only for the approval and regard of others were shallow and weak. Now the universe—through the agency of a US Navy senior chief petty officer—was calling his bluff. Put up or shut up. If Jules were still alive, he realized, this would have been a lot harder—making her dislike him along with everyone else. As it was . . .

"Well, a job's a job," Sam said.

For the first time, Navarro smiled. "Yes, sir."

CHAPTER SEVEN

5 December 2133
(one day later) ***(sixteen days from K'tok orbit)***

"Fillipenko, I appreciate you agreeing to step up like this to take over the tactical department," Sam said.

Sam and Filipenko had travelled in silence so far, floating side by side down the central transit tube heading aft, banking from one wall to the opposite wall and then back again every three meters to avoid the half-bulkheads, tacking as if they were sailing vessels heading into the wind. Now Filipenko, the former communications officer and now acting Tac Boss, looked at him, surprise showing clearly on her face.

"You mean you don't mind?"

"*Mind?* Hell, you're saving my ass. The admin duties are overwhelming, especially with all this repair work. You wouldn't believe how many forms I have to fill out."

Marina Filipenko's surprise changed to something close to disapproval. At least she had recovered from her distracted lethargy of the day before. Sam mentally shrugged. *A job's a job.*

"I've got some help for you, too. I got curious about our new engineering ensign when he told me his specialty was electronic warfare. Moe Rice looked through the personnel folders and noticed that Ensign Jerry Robinette is a rated line officer. He's just serving a tour with engineering right now, but I'm moving him over to head up your EW division, give you at least one other commissioned officer to work with. Supervising and training him won't hurt your resume, either."

"Pretty odd, putting a line officer in engineering, isn't it?" she asked.

"Well, that's the Navy for you. Good for us, though. We need the extra body."

He glanced over at Filipenko. She didn't seem too curious about Robinette, which was just as well. No point in maybe souring her on the kid. It turned out he'd bombed out of astrogation school and then out of communication. He'd barely squeaked through electronic warfare school, and the Navy must have decided he'd fit better in engineering until—and if—he found his footing. He hadn't even commanded a division of his own; he'd been deputy to Lieutenant (JG) Carlos Sung, commander of the Auxiliary Division—universally known as the A-gang, the people who handled the odds and ends of routine maintenance most of the time and damage control during and after a battle.

They drifted past a large yellow arrow pointing in the opposite direction, toward the bow. As with every compartment and stateroom on *Puebla*, the central transit tube had omnipresent visual cues indicating up and down, despite the absence of any such physical sensation in zero gravity. Everything toward the bow of the boat was "up," and everything toward the stern was "down." All pictures on walls, all signs, everything which suggested orientation rigidly followed that pattern. Without that it was too easy for people to lose their sense of spatial orientation in extended zero gee, and then it became more difficult to re-adapt to a normal environment afterwards.

"I think you'll like Menzies," Sam said. "She's kind of a diamond in the rough—*Quebecois* from the wrong side of the tracks."

"Wrong side of the tracks? There's an expression I haven't heard in a long time. I take it you're from the right side?"

Sam thought about that for a moment before answering. "Originally, but we sort of moved over as I got older. My dad had a pretty good job at Presidio Collective, but when the collective collapsed, it took out most of his equity and he was a little old to get as good a job anywhere else. None of the big outfits were all that crazy about hiring a former collectivist anyway, so things got . . . austere."

"It seems as if a lot of people moved across the tracks the last thirty years," Filipenko said. "You ever think maybe it was the tracks that moved?"

Filipenko was alright, and she meant well, but Sam didn't feel like talking about it. His family's decline wasn't really her business. He had described it as austere. Soul-crushing was more like it—his father's unwillingness to bend with the growing wind, his mother's slide into alcoholism and addiction and compulsive spending, trying to maintain the shabby façade of middle-class gentility in worse and worse apartment buildings. But the part of the process which at first confused and then frightened and then angered Sam most was the look of assessment in the eyes of strangers. It wasn't judgment or blame or contempt. It was just that he and his family had once mattered, and then gradually stopped mattering.

Only his father's decision to move his college fund into a separate trust early in the disaster, before the debts became overwhelming, had let Sam make it to UC San Diego and have a shot at getting back across the tracks. His younger brother Rico hadn't even had that, nor had he wanted it. He was doing okay, he claimed, although he was careful never to explain to Sam or their parents who he worked for or what he did, and none of them asked about the growing coldness in his eyes.

But Sam had pulled himself back across the tracks and up the lower rungs of the management ladder at Dynamic Paradigms, had gotten his MBA at night and on weekends, almost had his doctorate of financial management. If he could crack his way into the executive track at DP, his children would never *not matter*.

Anxious to change the subject, Sam remembered Filipenko's origin.

"What I said in the crew briefing about K'tok's biology—I never really thought much about it before all this blew up. But you're from Bronstein's World, right? Must be tough there."

She thought for a moment before answering.

"Tough . . . but beautiful, too. Maybe that makes it worse. My parents emigrated from the US of NA before I was born. I have dual citizenship. It sounds exciting to live on an alien world, to build a new home for Humanity among the stars, but that's just a romantic lie. It is hard, boring work, and it is dangerous in ways that are *so* mundane. My little brother . . . " She paused for a moment, looking away, and took a slow breath. "Well, it's like hell's garden. I finally had enough and the Navy would pay for my relocation back to Earth if I joined, so here I am."

She didn't say anything for a while and then she shook her head.

"The Varoki knew K'tok was compatible with our proteins. You know what they were trying to do? Ecoform it to suit their body chemistries. The only place in the whole galaxy that doesn't try to kill us, and they were trying to fix it so it would. What kind of people do that?"

Sam had the feeling Filipenko didn't talk about this very often. There was a bitterness in her voice she must keep bottled up most of the time. He also realized with a start that he now knew why she sniffed every bite of food before eating it. Living her entire life in a toxic environment where food could become contaminated and poisonous by the slightest mistake probably made everyone sniff every bite, every meal, every day of their lives. There was no chance of contamination here on *Puebla*, but habits like that don't just go away.

"Here we are." Sam said. He keyed the hatch from the main access passage into the port missile room and eased it open a crack, Loud, rhythmic electronic music escaped into the corridor. "You've been back here before, right?"

"Only once, on the tour when I first came aboard. No reason to since then." She squinted through the hatch and hesitated, as if afraid she would get dirty inside.

Sam nodded. As communications officer she never had to venture aft of officer's country, seldom interacted with anyone but officers and her division chief petty officer. This could be an assignment even less well-suited to her than Sam had feared.

Sam pushed through the hatch and into the missile room and Filipenko followed. Newly promoted Acting Chief Joyce Menzies and two ordinary mariners were on duty, the mariners at workstation consoles and Menzies at the maintenance station with a missile secured to the anchor bracket and the housing open to reveal its guts. Menzies saw Sam and Filipenko and came to attention, her feet locked through a deck handhold.

"Attention!" she barked and the two mariners came to attention at their work stations. Menzies was short and not exactly stocky, but solid, with the look of upper-body muscles. She wore her dark hair short, like most of the crew, and her nose looked as if it had been broken once and had not set quite right. She was almost invariably cheerful, but was also one of the last people on the boat Sam thought anyone who valued their health would pick a fight with.

"As you were," Sam said. "Someone want to secure the music for a couple minutes? Thanks. Just showing Lieutenant Filipenko around. She's your new department head. Ms Filipenko, this is Acting Chief Menzies, the best missile technician in the whole squadron. Speaking of which, how's it feel to be a chief?"

"Doesn't suck, sir," Menzies said, grinning. She turned to Filipenko, her face now blank, noncommittal. "Welcome aboard the Tac shop, Ms Filipenko."

Filipenko nodded and looked around, again squinting. The missile room was a wedge-shaped section of the boat's hull, about five meters across and over four meters fore-to-aft. Racks along the outside wall held fifteen missiles, with one empty set of clamps. That was the missile on Menzies's maintenance station.

"Damaged?" Sam asked, nodding toward the open missile.

"Not so's I can see, sir. We wasn't hit back here but we take some jolts. I pull open every bird, run the internal diagnostics, make sure no *ostie de crisse* parts got shook loose, yeah?"

Listening to her mix of English and bits of *Quebecois* slang again reminded Sam of the yawning social gulf between Menzies and Filipenko. It was more than just enlisted and officer, it also had to do with education, experiences, and mannerisms. Filipenko's background—growing up on Bronstein's World—had toughened her, but not the same way the slums of Ottawa-Gatineau had toughened Menzies.

Sam hadn't had a problem with her. He'd grown up with kids like her, at least when he was getting older. Also, he'd spent a year and a half in his company's Montreal service center and had acquired a smattering of *Quebecois* trash talk. Filipenko, though . . .

"Good thinking, checking out the missiles." Sam told Menzies. He turned to Filipenko and gestured to the massive cradles lining the hull of the missile room. "These are our real stingers and nobody knows them better than Menzies. Chief, do the honors."

"Aye, aye, sir." Menzies laid her hand on the open missile casing. "The DSIM-5 Bravo— Deep Space Intercept Missile Mark Five B. We call her the Mark Five Fire Lance. Manufactured by Lockheed-Siemens, this is the latest block four version: it has the better energy storage system and tweaked targeting mechanics."

"I know some of that," Filipenko said. "It has a nuclear warhead, right?"

"Yes, ma'am, here in the belly."

She patted the smooth composite housing of the missile on the maintenance station and then explained how the thirty laser rods up front all aligned on target and then, when the nuclear warhead detonated, were completely vaporized, but not before—for just an instant, fewer than five nanoseconds—they were engorged with energy and discharged that energy in thirty incredibly powerful bolts of coherent X-ray energy.

"If it has a nuclear warhead, why not just crash it into their ships?"

Menzies glanced quickly at Sam and then back at Filipenko, her face expressionless.

"The missile can evade and it releases two dozen radar decoys, which can get it closer to the enemy ship. But the point defense lasers—at a certain range they do not miss something the size of a missile. But the fire lance only has to get within five thousand kilometers. It detonates and the x-ray lasers do the rest, *tabarnak*."

Filipenko colored slightly with embarassment and frowned. "Yes, of course. I remember, I've just been away from this for a while. But why thirty rods? Why not just one big one?"

"Insurance, ma'am. At them ranges it don't take much deflection to miss: some vibration *faible*, the target starts to evade, you see? Thirty rods means a pattern of thirty shots, like the shotgun. Also we can independently target each rod *ostie*, take out up to thirty targets . . . or so they say."

"What makes you think it won't?"

Menzies looked back at the missile and frowned.

"Well, ma'am, is all new stuff, yeah? Lots of times this new *de saint-sacrament de câlice* stuff don't work as advertised. BuOrd says is fine, but they always say that. I hear talk—misaligned rods missing the targets in some tests, missing big."

Filipenko eyebrows went up a fraction but her expression remained cool. "The Bureau of Ordnance is responsible for testing and evaluation. From what I know, they are very thorough."

"Well, ma'am," Menzies answered, with an edge of challenge in her voice, "is hard to pull them apart and see why *mon crisse de missile* is broke-dick-no-workee after it's fired, being reduced to radioactive dust and all."

"Thanks for the briefing, Chief," Sam said quickly, now anxious to get Filipenko away before she and her chief petty officer started shouting at each other.

Sam led Filipenko back toward the spine of the boat. Sam had no idea which one was right about BuOrd—the Bureau of Ordnance. He knew nothing about their testing protocols, but he knew something about how the corporate world worked, and he knew there was a steady stream of former BuOrd officers moving into VP jobs at Lockeed-Siemens.

"You may be right about BuOrd," Sam said once they were back in the transit tube. "Hope so. But the real takeaway here is that Menzies knows her stuff."

Filipenko nodded. "Yes, I picked that up. I'm not crazy about her attitude, though. Wasn't there a discipline problem?"

Sam could have said the problem was Del Huhn's sexual frustration, his temporary mania for rooting out every sexual affair between enlisted personnel, but he couldn't say that, and what did it matter now anyway?

"Peacetime stuff," he said, "and nothing to do with her job performance. Don't worry about that. This is what's important." He gestured toward the hatches to the two missile rooms on opposite sides of the transit tube. "This is *Puebla's* reason for existing."

Filipenko frowned and looked at Sam for a moment. "You really love this stuff, don't you?"

Sam glanced around and shrugged. "I like hardware and I like tactical theory. I'm not sure I'd like throwing these monsters at living targets nearly as much."

Sam said the words because it would ease Filipenko's path, but it wasn't really true. He *did* want to fire these missiles into an uBakai naval formation and watch it come apart. Part of it was a hunger for revenge, whose growing heat had begun to replace some of the dead, black places in his heart. But part of it was something possibly more primitive still—the thrill of the hunt.

Filipenko looked around half-heartedly. "It all seems so . . . mechanical. The point defense lasers are controlled by that automated fire control system—what's it called again?"

"ATITEP," Sam said, "Automated Threat Identification, Tracking, and Engagement Protocol."

"Yes, that one," Filipenko said. "We don't make any decisions except to turn the system on or off—guns up or guns down. We maintain these missiles but most of the firing decisions on them are made by ATITEP, as well."

"You're mostly right," Sam said. "This is all pretty mechanical. Setting up the shot window, keeping the enemy from detecting you until you're in that window—those are the tough parts."

"But astrogation does most of that," she said. "What do I do other than . . . preside?"

"Presiding—if you want to call it that-is what a department head does. It's ninety-nine percent of your job: keep the equipment running, keep your personnel trained, disciplined, and effective. That other one percent is sitting in the Tac One seat when people are shooting at us, and you giving the captain the best tactical advice you can."

"Which I know nothing about," she said and shook her head.

Sam thought that the unspoken second half of that sentence might have been, *nor do I want to.*

"Look, Filipenko, I know you'd rather stay in Operations. Honestly, I'd be happier running Tactical. Somewhere on the boat there's probably someone who wants to wear ballet slippers and be called Princess Anastasia. But since none of that is going happen, why dwell on it?

"We've got a couple weeks to get ready, especially since they pulled us out of the first wave. I've got some drills slated that will sharpen your tactical thinking, bring back those course lessons from a few years ago. You'll get the hang of it quicker than you think. I bet you'll make a good Tac Boss."

"Well, thanks for the confidence," she said, although without much enthusiasm.

"Hey, it's not rocket surgery. I got pretty good at it and I'm just a dumb reservist. You're got The Ring of Power, so how tough can it be?"

She looked at her Annapolis class ring and smiled at that, but Sam knew words could only do so much. What Filipenko really needed was just to get into the routine of the job and build up some confidence. He pointed back to the missiles.

"Look, deep space tactics are easy. It's all a matter of speed and distance. If you can put a Mark Five Fire Lance within five thousand kilometers of an enemy ship, it will take care of the rest. In order to get it where you want it, you point the boat in the direction you want the missile to go and shoot it out of our spinal coil gun. The coil gun's a linear magnetic accelerator that runs from here all the way up to the bow, right through the boat, just ventral of this access tube. It kicks the missile out with an exit velocity of six kilometers per second. If you know the relative velocity of the target, it's grade school arithmetic to figure out whether you can put a missile moving six kilometers per second within five thousand kilometers of it."

"There's more to it than just that," Filipenko said.

"Well, sure. That's why they pay us. But that's the core of the problem: putting one of our missiles within killing range of a target. Everything else is a variation on that theme.

"This is your job now. To do it right you have to understand your tools—and your people. You've got a good weapons division chief in there. She may be a little rough around the edges, but she'll help you learn the ropes and she won't let you down in a crisis. You just need to get along with her."

"Sure. The way you get along with the captain."

CHAPTER EIGHT

5 December 2133
(six hours later the same day) ***(sixteen days from K'tok orbit)***

Vice-Captain Takaar Nuvaash, Speaker for the Enemy, ducked his head to avoid a low-mounted circuitry trunk line as he entered the admiral's tactical center in the rotating habitat wheel of the cruiser KBk Five One Seven. He already had one small patch of spray bandage on his forehead from an earlier collision with an equipment housing. In happier times Nuvaash had served as a liaison officer on two different Human warships and found them much more comfortable than Varoki ships. That was pointed to by some officers as further proof of the frivolous approach Humans took to war. But their ships had not struck Nuvaash as luxurious; their designers had simply paid more attention to their interior layout and to making them easier to use.

Nuvaash paused at the door to the admiral's office and heard music from inside. The office was soundproof but Nuvaash noticed the slight trace of light along one edge. The door had been left ajar and the bright beauty of the music from within stopped him in his tracks.

Instruments unaccompanied by lyrics painted a rich picture of sunlight and hope and love, and he rested his head on the doorframe, eyes closed, and let it wash through him. It was as if every note surprised him as he heard it, but then reminded him it was the only note which could possibly have followed the ones before, and that of course he should had known that all his life.

The music ended. Nuvaash breathed deeply for a few moments to regain his composure, then rang for entry. The admiral's voice sounded more gruff than usual and as Nuvaash entered he saw e-Lapeela rubbing his face with both hands, as if to scrub away whatever expression had been there a moment earlier.

"Admiral . . . I could not help but hear that music. I wonder . . . can you tell me the composer?"

"Some Human, of course," the admiral answered. He nearly snarled the words but then he frowned in thought and shook his head. "His name is—*was*—Jobim. He has been dead for over a century. Have you studied music, Nuvaash?"

"No, Admiral, although I have listened to a great deal of theirs, trying to better understand them. I often find it . . . quite moving."

e-Lapeela ran his fingers along the surface of his desk, tracing the outline of the visual icon of the music file, his eyes far away.

"As a youngster I studied music," he said. "I wanted to compose music like that, but I never could. I could understand it, duplicate it, but never create it. You are familiar with the concept of the Sequence of Creation?"

"I have heard of it, Admiral, but I am not familiar with its meaning."

"It is a simple mathematical progression, beginning with the numbers zero and one, which bracket the moment of creation, the instant when something emerged from nothing. Every number following those two consists of the sum of the two which came before, so: 0, 1, 1, 2, 3, 5, 8, 13, and on forever.

"It is not simply some mathematical curiosity; it is a sequence which repeats throughout the natural world. It describes the rate of creation of seeds in a plant, the multiplication of cells within an organism, the rate of decay of radioactive isotopes. Its ascending ratio perfectly defines every naturally occurring organic spiral, such as the carapace of many aquatic animals.

"All of the six races have studied it. How could they fail to notice something so omnipresent in nature? We call it the Sequence of Creation. The Katami call it The Pulse of God. Humans call it the Fibonacci Sequence. Trust them to name it after one of their own."

"I see, Admiral," Nuvaash said, although he did not see what this had to do with either music or their war.

e-Lapeela looked at him and his expression hardened. He tapped the icon on his desktop.

"Music follows a sequence of recurring and nonrecurring

harmonics, sounds at different frequencies. Given the natural relation between frequencies and their progressions, it is possible to chart the likelihood that a particular note will come next in a composition, and whether it will be of a certain length. I see that means nothing to you, but trust me as a former scholar of music, it is so."

e-Lapeela's eyes had grown wide, his ears lay flat back against his skull, and his voice became more intense as he spoke. Nuvaash felt a flash of danger, as people often do when they suspect they are in the presence of either madness or genius.

"Most music is communally generated, and is designed to be participatory" e-Lapeela went on. "As a result, it must rely on predictable and repetitive patterns of rhythm and harmonics. But Human music includes a class of compositions designed to be communicated from the musician to the audience. The different races have wide varieties of music, but for some reason only this Human presentational music consistently reaches across the racial and cultural barriers, and appeals to the souls of all the intelligent species of the *Cottohazz*. How can that be? How is that even possible? I will tell you.

"Mathematically generated music is produced simply by varying how closely the creation of the next note adheres to expectation, based on what has come before. If the probability is set very high, the music is rhythmic but repetitive, predicable, even dull. If it is set very low, the sound is nothing more than random noise. You understand that these are two extremes on a continuum?"

"I believe I understand that, Admiral."

"If you study Human presentational music Nuvaash, if you study it as I have, you will find the pattern of progression of harmonic frequencies and rhythms is, nearly—but not quite—predictable. It sometimes delays the satisfaction of expectation, sometimes anticipates it, but over and over and over again, its likelihood of matching expectation is described by the Sequence of Creation. The Sequence of Creation, Nuvaash. And when we hear it, without knowing exactly why, we sense that it is . . . *right*.

"How can they so instinctively know that? It is as if Creation itself whispers in the Human soul, and speaks to us through their music."

Nuvaash felt momentarily dizzy thinking about what that might mean. The admiral had not asked him to do so but he sat down in the chair facing the desk. For some time they sat together in silence.

"Do not let this information seduce you, Nuvaash," the admiral finally said. "The Humans do *not* speak for Creation. Are you religious?"

Nuvaash blushed. Religion was the most private of matters, seldom if ever discussed in public.

"It does not matter," e-Lapeela said. "My point is that I am not a mystic myself. I do not know that I believe in Creation. But I believe in blasphemy. How can the one exist without the other? I do not know how they can, only that there is something . . . *abominable* about Humans. If there is Creation, why would it speak through these crude, violent, evil beings? Why not speak through us?

"They are like demons, Nuvaash, and they *will* consume us. They are a plague. We must be the physicians who heal the *Cottohazz*, and the healing must begin here. Do you see?"

"Yes, Admiral, I see," Nuvaash said, but what he saw most clearly was an obsession in the admiral bordering on madness.

e-Lapeela's ears fanned out from his skull and his skin took on a slight orange anger tint.

"Our people are at a crossroads. Our governments are corrupt, the civilians softened by decades of luxury and now embittered when times grow only slightly harder. The coup in our own nation a year ago might have begun setting things right but we relied upon the ground forces to control the cities. Only one task did we entrusted them with, and they were not even capable of carrying that out!

"Now our navy is humiliated, many of our most visionary admirals and politician are in detention or dead, their voices stilled. Weak fools run the government."

That the government was weak and corrupt was not news to Nuvaash, nor was the fact that ever since the disastrous failed coup the uBakai Star Navy's loyalty had been an open question. But Nuvaash wondered why, given all of that, the government had authorized this reckless war.

The Admiral stood up and continued speaking, now more animated, more angry.

"The *Cottohazz*, which we Varoki created, which was once a bulwark of our primacy, is now only concerned with the rules and regulations of its massive bureaucracy—and satisfying the whining grievances of the lesser races.

"Only victory in this war can restore the Star Navy to its position of respect," e-Lapeela continued, his ears relaxing back again, his skin clearing, "and give our people a vision of destiny worth fighting for. Do you see it, Nuvaash? Only victory matters."

"Of course, sir," Nuvaash answered soothingly, "only victory. But in that regard I have . . . questions. What is our real objective? How are we to achieve it with such limited forces? And as you say, the Navy is demoralized, the government uninterested in anything other than shoring up its political security."

"Our objective is to destroy the Human will to resist, to question, and to expand. K'tok is only the pretext, the inciting event.

"Our resources are greater than you imagine, Nuvaash, because they are not limited to those solely of Bakaa. Others stand behind us, in the shadows, but they will emerge when the time is right.

"And the Humans will never understand what is happening to them until it is too late."

"Where the hell do you get off poaching my officers?" Lieutenant Larry Goldjune, the Ops Boss, demanded as he floated through the door to the XO's office.

Sam looked up from the script he was drafting for the hologram message he'd record and send to the parents of Machinist Mate Second Class Pulaski, Vincent J., of Joliet, Illinois. Pulaski had died when the first uBakai pellets hit *Puebla* and evacuated the forward machinery spaces where he was conducting routine maintenance on the thermal shroud retractor. Pulaski had not died immediately, nor easily, and Sam had been trying to find a way around sharing that information when Goldjune's outburst interrupted him.

"Where do *you* get off storming into my office without knocking and waiting for permission?"

"Don't pull that XO crap on me, Bitka. It's not going to fly."

"Tell you what, Lieutenant Goldjune, why don't you go back out into the passageway, count to ten, knock, and we'll try starting this conversation over."

"Why don't you go to hell? Now answer the goddamn question."

Sam leaned back in his zero gee restraint and looked Goldjune over. His fleshy face was flushed and he panted slightly, either with emotion or exertion.

"You're really pissed, aren't you? Well, if it makes any difference, I wanted *you* to take over TAC, but the captain overruled me. Filipenko was the only alternative. With Washington and Waring dead and me at Exec, there are only four line officers—two lieutenants and two ensigns—left to staff the two line departments—Operations and Tactical. Hard to figure out an arrangement that doesn't end up with one lieutenant and one ensign in each department. So which would you prefer: to run Ops with Barb Lee as your ensign, or run Tac with Jerry Robinette?"

The answer was obvious for several reasons: Goldjune was a diehard Ops man, Jerry Robinette was the most inept ensign on the boat, and it was an open secret that Larry Goldjune and Barb Lee had been having an affair for over a month.

Goldjune hooked his feet through a padded handhold on the wall and folded his arms across his chest, but Sam could see his anger slipping away, and Larry struggling to maintain it.

"So you wanted to stick me in TAC, huh? That figures."

"Yeah, it does, because you're better qualified than Filipenko. When the shooting starts, the captain better have the best brain he can get sitting beside him in the Tac One chair. At least that's how I see it. But he decided you'd be happier in Ops, and what the captain says goes."

Larry looked at him, thought that over, and for a moment Sam thought they might get past this wall of animus that separated them. But Goldjune's eyes narrowed again, and hardened.

"What do you know about what he'll need in combat? When did you become an expert on it? You think just because you guessed right once on an attack profile you're some kind of military genius?"

Sam could have told him that neither of them had ever heard a shot fired in anger, that all any of them had to go on was their training, but he was suddenly tired of arguing. No matter what he said, nothing would change.

"Filipenko is taking Tac and that's it. And while you're here, your affair with Ensign Lee is over, effective right now—or at least on hiatus until end of our deployment. It's none of my business after that. But she's your direct subordinate, for Christ's sake. Now get out of here so I can do some work."

★★★

An hour after Goldjune left, Sam's commlink vibrated and he heard the ID tone of the captain.

"Yes, sir."

"Bitka, come to my cabin at once," Huhn said, clearly agitated, and then he cut the connection.

"Aye, aye, sir," Sam said to the empty office around him. *Now what?*

As Sam unbuckled his restraint lanyard from the workstation he saw a flickering something out of the corner of his eye, just for a moment, and turned quickly, but nothing—or rather on one—was there. The image had been unclear but somehow familiar, familiar enough to make his scalp tingle, make his vision lose clarity and turn the colors pale, make his hands tremble. It had been Jules, hadn't it? The thought filled him with a familiar warmth and dread realization in equal measures.

Oh, that's great. First an interstellar war, and now I'm going nuts.

He looked around the office one more time, took a long breath to steady himself, and left.

Sam's office was forward, off the bridge, and Huhn's cabin was aft, in officer's country, but it still took him less than five minutes to reach the door. He touched the knocker and camera-mike, which would turn the inside surface of the door into a window and show his presence to Huhn.

"Sir, it's Lieutenant Bitka, reporting as ordered."

Huhn immediately opened the door. He hadn't shaved in at least a day, as near as Sam could tell, and pale stubble covered his cheeks, chin, and the sides and back of his head.

"Come in, Sam. Come in." Huhn stuck his head out into the corridor and looked both ways before closing the door and locking it. "Care for some coffee? Or can I offer you something stronger—got some pretty good bourbon over here." He kicked off from the door, gliding over to a cabinet behind his desk. Sam looked around and the cabin walls were still unadorned gray. A dirty sock was stuck to an exhaust ventilator.

"Thank you, sir, coffee sounds good. I still have some work to finish up later this afternoon. Better keep a clear head."

"Of course, of course," Huhn said. He punched in the order on his desk dispenser and in seconds handed a warm drinking bulb of coffee to Sam. He gestured to the padded restraints and handholds along the gray cabin walls. "Make yourself comfortable, please. No need to stand on ceremony."

Sam pushed off the deck toward a wall stanchion and clipped his restraint lanyard to it. So far this was not the conversation he had anticipated.

Huhn floated silently behind his desk for a few seconds, as if gathering his thoughts. "Sam, I want to talk to you about Lieutenant Goldjune."

Okay, here it comes, Sam thought and took a swallow of coffee. Maybe the bourbon would have been a smarter move.

"Yes, sir?"

"You and I have disagreed about him, especially in our assessment of him as an officer."

"I think Goldjune is a talented and capable officer, sir," Sam said, just to get it on the record.

"Of course he is," Huhn said, nodding, "as far as that goes. But you know, sometimes character's more important. Maybe that's especially true in wartime. The war's made me take another look at some things. I'll tell you something, Sam: I don't trust him. He's been acting funny for the last day or so, talking to people in the wardroom and then they stop and just look at me when I come in. What's that all about?"

Sam thought it might be about Del Huhn's guilty conscience, but he didn't say that.

"I don't know, sir, but I'll try to find out."

"You haven't heard anything? Any . . . disloyal mutterings?" Huhn searched Sam's face but avoided his eyes.

"No, sir, and if I had, they'd have stopped right there. I give you my word on that."

Huhn looked at him for a moment and then looked away and nodded.

"I believe you, Sam. I think you're a man of character, an honest man—too honest maybe. I suppose that's why we had our little disagreement. Seems a lifetime ago, doesn't it? Well, water under the bridge. Peace and war, different times, different *lifetimes*. Maybe it's only possible to be too honest in peacetime, you know, like I was saying, war and character . . . something about them going together, I . . . I don't know. But I trust you, Sam."

Huhn looked at Sam with eyes that shown with moist affection and entreaty, a combination Sam found pathetic, repellant, and vaguely alarming.

"Thank you, sir," he managed and looked away, his eyes fastening again on Huhn's family pictures, slowly cycling on the one small live area on the smart wall.

"That's Joey, my boy," Huhn said, and glided over to the video window. He stopped the display and enlarged it to show the family in yet another posed grouping. Did they ever vacation? Did they ever do anything together but pose for pictures? The son was in his late teens in this picture, beginning to look heavy in the face and upper body, and for a change staring directly at the camera in an apparent act of defiance with a hint of contempt.

"He's a few years older now. He tried the Navy—probably wanted to please the old man, follow in my footsteps, you know how sons are. It didn't work out, Navy wasn't for him. Joey's had trouble finding his niche, but he's a good boy. He's . . . well, he's a good boy."

Sam looked at the picture and nodded. The woman with her tentative smile, fleeing in quiet panic toward the safety of dowdy middle age, looking as if she needed permission to do anything, who might have been pretty when she was young if she'd let herself, if she'd just given herself permission. Married to a husband who tried to cheat on her when on deployment—probably thought it was what mariners always did, were supposed to do, made them somehow more manly and desirable. And Huhn couldn't even manage to do that right, could he? Jules had turned him down, and how many others before her?

When Huhn had graduated from Annapolis and, with a thousand other white-clad men and women, thrown his hat as high into the air as he could, he must have envisioned a life about to unfold before him. He had seen those plans realized, but distorted and grotesque, as if reflected by a funhouse mirror. Did he sometimes wonder where he went wrong? Did he ever stop wondering?

"We'll get through this, sir," Sam said. "We'll get through it, and we'll get back to our families."

Huhn put his hand on Sam's shoulder.

"I know I can count on you, Sam. Now, Goldjune?" Huhn looked aside, eyes focused farther away than the barren gray wall he faced. "After all I've done for him? Stood up for him? Covered up his mistakes and indiscretions? He's just a disloyal little shit. Sometimes I wish he was dead."

In the corridor outside Huhn's room Sam stopped and closed his eyes, but the flickering shadow he knew to be Jules persisted, dancing at the periphery of his right field of vision, always just out of reach. Her being there, watching, waiting for something, made his nervous, almost sick to his stomach. Who was crazier? he wondered. Huhn or him?

He squinted up the medtech's comm address.

Medtech Tamblinson. What can I do for you, Mister Bitka?

"Tamblinson, I've . . . I've got a headache," he lied. "Yeah, a real skull-buster, and I need to get some shuteye. Can you give me something that will knock me out for a couple of hours but not leave me punchy when I wake up?"

They don't call me Doc Feelgood for nothing, sir.

CHAPTER NINE

7 December 2133
(two days later) ***(fourteen days from K'tok orbit)***

PLAN OF THE DAY
USS *Puebla*, DDR-11
7 December 2133

LCDR Delmar P. Huhn, USN
COMMANDING OFFICER

LT Samuel M. Bitka, USNR
EXECUTIVE OFFICER

Uniform of the Day	Officers:	White shipsuit
	Chiefs:	Khaki shipsuit
	All Others:	Blue shipsuit

0000 Mid Watch drills and training
0500 Breakfast
0530 BLUE Watch relieves RED, LT Goldjune OOD, LT(JG) Ramsey DEO
0600 Morning Colors
0630 Morning drills and training
1100 Lunch
1130 WHITE watch relieves BLUE, ENS Lee OOD, LT(JG) Sung DEO
1200 Afternoon drills and training

1700 Supper
1730 RED watch relieves WHITE, LT(JG) Filipenko OOD,
LT Hennessey DEO
1800 Boat's company muster for inspection
1830 All hands General Quarters. Anticipated rendezvous
with Task Force 1
2000 Anticipated stand-down from General Quarters
2300 Late Supper
2330 BLUE watch relieves RED, LT Goldjune OOD,
LT(JG) Ramsey DEO

NOTES

1. MORNING COLORS: All hands not on watch will assemble for morning colors. Colors will be presented at half-mast in honor of Pearl Harbor Remembrance Day.

2. DRILLS: Departments will drill on-duty watch personnel as follows

OPERATIONS:	Navigation by HRVS optics only Reestablishing lost communication tight link in battle situation
TACTICAL:	Detection of hostile craft with HRVS optics using stellar occlusion method Simulated target engagement at high closing rate vectors
ADMIN:	Casualty clearance
ENGINEERING:	No drills. All available personnel tasked to damage repair

3. TRAINING: Department heads will insure personnel coming off watch immediately spend at least one hour on review training on their MOS and one hour mastering their next grade or a parallel MOS in their department. Review. Train up. Train across.

4. TASK FORCE RENDEZVOUS: All drills and training suspended during the Evening Watch due to rendezvous with Combined Task Force One. All hands will go to General Quarters following inspection.

5. CREW APPEARANCE: Crew to remove all facial hair and non-permanent ornamentation by inspection at 1800, haircuts high and tight. We will be holo-conferencing with other craft of the task force from this evening forward, including a large number of WestEuro craft, and every member of the crew must present a professional and squared-away appearance at all times. Don't make us look bad in front of the Europeans.

D. P. Huhn
LCDR, USN

Sam read the Plan of the Day again and shook his head. Two years ago he never would have imagined he'd be where he was, in the middle of an interstellar war, writing a Plan of the Day about haircuts.

He had never imagined that he would be in the first combatant action of the war, nor in the first craft damaged by such action, nor in the forward screen of the first offensive space task force assembled in Earth history, nor that he would suffer loss so early, nor that it would affect him so deeply that he would not be able to just put it from his mind and carry on. He did carry on, but it was as if Jules's ghost silently accompanied him, watching everything he did. He had seen her three times, fleetingly, out of the corner of his eye, after that first time when her presence had unnerved him.

Most of all, he never imagined that almost a week into the war it would remain so ordinary, so routine, as if that first burst of terror and violence, which had lasted less than half an hour, had been simply a dream. He never imagined that when the vagaries of war catapulted him into a position of responsibility for which he felt entirely unprepared, and while hurtling toward what could be the climactic battle of the first campaign in the war, he would spend his time filling out forms, posting plans of the day, and overseeing the minutiae of crew training and discipline. Was *this* what war was really like?

"*Haircuts*, Bitka? What the—?"

Sam looked up from his workstation to see Marina Filipenko, the new Tac Boss, floating in the open doorway.

"Yeah, haircuts. You want the Euros to laugh at us for looking like a pirate crew?"

She gave a soft tug on the doorframe and coasted into the XO's office. "So instead they'll laugh at us for looking like a bunch of circus geeks. Jesus, what'll he come up with next?"

Sam sighed and stretched. He'd argued with Huhn for fifteen minutes about this stupid order but hadn't been able to talk him out of it, not that Filipenko needed to know that.

"Just do it, okay? And get some perspective: nobody's life is going to be shattered by a haircut. While you're here, what's the progress on getting Ensign Robinette certified to stand watch as Officer of the Deck?" Sam had to make a conscious effort not to call the young ensign *The Jughead.*

"Slow. He's trying but he's got a long way to go." Filipenko looked away and her attention seemed to wander.

"Something bothering you, Filipenko?"

"Bothering me? We're up to our ears in a war, taking on the largest military power of the most technologically advanced race in known space, and we've got a weak spot in the crew roster." She paused and looked at him, eyebrows raised. "You know who I mean."

She meant the captain. Sam's first instinct was to bark her down, but he'd done a lot of barking in the last couple days. He took a deep breath instead.

"You want a coffee? Fresh brewed, right here in my dispenser."

She shook her head.

"It's been a lot to absorb in just a few days," Sam said after a moment, "a lot to get used to. You don't need to tell *me* that. But the person you're talking about is going to be fine—maybe not the easiest guy in the fleet to work with but so what? Best thing you can do about him is concentrate on doing your own job, okay? Stand one watch at a time."

"I'm not talking about being easy to work with, or this haircut silliness," she said. "I'm talking about freezing on the bridge in the first attack. I'm talking about who made the call to realign the boat."

Sam felt his face flush. He'd thought that was only between Captain Huhn and himself. If the crew were talking about it, that was trouble.

"Since the cloud missed us anyway it wouldn't have made a difference, but I think you have things mixed up, Filipenko. I recommended realigning the boat—which was my responsibility as TAC Boss—and asked the Captain for permission. He gave it and we realigned. End of story."

"That's not what Barb Lee told me. She said he froze and you gave the order. It'll be on the bridge hololog."

Sam shook his head. "I gave the order but only after the captain gave me permission."

"And the audio track will confirm that?" she said.

"No, the captain nodded to me. He didn't speak."

"And the permanent holovid track will confirm *that*?"

Sam shrugged. "At one frame a second, who knows if you can tell he nodded. But I'm *saying* he did. You calling me a liar, Filipenko?"

She looked away. "This really stinks. I'm trying to do the right thing, the responsible thing, but it feels ugly and small and . . . and dirty, like I should go take a sponge bath. I have this feeling no matter what I do, I'll end up dirty." She turned and looked at Sam. "The kind of dirt I'll never scrub off. You know what I mean?"

"I do. You want to *not* feel dirty? Stop trying to make judgments about things that are above your pay grade. When you leave here, go find Ensign Lee and kick her ass from here to Monday. Tell her what I told you about the captain nodding. Tell her to stop spreading rumors about things she doesn't know the whole story on, rumors that undermine the authority of the captain and endanger everyone on the boat. Those are breaches of Navy regulations and in wartime constitute a serious offense, punishable by loss of rank, separation from the service, and imprisonment. Explain that you're telling her that as a favor, because if I have to—as exec—it'll get ugly."

Filipenko again looked away. "There wasn't supposed to be a war, ever again," she muttered. "And if there was, it wasn't supposed to feel this way. I hate it, hate all of it. We didn't sign on for *this*."

"Amen," Sam said, but only to make her feel better. He didn't really believe it.

In fact all of them had signed on for exactly this. Filipenko had graduated from Annapolis in 2130, with a commission as a regular officer in the United States Navy, with all that entailed. Twelve years earlier, in the fall of '18, Sam had joined the Naval Reserve Officer Training Corps at U-Cal San Diego, and if it was mostly for access to the excellent NROTC gliders and sailboats, what difference did that make now? What difference did it make that when they had all agreed to serve, none of them had imagined that it would come to this? Did their lack of imagination relieve them of their obligation?

It occurred to Sam that lack of imagination might actually be an asset in the coming weeks.

His commlink vibrated and he squinted to see the ID of the duty communications petty officer.

"XO," Sam answered.

Sir, this is Signaler First Class Kramer, communications. I have an incoming request for a holoconference from USS Pensacola, *Task Force flagship.*

"They're about ten hours early. Have you notified the captain?"

Sir, the request is from a Commander Atwater Jones, Royal Navy, and it's for a one-on-one conference with you, by name, as soon as you're available.

"That's funny. I don't recall knowing anyone in the Royal Navy."

The second member state of the coalition was the West European Union, but the member states still maintained many of their pre-union national institutions, including their own armed forces. They operated under a unified command, but Sam still wasn't sure exactly how that all worked. He looked up at Filipenko.

"Lieutenant, can you excuse me? Royal Navy needs a face-to-face."

"What for?" she said.

Sam shrugged.

"I'm due on watch anyway," she said and pushed off toward the doorway. "I'll talk to Ensign Lee." She closed the hatch behind her.

Sam wondered if she'd bought his story about Huhn nodding. He thought she had, and in any case she seemed to understand the necessity to act as if it were true. He hoped Ensign Lee would as well. If it came to an official board of inquiry, he wasn't prepared to perjure himself, or torpedo Lee's career, just to cover for Delmar Huhn's lapse.

Sam put on his suit helmet, whose optics were necessary for the holoconference, and triggered his commlink again.

"Okay, Kramer, let's see what this Jones guy wants."

Sam waited for a few seconds while Kramer patched the tight beam communicator channel through to his commlink and then the ghostly image of a tall, attractive, red-haired woman in her late thirties or early forties appeared, wearing a dark blue Royal Navy officer's shipsuit and transparent viewer glasses.

"Um . . . I'm on the beam for a Commander Jones?" Sam said.

"Atwater-Jones," she said. "Right, that's me. You look surprised."

"I was expecting a man," he said, and her expression immediately darkened. "No, I just . . . it was the name. Atwater sounds like a guy is all."

She squinted at him for a moment and then shook her head. "It's my family name: Atwater-Jones, hyphenated. My first name is Cassandra."

Aware he might have gotten off to a bad start, and also aware she outranked him by two grades, Sam tried to think of a way to make amends. "Cassandra's, um . . . a nice name."

"Really? I think it's a perfectly dreadful name for a naval intelligence officer. Fraught with all sorts of unwanted significance. Wouldn't have chosen it myself."

"Well . . . what can I do for you, Commander?"

"Let me start by presenting my *bona fides*. I am N2, intelligence chief, to your Admiral Kayumati, part of the allied staff, Combined Task Force One. I believe both our services call the position Smart Boss. The commander of your destroyer division, Captain Bonaventure, forwarded your threat assessment but without any explanation as to how you came to your conclusions. I spoke with him and he had simply passed on the message sent by your captain. Huhn? Isn't that his name?"

"Yes, ma'am."

"Right. As Captain Bonaventure didn't know any more than I did, he recommended I ring you up. The only information in the burst transmission was as follows: 'Advise, Stinger Squadron attacked by pellet clouds on high velocity exact reciprocal course. Tac Boss Red Stinger Two believes identical profile attack likely main force. (Signed) Red Stinger Six Actual.'

"You are the TAC Boss?"

"Was. I'm XO now."

"Congratulations on your promotion. Well-deserved, I'm sure. Now, I'm afraid I'm all in bits over this second attack against the main task force. The only way I can see these attacks launched is as a result of an intelligence leak—two leaks, actually, as the departure times and flight profiles of both forces would have to have been independently discovered and communicated. My question is this: how would the tactical officer on a destroyer, deployed in advance of us, know about those two leaks?"

"Commander, I don't know anything about any intelligence leaks."

"Then how could you be so sure the same attack launched against your force could have been duplicated against ours? Our senior operations staff assures me the potential volume of space where we could emerge from interstellar jump renders chance detection of an arriving force almost impossible. Coincidental detection of *two* such forces?" She frowned and shook her head.

"Yeah, well . . . all due respect to your operations people, Commander, but they think like astrogators, not Tac-heads."

Then Sam explained in detail why the astrogation standard practices of arriving Earth forces had made it possible to detect them, the same as he had explained to Huhn and the others the day of the attack. Commander Atwater-Jones listened carefully, nodding her understanding, her face eventually creasing with anger.

"Knobbers!" she finally said when he was done, then she shook her head. "Oh, not you Bitka. Excellent piece of tactical reasoning."

She stared ahead for a moment, her eyes not on him, so she must have been studying information projected by her viewer glasses. Her focus returned to him.

"You're a reservist," she said, surprise in her voice.

"Yes, ma'am. Is that a problem?"

"Heavens, no! Why, some of my best chums are Royal Navy Reserve." She gave him a lopsided grin. "We just don't expect them to be prodigies, that's all. What's your secret?"

Prodigy? Sam felt his face warm a bit but he took a breath and made his mind work this through. He was on dangerous ground: he didn't want to say anything a British officer might interpret as criticism of the US Navy, and who knew what her agenda was? He did suspect that flattery from a naval intelligence officer was more likely a prelude to trouble than to good news.

"I'm no prodigy, Commander, and there's no secret, just excellent training at Pearl River—the Deep Space Tactical Warfare School. Fundamentals of interplanetary astrogation, sensor performance at light-second range, combat tactics on a high-closing-rate vector—they made it all seem easy and fun."

She laughed.

"Easy *and* fun? They must have changed some of the faculty since I read tactics there six years ago. An exchange assignment, you know. Beastly in the summer, isn't it?"

"It's not really the heat," Sam said with a smile, "it's the humidity."

"I rather thought it was both," she answered and she nodded thoughtfully, but Sam didn't think her mind was on the climate of southwestern Mississippi. After a moment her eyebrows danced up just for an instant and then settled back, as if shrugging.

"Right. Well, thank you *Leftenant* Bitka, you have been most helpful."

And the connection went dead.

Sam took off his helmet and clipped it to his workstation, then stretched his back and locked his fingers behind his head.

What *was* his secret? Did he even have a secret?

After college and his mandatory term of active duty service with the Navy, he'd spent seven years in the private sector, working his way up to assistant vice president for West Coast Product Support in the large-capacity fabricator division of Dynamic Paradigms. Had anything from his work helped him as a tactical officer? It had taught him how to figure out what his bosses wanted and give it to them, which got him through Pearl River with great marks. Then it got him strong fitness reports and glowing recommendations from the captains he served under before coming to USS *Puebla*.

The training really had been good, and something about it had appealed to him. It *was* easy and fun, but probably less because of the instructors and more because Sam had taken to it. It was a good mental fit, the way you sometimes meet a stranger but your minds are organized so similarly that within no time you feel like you've know her for years. But others took to the training as well. That wasn't his secret.

He started to sip coffee from the drink bulb tethered to his desk but it had gone cold. He flushed it in his drink dispensor's liquid recycler and switched to mango juice. He had enough caffeine in his system but a little sugar wouldn't hurt.

What was his secret? It wasn't his secret at all; it was the Navy's, and he didn't think they even knew they had one. A hundred years of peaceful space travel had left the Navy paying lip service to the violent part of its mission, and you could see it in something as simple as where officers sat at the wardroom table. Promising regulars, the ones with good marks and better connections, went into operations—astrogation and communication—not tactics. They had to do rotations in tactical departments, but when they did they usually opted for the sensor slots rather than weapons. Weapons were things you maintained and polished and practiced shooting, but never actually used. Sensors at least were useful for astrogation.

Sam didn't fault that. It wasn't for him to judge, and in any case it made sense. What the Navy did was move people and ships around, and to do that they needed astrogators, communicators, and engineers. The tactical people had been dead weight for a hundred years, they were the bottom rung on the social ladder, and as soon as a bunch of bright-eyed reservists started coming into uniform, as many of the old tactical officers as could manage it had switched over to operations, leaving their seats for reservists to fill.

But what Sam had said to the British commander was true as far as it went: operations people just didn't think tactically; they thought like astrogators. What he hadn't told her was that, as far as he could tell, right now the United States Navy was run, top to bottom, by astrogators.

He couldn't just come out and say that to some Limey.

Had he just gotten a number of astrogators in trouble? He hoped so. Those would be the same ones who got Jules and six more of his shipmates killed by cutting corners to make their jobs easier. If Sam survived this, they'd find out what real trouble was.

Speaking of trouble . . .

Sam keyed his embedded commlink and squinted up the connection to the duty communications petty officer.

Sig-One Kramer.

"Kramer, this is the XO. Notify the captain that the task force smart boss just called for a face-to-face with me by name, and send the captain the recording of the conference."

Aye, aye, sir.

"Oh, and Kramer . . . make sure you let him know *I* told you to send him the recording."

CHAPTER TEN

7 December 2133
(ten hours later) ***(fourteen days from K'tok orbit)***

Sam's relationship with Captain Huhn had proved as constant and predictable as the energy output of an eruptive variable star.

The day after the attack, and after the first promising conversation, Huhn had ignored Sam when in the same room and sent a series of increasingly brusque orders by commlink.

The next day Chief Navarro had given Sam a badly needed education in his duties.

The day after that Huhn had called Sam to his cabin during the afternoon watch, delivered his rambling monologue about his trust in Larry Goldjune having vanished, and sent Sam away with the admonition that the two of them needed to stick together in the face of their "enemies."

For the entire next day and the following one, Huhn remained in his cabin with orders not to be disturbed except for contact with the enemy or incoming communications addressed to him. Sam should handle everything else. Those were the two days before the scheduled rendezvous with Combined Task Force One. Sam knew that Huhn and Goldjune had been close and Goldjune turning on him must have shaken the captain up badly. He hadn't know the cause of the break then, but he now suspected that Ensign Lee's take on Huhn freezing on the auxiliary bridge the day of the attack was at the core of it. Lee had shared her thoughts with Marina Filipenko; wouldn't she do the same with her department head and lover?

Six hours after Sam's conference with Commander Atwater-Jones in the afternoon of the rendezvous, *Puebla* and the other boats of their division—Destroyer Division Three—received a tight-beam burst transmission to be ready for a holobriefing by senior staff of the task force in two hours. The briefing would include the command teams of all four DDRs of DesDiv Three: USS *Oaxaca, Tacambaro, Queretaro*, and *Puebla*, all patched into the same virtual conference space. Each DDR's command team was limited to three officers: captain, executive officer, and Tac Boss.

Perhaps Huhn would settle down after the briefing—it had only been five days since the attack, only five days of war. They knew the barest outline of a plan but no details, few specifics of what they were expected to do beyond hang back with *Hornet* and act as a reserve. Maybe this briefing would do the trick, give Huhn something to focus on. Sam hoped so.

Whatever animosity he had felt toward Delmar Huhn had faded, although he could not say why. He felt no affection for the captain, not even sympathy. Instead it was as if Sam drove an aged ground car across the desert and Del Huhn was its engine—sputtering, overheating, losing power. He felt no emotions for the engine except anxiety and desperation to keep it running until he reached safety.

Perhaps it would have been different if Huhn had stalked the boat, finding fault with officers and crew, delivering harangues, but Sam had not seen him in almost three days. As far as he knew no one had, except probably the mess attendants who delivered his meals. The captain communicated occasionally by voice commlink, more often simply by text memos. Perhaps Sam's animosity had faded because Del Huhn seemed to have faded.

Twenty minutes later, Sam's commlink vibrated and he squinted up the ID tag of Yeoman Fischer.

"What's up, Fischer?"

Sir, the captain said to ping you and say you won't need to show for the holobriefing. Lieutenant Goldjune will take your slot.

"Understood. Thanks, Fischer."

Now that was odd. As far as Sam knew, the task force staff's instructions had been specific. Huhn must have gotten permission to change the lineup. And had he patched things up with Larry Goldjune? Possibly. Or maybe he'd rather be surrounded by fellow regulars, not a reservist like Sam.

He tasted something sour, felt his face flush as resentment bubbled up within him. *He* should be in that briefing, goddamnit —either as executive officer or as Tac Boss. Huhn turning the tactical department over to Filipenko was asking for trouble. She was smart enough, but so far she hadn't shown the fire in her to own the job rather than just go through the motions. What was Huhn thinking? What was that coward, that pathetic emotional cripple, ever thinking about but his own sense of aggrieved entitlement?

Sam leaned back and took a deep, shuddering breath.

Damn! Get a grip.

Right, it wasn't about Del Huhn's grievances or disappointments, and it wasn't about his either. It was just about the boat.

So suck it up, Bitka.

Sam looked at his desk display. He had been in the middle of finishing the certifications for promotion of seven petty officers. Two of them, including Joyce Menzies, were to fill chief slots they badly needed to fill—actually were just formal confirmation of the acting promotions they'd already made. He already had his hands full with work that needed doing, right?

He looked around at the walls of the office, set to mimic the view from a small island in the Pacific, kilometers of slowly rolling ocean stretching all the way to a horizon made indistinct by low scattered clouds.

"This job stinks." he told the ocean.

He shook his head, pushed the mass of contradictory thoughts and emotions aside, and got back to work.

An hour and forty minutes later, when the holoconference was to start, Sam's commlink vibrated and he heard the ID tone of Captain Huhn.

"Yes, sir?"

Bitka, I know you think your paperwork should take precedence but I need you to helmet up for the briefing.

"Aye, aye, sir, if that's what you want."

Of course it's what I want. Why else would I say it?

"Well, Yeoman Fischer told me you wanted Lieutenant Goldjune to take my place, sir, but I'm happy to sit in."

Sam snapped on his helmet and immediately found himself in the holoconference, flanked by Huhn's virtual self to his left and Filipenko's to his right. Both of them looked embarrassed and he saw a variety of grins and scowls on the other faces, which made him realize he had been live to the conference during his exchange with Huhn. What had the captain said earlier that made Sam's words so embarrassing?

"I'll have to speak with Yeoman Fischer," Huhn said with anger in his voice. "There was apparently a misunderstanding."

Ah! Huhn must *not* have gotten permission to alter the conference attendee list, then when he'd been called on it had lied, and then had his lie exposed.

"I may have misunderstood, sir," Sam said. Whoever was at fault, it sure as hell wasn't Yeoman Fischer. Better for Sam to take the heat.

"Very well," Huhn said without looking at him.

Commander Bonaventure—Captain Tall, Dark, and Greasy, as Jules had once described him—captain of *Oaxaca* and commander of the Third Destroyer Division (*ComDesDiv Three* in Navy parlance), sat with his team to Huhn's left. The virtual images of the command teams of *Tacambaro* and *Queretaro* sat to Filipenko's right, all of them forming a shallow crescent.

The images of three senior officers faced them, floating slightly below their level and looking up. Two wore the white shipsuits of US Navy officers. The man on the right was vaguely familiar but Sam did not recognize the short, stocky, and formidable-looking woman in the center, who was clearly in charge. She wore the four stripes of a full captain—not the job, but the rank, one step short of an admiral. Her hair was gray, her expression ferocious, and her build reminiscent of a fireplug.

The third briefer wore dark blue: Commander Cassandra Atwater-Jones, Royal Navy. She seemed quite amused by whatever had gone before.

"So you're the famous Lieutenant Bitka," the gray-haired staff captain said, making *famous* sound like an epithet. Her mouth seemed sculpted into a permanent frown, accentuated by her heavy jowls and deep-set eyes. "I better let you know neither I nor Commander Boynton thinks much of your theory of the uBakai attack profile. Commander Atwater-Jones disagrees with us, but I do not believe either she or you appreciate how tricky the astrogation setup for that attack must have been."

Boynton. That name was familiar. Where did he know him from?

She glowered at him and after a second or two he realized she expected a reply.

"Understood, ma'am."

"I still believe the problem must have been an intelligence leak." She turned her glare on Atwater-Jones, who returned a cheerful smile. "Do you have anything to add to that, Commander?"

"If I had," Atwater-Jones said, still smiling, "and as it would involve an ongoing intelligence investigation of a most sensitive nature, it would of course be for your ears only, mum."

So apparently Sam was not the only one who occasionally felt the urge to bait the bear.

The formal briefing got going after that. The formidable gray-haired captain running the show turned out to be Marietta Kleindienst, chief of staff to Admiral Kayumati, the commander of the task force. Atwater-Jones was obviously there as the N2—smart boss. Sam still couldn't place the other officer.

The plan was essentially as outlined before: a direct descent on K'tok, two cohorts of mike troops landed to seize the needle, another cohort in reserve, the fleet to engage and destroy any uBakai warships in the area of operations, then provide orbital bombardment support and secure the orbital space from interference by any arriving uBakai forces.

Sam was unfamiliar with the terminology of the planetary assault itself, never having served in assault transports or in exercises involving deployment of ground troops. He kept squinting up glossaries to guide him through the maze of jargon. "Mike" stood for Meteoric Insertion Capable—soldiers dropped from orbit in individual re-entry capsules and accompanied by clouds of decoys to confuse missile interceptors.

The five heavy cruisers would hold Low Planetary Orbit (LPO), positioned to bombard the area around the Landing site. The four destroyers of DesDiv Four would form the outer screen in much higher Planetary Synchronous Orbit (PSO). The transports and logistical support vessels, along with USS *Pensacola*, the task force flagship would take station as needed.

Captain Kleindienst also told them a Nigerian and a British cruiser—NNS *Aradu* and HMS *Exeter*—had been detached to secure the system gas giant, Mogo. The four destroyers of DesDiv Five had been dispatched to Mogo; they would arrive later than the cruisers but relieve them on station there so the heavier ships could rejoin the task force.

"Any questions?" Captain Kleindienst asked and looked at the twelve men and women in the crescent.

To his surprise, Sam heard Filipenko clear her throat.

"I have one, ma'am."

Kleindienst's frown deepened and took on an added layer of impatience.

"Very well, but make it fast."

"I'm a communications officer by training and principle experience. Usually communication back to Earth takes weeks, because there is no communication except by data transfer by jump craft. This is only our fifth day of war.

"I know our emergency procedure calls for an automated comm packet dispatched by jump missile to Bronstein's World, where it will be received, transferred to a similar jump missile to Earth, where it will be received, acted on, and the procedure then repeated in reverse. But even the emergency process takes days, usually many days."

"Yes, what's your question?" Kleindienst snapped.

Filipenko took a breath, perhaps to steady herself, and then spoke.

"This plan was given to us in outline the day of the attack. I don't see how consultation with superior authority was possible. Is this attack authorized?"

That was a hell of a question. What Filipenko said was true, obviously true, but Sam hadn't thought to wonder about it. He faulted the astrogators for not thinking tactically, but Filipenko just showed him what it meant to think as a signaler.

Opposite them, Kleindienst paused, apparently to let her glare grow even more fiery.

"Given the very problems you enumerate," she said carefully and slowly, "and given the volatile nature of the situation here, Admiral Kayumati sailed with sealed orders covering a variety of anticipated contingencies. Yes, *Lieutenant*, this attack was authorized at the highest level. Admirals don't go around starting wars."

Sam did not find that particularly reassuring. Of course the attack was authorized. But if the task force had sailed with contingency plans this detailed, how peaceful had the original intention been? The uBakai had struck the first blow, taken the role of aggressor. But what if they hadn't? Maybe they had been very obliging to strike that first blow. Maybe that's just what the coalition had wanted when the task force was sent, but that left Sam more unsettled than the idea of a rogue admiral swept away by desire for revenge would have. If their side had wanted this to happen, then they had wanted Jules and the others to die. But that was a very big "if."

"Very well," Kleindienst said, eyes narrowed with irritation. "The smart boss will update you on our current threat assessment." She nodded to Commander Atwater-Jones.

"Right," she began. "Our best estimate, based on communication traffic analysis and sensor tracks over the last six months, is that the uBakai have four cruisers in the star system, of which two are currently in orbit around K'tok. One had been in orbit around Mogo but withdrew upon approach of Task Group 1.4—that's *Aradu* and *Exeter*. We don't know its angle of departure as it made its escape burn when Mogo was between it and our task force. Very clever boots, these uBakai. One cruiser is currently unaccounted for, but did depart K'tok orbit at a time consistent with Lieutenant Bitka's theory of the initial uBakai attack profile."

"That doesn't prove anything," the dark-haired male officer with a squat face and bulbous nose said. He wore the three broad stripes of a commander and Sam finally placed him: Holloway Boynton, who had been Ops Boss on USS *Theodore Roosevelt* where Sam served as a sensor officer until three months earlier. He knew him by name but had never spoken to him.

"No," Atwater-Jones answered, "but if that cruiser made both attacks, and if it made its final evasive course correction using its MPD thrusters at a low enough energy level to escape thermal detection by us, we have a reasonably limited sphere in which it must be."

"Commander, we've had HRVS optics looking in your sphere for days, and haven't found anything," Boynton said.

"Which means," Atwater Jones shot back, "either *Leftenant* Bitka's theory is incorrect *or* the vessel is where we cannot detect it by visual stellar occlusion—which is to say it is directly between us and the asteroid belt, which I note we have not completed mapping."

"That's enough," Kleindienst snapped. "This is a briefing, not a staff debate."

"Quite right," Atwater-Jones said. "As I was saying before I was interrupted, our best estimate is that they have four cruisers in the system, two around K'tok, one somewhere near Mogo, and one unaccounted for, but it's bloody-well somewhere and up to mischief.

"At present the surface objective is defended only by internal security forces, mostly military and civilian police. We rate their esprit and effectiveness as low. uBakai lift infantry and armor could be shifted back from the colonial frontier quite rapidly, but Operations is persuaded that our orbital bombardment assets can either prevent a large-scale move of mechanized forces or impose unacceptable losses on them. I must emphasize the importance of maintaining the orbital bombardment force on station in order to reduce the ground threat to manageable proportions."

She settled back in her chair and folded her hands over her lap.

That was an interesting way of putting it—that the Ops staff was *persuaded* that the orbital bombardment would work, as if Atwater-Jones did not share that opinion but it wasn't her job to question it.

"Any *more* questions?" Captain Kleindienst asked and glowered at them. "Very well. Now for Destroyer Division Three's specific part in this: Commander Boynton, the task force operations boss, will take over."

Task force ops boss? He must have moved up from *Bully*.

"Aye, aye, ma'am." Boynton put on a set of viewer glasses of his own and began speaking, probably reading from his prepared notes. "Because of the twenty-second burn the former captain of *Puebla* executed immediately after the first attack, USS *Puebla* is now seventy thousand kilometers in advance of the main body of DesDiv Three, and considerably farther in advance of the main body of the task force. Based on that, we've worked out the correction packages for *Oaxaca*, *Tacambaro* and *Queretaro* to use the thermal shroud of *Puebla* to occlude K'tok and mask their deceleration burns.

"At those distances the tolerances are very tight, but doable if you follow the burn schedules *precisely*. Let me beam that data bundle over now and you can pass it to your Ops people. For what it's worth, and considering the mission change for the division, I think Captain Huhn was right to want his Ops Boss in the conference. Not sure why we need the tac-heads."

"Noted," Captain Kleindienst said dryly.

Sam saw Huhn's holographic image shift beside him.

"Who will we use to mask our deceleration burn?" Huhn asked.

"No one," Kliendienst said. "Change in plans. You are detached to direct control of the task force commander for the duration of the assault phase. I think the admiral's going to chop you to DesDiv Four but we'll see how things shake out."

"You mean we're going in with the assault force after all?" Huhn said, his voice wavering a bit. "I thought . . . I mean, we took a lot of damage, ma'am. And we're very shorthanded, particularly officers."

Kleindienst said nothing but moved a pair of viewer glasses down from on top of her head onto her face and for a moment her eyes lost focus as she studied the data projected by them.

"I'm looking at the list of repairs and you must have one hell of an A-gang, Captain Huhn. With the exception of being down one point defense laser, *Puebla's* in better shape than any of the other three boats in the division. How are you dealing with only having seven PDLs?"

After a moment of silence Huhn turned and looked at Sam, as did Filipenko on his other side.

"Software patch on ATITEP is all we can manage for now, ma'am," Sam said. "Engineering says we can still get full coverage. We just won't have as much redundancy."

"Less defensive firepower in a stern-on engagement," Kleindienst said.

"A destroyer's preferred angle of engagement is bow-on, ma'am."

Boynton, the task force operations chief, shifted in his chair and scowled. "Is that your *professional* judgment, Lieutenant? Sounds like hot air to me."

Kleindiesnt's eyes narrowed slightly and she turned to her left. "Commander Boynton, he's quoting our basic manual on deep space tactical principles: DSTP-01, chapter four, something like section seven or eight. Which is it, Bitka?"

"Sorry, ma'am, I don't remember. It was just something that stuck in my mind."

"Well, I suppose there are worse things to stick in there. Anything else?"

Sam thought for a moment, unsure whether he should press his luck, but there was a problem they needed to address while they still could.

"Yes, ma'am, I am concerned about our ability to deal with another round of damage. We took a hit in an engineering parts bay, so a lot of our key replacement parts are gone, over and above the actual damaged components we had to replace. If you want us up front and active, we could really use a component resupply."

"It's not possible, Lieutenant," Commander Boynton said, taking off his view glasses and tossing them on his workstation in anger. "If you had an astrogation background you'd understand that. You know *Hornet's* crippled. You want one of the destroyers in your division to shuttle back and forth to *Hornet* for parts? It's not feasible, either from the point of view of reaction mass or available time."

Sam fought a momentary urge to answer that arrogant prick the way he deserved, but swallowed it and nodded seriously instead.

"You're absolutely right, sir, which is why that's not what I had in mind. I bet most of the parts we need are on the other three division boats, and as they're heading back to *Hornet* anyway—"

"W-wait!" Captain Bonaventure of *Oaxaca* said, as if suddenly waking from a nap. "What's that?"

"Make up your list, Bitka," Kleindienst said, "but light a fire under it. Captain Bonaventure, you fill that list, but spread it out. No more than two cargo pods per boat. I want your three division boats headed back to *Hornet* ASAP. The admiral detached an Indian cruiser—INS *Kolkata*—as close escort back there but he wants it up front in his line of battle when the shooting starts. Our two cruisers at Mogo won't get to us until at least two weeks after we reach K'tok orbit. Until INS *Kolkata* can rejoin, the cruiser force is down to four heavies."

"Ma'am, I'm not happy about cannibalizing my parts lockers," Bonaventure said. "As beat up as *Hornet* is, what guarantee is there she'll be able to restock us when we get there?"

"None," Kleindienst said. "Make it happen anyway."

Then she turned to her right and glared at Atwater-Jones. "And what are *you* grinning about?"

Atwater-Jones smiled sweetly at the chief of staff. "Nothing in particular, mum. I hail from a green and pleasant land and it makes me cheerful by disposition. Sometimes just thinking about Old Blighty makes me smile."

Kleindienst turned back with a sour look. "Now, if there are no more questions, we've all got work to do. Let's get on it."

She cut the connection and all of the holo-images vanished, leaving Sam alone in his office. He waited for his commlink to vibrate, waited for the accompanying ID tone of the captain, but it did not come and Del Huhn faded a little more. After five minutes he gave up, squinted up the boat's directory, and pinged Rose Hennessey, the chief engineer.

"Hennessey, I got six two-cubic-meter cargo pods worth of replacement parts lined up from the other three division boats, but I need a prioritized list of what you want and I need it fast."

"*Six pods?* Bitka . . . I want to have your babies!"

CHAPTER ELEVEN

19 December 2133
(twelve day later) ***(two days from K'tok orbit)***

"They're gone," Delacroix said, her eyes on the sensor repeaters.

"Looks that way to me," Robinette agreed.

Petty Officer Second Elise Delacroix sat Tac Three and Ensign Jerry Robinette sat Tac One on the bridge, with Sam in the command chair. They'd been at Readiness Condition Two—half of the crew on watch—for the last day. An hour ago Sam had taken over for Ensign Barb Lee as OOD to give her a breather.

They were coming up on K'tok. The transports and fleet auxiliaries had already begun their deceleration burns preparatory for entering orbit. The warships had more powerful drives and so could put off the burn longer, then make it short and hard. They'd go to general quarters then, but not until they had to. They could only keep everyone at their battle stations so long before performance went into the toilet.

Sam looked at his own sensor repeaters, showing the radar return echoes from the sensor probe far out ahead of the task force, far enough to have cleared K'Tok's orbital track and look "behind" it, into the space the planet occluded. Nothing there.

"Those two uBakai cruisers only disappeared two days ago," Sam said, as much to himself as the others. "Where did they go?"

"Hiding with the asteroids behind them, like the Red Duchess said about the other one?" Robinette said. "And how come we don't have a decent data map of the asteroid belt in this star system? All our stellar occlusion detection routines freak out as soon as we dump any data in with the asteroids in the frame. A million bogies, maybe more."

The "Red Duchess" had become Commander Atwater-Jones's nickname throughout the boat, and apparently throughout the task force. Red came from the color of her hair. They called her a duchess partly because she was English, but also because she had an Oxford accent and money, judging by the fact her Royal Navy shipsuit was not standard issue but tailored, apparently by some famous "Old Bespoke" designer on Saville Row, if you believed all the scuttlebutt, which also required you to believe she had had sex with most of the male and half the female admirals in the Royal Navy, and possibly several members of the royal family. Sam's state of mind, particularly concerning Jules's death, had been such that he had not taken much notice of the British officer's looks in their first encounter, but everyone else had.

This all confirmed Sam in his belief that mariners on long deployment were like old men and women with nothing to do but make up gossip. Atwater-Jones was certainly attractive, but he wouldn't call her vid-star beautiful. She did have an interesting attitude. He wondered if Jules would have liked her. Atwater-Jones was almost old enough to have been Jules's mother—*was* old enough if she'd been naughty very early, and of course the gossips suggested exactly that. He saw a familiar flicker in the corner of his eye, turned to ask Jules, but of course she wasn't there.

Focus: cruisers and asteroids . . .

"I think Survey is working on a data set of the asteroids," he said, "but that's not the problem here, Ensign. We're coming down on K'tok from straight above the plane, galactic north, so they can't be hiding in the background clutter. Only direction for those two cruisers to run and keep K'tok between us and them is straight down, below the plane, and there's no asteroids down there to hide in—nothing but stars and hard vacuum. Your stellar occusion routines are working fine."

So where the hell had they gone?

Sam closed his eyes and concentrated on the problem. To keep K'tok between them and the task force left a very narrow cone where they could be. The uBakai could have gone cold, turned their thermal shrouds toward K'tok, and coasted away once they'd made their burn, but the probe was pumping active radar energy down that cone and getting no bounce-back. A thermal shroud didn't stop radar echoes and there were no known means of defeating the multi-wavelength variable-pulse radar mounted on the US Navy sensor probes. Even if the uBakai had some new stealth trick up their sleeves, these cruisers were both from a familiar class of uBakai warships that ground-based radar had tracked with no trouble earlier. They couldn't just have turned invisible.

"Maybe they jumped out-system," Robinette said. "I mean, we outnumber them—what—five to one in combatants? I'd sure get the hell out of Dodge."

"Smartest thing you've said so far, Ensign. I'm just reluctant to assume all our problems are over and they jumped back to Akaampta or someplace else. Would they give up the system that easily? Why start a war and then run away?"

His commlink vibrated and when he squinted he saw the ID tag for the engineering officer, Rose Hennessey.

"Yeah, Hennesey, what's up?"

"Mr. Bitka, we have a situation in the wardroom and we need you here, right away."

"I'm standing watch for Ensign Lee."

"She's here, and I'll send her forward, but you need to get here as soon as you can."

She sounded frightened, or maybe just out of her depth, off-balance. Sam couldn't remember ever hearing her sound quite like that.

"On my way," he said and cut the connection. He turned to Ensign Robinette, who had still never stood a watch as Officer of the Deck.

"Big day for you, Ensign. The boat is at Readiness Condition Two, Material Condition Bravo, on task force course for K'tok. Power ring is fully charged, reactor on standby, shroud deployed, sensors passive. Expect your relief by Ensign Lee shortly, but until then it's your boat."

"I . . . I relieve you, sir," Robinette said, his eyes larger than a moment before.

I'm turning the boat over to The Jughead, Sam thought to himself as he unbuckled his harness. *What could possibly go wrong?*

Sam passed Lieutenant Barb Lee going in opposite directions in the central trunk, her normally pinched features looking even more distressed.

"What's going on?" he asked.

"If I say, you'll probably arrest me for conduct unbecoming," she answered as she glided by, avoiding eye contact.

Maybe he had overdone it in telling Filipenko to come down hard on her. Lee hadn't spoken to him much since then, come to think of it. He should have noticed, but everyone had been busy getting ready to enter K'tok orbit and almost certainly fight a major ship-to-ship action. Well, angry with him or not, it sounded like the problem was with Huhn.

A minute later Sam pulled himself through the door of the wardroom and saw a tableau which would not have been all that unusual were it not for the awkward and distressed expressions on the participants' faces—that and the fact Captain Huhn was in his dress whites complete with all decorations. Dress whites weren't really made for zero gee and Sam noticed the trouser cuffs floating up high enough to show a band of pale hairy leg above the socks. Huhn floated at the head of the wardroom table with Goldjune to his right and Rose Hennessey and Moe Rice, to his left. Chief Navarro and Tamblinson the med tech floated near the end of the table as well. Actually, the presence of two enlisted crew in the wardroom was unusual.

Everyone's eyes turned to him as he entered. Huhn's visage was unreadable, but from the expressions on everyone else's faces Sam had the feeling he was in trouble—a lot of trouble. Maybe those mass-approved damage survey reports were coming back to haunt him. Or maybe one of the two enlisted crew were the ones in trouble. Somebody sure was.

"Sam, come over here," Huhn said. Sam kicked lightly off the door and floated over to the table. Goldjune moved down the table, making room for Sam next to the captain. Sam clipped his tether lanyard to the table and held a bracket, mostly to keep his hand from trembling.

Huhn fingered his decorations, particularly an odd one, a large silver, gold, and red multi-pointed star or flower—Sam wasn't sure which—that looked foreign and out of place below the orderly ranks of colored rectangular ribbons that represented his US Navy awards. Huhn's index finger traced the edge of the star, lingered on one of the points.

"Sharp. Could hurt someone with this if you weren't careful," Huhn said. "Order of the State of the Republic of Turkey. Got it back in '29. I saved the daughter of the Turkish ambassador to Bronstein's World.

Just a teenager, got caught in an airlock without a vacuum suit, but I kicked a circuit box open and shorted it out, so we could pop the hatch manually. Just used my head is all, but everybody else panicked. Saved that girl's life and got this for it. Proudest day of my life."

Sam wondered if he meant the day he saved the girl's life or the day he received the medal.

"It's very impressive, sir. What was it you wanted?"

"Sam, some of us are cut out for certain things, but not others. You know what I mean?"

"I think so, sir."

"Sometimes we have to face hard truths about ourselves, look in the mirror and see things we don't want to see, would rather look away from. But we've got to look, Sam. We've got to look hard."

Huhn stared at him as if he expected a reply but Sam said nothing.

"We're about to go into battle, Sam, and we all need to ask ourselves, 'Am I cut out for this?' It's hard, but a lot of lives depend on us answering that question as truthfully as we know how. Do you agree with that?"

"Yes, sir," Sam answered and licked his dry lips.

He *had* wondered this, many times, and also wondered if seeing ghosts might be a disqualification for duty. But he had no idea how to answer those questions except to see it through, do his duty as well as he could, and on the other side of it find out if that was good enough. He'd done okay in the first battle, but it had caught him by surprise. This coming fight filled him with a growing dread. He'd looked forward to their arrival, going to general quarters, facing whatever stood before them, but not because he longed for danger. It was only because he wanted this awful uncertainty, this dark foreboding, to end.

"Well, I've been looking in my mirror," Huhn said. "I've spent a lot of the last week looking in it, and I know now: I'm not cut out to command this boat in battle. I'm cut out for a lot of things in the Navy, but not that. I think. . . I think I need a rest is all. That's why I asked Medtech Tamblinson here, to certify me medically unfit for command."

Sam looked at Tamblinson, whose eyes were larger than Robinette's had been earlier when Sam turned the watch over to him for the first time. He looked at Goldjune and faced cold hostility, at Hennessey and faced anxiety bordering on panic, and he realized the trouble he was in was real, but was entirely different than he had originally thought, had in fact never imagined, and he felt this heart rate climb and chest constrict with the beginning of panic.

"Captain, I. . . I wouldn't do anything too hasty. You need to be—"

"What? *Certain?* You think I'm doing this on the spur of the moment? Haven't thought it through?"

Sam licked his suddenly dry lips again, and swallowed to loosen his tight throat. "Nothing like that, sir. It's just. . . if you do this, it's going to change your life, and there's no changing it back."

That was dishonest. Sam didn't give a damn about Huhn's future. He simply wanted no part of being captain. This was a job on which the lives of nearly a hundred people depended, and a job which he was so totally unprepared for he could not imagine any outcome but disastrous failure.

Huhn looked down at the table for a moment and then looked back up into Sam's eyes.

"At least my conscience will be clear."

Sam wanted to scream at him, wanted to slap sense into him, wanted to get up and leave the wardroom, come back in and try again from the beginning. Instead he floated by the table and stared dumbly at Captain Huhn. . . no, not captain anymore. . . at Lieutenant Commander Huhn.

Sam noticed that, while the grim-faced image of Captain Marietta Kleindienst, the task force chief of staff, remained fixed in his view, the ghosted image of the work area behind her floated gently, so she was holoconferencing by helmet from the flag bridge of *Pensacola*, not from the conference room up in the rotating habitat wheel where there was spin-induced gravity and a full holosuite. Sam couldn't see her helmet, any more than she could see his, one of the odd effects of the helmet optics. The internal optics looked in and recorded the speaker's face and head while the external optics looked out and recorded the nearby environment, but neither of them recorded the helmet itself.

"Mister Bitka, exactly what in the Sam Hell is going on over there?" Kleindienst demanded. "Lieutenant Colonel Okonkwo just got off the link and sounded like he was going to have a stroke."

No one on *Puebla* had been sure who to notify about Huhn's action, but Moe Rice had recommended the task force personnel department.

Okonkwa was the task force N1—personnel chief—and Sam's own conversation with him a quarter of an hour earlier had been difficult, eventually becoming heated.

"Yes, ma'am. When I spoke with him the situation seemed . . . beyond his personal experience. I don't know that any ship captain in the Nigerian Navy has ever requested relief from command and duty on medical grounds—at least for this reason. But that's the situation with Lieutenant Commander Huhn."

It sounded strange not to call Huhn "captain."

Sam didn't know much about the Nigerian Navy, but Okonkwo 's rank was lieutenant colonel, not commander. The fact they used the same rank titles as the army instead of most other nations' navies was a small thing, but it still seemed like a strike against them.

"And do I understand that those medical grounds are 'pyschological exhaustion?'" she asked.

"Yes, ma'am."

"And you actually went along with this?"

"He didn't give us a lot of options. As long as he was in command, we had no choice but to obey his orders, and his last order was, 'Take command.' "

"It sounds pretty fishy to me. I just spoke to him on commlink but he won't holoconference so I can't tell if someone's holding a gauss pistol to his head. If you're pulling some kind of fast one over there, you will spend the rest of your natural life in a Navy brig. Do you read me?"

"Ma'am, you can commlink anybody you want to on this boat. If you think there's some kind of conspiracy and *everyone's* in on it . . . well, then I don't know what to tell you. We don't have a holoconference suite over here, just our helmet optics. Lieutenant Commander Huhn won't holoconference because he's in his dress whites and won't change out of them for a shipsuit, so he's got no helmet mount."

"No shipsuit? Is he crazy?"

Sam didn't answer. Kleindienst studied him for a moment.

"Has he been acting . . . odd?"

Sam paused to think about his answer, to choose his words carefully.

"Nothing he did was outside the behavioral latitude enjoyed by a commanding officer on his own vessel, ma'am."

Kleindienst's scowl deepened. "Meaning all captains get to act a little nuts? Alright, maybe you got a point. If you'd come running to the squadron medical officer with a list of peculiar behaviors, I'd have slapped you down as a disloyal bellyacher. And I'd have been right."

Sam said nothing.

"Atwater-Jones thinks you're smart, Bitka. Maybe so. But I never thought 'smart' was the most important attribute of a successful ship captain. What do you think?"

"I think I'm smart enough to know I'm in over my head."

She nodded.

"I agree. You're short line officers, too, aren't you? I've got someone in mind to send over to take command: Lieutenant Commander Barger, in the operations shop of the task force staff. Good man: Annapolis, class of '17. The shuttle can take Huhn off at the same time, bring him over here and we'll see if he can handle some light staff duty. But Barger's coordinating the orbital bombardment plan and I'd rather not bring someone else up to speed between now and the landing. Can you keep things together over there for, oh, let's say five days?"

"Yes, ma'am."

Kleindienst cut the link without saying anything more.

The uBakai Star Navy had left K'tok orbit, so the task force shouldn't encounter any resistance when they made their strike, and *Puebla* would be with the auxiliaries anyway. Five days—the duration of the short and hopefully uneventful career of Captain Sam Bitka, USNR. Chief Navarro should be able to keep him from screwing up too badly for that long. Then he would help Barger however he could, get through this war, and get back to his job on Earth.

He remembered joking with Jules that this was like Space Camp with better food, but that was before people started dying.

He triggered his commlink, squinted up the link for Ensign Lee—officer of the deck—pinged her, and had her patch him through the boat-wide announcement channel.

"All hands, this is Lieutenant Bitka speaking. At 1421 hours today Captain Huhn relieved himself of duty on medical grounds and turned over command of USS *Puebla* to me. I've just spoken to the task force chief of staff and we can expect a replacement captain once the initial operations in K'tok orbit are completed. Until then I will serve as acting captain.

"Lieutenant Commander Huhn will remain onboard until my relief arrives. He will be treated with the utmost respect and rendered every military courtesy by the crew at all times.

"Carry on."

Sam cut the channel and went back to clearing the last of the paperwork on the replacement parts received from the other boats in the division, the repairs undertaken onboard, and the work that a proper shipyard needed to address the next time they saw one. He had already decided to continue with the XO job as well as command until his relief showed up. He saw no need to further disrupt the schedules and responsibilities of his fellow officers, short-handed as they already were. Everyone had to carry more water, and that included him.

He finished the report and moved on to an intel bulletin from the task force. Sensors had picked up a strong energy glow consistent with starships running their fusion plants to recharge their power ring, probably after emerging from jump space. The contact was over eighty million kilometers galactic south of the planetary plane and whoever it was they weren't making a secret of their presence. If they were coming to K'Tok from there, the task force would have plenty of time to get ready. He made sure the Tac department was on the distribution list.

A half-hour later his commlink vibrated and then he heard a feminine voice in his head.

Sir, this is Signaler Second Lincoln, duty comm. I have another incoming tight beam for you from USS Pensacola, *a Lieutenant Commander Barger.*

"Right, patch him through." Sam heard the click of the circuit changing. "Bitka here."

Lieutenant Bitka, this is Lieutenant Commander Lemuel Barger. Captain Kleindienst has just told me what's going on and that I am to take command and straighten things up over there as soon as the landing force is down and has secured the objective.

"Yes, sir, I—"

Do not interrupt me, Bitka.

"No, sir."

I know Delmar Huhn. I cannot say we are close friends, but I believe he was capable of handling command of a vessel in combat, especially as part of a larger task force, provided he received the support of his subordinates. Given his emotional collapse, I can only assume he did not receive that needed support. I am made of sterner stuff than Delmar Huhn, Mister Bitka. I will not tolerate disloyalty among my officers, and I will get to the bottom of what went on over there once I take command. Is that understood?

"Yes, sir."

A reckoning is coming, Mister Bitka. I hope you will share this information with your fellow-officers and the senior chiefs.

"Understood, sir."

The connection broke and Sam sat there for a while, staring at the open report on remaining food consumables without really seeing it.

Well, Barger hadn't actually ordered him to poison the morale of his officers and chiefs, he had just "hoped" he would do so. Barger outranked Sam, but he had no authority to dictate what Sam did as captain of his own boat. And Sam had not promised to do so; he had only said he understood what Barger hoped for.

So at least for the next five days the officers and crew would go about their duties as if their loyalty were not under suspicion. They would go into battle with pride, believing they were appreciated and that their sacrifices so far, and their efforts to overcome battle damage and crew casualties, were valued by their superiors. Sam could at least see to that.

And for those next five days, until Lieutenant Commander Lemuel Barger was actually captain of USS *Puebla*, he could hope in one hand and piss in the other, and see which one filled up quicker.

CHAPTER TWELVE

19-20 December 2133
(later that day and the next) ***(one day from K'tok orbit)***

Before turning in, Sam had a visit from Lieutenant Marina Filipenko, an official visit that he had requested. She accepted a hot green tea and the two of them floated in his stateroom tethered to stanchions and at first just looked at the star field displayed on the smart wall.

"Filipenko, I'm kind of skipper and XO rolled into one for now. I'm supposed to make sure the crew functions as a team, you know? Something's eating at you. It's hard enough dealing with a war none of us expected, but something else is going on with you. I don't want to intrude in your private life, but you've become an essential officer, a keystone member of the crew. If there's anything I can do to help, let me."

She floated silently for what seemed like a long time, looking down at the deck, thinking. Finally she shook her head.

"I don't know that there is anything you can do. I think I made a terrible mistake leaving home. You don't . . . I don't know that any of you can understand the sort of bond there is between folks on the BW—that's what we call Bronstein's World most of the time, the BW. It's like a club, but everyone has to pay dues to stay a member, and the dues are really high, and you have to pay them every single day. But everyone there does—or they die and that's that."

She was silent for a while and finally Sam said, "Gotta be tough. But you got away. Took control of your life again."

She shook her head.

"I ran away. I ran, and I abandoned my family, my friends, everyone on the BW. I said, 'I'm not like you. I can't do this.' But I didn't understand how important it was to *be like them*, to belong to that tribe, until I quit. That's what it is, a tribe. None like it anywhere.

"I thought I'd find it here in the Navy, a new tribe, but . . . " she looked around and then shook her head.

"Strikes me as pretty tribal," Sam said. He'd never thought of it in quite those terms, but it fit.But once he said it, the thought made him uneasy.

"Yes, but a very silly tribe," she shot back and glanced up at him, gave him that long, penetrating stare, and then shrugged. "Not supposed to say things like that, I know. But at Annapolis, everyone was so proud of what they had endured to get through each year, so proud of what they had accomplished by the end. All I could think was, twelve-year-olds on the BW have gone through more, endured more, had to shoulder more personal responsibility for their survival, than anyone at that graduation, and nobody ever told they to throw their hats in the air and crow about how exceptional they were. Now all my classmates do is preen and bicker and jostle for the right place at the wardroom table.

"God, I hate it! I *hate* the Navy."

The passion and bitterness in her voice took him back, and Sam took a while thinking about it before answering.

"It's funny, before this whole war thing started Del Huhn and I got into it over disciplining two of my petty officers and I told him it was stuff like that made people hate the Navy. To tell you the truth, I think I was talking about myself as much as anyone. But that was before the war. War has a way of . . . broadening your thinking, you know?"

She shrugged, not meeting his eyes.

"I guess there are different versions of the US Navy, different layers. I don't hate them all, and I don't think you do either. There's one I think of as The Entitled Navy. That's the one where politically well-connected officers take for granted that their superiors will treat them with circumspection and wink at their shortcomings, and it turns out they're right—that one I hate."

Her eyes narrowed and she nodded.

"There's another one where everyone's got an eye on what comes next, whether it's the next assignment or the job after you're done with the Navy, and puts smoothing the way for that above doing their job here and now. The Nest Feathering Navy. Not crazy about that one either."

"No," she said.

"Tell you what I am crazy about, though. I'm crazy about my tactical department—yours too now. Joe Burns stepped up to Bull Tac like he was born for the job."

"Yes! God, I don't know how I'd have managed the department without him."

"Joyce Menzies is like some sort of missile savant, and we might even make something of Ensign Robinette, too."

"He's trying hard," she admitted.

"Got a pretty good engineering department, world-class A-gang. I'm even getting used to Ops. Goldjune and I are never going to bosom buddies, but so what?" Sam paused and looked around his cabin. "I'll tell you what I'm crazy about: this boat. I don't mind telling you it comes as something of a surprise."

"It's a fine boat," she agreed.

"This is our tribe, Marina. Maybe tribes are like cats: you don't find them, they find you."

For the first time Sam could recall, Filipenko chuckled.

After two hours of floating and sweating in his sleep cubby, Sam awoke from a nightmare of *Puebla* dying under a hail of uBakai laser fire because he had forgotten how to maneuver the boat, forgotten how to order the weapons division to fire, been unable to form the right words, and so they had drifted impotently into the uBakai killing zone.

He turned on his stateroom lights and checked the time: 0030 hours, literally Oh-Dark-Thirty. He felt on the edge of panic, needed help. Then he had an idea where he might find it. Over a decade ago he had taken several courses on leadership. Everyone made light of "the book," acted as if true enlightenment could only come once you had gone far past its simplistic lessons and formulas. Sam didn't care. At that particular moment he was willing to take any help he could get.

He put on viewer glasses and scanned several manuals, but of course there was no single guide explaining how to be a crackerjack boat captain. Finally he came across something, something he had once known by heart. Every officer candidate learned it: the eleven principles of naval leadership. Even as he read them, they came back. They didn't answer any specific question he had, but the first one got his attention right away.

First Principle of Naval Leadership: Know yourself and seek self-improvement.

Well, that wasn't a bad place to start.

Six hours later Chief Constancia Navarro, one foot hooked through a handhold, floated before Sam's desk in the captain's office, her face a blank mask.

"Chief, I sent for you because I need your help," Sam said. "I need it bad. I'm only captain for five or six days, but I can't afford to screw this up."

Sam gestured in invitation to the drink dispenser on his desk but Navarro shook her head.

"No thanks, sir. You move your gear into the captain's main cabin yet?"

"I figured Lieutenant Commander Huhn can stay there until Commander Barger shows up. No point in moving twice in one week. Chief, my problem is I'm having a hard time getting a handle on commanding the boat. I sort of know the administrative end of things, but that's not what I mean. I'm having trouble getting some of the officers on board. I could come down harder on them but I don't want to rock the boat too much before the new C.O. gets here. What do you think?"

She squinted at him for a moment before answering. "It's your boat, sir. I'd say rock it as much as you want."

She continued looking at him and showed no more inclination to volunteer additional advice. Sam sipped his coffee, unsure if he'd done something to offend her. A captain maybe shouldn't worry about that—it wasn't a popularity contest—but he needed Navarro's help. He needed *somebody's* help, that was for sure,

Navarro shifted and looked away.

"Chiefs," she said.

"How's that?"

"Chiefs," she repeated and turned to face him. "All due respect, sir, but you spend too much time thinking about the commissioned officers. They're fine when somebody's shooting at us, but the chief petty officers run the boat, day-in, day-out. You don't need the officers to run a tight boat if you've got the chiefs."

"Go on," Sam said.

"Well, the problem is, chiefs aren't going to piss off their department officers to please a captain who's only going to be around to cover for them for five or six days."

"Meaning I can't really count on them," Sam said.

"No, sir. Meaning you can't count on them to walk the plank for you if you're not even willing to move into the goddamned captain's cabin."

Sam straightened a bit, surprised at the animosity Navarro's words revealed. "You really want me to move into that cabin?"

"No, sir. What I really want is for you to decide what you want from this crew. Now, if that's all. I got a pile of work I need to get back to."

He nodded. Navarro started to leave but she paused by the hatch, her back to him.

"So far the crew's running on inertia and rage, and that's okay for now. But pretty soon that'll run out and they're going to figure out what a really tight spot they're in. You want to do something for them? Something that'll make a difference? Tell them why they're here. Tell them what they're fighting for. Tell them why someone killed their shipmates and is trying to kill them, and why maybe it's worth their lives"

"I'm not sure I know," Sam said. "It's something about K'tok's biochemistry."

Navarro left without looking back and Sam stared at the closed office door for a long time, thinking about how empty his words had sounded even to him.

That hadn't gone very well. She'd told him what she thought he was doing wrong, she'd said it in plain standard English, but he had no idea what it meant. What was he supposed to do? Sure, he was the captain, but only for less than a week and with his relief already appointed. And how the hell was *he* supposed to know what the war was about? He just followed orders, like everyone else.

He saw a shadow in the corner of his eye and he looked away. He didn't want her or anyone else to see him like this: confused, indecisive, a powerless captain because he didn't know how captains exerted authority except by brute force of law and navy regulations—and he knew that was the worst possible course he could take.

Maybe the only way to handle this was to just go on acting as the executive officer for an imaginary, invisible captain. He knew how to do that much. But something nagged at him, something Navarro had told him in their first conversation after the war started: for the crew the captain *was* the Navy. And didn't they deserve to hear from the Navy why they were going into harms way? He'd even read it the previous night.

Fourth Principle of Naval Leadership: Keep your subordinates informed.

Sam pinged the duty communications technician.

This is Signaler First Class Kramer, sir. How can I help you?

"Kramer, get me a tight beam to the flagship. I want to talk to someone on Captain Kleindienst's staff, whoever you can raise."

This is Lieutenant Alice Fong, Captain Kleindienst's aide, Sam heard in his head once the tight-beam connection went active. *What do you need, Lieutenant Bitka?*

"Well, you can start by calling me Captain Bitka."

Um . . . I understood your appointment was only temporary.

"Correct, which is why you'll only have to call me captain temporarily too."

Sam waited.

Of course. Captain Bitka. What do you need?

"What I need is to know why we're fighting this war."

We're very busy here, Captain Bitka. Do you have a request affecting the combat efficiency of your ship?

"First off, *Puebla* isn't a ship. Destroyer riders don't have jump drives, so they're boats, which I assume you just forgot. Second, I'm not screwing around, Lieutenant Fong. I've got senior chiefs asking me what the hell's going on and I don't know what to tell them. Why are my people supposed to go into battle and risk their lives?"

Because they are under orders to do so.

"Not good enough. These are American mariners. They aren't robots and they aren't galley slaves. If you think this is the only place crews are asking questions like this, you're kidding yourself. If you want these people to fight hard, you better figure out what it is they're fighting *for*, and let them know. Or let me know and I'll pass it on. You might want to let the West European, Indian, and Nigerian crews in on it, too."

I'll . . . have to get back to you, Captain Bitka.

"Fine. Just see that you do. Oh, and Ms. Fong? We lost people in that first attack, friends and shipmates, gone forever. The reason better be pretty good."

Twenty minutes later Sam was finishing up the new incoming parts inventory when his embedded commlink vibrated.

Captain, this is Signaler First Kramer on the bridge. I have an incoming audio tight beam from the flagship for your ears only.

"Okay, Kramer, patch it through."

Sam expected to hear the voice of Lieutenant Fong, or perhaps someone with more rank. He suspected that the more rank behind the incoming comm, the angrier it was likely to be. Instead the voice in his head vibrated with barely contained mirth.

Captain Bitka, are you there?

"Commander Atwater-Jones? I was expecting someone else."

I daresay, and I won't keep you long. Just thought I would congratulate you on making the most of what will undoubtedly be the shortest command tour in the history of your navy. Good heavens, you've got a knack for asking the most awkward sorts of questions! Next you'll be demanding to see the emperor's new clothes.

"Well, I think it's a pretty reasonable question."

Of course it is! That's what makes it so bloody awkward. Well, buck up. Dame Marietta will probably try to frighten you to death, but I felt obliged to ruin her fun. They—which is to say the admiral's senior staff—have already decided your question does require an answer, and one spread throughout the task force, so you are not to be drawn and quartered—at least not yet. Not that you've gained an ounce of their respect or gratitude, you understand.

"Commander, I don't want to sound ungrateful or anything, but you being part of the admiral's senior staff, I'm having a hard time figuring out where you stand in all this."

I wouldn't worry about it, Bitka, as long as you know where you stand. Toodles.

Sam received the predicted comm from Captain Marietta Kleindienst within another half hour and, as anticipated, it alternated between anger and expressions of disappointment, as well as containing a veiled threat to sent Commander Barger over sooner than originally planned. Sam responded respectfully but managed not to buckle under the assault. Perhaps he'd have held up anyway, but Atwater-Jones having tipped him to the bluff certainly helped. As it was, Kleindienst left him with an admonishment to "shape up."

"Yes, ma'am," he had said as she cut the connection.

Dame Marietta. That's what Atwater-Jones had called her and Sam chuckled. He respected the chief of staff, both personally and the authority of her office, but it was going to be hard to find her frightening from now on. There were just too many more-dangerous things in the universe for him to take her cross words very seriously. Besides, what could they do to him? Send him to K'tok?

CHAPTER THIRTEEN

22 December 2133
(two day later) ***(first day in K'tok orbit)***

The task force reached orbit and conducted its bombardment and assault as planned. To much relief and some surprise, everything went off without a hitch. Ground resistance was sporadic and unorganized, surprise apparently complete, casualties minimal, success absolute.

That evening Vice-Admiral Leman Kechik Kayumati went live via holovid to the entire task force. Sam watched and listened in his cabin, through his helmet optics. He had never seen Kayumati before and the admiral was older than he expected, well into his sixties, and slight of stature, but with rigid posture. He had a steady, confident manner and intelligent eyes in the broad, brown, high-cheekboned face that showed his Malay ancestry. With his thinning gray hair and bushy white eyebrows, he looked a bit like the tough old patriarch of the family in so many adventure holovids—strong, seasoned, and wise. Sam didn't know much about how good an admiral Kayumati was, but he had to admit the guy looked the part.

"As you know, this morning we entered orbit above the planet K'tok," Kayumati began. "We have been at war for twenty days, although the only hostile activity to date has been a single cowardly sneak attack, launched by the enemy before a formal state of war existed. That attack cost us a lot of good men and women, but since then the uBakai haven't shown much stomach for a fight. They ran away from us at Mogo and it looks like their fleet's run away from us here at K'tok as well."

Pretty good start, Sam thought. Can't have an interesting story without a good villain. From there Kayumati went on to caution everyone that, although the uBakai had run, they'd be back, because K'tok was too important to them to let it go without a fight. Then he told them about the protein chain differences, why they made K'tok the only place anyone had found other than Earth where Humans could eat the food grown in the ground, instead of in a hydroponic tank.

Humans had started settling the Utaan Archiapelago in the western hemisphere of K'tok. The uBakai claimed all of it, even though no Varoki had ever settled anywhere but the two continents in the eastern hemisphere. There had been clashes, both sides had sent military forces as observers, but the coalition of Human states that backed the colonists had agreed to arbitration by the *Cottohazz Wat.*

"That's when those cowards hit us," Kayumati said, his voice rising in anger. "Why? Because they knew the arbitration would go our way, leave our colonists in their homes on K'tok. Most of the *Cottohazz* is with us on this, is tired of the Varoki having everything their own way. Well, we deserve our chance at the stars too, by God! We shouldn't have to fight for it. We didn't want this fight. They started it, but so help me we're going to finish it!

"And we got a good start on that today. Every objective secured with no naval casualties and very light casualties among our Marine and allied ground forces. That's because every man and woman in the task force carried out their duty with courage and professionalism."

He had them. Sam could sense it, could almost hear men and women cheering that line. This was good, simple, and to the point. He'd shown them an injury to avenge, a prize worth fighting for, and bad guys to smack down. All he had to do was end on a high note and the task force would follow him to hell.

"You know," Kayumati continued, "those Varoki think they're entitled to everything, just because they developed the interstellar jump drive first. And then they fooled us and everyone else in the *Cottohazz* into signing on to their intellectual property covenants. Maybe you don't understand the importance of that, but let me explain."

Sam stared at the hologram in front of him. What was Kayumati doing? He *had* them. Make the sale, close the deal, and say goodnight. But he kept on talking.

First he gave a long explanation of how *Cottohazz* intellectual property law screwed everyone but the Varoki. Then he started in on how Humans were training fewer and fewer scientists every year. He had a lot of statistics to back that up and some colorful three-dimensional graphics. When he started in on the history of the settlement of K'tok and the Varoki ecoform project, Sam took his helmet off and cut the feed.

"Shut up!" he yelled at the silent walls of his cabin. "What are you thinking? Just shut up, you doddering old fool!"

Sam knew the feed was still coming in and though he didn't watch it, he watched the incoming feed light on his data pad. Kayumati talked for another twenty minutes. Sam did a quick keyword search of the speech recording by topics and came up with:

The First K'tok Campaign of 2130
Spacecraft design
Destroyer Riders
Fire Lance Missiles
Contemporary Music
Adventure Holo-Vids

There were more entries but he stopped the scan, closed his eyes, and simply floated in the center of his cabin for a while.

Sam had worked his way up the ladder of lower management at Dynamic Paradigms, onto the rungs of middle management, and although he'd found customer fulfillment most to his liking, he had done his share of sales as well, and he wasn't bad at it. One thing he knew was when to shut up. Over and over again he'd seen inexperienced sales people get the sale and then keep talking—and talk the customer right out of it. Sam understood why.

One thing people are very good at: they know, without even having to think it through, that if a salesman keeps talking after the customer is convinced, it's because he's still trying to convince himself.

Vice-Captain Takaar Nuvaash, Speaker for the Enemy, covered his face with his hands to hide his shame and anger.

"Nuvaash, what are you doing here?"

He looked up and saw Admiral e-Lapeela. He had not heard him enter the briefing room. Now he rose to the position of attentive respect.

"I am composing my resignation, Admiral."

A flicker of irritation passed across the admiral's face. "Resignation? You would flee from your duty at the first sign of adversity?"

"Admiral, I will serve in whatever position the fleet demands of me."

The admiral said nothing and soon Nuvaash realized the silence was his to fill.

"I believed I anticipated every enemy approach to this problem. Our heavy ground elements were well-dispersed to avoid destruction by orbital bombardment, our mobile troops placed to contain and isolate enemy landings, our aerial defense systems optimized to prevent reinforcement of their colony enclaves."

He paused and shook his head.

"Never did I imagine they would undertake an operation so . . . *audacious*. To seize the needle itself? By meteoric assault from orbit? Capture the administrative capital of the planet, and do so with only *three cohorts of troops?* This will be my legacy—I will be forever remembered as the Speaker for the Enemy who allowed the only capture of a needle in history. I have shamed you as well, Admiral. All I have left to offer is my resignation, insignificant as that is."

e-Lapeela stood silently for what seemed an endless interval, but which may have been no more than a minute. When he spoke, his voice was level and backed with authority but no contempt, so far as Nuvaash could detect.

"Sit, Nuvaash," he said, and he sat down as well, across the conference table.

"You are humiliated, and you think you understand why, but you do not. I will explain your humiliation to you, as one who has faced that same hopeless black night of the spirit.

"You have known Humans, interacted with them, and I imagine liked some of them. You respected many of their achievements, and in your interactions with them undoubtedly earned their respect as well. This lulled you into the illusion of equality. Today shattered that illusion, and that is the true basis for your humiliation. You finally, at long last, understand that *we are not their equals.* They are monsters, Nuvaash—but diabolically clever monsters. There can never be any question of a fair fight with them. You understand that now, don't you? We cannot *allow* them a fair fight, because *they will best us!*

"You will not be remembered for the capture of the Needle at K'tok. That will become a minor incident in a war which will be remembered for a thousand years. Let them enjoy their triumph for now. So rich and glorious a prize will hold them to this place, demand they defend it, pin their fleet in place for us to destroy.

"Your observation of their astrogation procedures, and the extent to which they rigidly follow their standing peacetime practices, let us surprise them once and I believe will let us surprise them again. *Audacity?* If you are remembered for anything, it will be for the brilliance and audacity of this next attack."

Nuvaash straightened in his chair but shook his head slightly.

"The attack plan was yours, Admiral."

"*You* showed the weakness, Nuvaash. Together we devised the means to exploit it—over the objections of our own fleet astrogator, you may recall. It is as dangerous as he counsels, but I believe the danger ensures surprise. I believe the Humans will never expect it from us for that very reason. It is too *Human* a risk. You believe that as well, do you not?"

"Yes, admiral, I do."

"What you do not know, Nuvaash, is that the surprise will be twofold. Our fleet munitions vessel ABk Seventy-One brought a special shipment of electronic warfare missiles of a radically new type. Even now they are being moved to the cruisers which will spearhead our attack. These missiles will shatter their fleet, and with it their morale. In two days we will decisively alter the naval balance of power forever. *That* is what you and I will be remembered for."

CHAPTER FOURTEEN

24 December 2133
(two day later) ***(third day in K'tok orbit)***

Seventh Principle of Naval Leadership: Train your crew as a team.

"Missile away," Filipenko said from the Tac One seat beside him.

"Time?" Sam asked.

"Three minutes, forty-two seconds."

The spinal mount electromagnetic coil gun, which launched their missiles, ran over two thirds of the length of the *Puebla's* hull, through the center of it, and could only be aimed by physically turning the boat itself. It took that much barrel length, and almost three gigajoules of stored energy from the power ring, to accelerate a missile to a velocity where it could get close to an enemy ship within a few hours, or maybe less. It came out the pipe at about six kilometers per second, which sounded fast until you realized that meant it would still take half an hour to cover ten thousand kilometers.

Other than physically realigning the boat, the main delay in firing was going through the simulated Identification-Friend-or-Foe—or IFF—procedures.

"That's pretty good time," Sam said. "Chief Menzies has your missile rooms ready to wreck ships and kill people. Our only delay is identifying the target and getting the boat aligned."

"Yes, sir," Filipenko said with a grateful smile. "I don't know what we can do to shave target identification any closer, given the IFF protocols."

"Neither do I. Okay, give me the all-boat channel."

"You're live, sir," Signaler First Kramer answered from the Comm One seat.

"All hands, this is the captain. Okay, three minutes and forty-two seconds. Well done, people, especially weapons division. Exercise is terminated. Secure from general quarters. Readiness Condition Three. White Watch, you're up. First beer's on my tab tonight, and nobody gets a second one. We're sharp; let's stay that way. Carry On."

Sam turned back to Filipenko. "You're on duty in a couple hours. Ensign Lee's Officer of the Deck and I'll hold down the bridge until she comes forward. Go ahead and get something to eat or grab some sack time."

"Thanks," she said, but she hesitated. As most of the rest of the bridge crew unbuckled and made way for their reliefs, and the bridge filled with a low babble of conversation, Filipenko leaned over toward him and spoke softly.

"Captain, why are we doing all these drills? Just to keep the crew busy? I mean, the troops landed successfully, the cruisers pounded the only mobile troops the uBakai had near the downstation, and their fleet has run away. Besides, even if they're out in the asteroids, we'll see them coming with days to get ready, or at least hours. Counting seconds . . . well, seconds don't matter, do they? Isn't it really about thinking it through and making the right call?"

Sam linked both hands behind his head and stretched his back, looking at the long-range sensor display on his workstation. Everything Filipenko said made sense, was all correct doctrine, but something nagged at him, something he couldn't put his finger on.

"That's standard operating procedure, and you're probably right. The thing is, I keep coming back to '*Why?*' Why would they start a war and then run away? It doesn't make any sense, unless they know something we don't. And remember what the Red Duchess said? 'These uBakai are clever boots.' I've got this feeling they're going to hit us some way we're not figuring on."

"What way?"

Sam laughed. "Hell, if I could figure that out they'd make me the next chief of naval operations, which would piss off Lieutenant Goljune's uncle, right? Isn't he in line for the job?"

"Sir, I've got an incoming hail from *Pensacola*, for the duty officer," Kramer said.

"Right, I'll take it," Sam said and waved Filipenko toward the bridge hatch. "Captain Bitka here," he said on the tight beam channel. Sam suspected he knew what this comm was about and he said *'Captain Bitka,'* perhaps for the last time, and with some regret, which surprised him. He hadn't enjoyed anything about the last five days—frustration was closer. But he'd felt a little satisfaction now and then. He had the feeling he'd been doing something important, and actually doing it passably well under the circumstances. Maybe Navarro didn't agree, maybe half his officers didn't agree, but he thought he'd done okay. This was probably his scheduled relief, and he should welcome it. After all, it came before he'd encountered a situation he couldn't deal with and had a chance to screw everything up. He'd be leaving the boat is as good a shape for Barger as he knew how.

Bitka, this is Lieutenant Commander Barger. I'm on board shuttle Papa Echo One Seven and we are approaching your orbit track from planetside. The pilot estimates docking in twelve minutes. Be prepared to execute the change of command as soon as I arrive aboard.

"Understood, sir."

Sam looked around the bridge, possibly for the last time from the command chair. The bridge hatch opened and Ensign Lee pulled herself through. He nodded to her and unhooked his tether as she pushed off to drift to the command station.

"Ensign Lee, the boat is at Readiness Condition Three, Material Condition Bravo, in low planetary orbit above K'tok, in formation with Task Group 1.3. Shuttle Papa Echo One Seven, carrying my relief, is approaching from retrograde and planet-side to dock in approximately ten minutes. The power ring is fully charged, reactor on standby, shroud secured, sensors active. The boat is—"

"High Energy Discharge!" Ron Ramirez called out from the Tac Three seat. "Multiple unidentified contacts!"

Sam turned and saw his workstation display light up with several flashing yellow contact markers. He punched the General Quarters alarm on the command console and immediately heard the gong of the alarm fill the bridge, knew it spread through the boat as well.

"Lee, take Maneuvering One," he ordered, but she was already strapping in when he glanced up.

"Mean bearing two four seven degrees relative, angle on the bow one two zero, range . . . " Ramirez said, his voice rising, "*six thousand kilometers?* That can't be right! They're right on top of us. And they're closing at twenty-one kilometers per second!"

Sam tried to see the situation in his mind but the numbers made no sense. He enabled the holodisplay on his workstation and he pulled it into larger scale with his hands: K'tok at the center, the string of cruisers and other vessels, including *Puebla*, strung out in orbit around its equator, most of them about seven thousand kilometers out. But the tight cluster of contacts glowed about six thousand kilometers *above* them and the planet, visibly advancing down toward K'tok's north pole at a sharp angle. It was hard to make out the number of ships in the enemy formation. They were obscured by some sort of debris or energy cloud.

Where did they come from? How had the destroyers, or the deep sensor drones, not picked them up before this?

"Kramer, make to Shuttle Papa Echo One Seven: 'Am preparing to maneuver. Stand off.'. Lee, prepare to align the boat on those contacts. No . . . look at their track. They're going behind K'tok, putting it between them and the main cruiser packet. Align on K'tok's horizon where they'll depart line of sight. Ramirez, all eight iris valves open and get our laser heads deployed."

Sam's thoughts raced. The uBakai were almost on top of them, but their velocity was the real complicating variable. They were moving over three times as fast as *Puebla*' missiles would leave the coil gun. Instead of overtaking them, the missiles would fall behind. Once the uBakai were past them, there wouldn't be a target solution. He glanced over at the Tac One seat—Filipenko wasn't back yet. He could use someone else running the numbers but he didn't know if they had enough time to put a missile over that horizon before the enemy ships disappeared into K'tok's shadow. He squinted up the duty missile rating and pinged.

Port Missile Room, Chief Menzies.

"Menzies, glad you're still on duty. This is no drill. Get ready to cycle missiles as fast as you can. How soon?"

Sir, you can fire as soon as you get this de crisse *boat aligned on target. I'll have one in the pipe by then and we'll keep it up from here until the starboard missile room is manned and ready as well."*

"Load 'em up, Menzies. We'll fire from here once the boat's aligned on target.

"Ready to align," Lee shouted from her station.

"Hit the klaxons and align the boat," Sam ordered.

The acceleration warning klaxons sounded and Sam took a deep breath, tried to steady his thinking, slow things down, but the seconds tumbled past with undiminished velocity.

"Multiple ordnance launches from bogies," Ramirez reported, his voice still tense but more business-like than in the first excitement of the contact."

"Not bogies, Ramirez," Sam said. "Those are hostiles—*bandits*. Code 'em red."

"Task Forces hasn't unlocked IFF yet, sir."

"*I* just did, damnit!"

"Aye, aye, sir. *Bandits* have launched missiles, individual contacts tracking on all our vessels: outer screen destroyers, cruisers and transports. *Bully* just launched ordnance in reply!"

Bully—USS *Theodore Roosevelt*—one of the leading cruisers in the bombardment group. If anyone could get a missile off that fast, it would be Captain Chelanga. She couldn't have a good target solution yet, but at this range did she need one? Just get the missile within five thousand kilometers of the target and let nature take its course. That was a hell of an idea.

Sam checked and saw Elise Delacroix had finished strapping into the Tac Four seat. Marina Filipenko and two others came through the hatch and pushed toward their stations.

"Delacroix, the laser heads are deployed. Guns up. Hit those missiles tracking on the flag and transports with our point defense lasers."

"Guns up. Engaging," she answered.

"Sir, incoming burst transmission from Papa Echo One Seven," Kramer said, her voice unnaturally calm amidst the chaos. "Text reads: *'Belay maneuver. Prepare to take me aboard.'* Signed Barger.'"

"There's no time. We've got maybe a minute before those uBakai missiles are within discharge range. Make to Shuttle Papa Echo One Seven: 'Stand off—Expedite.' and demand an acknowledgement from the *shuttle pilot*, understand? Lieutenant Commander Barger is just a passenger over there."

"Sir, incoming text from Task Force Flag," Kramer said, her voice now cracking with excitement. "Text reads: *'Cease fire at once. Targets not positively identified.'* Signed, Klinedienst, Chief of Staff.'"

Part of him wanted to give in, to surrender responsibility to Klinedienst, let her take the heat if the decision was wrong. Another part of him saw the missile tracks closing on them, knew they were coming to kill them, *knew it,* and wanted to scream in panic.

"Kramer, make to flag: 'Negative.' Sign it Bitka, Captain.

Well, ignoring IFF protocols was one way to cut a minute or so off the reaction time

"Enemy missile destroyed." Delacroix said. "We got another! Continuing to engage."

Sam saw an energy flare from the uBakai ships on his tactical display.

"What's that? Did someone hit them?"

"Negative, sir," Ron Ramirez said. "They're firing their direct fusion thrusters. Those guys are headed for the barn."

Ramirez was right. Sam could see the velocity numbers changing on his display. The uBakai must be pulling well over one gee, possibly over two gees. He felt *Puebla's* attitude control thrusters kick in and the boat's alignment begin to shift. Sam turned to Filipenko, who was now in the Tac One seat with her holodisplay activated. He took a second to gather his thoughts, try to put them in an order that would make sense, make what he saw developing clear to her. He couldn't afford many seconds, though.

He took a long steadying breath,

"Okay, Tac, Delacroix's on guns, you're on missiles. Set the missiles on TeeOpp mode—targets of opportunity—code everything you see in that bandit cloud as hostile, and start launching as soon as our bow's within, oh, twenty degrees of them.

"Now look at your display. Think about what you're seeing. They've fired off their missiles, lit up their fusion drives, and they're passing on the far side of K'Tok from us and the cruisers. We've got maybe three or four minutes until they're occluded by K'tok's disc. They're past the lead cruisers already and by the time our cruisers get missiles out the tube, the uBakai will be in K'tok's shadow and they'll have so much velocity built up the cruiser's missiles won't catch them."

"Where did they come from?" she asked, eyes wide with something close to shock.

"I don't know, but they're here. Just focus, okay?"

She nodded wordlessly.

"We're retrograde from the cruisers in the orbit track so we're better placed to lob missiles back and around to hit the uBakai when they pass on the far side, but not by much. Maybe we'll get lucky. It's going to be close, though, so as soon as you've got anything approaching a shot, just spit missiles out as fast as you can. I'm going to keep Lee rotating the boat past the horizon to shoot galactic south and try to get a piece of them as they emerge from K'tok's shadow on the down side, although that's a pretty forlorn hope.

"Here's what I need you to do: once you start firing, put the coil gun on auto-fire and start crunching the numbers on the firing solutions for the salvo we'll fire on the down side. Understand?"

"Yes, sir," she answered and turned back to her console.

Puebla suddenly lurched hard to the side, hard enough to send a lance of pain up Sam's back and neck. He felt the explosion more than he heard it, coursing through the solid structure of the boat. The main lights went out but the consoles continued to glow. He heard the whooping siren of the hull breach alarm and voices crying out in terror. For a moment he almost joined them, but the lights came back on and he took a long shuddering breath.

"Damage report," he said, and it came out coarse and angry-sounding.

"Hit—dorsal starboard, aft of frame sixty-eight," the engineering tech answered."Power spike caused some shutdowns but all internal systems back on line . . . we're losing hydrogen reaction mass and I think another point defense laser is down, still trying to reboot its director. I think we lost a radiator, too."

"Do we still have our coil gun?" Sam shouted.

"Yes, sir."

"Okay, what else is—"

"They got *Bully*!" Delacroix said from her station.

"I've got a target solution!" Filipenko called out.

"Commence firing missiles," Sam ordered and then pulled the scale up on his holo-display. In the cruiser formation the ID tag for CGS-218, USS *Theodore Roosevelt*, had turned red and flashed rapidly. Sam swallowed hard. *Bully Big Dick* had been the first starship he had served on as an ensign, following his commission back in '22, and then was his first ship assignment after his reactivation earlier this year. He didn't know if it was better or worse than any other cruiser in the fleet, but he'd walked its habitat wheel, served watches there, and he had admired and respected Captain Chelanga. He owed his current position to her glowing recommendation. How many casualties had they suffered? How many crew had survived?

Another cruiser tag went red. Then a transport. Then a fleet auxiliary.

And then another cruiser.

CHAPTER FIFTEEN

24 December 2133
(four hours later) ***(third day in K'tok orbit)***

Sixth Principle of Naval Leadership: Insure the task is understood, supervised, and accomplished.

"Hand me that pinhole nitrogen blower, would you, Chief?" Sam said.

Chief Pete Montoya's beefy hand holding the nitrogen blower appeared below the fabricator's support frame. Sparks from a flux welder cascaded behind him and Sam heard the babble of shouted orders and clanging of heavy equipment maneuvered into place on the forward engineering maintenance deck. Sam took the blower and started to clean the injection nozzles on the fabricator's "underside," which is to say the side secured to the bulkhead which would have been "down" had there been gravity. The first high-pressure squirt pushed him away from the nozzles, first against the deck and then bouncing back against the frame.

"Damnit!"

Montoya's face appeared. "You okay, sir?"

Sam laughed. "Yeah, I'm fine, Chief. Last time I did this was in one gee, that's all."

He braced himself, one foot against the deck, one on a support arm, and went back to work.

"Try it now." Sam heard the fabricator, centimeters from his face, hum with power, followed by Montoya's bark of satisfaction.

"That's got it, sir! Green lights on the board."

Sam pushed himself out from under the fabricator and turned to the machinist mate standing by.

"DeWilde, isn't it?" Sam asked. "I'm sure you guys follow all the preventive maintenance schedules, but the bottom injectors on these large-cap DP fabricators are always getting clogged up, especially if you get an in-job stoppage. If you trip a breaker or something, you get blowback in those bottom nozzles. So after you correct the main problem, always take a look underneath for trouble."

"Okay, sir," DeWilde answered, looking surprised.

"Thought you were a Tac officer, sir," Pete Montoya said, the same questioning look on his face. "You do a hitch as a snipe?"

"Nope. Back in The World I used to install and maintain these pigs," Sam said, gesturing to the large fabricator. "So tell your boss, Lieutenant Hennessey, she's got her number three fabricator turning out high-temp pipe again. I need that dorsal radiator back on line by 2400 hours."

The fusion reactor generated enormous energy—one and a half gigawatts at full power—but also enormous waste heat. Some of that was released with the thruster's reaction mass, some was converted to electricity by the Seebeck generator, but the excess waste heat was bled off by the boat's four large radiators, extending radially from the stern of the boat. Each radiator not in service cut the maximum safe power output of their reactor by a quarter.

"Aye, aye, sir. And thanks for the help." Montoya gave him a crooked grin as he took the nitrogen blower.

The tone for his embedded commlink sounded and he saw the tag for the duty commtech. He dismissed Montoya with a wave.

"Captain here."

Chief Gambara, sir. I've got a request from the flagship for a holocon with you.

"How soon, Chief?"

Right now, sir. I think it's the chief of staff.

"Okay, I've got my helmet. I'll plug in and take it down here."

Sam lifted his helmet and felt a surge of apprehension. This was where he got chewed out for ignoring Captain Kleindienst's direct order to cease fire during the battle, and maybe for his refusal to take Barger on board during the battle, and who knew what else? But the apprehension faded immediately, replaced by irritation at being pulled away from repairing his boat, and impatience to get back to it. He clicked the helmet in place and activated the holocon link.

Instead of Marietta Kliendienst, he faced Admiral Kayumati himself, and his irritation vanished. The admiral looked more haggard than when he'd given his long rambling speech two days ago. He looked older. Had it really been just two days?

"Bitka, you disobeyed a direct order," the admiral's holoimage said.

"Yes, sir, I did." Sam let out a short huff of breath and shrugged." Truth is, Admiral, I imagine I'd do it again. I'll turn over *Puebla* to Lieutenant Commander Barger as soon as he docks. Am I under arrest?"

For a moment the admiral looked even more tired. "No, you're not under arrest. We don't usually throw captains in the brig for disobeying orders when it turns out they were *right*. Sometimes we do, but not usually. Besides, Lem Barger didn't make it. He got it from an uBakai fire lance when his shuttle maneuvered between the missiles and *Pensacola*. Not sure whose idea it was, but I'm putting both him and the shuttle pilot in for Navy Crosses. Posthumously. Lots of posthumous medals today.

"Where are you? Looks like engineering. How badly did you get hit?"

"We were lucky, sir. Glancing hit, probably because we were realigning the boat for our shot. We have seven crew injured but none seriously. The hit took out about two hundred tons worth of hydrogen honeycomb tankage, but the internal bulkheads held and we didn't get any O2 contamination. Our dorsal radiator's almost a total loss, so our fusion power plant's capped at about seventy percent if we need to go hot. But we're fabricating high-temperature composite-alloy pipe to replace it and we should be back up to about ninety per cent by tomorrow. We lost another point defense laser, some sensor redundancy, and the boat's axis is slightly bent."

"Bent?" Kayumati said. "Can you maneuver with your drives out of alignment?"

"Not at the moment, sir, but we can magnetically bias the thrust angle a little and that's all we'll need. My Ops Boss is working on a software fix. We're going to need some serious orbital spacedock time when we get home, but we've got atmosphere, power, and weapons, and we'll be able to maneuver as soon as we get that software patch in place. Maybe three hours on that."

Larry Goldjiune had been surprisingly pliant and cooperative when Sam gave him the task of getting the drives realigned. Perhaps the pounding the uBakai had delivered to the task force had sobered him, or frightened him, or made him less anxious to take command responsibility for what was shaping up as a disaster.

As Sam spoke he saw the ghostly shadows of officers and crew moving behind Admiral Kayumati, a constant flutter of movement. One officer briefly came into sharper focus to hand Kayumati a data pad. The admiral nodded and handed it back, then looked at Sam again.

"Three hours is better than I expected. How many missiles you get off?"

"Nine, sir," Sam answered. "Six over the north horizon of K'tok, the others south as they were departing. After that we didn't have an intercept solution any more. They were just moving too fast."

"Any hits?" the admiral asked.

Sam's mind returned to the final frantic minutes of the engagement, when all their missiles were away and the bridge crew waited for some indication of success—Filipenko hugging herself, arms crossing, as if keep herself from flying apart with nervous energy, Ron Ramirez's face tear-stained although he seemed unaware of it, Elise Delacroix calling off range to target in her nasal *Quebecois* accent.

"Their point defense took out at least half our missiles," he told the admiral, "and once the rest started detonating we couldn't see much past the plasma cloud, so I can't be sure, but . . . I don't think so. No sign of heat spikes from any of the bandits, no visible debris."

Admiral Kayumati nodded. "Good honest answer, son. No, I don't think you touched them—same as the other destroyers. The cruisers got a hit or two, and we took out at least one enemy ship. I say at least one because we blew it into so many pieces we couldn't tell if all that junk was parts from one ship or two. But I think something's seriously wrong with those fancy new Block Four missiles you destroyer folks are carrying. You may as well have been shooting blanks."

Sam tasted something bad in his mouth, felt different feelings tugging at him. At least it wasn't just *our* shooting that was bad. It wasn't something *we'd* screwed up. But the price for that absolution had been universal failure, and a problem that might be much harder to solve. He'd far rather have had two or three more dead uBakai warships, and let someone else get the credit.

"How bad were the casualties on the cruisers, sir? Some of the crew . . . they have friends over there, former shipmates."

Kayumati looked at him for a moment, eyes empty. "We're still searching, but as near as we can tell casualties on the three cruisers, the two fleet auxiliaries, and the one transport which were lost were one hundred percent. We lost two destroyers as well, but we got an emergency signal from survivors in *Vicksburg* and we have a shuttle on the way to check *Shiloh* for survivors."

"One hundred per cent? But . . . how is that possible? Somebody usually survives, in an airtight compartment or in escape capsules . . . don't they?"

The admiral looked away for a moment and then back. Just moving his head looked as if it took most of his remaining energy.

"From a fire lance hit, yes. But they used some sort of electronic warfare on us, a version we've never encountered before, never even dreamed of. Atwater-Jones is still going over the signal intercept data. We'll put together a briefing as soon as she and her staff figure out more pieces of the puzzle, but the bottom line is this: somehow they caused six of our ships to engage their interstellar jump drives. The electronic jump signature is clear as a bell, but mostly they didn't go anywhere." He paused and sighed, then shook his head.

"This deep in a gravity well, the jump impulse was what the engineering people call 'noncoherent'. Pieces of the ship and crew—very small pieces—jumped, but apparently only a few millimeters, and caused a whole bunch of annihilation events. Not much left but wreckage and . . . well, human remains. I don't know how they did it, but somehow the leatherheads can turn our own star drives into weapons against us."

For a moment Sam's mind was occupied trying to stave off the imagined picture of Captain Aretha Chelanga and others on the bridge of *Bully* with *pieces* of them missing. No, he realized, they would mostly have exploded. He pushed the vision out of his mind, made himself think about the problem at hand.

"But weren't the jump drives powered down, sir?"

"Yup. Didn't matter. Like I said, we can't figure out how it's even *possible* to do what they did, and until we do, we don't know how to protect our remaining ships from it."

A shiver of fear made Sam lift his shoulders, and then he realized something important, something that affected him and the *Puebla* directly.

"Admiral, then that means—"

"That's right, Bitka," the admiral said, cutting him off. "The only combatant vessels we have that we can count on to stand up against this weapon are ones *without* jump drives, which means your destroyers—and for the moment we only have three left in K'tok orbit. *And* there's something wrong with your blasted missiles. I hope we can figure that out and fix it quick." He shook his head again, looking down, but then looked up at Sam and straightened.

"Captain Bitka, you are chopped to DesDiv Four effective immediately. I just field bumped Juanita Rivera on *Champion Hill* up to O-5 to take over what's left of the division. She's your new boss and she'll brief you—as soon as *we* figure out what the heck our next move is and tell her. You got any questions, son?"

"Just one, sir. Any idea when you'll have another replacement captain to us?"

Kayumati squinted at him, a flicker of irritation flashing across his face.

"I'm a little short of officers myself at the moment, Bitka. You didn't completely foul things up this morning so you're going to have to run *Puebla* until we get some reinforcements or . . . well, something turns up. I'll see about taking Commander Huhn off your hands, but no promises. For the next thirty or so hours all our orbital transfer assets are going to be busier than a long-tailed cat at a rocking chair convention."

CHAPTER SIXTEEN

24 December 2133
(thirty minutes later) ***(third day in K'tok orbit)***

The wardroom was crowded, holding all the off-duty officers in white as well as the khaki-clad senior chiefs, almost a dozen total. Sam paused at the open hatch. He'd had the mess attendants set the wardroom's smart walls to mimic the HRVS optics pointed laterally, so K'tok—enormous, blue, and cloud-wrapped—dominated the view to port. They were just coming up on the needle, a shining golden thread impossibly long, stretching all the way down into K'Tok's atmosphere and over forty thousand kilometers up to its orbiting counterweight. Somewhere down at the bottom of it, Human troops held a small bridgehead on the planetary surface, and were counting on support from a task force that had just been shot to pieces.

But that wasn't his immediate problem.

Realistically, he figured he had one chance to win *Puebla's* officers and chiefs over. He knew he'd have plenty of chances to lose them later, but that wouldn't make any difference if he couldn't even make this first meeting click.

No pressure.

"Atten-*shun*!" one of the chiefs barked and the officers and chiefs snapped to smartly enough, although several of them weren't tethered and so started drifting slowly across the compartment.

Sam took in a slow breath.

Okay. It's a staff meeting. You've run these before. Maybe not in space, not in the middle of a war, but the principle's the same: don't let them see you sweat.

"As you were," Sam said. "I'm having this meeting piped to the crew so we're all on the same page. I just talked to Admiral Kayumati half an hour ago. We'll get a complete report later, but what it boils down to is we got our asses kicked. We were very lucky on *Puebla* to come away with just a few bruises. Eight vessels are total writeoffs, including three cruisers and two destroyers, and most of their crews are dead."

They had suspected bad news but he could see from their faces this was worse than expected.

"We probably all lost friends today. I had friends on *Bully Big Dick*. Captain Chelanga . . . well, she was a hell of a lady. When you're back in your cabins, take a moment, remember them, but right now we've got too much work to do.

"I wish like hell I could tell you *Puebla* got a piece of those bastards, but we didn't. It wasn't your fault. You got our missiles out the tube faster than any other unit in the task force, except *Bully*, and near as I can tell we had the best target solutions. The problem is our damned missiles are broken. None of the destroyers got any hits, so it looks like the problem is in the Block Four missile design."

Sam scanned the group and was pleased—and a little surprised—to see Marina Filipenko and Joe Burns, his Tac Boss and Bull Tac, floating side-by-side.

"Lieutenant Filipenko, Chief Burns, that's the tactical department's big job. Figure out what's wrong with the missiles and fix it. Get Chief Menzies in on this, too. Nobody knows those Block Fours better than she does. Contact the other destroyers and get together with their tac-heads. Tight beam *Hornet* and see what their squints have to say. We've got a machine shop and fabricators, so you should be able to jury-rig something. Understood?"

"Yes, sir."

He turned to the operations staff next but found Gordy Cunningham, the Bull Ops, floating next to Constancia Navarro and Chief Pete Montoya from engineering, with Ensign Barb Lee on the other side of the wardroom.

"Ensign Lee, Chief Cunningham, I've got two jobs for the operations department. First, figure out a way to get a quick and dirty map of the asteroid belt so we can detect ships by stellar occlusion, even with asteroids behind them. This time they hit us from above, but those uBakai shitheads like to play hide-and-seek with the asteroids, and I'm sick of it."

"Sir, I don't know how we can manage that," Lee said.

Lee had been calm and confident under fire only two hours earlier. She had been the same, he remembered, during the first attack three weeks ago. It was odd seeing her hesitant and unsure of herself in a meeting. Maybe her brain needed a good shot of adrenaline to get going, or maybe she'd settle down once she got away from the crowd and back to a workstation.

"Genius, Ensign Lee. Give me an act of genius.

"Now here's operations department's number two job. Lieutenant Goldjune will take this one when he's done with the software patch he's working on, but you pass it on to him. We lost six ships today that the uBakai never touched with a fire lance missile. They made their jump drives cycle and it killed the ships and everyone in them. Nobody knows how they did it.

"Get with Task Force intel, pore over their data, our data, ship specs, whatever we have. How come *those* six ships blew up and the other eight jump-equipped ships in the task force didn't? Start there. If we don't figure out a way to keep our cruisers from blowing up, there's going to be nobody left to hold the fort but us and two other destroyers. Anybody here think that sounds like a good plan?"

He looked around and got a lot of shaking heads and a smattering of *no*'s.

"Okay.

"Lieutenant Hennessey, Chief Montoya, engineering's only job is to get us operational, and as quickly as possible. Any off-watch personnel from any other department with usable skills, you take 'em. Lieutenant Goldjune's finishing the software patch to bias the thrust nozzles, and I just told Admiral Kayumati we'd be ready to maneuver in three hours."

"*Three hours?*" Hennessey repeated. "How long before Goldjune's done with the software patch?"

"No idea, but it was advertised as 'soon.' Don't look at me like that, Lieutenant. I'd give you an easy job if I had one, but there just aren't any today.

"And Lieutenant Rice, our supply officer. The task force lost one transport and two fleet auxiliaries today, almost half our support vessels. That's going to mean trouble supplying the troops on the ground. Find out how bad the situation is and what they may need. It's not our job yet, but it might end up that way, so if it does, let's get out ahead of it mentally."

"I'm on it," Moe answered.

Sam scanned the faces. The men and women in front of him didn't look happy or cheerful, but they didn't look in shock either. Their minds were engaged, every department had a job to do, and for now that was as good as he could manage.

"Questions?"

"Yes, sir, I got one," Gordy Cunningham, the Bull Ops said. "What the hell collided with us during the battle? Was that *Pensacola's* shuttle?"

"We took a hit from an uBakai fire lance missile, Chief," Sam answered.

"You mean it ran right into us? I thought they just shot a laser."

"That's right, it shot a laser and the laser hit us."

Cunningham shook his head. "No, a laser would've cut through, right? This felt like something big slammed right into us."

Sam heard a mutter of agreement from the others, all except Chief Burns who looked at the others as if they were crazy. Joe Burns had been the chief of the weapons division before he moved up to Bull Tac, so he knew fire lance missiles and what they did. Didn't everyone? No, apparently not.

"Okay. Um . . . you're right about lasers cutting the target, but only if the laser is at lower power and has a long burn time, say a second or more. A fire lance, when its warhead blows, pumps its laser rods once, and then they're vaporized by the detonation within a nanosecond or two. That's one or two *billionths* of a second. So the actual pulse of the rod is less than that, but in that instant it delivers about a gigajoule of energy to the target. That's the equivalent of, what, Chief Burns? Isn't that about two hundred kilos of explosives?"

"Two hundred and forty, sir," he answered.

"Right, two forty. The thing is, it's transferred so quickly—a lot quicker than a conventional explosion—it converts a section of the hull to plasma which is trying to expand, but it can't expand fast enough to just drift away. Instead it whacks the boat about as hard as a quarter-ton explosive shaped charge attached to the hull: same concussion, same shear effects. We're lucky we only caught a glancing blow."

He looked around and saw men and women exchange frightened looks. Somebody should have told them this sooner. Somebody should at least have explained how their damned weapons worked, even if they didn't need to know it to do their jobs.

"Any other questions? Okay. Chief Navarro, I want you to keep on top of progress, see where we need some extra help."

"Aye, aye, sir," Navarro answered, her face expressionless.

"Well," Sam said, and thought for a moment about how to send them on their way. "Merry Christmas, or it will be tomorrow. Kwanza starts in two more days, Chanukha in three. The winter solstice was two days ago, Mawlid a month back. Bodhi Day was . . . what? . . . two weeks ago? The day some of you celebrate the enlightenment of the Buddha. Not much enlightenment to celebrate this year. Maybe it seems like there's not much to celebrate at all, but we're still alive, and that's something.

"We got punched pretty hard today. Next time it's going to be different. So let's turn to."

As the officers and chiefs cleared out past him, Sam noticed Del Huhn floating at the rear of wardroom, his tether clipped to a wall stanchion. He looked a lot better. He was wearing a standard shipsuit and his face appeared rested, more relaxed. He held a drink bulb in his hand and looked at Sam, an odd knowing smile on his lips as if he and Sam shared a secret no one else knew. As the last of the chiefs left, Huhn cocked his head to the side. Sam kicked off and drifted over to him.

"So, how do you like being captain so far?" Huhn asked, and the smile became something closer to a smirk.

"Enjoy your coffee, Lieutenant Commander Huhn, but in the future I want you to clear the wardroom when I'm having a meeting with my officers and chiefs."

"I'm still an officer on this boat," Huhn said.

"With respect, sir, you are a passenger on this boat. And by the way, since you were already packed for the transfer to *Pensacola*, we'll swap cabins in two hours."

Sam turned and glided through the wardroom hatch only to find chief Navarro waiting on the other side.

"Satisfied?" he asked, but from her grim expression he didn't think so.

"I got a little girl seven years old, a little boy five," she said. "I don't want them growing up *sin madre*. What do we do when *El Almirante* pulls everyone out of orbit except our three destroyers?"

Sam had suspected Admiral Kayumati might do that—pull all the jump drive-equipped ships out of harm's way—but he wasn't as certain as Navarro seemed to be.

"I don't know yet, but I'm working on it."'

Her face remained rigid for several seconds, and then she nodded. "With the captain's permission, I think it's time we had a talk."

Ten minutes later they tethered themselves to restraint rings in Sam's stateroom. It didn't feel like his anymore, now that he'd made the decision to move, and he was glad he had. He was probably going to have a lot of private conferences like this and the captain's cabin had more room. This had been Del Huhn's cabin before Sam moved up to XO and he remembered how crowded that first officers' meeting had felt.

Sam offered Navarro something to drink and for a change she took him up on it.

"Orange juice if you've got it, sir."

After they took a moment to sip from their drink bulbs, Navarro cleared her throat and started.

"Near as I can tell, you did real good today, sir. With respect, how much of that do you figure was luck?"

It wasn't the question Sam was expecting, although he couldn't have said which one was expected.

"I'm not sure. Maybe most of it."

She shook her head, her mouth a hard line.

"Captain, if you follow my advice, you will never say anything like that to another living soul on this boat. You can be all modest and stuff for the brass and for the folks back home, but for this crew, since you aren't a career officer and you aren't an operations officer, you better be a goddamned tactical genius. Everyone had lots of questions about whether you were up to this job. If we had a nice long peacetime cruise, you'd have time to work into this gradually, but that's not our situation."

"Not being from operations, not being a regular—does the crew really care that much about it?" Sam asked. He'd thought that pecking order was important only to the officers.

"Sure they care. *I* care, sir. I came up through maneuvering, promoted from quartermaster first to chief, operations all the way. All my career, most tac-heads I ever saw were just ballast, and some of them weren't even very good at that. And as for being a reservist, the things you have to figure out, think through, the regular men and women know by instinct. They've been doing it every day for years."

"That didn't seem to be a problem for you when I got the XO job," he said.

"XO ain't captain, sir. But you may have noticed I said everyone *had* questions about you. All those drills everyone thought were a waste of time—seeing how fast we can get to general quarters, how fast we can get missiles out the tube—everyone knew speed and quick reaction time wasn't important, right?

"But earlier today when our task force got hammered, we survived, and we were one of the only boats to get missiles fired. Even if the missiles ended up being broke-dick-no-workee, *we* looked pretty good. Now, the fact everyone *but you* thought those drills were stupid, makes you look like some kind of mastermind. And that's good, because over a thousand men and women died in orbit earlier today, and as bad as everyone feels about it, they'd feel a lot worse if they were dead too.

"Why are those other people dead and we're alive? The crew thinks it's because of you. Whether you're smart or lucky, they don't much care. In their minds whatever mojo you have going is keeping them alive, and that's good enough for them.

"I'm not saying to swagger around this boat as if you were Bull Halsey. I'm just asking you, please, to never let on to anyone that you don't think you've got what it takes. The belief that you're on top of this—even if it's a lie—is all that's holding these kids together.

"Oh, and by the way, pitching in to help with the repairs was good. Most of the time I wouldn't encourage a captain to do that, but you've got a kind of eccentric genius thing going with the crew that makes it work."

She stopped and took a long drink of orange juice. When she finished Sam expected her to resume speaking, but instead she just looked at him and he realized it was his turn to talk.

"Eccentric genius, huh? Not at all the way I think of myself, but I can live with it."

"Don't get me wrong, sir. I'm not telling you to try to be something you're not, even though it may sound like it. But that won't work either. You can't act like the captain. You've got to *be* the captain."

CHAPTER SEVENTEEN

26 December 2133
(two days later) ***(fifth day in K'tok orbit)***

The four holoconference attendees seemed to float in space, each one surrounded by a small sphere of imagery—a cabin, a wardroom, a work station, an empty conference room—the spheres forming the four corners of a small square surrounded by dimensionless gray. Atwater-Jones was holo-conferencing from the unarmed command ship, USS *Pensacola,* but from a conference room somewhere other than its habitat wheel, so she was in zero gee. Her long red hair was tied back into a ponytail, but a very loose one, so her hair floated around her head in a soft cloud, as if she were under water. It was a little distracting. The three destroyer captains, of course, floated in zero gee as well—they had no other option.

Sam had balked at another holoconference—he had too much to do as it was without another meeting to attend—but he found himself looking forward to seeing Cassandra Atwater-Jones again. He liked her sense of humor, After five minutes, though, he wasn't laughing; he found himself staring at the image of the British officer in disbelief.

"They hit Bronstein's World? But the BW's neutral, isn't it? They don't even have a military, just a police force."

"That is quite correct, Captain Bitka," Atwater-Jones said. "However, the US Eleventh Fleet Headquarters is located on land leased from the planetary authorities, close by the needle downstation and in the administrative capital. There are also several orbital facilities owned by the United States Navy, as well as one owned jointly by India and Brazil. All of the orbital installations were destroyed and the Eleventh Fleet ground facilities were attacked from orbit, with considerable loss of life both in the facility and the surrounding civilian community."

Sam shook his head and for a moment thought about Filipenko—this would hit her hard.

"Beyond that," she went on, "the coalition task force assembling near the system gas giant was taken under attack as well and has suffered casualties similar to ours, both in scope and apparent cause."

"What does that mean for us getting reinforcements?" Juanita Rivera on *Champion Hill* asked.

Rivera was the acting commander of the destroyer division, and Sam had spoken to her several times about readiness and repair progress. She hadn't been able to tell him what the long-term plan was, because task force hadn't told her yet. They'd both hoped this briefing might answer that question.

In sharp contrast to Atwater-Jones, Rivera's raven-black hair was cut to a uniform length of five centimeters and in zero gee stuck out like a porcupine's quills. She was big, with big hands and a strong, squared-off jaw. She looked as if she lifted weights normally, but the extended zero-gee was getting to her, rounding her face and body. She probably wasn't getting as much exercise as she should, but she still looked as if she could kick down doors that got in her way. So far her command style was just about as subtle as that, which was fine with Sam. The time for subtlety had passed, in his opinion.

Atwater-Jones said nothing for a moment.

"Our two detached cruisers—*Exeter* and *Aradu*—are en route to join us, as are the three destroyers under Commander Bonaventure escorting USS *Hornet*. They will be here in three days. The admiral has also ordered your four remaining destroyers to leave orbit around the gas giant Mogo and join us. But as to reinforcements from Earth . . . well, that's off, at least for the immediate future."

"*Mierda*," Rivera said. "Any more bad news?"

The British intelligence officer shifted uncomfortably—the first time Sam had seen any hint that anything might put her off balance.

"I am afraid so. It seems our initial assessment that we destroyed an uBakai cruiser in the battle was incorrect."

Sam sat back in his chair.

"But I've seen the wreckage imagery," he said. "We all have. Now you're telling us we didn't kill a *single* uBakai ship? How is that possible?"

The other two destroyer captains in the holo-conference made noises of agreement, and Atwater-Jones's expression didn't change as she listened. Her briefing had already made clear that the task force still had no idea how the uBakai had turned their jump drives on remotely. Now this.

"Yes, I know it's a bitter pill to swallow," she said. "Believe me, the cruiser captains were even more distressed. They had thought to have been responsible for the one uBakai ship destroyed. But careful study of the sensor records indicates that the single enemy craft lost was destroyed well before any ordnance was launched by any of our vessels."

"You mean the uBakai blew up one of their own ships?" Rivera said. "Bullshit! They aren't that *loco*."

"Blew up their own ship? Not deliberately," Atwater-Jones answered, ignoring the implied challenge. "It appears to have been an accident. They were able to arrive seemingly out of nowhere because that is in fact precisely what they did. You see, they exited jump space well within the plane of the ecliptic, under ten thousand kilometers from K'tok. Our sensor records clearly show the energy signature of a jump emergence at the point we first detected them."

"And no one in the task force saw it coming?" Rivera said, her voice taking on more of an angry edge.

"*Sane* people like us never do that sort of thing," Atwater-Jones said quietly, "because the plane of the ecliptic is full of debris, dust, asteroids—widely spaced to be sure, but chance emergence in the same space as even a fairly modest-sized piece of rock can be catastrophic, as you all know very well. That appears to have been what happened: one of their ships exploded immediately upon exiting jump space." She glanced briefly at Sam and raised one eyebrow.

"Sane people like us listen carefully to what *our* astrogators say, and follow all the rules, even after the rules cease making sense."

"So their admirals are smarter than ours, is what you're telling us," Rivera said.

"I'd say they gambled and won," Atwater-Jones replied.

"I'd say they just revolutionized interplanetary warfare," Sam said.

The others turned to look at him. "Think about it. All of our tactics are built around the assumption jump drives get us from star system to star system but Newton thrusters move us around *in* the system. It makes perfect sense in peacetime, but these in-system jumps are the way tactical surprise returns to the battlescape. Sure, there's a risk, but there's a hell of a payoff if it works."

Sam did not add that in a single stroke the uBakai had also rendered the destroyer rider concept obsolete, or at least a great deal less useful. The others sat silently for several long seconds.

"So we didn't even get a *piece* of them?" Captain Mike Wu of *Petersburg,* finally said. Wu looked as if he was well over the fleet mass limit for his height. He frowned and rubbed the top of his shaved head with his small but fat-fingered hand—or at least seemed to, but the hand moved back and forth several centimeters above his head, rubbing the top of his invisible helmet.

"I've looked through the data dump on the attack. There are heat spikes, additional debris, even some outgassing."

"Yeah, how do you explain *that*?" Rivera demanded.

"Oh, they did not escape entirely unscathed. One of USS *Theodore Roosevelt's* missiles certainly hit an uBakai cruiser. We cannot tell how serious the damage was—not enough to disable it—but a fire lance hit can cause quite a lot of mischief short of that. And Captain Rivera, you may find this particularly heartening. USS *Shiloh,* one of your destroyers, was effectively overrun by the uBakai squadron as it passed behind K'tok, and as you know was destroyed with considerable loss of life. But in recovering survivors we also recovered its intact bridge data log.

"The late Captain Rothstein of *Shiloh* fired six missiles at the oncoming uBakai, and although they caused no hits their close-in detonation provided her with an interference barrier against the uBakai sensors. That kept them from hitting her boat until they were quite close. Rothstein redirected her point defense lasers to engage ship-sized targets instead of missiles, and appears to have done considerable damage to several of the four remaining uBakai cruisers."

"Someone better put Miriam in for a decoration," Rivera said. "It's not much, but it might mean something to her husband and kids."

"I quite agree," Atwater-Jones replied.

Sam cleared this throat.

"I've got one more question. Why is this war so important?"

Atwater-Jones shifted in her chair and gave him a look partly quizzical, partly mocking.

"Important? I thought the admiral's address made that clear. The salient point is the biocompatibility of—"

"No," Sam said, cutting her off. "I understand why it's important to *us*. But we didn't start the war, they did. And now they've escalated it by hitting Bronstein's World. K'tok is just one of more than a dozen Varoki colony worlds, and some of them are Varoki biocompatible. So why is this one so important to *them*?"

"Well . . . " Atwater-Jones began but then stopped. She frowned for a moment and looked away, perhaps to gather her thoughts, and then her face cleared.

"Damned if I know," she said. "I really had better find out, hadn't I?"

"Let me just make sure I got all of this squared away," Rivera said. "The uBakai are cranking up the heat in the war, from everything I read in the intel brief they can double or triple their available ships here, our cruisers blow up when they look cross-eyed at them, and the missiles on our destroyer don't work."

"Yes, that last bit's something of a challenge. I'd get on fixing those missiles right away," Atwater-Jones said.

"We're screwed," Rivera said, barely containing her anger, or was it fear?

"Oh, I wouldn't say that," the intelligence officer replied.

"No? Why not?"

"Because I am paid not to. Come to think of it, so are you. I believe what you are paid for is producing good results under trying conditions. I doubt you will ever in your career get a better opportunity to demonstrate that aptitude than you have right now."

For a moment all Sam heard was the faint whisper of the air circulation system in his cabin.

"Easy for you to say, sitting on the command ship," Rivera answered. Sam looked over at her holoimage. She gripped the arms of her acceleration rig hard enough to make her knuckles white, and her eyes had narrowed to slits. Sam didn't like the situation much either, but he didn't see how insulting the task force N-2 was going to improve things.

"Not *altogether* easy," Atwater-Jones replied carefully. "Of course the real trick is to make difficult jobs *look* easy. You might work on that, Captain Rivera."

And then she cut her transmission.

"Nice one, boss," Sam said to Rivera. She looked at him for a moment, eyes cold, and then cut her own feed. Sam looked over at Captain Wu on *Petersburg*, who gave an elaborate shrug and then cut his transmission.

Well, the situation may be hopeless, but at least we'll die among friends.

Sam kept his faceplate down so his next conversation would be private. He squinted up the commlink code for Marina Filipenko. She should hear the news of this attack on her home directly from him.

Vice-Captain Takaar Nuvaash, Speaker for the Enemy, made way as a damage abatement party glided past in the weightless operations core of KBk Five One Seven, then continued to grip the handhold as two other crewmen passed, guiding three long bundles—bodies of crewmen wrapped in white death shrouds. The composite liner of one must have been torn because Nuvaash saw a red stain spreading along the side of the bundle. He closed his eyes and tried to master his growing anger and confusion.

A hand touched his arm. His eyes jerked open and he saw Senior Lieutenant e-Toveri, one of the few officers on the cruiser whose company he enjoyed.

"I am sorry, my friend, if I startled you," e-Toveri said. He tethered himself to a wall stanchion, then dug a short length of crushed *Taba* root from a plastic pouch and slipped it into his mouth between this gum and lip. He shook his head and nodded toward the two crewmen and their somber cargo.

"A difficult business this is turning out to be. Two more dead forward who we could not get to without hard suits and cutting torches, these three here, and I hear three more in engineering. Koomik'koh is one of them."

Nuvaash felt the news course through him like a wave of electricity, searing the nerves it surged through.

"Koomik'koh. I knew him," Nuvaash said, the traditional acknowledgement of the passing of a friend—the only other officer on the cruiser Nuvaash could honestly say that of.

"As did I," e-Toveri responded. "He inspired me to rise above the commonplace. He drove me to become better than I am."

"He made me laugh," Nuvaash answered honestly. Koomik'koh was the only officer on the cruiser who had.

e-Toveri touched his arm again and then pushed off to glide down the corridor, and soon Nuvaash was alone.

None of this made any sense!

Why would the home government support a war of aggression against the Humans when that war would bring glory to the Navy, the main agents of the failed military coup a year ago? Why? There must be a hidden reason.

Then he remembered—a report had arrived shortly after the battle describing the course of ground combat on K'tok. Something about it had struck him as odd, but his attention was absorbed in helping stem the loss of atmosphere and directing damage-abatement parties, and in the chaos and urgency of saving the ship the message had slipped his mind. Now it was back with its annoying itch of vague wrongness. He rested the back of his head in one of the wireless datalink alcoves spaced along the corridor. Not all of them were still live, after the damage they had sustained, but this one was. He activated his surgically embedded commlink and contacted the ship's e-synaptic memory core.

Load ground status report received Day Seven, Tenmonth Waxing.

Loaded

Access visual.

Nuvaash donned his viewer glasses and scanned the virtual image of the report which appeared in his optic centers. What had caught his attention? Then he saw it, at the bottom, the signature: Villi Murhaach, Governor Plenipotentiary of K'tok. That wasn't the name of the governor he remembered.

When had they arrived in-system? About two and a half months ago.

Identity of Governor Plenipotentiary of K'tok, Day Seven, Sevenmonth Waning.

Tinjeet e-Rauhaan

Yes, his memory was not betraying him. When had that changed?

Circumstances of replacement of e-Rauhaan by Murhaach as governor.

Tinjeet e-Rauhaan killed in groundcar accident on Nine of Ninemonth Waxing. Replaced same day as governor plenipotentiary of K'tok, in accordance with statute, by deputy governor Villi Murhaach.

Killed in a groundcar accident? e-Rauhaan must have been the unluckiest governor in history. Nuvaash could not remember the last time he had heard of an autocar malfunctioning dramatically enough to result in a fatality.

Day Nine of Ninemonth waxing. Now why did that date stick in his mind? Oh, of course.

List date KBk Five One Seven fired first multiple target ordnance in K'tok system.

Ten of Ninemonth Waxing.

Yes, they had fired the first shot of the war the day after e-Rauhaan had died and was replaced by Murhaach.

Nuvaash accessed background files on both the former and current governor. Tinjeet e-Rauhaan, a politician widely known for his moderate views, had worked to reduce violence with Human colonists along the frontier zone. Not the sort of politician who would have approved of this war at all. News feeds described Murhaach, on the other hand, as a firebrand, an extreme anti-Humanist, who had been appointed to the largely ceremonial position of deputy governor only as a political concession to the opposition. But then, suddenly and unexpectedly, he had become governor, and heir to the governor's plenipotentiary power.

Nuvaash broke the link to the ship's memory core and floated in the corridor, thinking the puzzle through, arranging the pieces.

Plenipotentiary powers: plenipotentiary meant the governor spoke with the full force of the home government and could act locally in its stead. Technically it meant *the governor* could launch the nation upon a war, but Nuvaash had never heard of that power being used—at least before now. The preemptive attack was not the sort of thing e-Rauhaan would ever have countenanced, while Murhaach would have embraced it immediately, used his extraordinary powers to authorize it, all of which was unprecedented and irregular, yet entirely legal. But . . .

But Nuvaash had been briefed on the attack plan four days *before* e-Rauhaan's death, and at that time KBk Five One Seven had already been on its firing course for two days. The plan must have been made even earlier.

Why would anyone make a plan which relied upon the complicity of a planetary governor who would never agree to it—a plan which could be carried through only by virtue of the convenient, but presumably unforeseeable, death of that governor, and his replacement by the fanatical Murhaach?

Nuvaash knew the answer to that question, and the answer froze him in place in the corridor, momentarily paralyzing his muscles and emptying his mind.

Nothing had made sense since this operation began, but now Nuvaash saw clearly it was because of their habitual Varoki willing embrace of secrecy in every aspect of their lives. The shadow brotherhoods which formed a hidden layer of cross-cutting ambitions and allegiances below the surface of Varoki society, the complex jostling of wealth and ideology, privilege and pride in successive layers of political and corporate governance, had rendered the true motivations for public acts seemingly unknowable. The Varoki were used to things not appearing to make sense, used to the idea that the real reasons for actions were complex and concealed—so used to it that it no longer occurred to them that someone might simply be lying. Their suspicious nature did not protect them from deceit; on the contrary, it made them defenseless against it.

We are dupes, Nuvaash thought, *a race of dupes.*

CHAPTER EIGHTEEN

26 December 2133
(one hour later) ***(fifth day in K'tok orbit)***

The forty-eight hours following the uBakai attack had been filled with frantic work, first trying to recover survivors from the two disabled destroyers, then making the surviving ships fully operational, and finally trying to find answers.

The big questions were simple. What was wrong with their missiles? How had the uBakai reached out and killed six of their starships? How could they execute their mission with the forces and resources they had left? The smaller, softer question, the one hardly anyone asked out loud, was much more complicated: *what were they doing here?*

Sam had no answers to any of those questions, even after the briefing from Atwater-Jones. If he would find them anywhere, he thought it would be in the boat and from the crew, not sitting in solitude in his cabin trying to think deep thoughts.

Third Principle of Naval Leadership: Know your subordinates and look out for their welfare.

He was about to set out on a tour through the boat, just to show his face and talk to some of the crew on duty, when his comlink vibrated.

"Captain, here."

Sir? It's Lieutenant Filipenko. I think we may have something you should see.

"Something good, I hope. Where are you?"

Port missile room, sir, and yes, it's good.

Ten minutes later Sam pulled himself through the hatch to the missile room and Lieutenant Filipenko held out her hand to him with two small, shiny metal pieces in it. Sam took them and examined them closely. They appeared to be a single lightweight metal part broken in half, and the broken area on each half was dramatically deformed, almost as if they had melted, but the break was sharp, jagged in places. Whatever had done this had done it violently. He looked up and saw Chief Joyce Menzies by her workbench, watching him with interest. The bench had a partially disassembled missile clamped to its work area.

"Is this your work, Chief?"

"All of us, sir," she said and glanced at Filipenko. "Me and the lieutenant here, and two of my missile monkeys: Warwick and Guerrero. And Machinist First Hasbrow back in engineering, who set up the horizontal compression machine. Oh, and Ensign Robinette ran the stress numbers for us."

"Stress numbers, huh? Okay, what am I looking at here?"

"Sir, that's why our *de crisse missiles* are all broke-dick-no-workee."

Filipenko took over. "That is the angular brace for one of the rod aiming subassemblies out of that Block Four Fire Lance over on the workbench, sir. It's why when our missiles detonated the laser beams went all over the place instead of at the target. We've got the diagrams up on a workstation over there."

Sam glanced over and even from two yards away could see a diagram cluttered with parts and notations.

"Just tell me what it means."

"BuOrd changed the layout of the rod aiming assembly not long before we shipped out," Filipenko said, "and they re-fitted all our missiles. There were problems in the tests and this was supposed to fix them."

"Let me guess: it didn't."

"It might have, sir, but it made a different one. They moved the angle of these braces and apparently forgot they were only rated to take the stress of the acceleration in their original position, which was perpendicular to the acceleration vector when the missile was fired. They moved the brace about twenty-five degrees off-angle and so when it goes through the firing acceleration, it sheers in half. Then the rods just sort of rattle around up there when the laser pointer tries to align them."

Sam looked at the metal parts again, looked at the distortion around the break lines, how the metal had changed color..

"You broke this under pressure in the machine shop? How much force does this part have to take, anyway?"

"A little over twenty thousand gees, sir," Menzies answered.

"Twenty *thousand*? Are you serious?"

Menzies shrugged. "Zero to twenty-one thousand kilometers an hour in less than a tenth of a second—the math's pretty simple, sir."

The part seemed warmer somehow, just from Sam thinking about that sort of acceleration force.

"Okay, what can you do about it?"

Filipenko looked at Menzies and the chief answered. "We're still looking over these assembly diagrams and the earlier test results. See, we can't just back-build everything the way it was before, 'cause the tests say they weren't hitting right most of the time."

"Remachine the part to take the strain?" Sam asked.

"Maybe we can manage that, sir. Engineering's got a pretty good precision-tolerance fabricator. The problem might be weight and space. There are thirty of these *de câlice de crisse* things in each warhead. Heavier part might be a little bigger, and that could be tricky. A little more weight could mean it's going to be slower coming out of the pipe, shave maybe a couple hundred klicks an hour off its launch velocity." She shrugged again.

"I don't care. Give me missiles that kill, Menzies. If we have to get in closer to launch them, we'll figure out a way to do it."

Sam handed the broken pieces back to Filipenko. "Filipenko, Menzies, well done. Let's get the word out to the rest of the squadron so we can all work on a solution, but my money's still on you guys coming up with the fix we'll use. You go ahead and set up the tight beam and do the honors."

"Yes, sir," she said, and it was the first time he could remember her saying that with enthusiasm and some pride.

Now that was some good news, and Sam felt his mood lift a little as he headed back forward to officer's country. One problem down and it wasn't much past breakfast. Maybe he could line his other problems up and knock them over in just as orderly a fashion.

Vice-Captain Takaar Nuvaash, Speaker for the Enemy, looked at the admiral floating behind the workstation, the admiral he knew to be complicit in the murder of a planetary governor and part of a conspiracy which had launched a war which had already cost hundreds of lives, perhaps thousands when the casualties from the ground combat and the attack at Bronstein's World were added in.

"Nuvaash, how badly did we damage the enemy?" Admiral e-Lapeela demanded.

Nuvaash closed his eyes for a moment to suppress his warring emotions and order his thoughts.

"Less than we anticipated, but we still materially reduced the capabilities of the enemy squadron. It also revealed a critical weakness: the missiles fired by the Human destroyers failed to hit, without exception, even though several of them evaded our point defense weapons and detonated."

It was a very good thing—Nuvaash thought but did not say—that they failed to accurately target the uBakai ships. The position of the distant picket destroyers guaranteed that two of them had excellent shots at the fleet as it overshot K'Tok's north pole, and a low orbit destroyer had also managed to launch its missiles well before Nuvaash would have thought possible. The destroyers' missiles had proven unexpectedly difficult to destroy.

"That last destroyer we killed seriously damaged our ship and two others," the admiral said. "Their missiles did not do that. Their point defense lasers did. Why did we not know they had this lethal close-in offensive capability?"

He seemed more distant than he had in the past, as if preoccupied with a different problem.

"The destroyer did not display any new or unknown capability," Nuvaash said. "Its captain simply used its close defense weapons in a novel manner, as offensive weapons. None of our simulations predicted this because the tactic was suicidal, as was demonstrated by the destruction of the craft."

That much was true, but he looked away from the admiral. He should have anticipated something like this.

"Humans do not put the same value on life as we do," the admiral said, "not even their own. A Speaker for the Enemy should understand this."

"The admiral is correct."

e-Lapeela gestured dismissively and for a moment returned his attention to his desktop.

The truth was, Nuvaash had never noticed Humans to be any less attached to life than were Varoki. But what in a Varoki would be seen as an act of courage and self-sacrifice was, in a Human, always judged differently by e-Lapeela and others like him, including the new governor of K'tok.

Nuvaash had spent many months with Human staffs when serving on combined fleet exercises. Humans displayed a barely contained nervous energy, like a powerful caged animal, which he had never seen completely unleashed except perhaps in some of their appallingly violent athletic contests. In contrast, they possessed enormous capacity for beauty, surrounded themselves with it to the point that it became invisible to them. Nuvaash remembered riding in the lift of a tall office building on Earth and in the lift hearing the most hauntingly beautiful music he could ever remember, music so sweet and melancholy it had nearly reduced him to tears, while the Humans ignored it, or in some cases hummed along. Most of them could whistle or sing, could do so beautifully, and simply took the gift for granted. Didn't they see what they had?

Nuvaash partly understood e-Lapeela's aversion to Humans, at least the part based on fear and envy. He felt its tug as well, more strongly of late, But if he let himself become slave to those base instincts, what was to become of him?

"How can a close defense laser do the sort of damage we experienced?" the admiral said, pulling Nuvaash's thoughts back to the cruiser and the present.

"It was designed in response to the new armored nose caps we began deploying on missiles two years ago, Admiral. It has a diameter of ten meters and a virtual focal array of twenty, which is why the mounts are so clearly visible on the exterior of their destroyers. Some of their cruisers have been refitted with them as well. They emit in the ultraviolet part of the spectrum and the combination of short wavelength and very large focal array gives them considerable power at range.

"How serious was the damage?"

"Cruiser Four-Two-Eight was a total loss, of course, when it exited jump space into a planetoid. A fire lance hit disabled the jump drive of

Four-Two-Nine and the captain jettisoned the entire module to avoid contamination. It can maneuver but will use most of its reaction mass to decelerate and return to our fleet rendezvous. It will arrive in twelve days. Five-Two-Two has only intermittent power, has lost its coil gun and most of its sensor array, and is not immediately repairable. Five-Oh-One is lightly damaged and will be operational as soon as we are."

So—discounting Cruiser Four-Two-Nine, which could not jump and so could not join the other ships in their next attack maneuver—they had only two operational cruisers left, including the flagship. Two ships to face whatever remained of the Human fleet, which included at least two cruisers and three destroyers at K'tok, two cruisers at Mogo, and seven more destroyers unaccounted for. The First Fleet had had fewer ships destroyed, lost fewer lives, than had the enemy, but the balance of force had changed hardly at all. Nuvaash took a breath to steady his voice before speaking.

"The new missiles performed well, Admiral."

e-Lapeela looked up sharply but Nuvaash met his gaze and after a moment the admiral cocked his head to the side in a shrug.

"We expected to take out every starship. It worked well in testing but the test sequence, for reasons of secrecy, was limited. No weapon ever seems to perform as well in the field as in the tests. Still, we dealt them a shattering blow: eight ships destroyed versus only one of ours. It may not seem so here, surrounded by casualties and damage, but this was a great victory."

"But to what end?" Nuvaash said. "They still hold K'tok."

"To what end? I told you others waited in the shadows to join us. Victories steel their courage, quicken their blood, broaden their vision. Because of this victory—and that is exactly how it will be perceived, regardless of how much damage we sustained—others will join us. First a trickle, but like water cutting a sand bar, a trickle widens the passage and more water follows.

"And I have just received word by jump courier. The government has released the cruiser division on Akaampta from *Cottohazz* duty to my command, and the Home Fleet is readying another squadron to join us. Our enterprise prospers."

"Not on the ground, I am afraid," Nuvaash said. "We are stalemated. Human orbital bombardment has become less effective both in terms of volume and accuracy, and the Human ground forces have taken casualties which they seem unable to replace immediately. These are both fruits, in my opinion, of our earlier attack. All of our heavy ground force units took severe casualties in the aftermath of the invasion, however, and our three regular mobile cohorts have been rendered ineffective for offensive operations. If we are to resume the ground offensive we must reinforce out ground forces."

"Reinforce? How?"

"We are receiving three transports from home, carrying between them a reinforced ground brigade. I believe we can land part of a lift cavalry squadron by reentry gliders."

"Reentry gliders?" the admiral demanded. "While the Humans hold orbital space? That would be suicidal for the transports."

"If we used the transports, that would be so. But out cruisers have the ability to carry a limited number of reentry gliders in place of external ordnance modules. The extent to which the detonation of Human nuclear warheads interfered with our sensors during the last attack suggests a way for a ship or two to make a high-speed approach and exit, dropping the reinforcements into the atmosphere as we pass."

"We?" the admiral said.

Nuvaash shifted his position and let his earns fold back slightly in the position of respect.

"As the attack profile I am outlining is hazardous and untested, I assumed the admiral would lead the first raid in the flagship."

e-Lappela leaned back in this chair and smiled. "I am surprised, Nuvaash. You strike me as cautious rather than aggressive, and yet now you recommend another audacious attack."

"I recommend nothing, admiral. I only point out the facts as I understand them."

And one of the facts he understood now was that the admiral was a murderer. But how many supposedly glorious triumphs throughout history, he wondered, were secretly purchased with murder?

Sam glided through the hatch to the wardroom and clipped his tether to end of the main table. No other officers were present and so Sam ordered cheese enchiladas for lunch and prepared to eat alone. That was fine; he had a lot of reading to catch up on.

Second Principle of Naval Leadership: Be technically and tactically proficient.

He put on viewer glasses and started rereading *TM-01 Deep Space Tactical Principles.*

After five minutes Lieutenant Rice, the boat's beefy supply officer appeared, drew a bulb of coffee from the dispenser, and clipped his tether next to Sam's.

"How's it going, Moe?" Sam asked, taking off his viewer glasses.

"Not too good, Cap'n. I mean, we're in good shape, but the grunts down in the dirt are in trouble. With most of the cruisers gone we've only got ground bombardment coverage about a third of the time. The uBakai are starting to close in with mobile troops whenever there's no one in a firing position. For now they're okay but that Limey battalion is going to run short of ammunition if things heat up much."

"Ammunition? Don't they have their fabricators with them?"

"No, sir. The cohort's fabricator platoon never got down to planet surface. It was going to come down the needle with its gear but was still onboard HMS *Furious* when the uBakai attack came. That's the British transport that got nailed."

"Aren't there backup British fabricators in the fleet train?"

"There were, sir. They were aboard FS *Mistral*, the French auxiliary vessel we lost."

That was a problem, but Sam didn't see it as insurmountable. He'd spent enough years in the fabricator business to understand their versatility.

"The other two cohorts down there have their own fabricators, right? There's nothing the Brits need they can't fabricate for them."

"Not quite, sir. Seems like no one has the software code to load the output specifications for the British munitions into the US or Indian fabricators. The British cohort HQ has the specs in their tactical database. They just can't get the other cohort fabricators to accept it. I talked to the task force N-4 and he says they're trying to get the go-codes from home by jump courier missile, but they're still negotiating with the fabricator manufacturers."

"Who's that?" Sam asked, but was suddenly reluctant to hear the answer.

"SubcontininenTech made the Indian fabricators, Dynamic Paradigms made the US ones."

Of course, the company he worked for, squabbling over intellectual property while people's lives were at stake.

"Okay, keep me apprised, Moe. Any deterioration on the ground, let me know right away."

Moe raised his eyebrows slightly in surprise, but nodded. Of course, he was surprised. Why would a destroyer captain in orbit be this interested in whether or not fabricators were working on the ground?

"Remember, I worked for Dynamic Paradigms until I got activated," Sam explained. "Professional curiosity."

It wasn't the truth, or at least not the entire truth, the important truth, but it satisfied Moe, and for now that was all that mattered. Still, this new wrinkle was one more thing for him to worry about, one more tough call he might have to make fairly soon.

In his seven years at Dynamic Paradigms, he'd done a variety of jobs, but most of his time was spent in the Product Support Division, making sure installed fabricators worked as advertised. Sometimes all the different interfaces got scrambled, the processor locked up, and you had to just reset everything. Even when power was pulled from the unit, even when there was no available interface, the e-synaptic core of the processor was still alive, still barely powered by waste heat generators, waiting for the master cheat code which would reopen the system and let technicians reprogram it.

The code was all but unbreakable, a precise series of signals of different intensities, durations, and at different radio frequencies. But a handful of product support supervisors knew the code, and Sam had eventually been one of them. He knew the code which would unlock the Dynamic Paradigms fabricators in the US Marine cohort's support platoon and let it accept the production instructions for the British munitions.

The problem was those codes were among the most closely guarded corporate proprietary secrets Dynamic Paradigms had. He had signed more nondisclosure agreements than he could remember. In addition, each code shared with an employee contained one signal sequence which was unique to that employee, so any use of it was immediately traceable. If he revealed that code now he was never going back to his old job, or any other job for any fabricator firm, or any corporate position anywhere that involved access to proprietary information. He would make himself unemployable, permanently, and in a pretty lousy job market to boot.

But his old company still might come through, do the right thing, and turn over the cheat codes. If not . . . well, no point in dwelling on that now.

CHAPTER NINETEEN

29 December 2133
(three days later) ***(eighth day in K'tok orbit)***

Larry Goldjune had already moved to the Maneuvering One chair by the time Sam got to the bridge.

"Sir, the boat is at Readiness Condition Three, MatCon Bravo, in stationary planetary orbit above K'tok, in formation with DesDiv Four. Power ring is fully charged, reactor on standby, shroud secured, sensors active. We are on alert for a captain's holoconference with task force command in six minutes," Goldjune reported as Sam strapped himself into the command seat.

"Thank you, I have the boat, Mister Goldjune. Did you say task force? I thought this was Captain Rivera's meeting."

"Was sir," Goldjune answered, "but Captain Kleindienst, task force chief of staff, wanted in. Guess she's got some news."

Sam looked at him and Goldjune just shrugged, but the gesture had the look of resignation about it. The bridge crew didn't look up, concentrated on their workstations more than this routine period in orbit would suggest. Sam sensed their anxiety and it make him nervous as well.

He nodded a greeting to Chief Joe Burns in the Tac One seat. Unflappable Joe, he'd heard one of the crew call him, and it fit. He was a rock, the steadiness the tactical department needed after all the changes, after Jules's death. Strange that he could think that phrase now and it didn't leave him short of breath, although he felt the now-familiar flutter just out of his field of vision—watching what he'd do here, watching how he'd handle more wheels flying off this wreck.

Chief Adelina Gambara sat in the comm chair. She'd taken over the communication division when Marina Filipenko moved over to Tac. She must have been in her late twenties but looked younger because of her slight physique. Her jet-black hair pulled back in a tight bun and her olive complexion complemented the lighter tone of her khaki shipsuit. Of course, he'd always known she was attractive, but Sam now realized she was strikingly beautiful. It had never occurred to him before.

I only had eyes for you, he thought to the shadow in his mind.

Ron Ramirez sat the Tac Two chair and Rachel Karlstein from engineering was at the boat systems station, two of the people who had been with Sam in the auxiliary bridge the day of the first attack. A petty officer first named Zimmer sat in the Maneuvering Two chair. All three of them were part of the nearly invisible—to most officers—rank layer called acey-deucies, petty officers first and second class, the people who actually made the boat work. Chiefs and officers, the folks above them, supervised. Those below, the petty officer thirds and the ordinary mariners, usually didn't know quite enough to let near the really critical jobs. If damage got fixed, if something important got done, most of the time an acey-deucie turned the wrench, or recalibrated the thingamajig.

Sam shook his head. Why was he thinking this way, almost sentimentally, as if taking stock of the crew before taking leave of them? None of them were going anywhere. Well, they were all going into the future, a fog-shrouded land which would take on a more distinct shape after this holoconference, but would probably look no more inviting.

"I've got a preliminary ping from *Pensacola*, sir," Chief Gambara said. "Setting up the conference network now."

"Thanks, Chief," Sam said and plugged the life-support umbilical from the work station into the socket at the waist of his shipsuit. No telling how long the conference would last and if the air in his helmet started getting stale he didn't want to have to fumble with it later. Once those were in place, he put his helmet on and clicked it into the neck ring, slid the faceplate down, and checked the diagnostics on life support and the holoptics: all green lights. He slid his faceplate up and leaned back against the acceleration rig.

"Any time, Gambara."

After ten seconds she gave him a thumbs-up gesture. He slid his faceplate down and the manufactured environment of the holoconference replaced the bridge around him. Marietta Kleindienst hovered at a briefing station, ahead and slightly below him, with captains Mike Wu of *Petersburg* and and Junaita Rivera of *Champion Hill* on Sam's right. To his surprise, Captain Bonaventure of *Oaxaca,* and commander of DesDiv Three, sat to his left.

Bonaventure and the rest of DesDiv Three had missed the First Battle of K'Tok, but they were approaching, escorting the crippled *Hornet,* and in all the excitement and distraction Sam had momentarily forgotten. Three more destroyers wouldn't hurt. Bonaventure hadn't changed much: he was tall and large-framed without being very heavy, and he still had a vaguely greasy look, possibly from his shiny black hair, possibly from the fact that he tended to perspire more than most. Sam nodded to him and Bonaventure's eyebrows rose in surprise.

"Where's Captain Huhn?" he asked.

"Relieved on medical grounds . . . his own call."

Bonaventure's eyebrows rose even further.

"Really? So, 'Bow-on' Bitka has the *Puebla*. Did you have command during the battle or did Huhn?"

"Enough socializing," Klelindienst said sharply from the briefing station. "You'll have plenty of time to gossip and exchange war stories later. Now we have urgent task force business to go over and only so much time."

Bonaventure shrugged and turned to face the task force chief of staff. Sam did as well, but with an odd feeling. Before this he had hardly exchanged a dozen words with Bonaventure. Different boats, two pay grades difference in rank made even more pronounced by Bonaventure's additional command responsibilities, and the still wider yawning chasm of regular versus reservist, had all meant they lived in separate worlds. Sam realized he didn't even know Bonaventure's first name, but suddenly those differences seemed not to matter, at least not to Bonaventure.

Bonaventure displayed a familiarity toward him which Sam did not find exactly unwelcome so much as inexplicable. Was it because they were all in this together? Or was it because Sam had performed well? No, that couldn't be it, as Bonaventure had not even known he was in command until just now. Perhaps it was simply that Sam had been part of this first terrible battle and Bonaventure had not, but wanted some sort of a claim on membership in that exclusive fraternity. Sam had the feeling membership would not stay exclusive for very long.

And then there was the name: *Bow-on' Bitka.* Is that what they called him in DesDiv Three now? It must have been from the holoconference when he had quoted from DSTP-01: *A destroyer's preferred angle of engagement is bow-on.* No one in DesDiv Four called him that, but they hadn't been plugged into that conference and Sam had all but forgotten. Obviously someone remembered.

"I've asked Captain Bonaventure to join this briefing because his destroyer division will enter K'tok orbit tomorrow and reinforce the defense here," Kleindienst began. "As he has seniority, he will assume overall command of all your destroyers as Task Group 1.2, with the acting rank of commodore.

"His destroyers are currently escorting USS *Hornet*, which as you know is severely damaged. Although his destroyers will remain here, *Hornet* will not enter orbit. It will do a correcting burn and slingshot back to orbit the gas giant Mogo, beyond the asteroid belt. The surviving cruisers of Task Group 1.1 will take over escort duties for it. The transports and auxiliaries of Task Group 1.3 will accompany them. All ships vulnerable to the uBakai jump drive scrambler will move out to Mogo."

Jump drive scrambler. It was as good a name as any, Sam thought. But all ships vulnerable to it meant every single starship in the task force. They were pulling out with everything except the three destroyers—well, six destroyers, once Bonaventure joined them.

Navarro had seen this coming, and Sam had as well, perhaps with less certainty. Admiral Kayumati had hinted at it in his and Sam's only holoconference. But the task force staff could have given them some warning. Were they that worried about how the destroyer crews would react? Or had they just not made a firm decision until now? Sam wasn't sure which option sounded worse.

"Captain Bonaventure, you will detach DDR-10, *Tacambaro*, to remain with *Hornet* as a close escort," Kleindienst continued.

Bonaventure's face colored and his eyebrows rose.

"*Tacambaro*? Ma'am, we lost the coil gun on *Oaxaca,* and *Queretaro* lost half its power ring. *Taco's* my only fully operational boat. You can't pull it and expect us to . . . what is it you expect?

"I can pull it and I just did," Kleindienst said. "The task force is only taking a single destroyer so it needs to be fully operational. Your mission is to hold the orbital space above K'tok until relieved by friendly forces, and support the ground troops to the extent of your ability."

"What friendly forces?" Bonaventure asked, his eyes still wide with exasperation.

"Destroyer Division Five is inbound from Mogo orbit and should reach you within the week. In addition, reinforcements are being prepared for dispatch from Earth. They may already be on the way, we don't know for sure."

"How are we supposed to support the ground troops?" Bonaventure demanded. "We don't have orbital bombardment munitions, or any way to launch them if we did."

"The two surviving cruisers are off-loading their bombardment munitions dispensers in low orbit. You will have to improvise a means of aiming and firing them, but the task force operations department is working on a communications network upgrade for you now. We're also leaving a two-seater orbital tug with each group of dispensers to aid in repositioning them."

Kleindienst's answers sounded rehearsed, which made sense. She'd clearly thought through the obvious questions they would ask. For a moment Bonaventure stared at her, mouth open. Sam exchanged a look with Captain Mike Wu of *Petersburg*, who shrugged.

"Excuse me, Ma'am," Wu said, "but if the cruisers are off-loading ordnance in orbit, we could use some of their Mark Three missiles as well. We can reposition them in a higher orbit and once they're powered down they'd be all but undetectable."

"Yes, good idea," Bonaventure said, nodding vigorously. "When the uBakai show up, we can give them a nice surprise."

"You'll have to use some of your own missiles for that," Kleindienst answered.

"Beggin' your pardon, Ma'am," Wu said, "but our Mark Fives are designed for launch by coil guns. They don't really have any thrust of their own, except for some ability to take evasive action. But those Mark Threes are self-flying, with their own thrusters. We can—"

"The cruisers need all their missiles," Kleindienst said, cutting him off. "Any other questions?"

Bonaventure shook his head, more in exasperation than negation, Sam thought. The silence stretched out for several seconds.

"What about logistics?" Sam finally asked. "Not ours, but the troops down in the dirt."

"The composite brigade's rear support company has secured the needle highstation," she answered. "The fleet auxiliaries have off-loaded the supplies the troops on the ground need, in proximate orbit with the highstation. The support company will see to moving it down the needle, but if they need some help, pitch in."

"Yes, but what about the lost fabricators for the British cohort?" Sam said. "Did they ever get the codes to let the other units fabricate for them?"

Kleindienst's eyebrows went up for a moment, perhaps surprised that Sam knew this detail of the supply arrangements.

"The British are stretching their own supplies by using captured small arms and ammunition," she said.

That would be a no.

"Speaking of logistics," Bonaventure said, "we could sure use *Hornet* here in orbit to support us. It has the best facilities for retrofitting the warhead patch on the Mark Five Block Four missiles, so we could get up and running quicker. I think Commander Rivera's division could probably use a missile resupply as well, and *Hornet's* magazines are full."

"*Hornet's* too vulnerable to leave here in orbit," Kleindienst said, "and we'll need its workshops to support the task force at Mogo. Transfer whatever material you need from *Hornet* today, before you start your deceleration burn. Clear it through the task force N-4 first."

"That's only about six hours, Ma'am," Bonaventure said.

"Noted."

Sam looked at the others and saw grim expressions. Everything he'd heard so far sounded as if they were being written off.

"Ma'am, our crews are coming up on six weeks in zero gee," Sam said. "Any chance of rotating them to the cruisers and transports for at least a day in a spin habitat wheel?"

"No, there isn't time. We expect to have a relief force to you well before you experience serious zero gee health issues."

Or else we'll be dead by then, Sam thought.

No one said anything for several seconds, then Juanita Rivera spoke, the first time she had spoken in the meeting.

"Yeah, let me get this right."

Sam looked at her. She looked about as angry as she had by the end of the Atwater-Jones briefing.

"The task force is taking three combatants—two cruisers and a destroyer—and leaving *six* combatants—our destroyers—here to carry out the primary mission, with four more destroyers on the way."

"That is correct, Captain Rivera. Did you have a question?"

"*Si, Señora.* Which of our destroyers is Admiral Kayumati moving his flag to?"

Sam suppressed a smile. She had a bigger set than he did, or just the confidence which came from being a long-service regular who had spent years preparing to be a boat captain. Wherever it came from, sometimes it took real guts to point out the obvious: that the commanding admiral's place just might be at the point of greatest danger and strategic importance.

Kleindienst straightened, her eyes narrowed, and color came to her fleshy cheeks. "There will be *five* combatants at Mogo once we rendezvous there, including our heaviest elements. That will be the task force center of gravity, and that is where the admiral needs to be."

"*Five?*" Sam said. "I thought the two cruisers at Mogo were inbound and due here in six days."

"Their jump drives make them too vulnerable. They will do a fly-by and slingshot maneuver to follow the main body to Mogo."

So they really were on their own. The chief of staff glared at each of the ship captains in succession, as if daring them to ask another question. After several seconds of silence, she cut the connection.

Kleindienst disappeared, along with the virtual briefing room background, but the four captains, surrounded by ghostly details of their cabins, continued to float in what was now a featureless, dimensionless gray void. Looking into it gave Sam a sensation of vertigo and so he looked at Bonaventure, concentrated on his face.

"I kept the connection open because I wanted to add something," Bonaventure said. "This sounds like a raw deal. I don't like it any more than anyone else. But you got a big mouth, Juanita, and you came real close to open insubordination with the chief of staff. You need to put a lid on that defeatist bullshit, understood? All of us need to work together to get through this."

"Bullshit? *Jesús*, listen to you, Pablo! A commodore for five minutes and already you talk like *el almirante grande*. You want me to shut up? Sure-sure, *no hay pedo,* I shut up. But you know where the bullshit was coming from in that briefing, and it wasn't from Juanita Rivera."

CHAPTER TWENTY

31 December 2133
(two days later) ***(tenth day in K'tok orbit)***

The general quarters gong still sounded and Goldjune had already moved to the Maneuvering One chair when Sam arrived on the bridge. As he strapped into the command chair he studied the tactical schematic on the smart wall ahead of him—already obscured by the interference of a nuclear explosion in orbit, but almost on the far side of K'tok from *Puebla*.

"What the hell happened? Is it an attack?"

"Yes, sir," Goldjune said. "Captain, the boat's at general quarters, MatCon alpha, task group standing orbit and speed, reactor on standby, full charge on the ring, shroud secured, sensors active. No change in orbit since last watch change. At 0721, we had two sudden new contacts—looks like another jump emergence—and I sounded general quarters".

"Very well, Mr. Goldjune, I have the boat. Where are they? Behind K'tok?"

"Yes sir. Another polar approach, only two cruisers this time. By the time I had the boat aligned, they had passed our firing window."

Sam brought up his own tactical display and walked it back to the contact point. Only two uBakai cruisers?

"Helm, give me a lateral acceleration warning and then align the boat on his transit point, where they'll break the disk."

"Aye, aye, sir."

The claxon sounded as Marina Filipenko came through the hatch.

She waited for the initial burn to start and then climbed up and into the Tac One chair.

"How many of them?" she asked.

"Two. They're over there on the far side of K'tok"

Filipenko brought up her own display. "Um . . . Captain Rivera's boat, *Champion Hill*, is in low orbit, tending the bombardment munitions."

Sam pulled up the tactical recording, ran it forward at high speed and then backwards and couldn't make any sense of what was going on. The one thing he was sure of was that the bandits had fired the missiles that had detonated and cluttered up their sensors. He glanced down to check who was in the Tac Two seat.

"Chief Patel, you take the long-range sensors, up and active. This can't be the whole story. There may be more leatherheads on the way. There *have* to be. Don't let them sneak up on us."

Two cruisers, popping out of jump space at ridiculously close range, doing a fast fly-by. . . what was this supposed to accomplish?

"There he is, breaking the disc!" Filipenko called out.

Sam saw it on his own display, the uBakai cruisers emerging from the sensor shadow of K'tok, emerging from behind the disc of the planet. The data tag showed their range increasing at over twenty kilometers per second.

"No firing solution, sir. They're going too fast and on a receding vector."

Sam nodded but still couldn't figure out what had just happened.

"Captain, I'm picking up an SOS from *Champion Hill*," Chief Gambara in the Comm Chair said. "It's an automated transmitter, not audio. They may be fucked up pretty bad, sir."

"Helm, who's in the best position to render assistance?" Sam asked.

"*Cha-cha*," Goldjune answered, and then he turned to look at Sam. He didn't look smug, he didn't wear that half-sneer of contempt he used to specialize in. No, Larry Goldjune looked scared and confused, and hoping Sam had the answers he didn't.

Sam.

Wasn't that interesting?

It took all of the morning and part of the afternoon to sort through the data records and figure out what happened. At 1130 hours it became Sam's job.

Bitka, Commodore Bonaventure had said via tight beam commlink, *I see in your service folder that when you were at Pearl River you took the course on squadron-level intelligence analysis, and ended second in the class. Say something smart about how to look at all of the data we are collecting*

Sam thought for a moment and said the first thing he'd learned in the course that struck him as genuinely interesting. "Don't waste your time trying to guess what the enemy's going to do. Concentrate on what he's capable of doing."

Huh. Bueno, *you're hired. You are now the task group's acting N-2. Find out what just happened.*

And so he had. The hardest part had been trying to reconstruct what happened to *Champion Hill.* He didn't have any crew interviews to work from yet since *Cha-Cha* was still recovering the survivors and they were undergoing medical triage. He did eventually have a copy of the data record from *Champion Hill's* engineering department, which also included the command log up until the last moment. He also had an external video survey of the boat which made him dizzy the first time he looked at it.

The forward third of the boat was nothing but twisted, spidery wreckage. The bow itself, all the way back to about the bridge, was completely gone. A fire lance hit wouldn't do this much damage. It wouldn't do this *sort* of damage. This looked as if something had torn the nose off and shredded everything behind it, just peeled it back in places like a banana skin. Another new uBakai secret weapon?

The answer was hidden in the command data logs. Once he made sure he understood what the uBakai cruisers had been doing in their high-speed fly-by, he contacted Bonaventure.

"Commodore, that was a transport mission. The cruisers dropped sixteen large-capacity reentry gliders. It wasn't easy to see them through the noise of that nuke they set off, which was probably the intention, but we've got a good composite picture from a couple different platforms. I've narrowed the likely landing area. It's six hundred kilometers northwest of T'tokl-Heem, the colonial capital."

What for, do you think? Bonaventure asked.

"All I can tell you is what those gliders are capable of carrying:

about fifty tons of cargo each or one hundred and fifty passengers, or some mix of that, depending on their configuration. The most likely cargo, given the situation, is military, but that could be better-trained ground troops or heavy equipment—either armored vehicles or surface-to-orbit weaponry. I'd recommend keeping an eye on the landing site."

Huh. In and out fast to drop off high-priority cargo. Stretched as thin as we are, it makes sense. And what about Champion Hill?

San shook his head. "I was worried about some new super-weapon, but Captain Rivera just had some really bad luck—no other way to put it. The recovered logs show she was firing a missile exactly when the uBakai hit her with a fire lance forward. The fire lance strike must have compromised the coil gun shaft, but the missile was still coming. It hit the shaft blockage already going between five and six kilometers a second. Fortunately, the warhead didn't fire or no one would have survived, but it still packed a hell of a lot of kinetic energy."

Yes, enough to blow the nose off and shred everything forward of about frame forty, Bonaventure said. *Some of the wreckage is hot—radioactive hot. That would be the material from the warhead's fission trigger, yes?*

"Yes, sir. How many survivors?"

Fifty-two, but three of them might not make it and we're going to have to freeze a lot of the other injured. Juanita Rivera was on the bridge. I doubt we'll ever find her body, or any of her bridge crew. It took out the forward crew bay as well. We'll shift as many survivors as we can to the Highstation. We don't have the medical facilities to deal with them. The admiral should have left Hornet *behind. Even just parked in high orbit, it would have been doing something—repair work, a hospital suite, letting our people rotate through for some plus-gee time. Something.*

Sam knew his boss was right, but being right didn't get them much.

CHAPTER TWENTY-ONE

31 December 2133
(later the same day) ***(tenth day in K'tok orbit)***

Sam had finished his dinner and evening administrative work when he heard the chime at his cabin door. He turned the hatch transparent and was surprised to see Lieutenant Commander Delmar Huhn in the corridor.

"Sam, do you have moment?" Huhn said to the door, still an opaque gray on his side.

Sam's first impulse was to say no, to plead pressing business, but his own orders to the crew had been to extend Huhn the courtesy and respect appropriate to his rank.

Fifth Principle of Naval Leadership: Set The Example

He released the hatch lock.

"Of course. Come in, Commander Huhn."

Sam noticed he carried an oblong brown plastic or composite box under his arm, no more than twenty centimeters square and twice that in length.

Hope it's not a bomb, the paranoid guy that lived in the dark back of his head thought.

Sam gestured to the two zero-gee "chairs"—actually padded torso frames—along one wall. Both men kicked gently off and glided over to them, Huhn from the hatchway and Sam from his workstation. Once they were tethered in, the silence stretched out until it became awkward, at least for Sam. Huhn seemed lost in his own thoughts. Finally he looked up.

"Once it was done and I had time to think, I figured I made an awful mistake, giving up command. I was always an ambitious man, but not . . . well, not crazy. Not unrealistic. Never thought I'd retire with an admiral's star. Captain of a cruiser—that was the pinnacle of my ambition. Four broad stripes on my sleeve."

"It must have been a difficult decision," Sam said, although the words tasted trite to him as soon as he spoke them. Huhn looked at him for a moment but Sam could not read his expression. Huhn's face seemed blank, as if the life had left him.

"Threw my future away," Huhn said after a moment, and then he looked around the cabin he had briefly occupied. "No getting it back. Hated you for a while, for doing what I couldn't. Still do, a little bit . . . hate you, I mean."

Sam didn't know what to say so he said nothing. He wished he'd poured them bulbs of coffee, water, something to keep his hands occupied.

"I've been reading about the Royal Navy," Huhn said, "back in the olden days, the Age of Fighting Sail. Know much about it?"

Sam shook his head,

"The ships had contingents of Marines, for boarding actions and such, commanded by a sergeant or a lieutenant on the smaller ships. On the big ships of the line those Marines were commanded by a captain. But onboard the ship he was always addressed as major. You know why?"

"No, why?"

"Because a ship can only have one captain."

Huhn took the box from under his arm and handed it to Sam, who took it with a measure of reluctance. Gifts suggested obligations. An unknown gift carried an unknown burden of obligation. He opened the box and saw a bottle of bourbon.

"Booker Beam," Huhn said. "Seven years old. About as good as it gets."

"I don't. . . "

"It's not for you, Bitka. Not personally, anyway. It's for the captain, in case you want to share a drink with your officers."

Sam stared at the bottle, uncertain what he should say or do about this, uncertain in fact how he felt about it.

"Will you . . . will you have a drink with me, Commander Huhn?"

"Nope. I'm not one of the ship's officers any more, just a passenger." He unbuckled himself from the chair and Sam felt his face flush.

"I regret that remark, sir."

"It was the truth, and it needed saying. Don't be sorry for that. Besides, it means I don't need permission to leave."

He pushed off the wall and left the cabin.

Sam stared at the bottle of bourbon. What was going on in Huhn's head? Was this gesture well-intended or ill? Did Huhn himself know? Sam shook his head.

"Back home we got an expression for a guy like Admiral Kayumati," Moe Rice said with the careful enunciation characteristic both of his West Texas accent and of a drunk. "All hat, no cattle."

Laughter flashed around the circle of officers, from Marina Filipenko's bell-like tinkle to the loud guffaws of Rose Hennessey. The five of them—Sam and his four department heads—floated in Sam's cabin and had been drinking the bottle of bourbon formerly belonging to Delmar Huhn.

The bourbon had been a small compensation—or at least a chance to unwind—for the officers after over seventy hours of near-continuous work and omnipresent tension, punctuated by the final horror of what happened to *Champion Hill*. Sam needed a drink himself, but didn't like the idea of drinking alone. Besides, it was New Years Eve. He had stood the crew to a beer at mess, which slightly assuaged his sense of guilt at this exercise of exclusive privilege—slightly, but not entirely.

As the laughter faded, Sam was tempted to pass on Juanita Rivera's final question in the briefing, knew it would find sympathetic ears here, especially now that she was gone, but he did not. Instead he thought he should reprimand Rice, shouldn't let disrespectful talk like that about the chain of command—*injurious to good order*—go unchecked, but he just said, "Moe, maybe you've had one too many bourbons."

Moe nodded. "Yup, that's muh story and I'm stickin' to it." Then he grinned.

They all laughed, except Larry Goldjune.

"Go on, Rice, get drunk, play the clown," he said. "You can afford to. Take a couple days off if you like. Nobody will even notice you're gone."

The laughter stopped and Moe's face cleared, the drunkenness—or perhaps its pretense—gone.

"Mister Goldjune, if you have some duty I can assist your department with, I will be happy to do so. I will do whatever I can to help make this ship combat—"

"*Boat,* Rice!" Goldjune interrupted him. "Christ, how long do you have to be on a destroyer before you learn it's called a goddamned *boat* instead of—"

"That's enough, Larry," Sam said, and to his surprise Goldjune stopped talking and settled back. For a moment Sam hated Goldjune, wanted to push his sour ass out the nearest airlock. All Rice had been trying to do was take their minds off the last twelve hours, the last two days, the last week. Sam took a deep, slow breath and let it out.

"Maybe this wasn't such a good idea after all. I guess part of me thought we might bond under all this pressure, loosen up with some alcohol. Well, that doesn't matter. You all worked your asses off the last couple days, and under lousy conditions. You earned a nightcap. So let's finish our drinks, get some rest, and we'll start again tomorrow."

They drank in silence for a moment, and then Marina Filipenko spoke.

"Any progress on the jump drive scrambler, Larry?"

"What's that supposed to mean?" he snapped.

Marina recoiled slightly, her eyes widening in surprise and distress.

"Take it easy, Larry," Sam said. "She didn't mean anything, except the jump drive scrambler's on everybody's mind. If we figure it out, we may have a handle on this whole mess."

Goldjune looked down at his drink bulb, and for a moment Sam thought he was going to throw it against the bulkhead.

"No progress."

Goldjune lifted his face and Sam looked at him, looked carefully, maybe for the first time, and under the anger and frustration and contempt, he saw something he had never seen before, although now that he thought about it, it must always have been there, back behind everything else. He saw fear.

They were all afraid. This was war, and a war they were losing, a war that was killing people at so alarming a rate that their own chances of survival seemed more remote by the day. Who wouldn't be afraid? But Goldjune's fear had always been there, hadn't it? And what did

Larry Goldjune, the son and nephew of admirals, the honors graduate of Annapolis, the officer clearly foreordained to wear stars on his shoulders one day, have to fear *before* the war?

"Okay, Larry, tomorrow put together a data dump with all the stats you think might be relevant and pass it to Hennessey. Rose, somebody in your engineering shop has to have pulled duty in a J-drive room. See if anything sets off an alarm with them and if so get it back to Larry. We've got to figure this thing out so our cruisers can back us up."

"I think that fleet already sailed," Larry said, again looking down at his drink. "Two days ago."

"Bush league," Moe Rice said after a while, staring down at his bourbon. They all looked at him but even Larry Goldjune said nothing. Moe raised his head and looked around at them. "I mean, I'm just a supply officer, right? But that's how this feels to me: fucking bush league. We're supposed to be the United States Navy and it's like we can't even get out of our own goddamned way. Every time we turn around those guys bitch-slap us. Our missiles don't work right. We've been hanging around with the Varoki for a century and all of a sudden they've got weapons we've never *heard* of? How'd *that* get past us? Our mission is to support a ground force with orbital bombardment and so we pull every bombardment-capable ship *out*? Now all the admiral can figure to do is run away to some gas giant it's just as easy for them to get to, but isn't *worth* as much, so maybe they'll leave him alone. Jesus *fucking* Christ!"

It was the longest, angriest speech Sam had ever heard Moe make, and he was right. He was right enough Sam felt his face burn with shame.

Marina Filipenko touched Moe's arm and smiled softly. "If you didn't know any better, you'd think we'd never been in an interstellar war before."

Rose Hennessey nodded. "It *is* taking some getting used to."

"Boy, howdy," Moe said.

They looked at each other for a few moments and then finished their drinks in silence.

CHAPTER TWENTY-TWO

1 January 2134
(the next day) ***(eleventh day in K'tok orbit)***

Sam floated out of his shower sphere, pulled off his shower mask, and checked the time: 0615, January First. Welcome to 2134, and just in time. Sam had had about all of 2133 he could handle.

The shower sphere was only about a meter and a half in interior circumference, with high pressure water jets on one side and vacuum intakes on the other. You had to wear an oxgen feed mask while you were in it to keep from drowning. Sam had to curl up almost in a fetal position to fit, and the pressure of the water jets spun him in the compartment, making him slightly dizzy, but despite all that it was one of the real luxuries of a senior officer's cabin. The junior officers and enlisted crew made do with a communal shower shared with a half-dozen other crew once every week and sponge bathing in between.

He toweled off and checked his stored messages, and he saw a flashing attention notice by one from Commodore Bonaventure, logged in five minutes ago. Bonaventure was up early.

Bitka, as the task group N-2 I've got two bones for you to chew on.

First bone: we picked up some acceleration signatures, multiple ships, out past the asteroid belt and almost on the opposite side of the primary, so presumed hostile. We sure don't have anything out there. Looks as if the task force main body wouldn't have a line of sight to them, and neither would the ships out in Mogo orbit. We copied them and the raw data's in the latest intel update but I want you to take a look yourself, bring that famous tac-head concentration to bear. Let me know if you have any ideas.

Second bone: we did a fly-over this morning of the landing site for those glide canisters and picked up vehicular movement heading south. They're keeping dispersed, but the ground speed is consistent with gunsleds. Looked like they landed some lift cavalry and they're headed toward the downstation. Give me some options to deal with them.

Enjoy your breakfast.

He cut the connection and then checked the intel updates, and found the report of thermal signatures of an acceleration burn, starting north of the plane of the ecliptic and then cutting out once they reached the plane. Four or five separate signatures, hard to tell for sure at that distance and with a lot of thermal "noise" from the primary—the system's sun.

He checked the watch rotation just to be sure, but knew what he would find: White Watch was on, had just taken over forty-five minutes ago. Ensign Barb Lee would be officer of the deck, already strapped into the command chair. The update had come in four hours ago when Blue Watch was on duty.

Jerry Robinette had finally qualified as officer of the deck and had taken over Blue Watch from Larry Goldjune three days ago. Robinette would probably be in the wardroom now, getting breakfast, having just come off watch. He'd come along surprisingly well since they moved him back to the tactical department from engineering. He took his responsibilities seriously, had worked hard to qualify as OOD, and had pitched in on the missile problem, done the force analysis calculations they needed to stress-test the parts. Sam had even gone several days without thinking of him as *the Jughead*. He wondered if Jerry might be one of those legendary diamonds in the rough, who never shine until they need to. Maybe it was time to find out.

Sam squinted up his contact code and pinged him.

Yes, sir? Robinette answered.

"Ensign, did you notice an updated intel packet concerning thrust signatures out beyond the asteroid belt?"

Yes, sir. I flagged it for Lieutenant Filipenko's attention, as Tac-boss, but it didn't seem immediately pressing. I think she may still be in the rack. Is there a problem, sir?

"No problem, Ensign. You're right, it wasn't coded as critical and a burn that far away—at least one like this—isn't an immediate problem. What do you suppose it means?"

There was a moment's silence

Mean, sir? In what way?

"Well, when the uBakai hit us here, they came out of jump with a high residual velocity. That means they had to do a long, hard burn before they jumped."

Sir, are you saying the uBakai could be getting ready for another attack?

Sam heard the rising alarm in Robinette's voice.

"I don't think so, Jerry." Sam used Robinette's first name to calm him, put him more at ease. "Besides, we'd have seen the energy signature of a jump if they'd done that, right? So if you take a look at these burn tracks, it is pretty clear they are moving slower as they approach the plane of the ecliptic, not faster. So they aren't accelerating, are they?"

No, sir. They must be decelerating.

"Right. So what do you think that means?"

More silence.

That they're slowing down? I'm sorry, sir, I don't know. It means they decelerated, but . . . I don't know exactly what you mean by 'mean,' sir.

Sam took a breath and swallowed to keep the impatience from his voice.

"Okay, Jerry, I'm not trying to stump you, but if you're going to be a tactical officer you've got to learn to think tactically. Everything means something. Every piece of data like this is the result of a sentient being making a decision to do something. The question is, what did they decide to do, and why?

"In this case, four or five unknown and previously undetected ships approached the plane of the ecliptic from galactic north at a fairly steep angle, then they decelerated and dropped into an orbit around the primary, out past the asteroids. They did it out there to use the primary and the asteroids to partially cloak themselves, right?

"But who are they? They had to come from somewhere and probably jumped to above the plane. But they've got a very different residual vector than the uBakai fleet had last time we saw them."

Yes, sir. Theirs was flat, almost parallel to the plane.

"That's right. So why would they change their vector into a

north—south orientation, then jump north of the plane, and then decelerate to burn away that new vector? And why wouldn't we have seen their burn when they made that original vector change?"

More silence.

I . . . I'm sorry, sir, but I just can't get it. I don't know why.

Sam sighed.

"Robinette, you can't think of a good reason for them to do it because there is no good reason. And we probably *would* have seen a major course change burn anywhere near this system. Those are uBakai reinforcements arriving, possibly the four cruisers they had at Akaampta."

Sam cut the connection and shook his head. Well, that had been a pointless exercise, a waste of both their times, except for what it showed him about Robinette.

The Jughead.

Sam wanted to teach the young ensign that sometimes if you can't think of a reason for something, there might not be one. The problem was, Robinette apparently could not figure out a reason for anything. Sam didn't think he had much future as a tactical officer, which was too bad. They needed someone good to back up Marina Filipenko. She was rising to the job, but if anything happened to her, they were in big trouble.

He turned back to his desk and loaded the report on ground vehicle traffic down on K'tok.

"Curse the *Cottohazz* and curse the uZmataanki!" Admiral Tyjaa e-Lapeela raged. Vice-Captain Takaar Nuvaash, Speaker for the Enemy, listened in what he hoped gave the impression of respectful silence. "The rotating commander of the *Cottohazz* peacekeeping force at Fleet Base Akaampta is Hue e-Puttazhaa. You know him?"

"No, Admiral, I do not have that pleasure."

"*Pleasure?* Baa! He fancies himself a man of cunning, and he imagines his tricks are amusing. Also he has never forgiven Bakaa for the death of his son in the K'Tok War. I suppose they will now call that the *First* K'tok War and ours the Second."

"I believe the admiral's insight on that matter at least is correct." Nuvaash waited to see if the admiral would react to his careful phrasing but e-Lapeela was too involved in his own anger to notice

"E-Puttazhaa has invoked the noninvolvement clause of the *Cottohazz* charter and refuses to release the Akaampta squadrom from service. He claims doing so would constitute using the Akaampta base as a support facility to sustain a war by one member against another."

"Yes, so I understand. It is unfortunate, Admiral, that simply the fact that our cruisers there are carrying munitions manufactured under *Cottohazz* contracts, and fuel purchased and refined for *Cottohazz* use, allows Admiral e-Puttazhaa to exercise this inconvenient technicality of the law."

e-Lapeela looked up and a hint of suspicion flickered in his eyes, or perhaps Nuvaash imagined it. e-Lapeela always looked a bit suspicious of everything. Nuvaash made sure his ears were spread wide and his eyes bore a look of sincere and respectful sympathy.

"That is why the Akaampta squadron has not arrived," the admiral continued. "They may have to jump back to Hazz'Akatu and conduct a nominal refit before joining us, assuming our government can secure their release at all. I wonder how hard they are trying."

That was an interesting observation, Nuvaash thought.

"This news came with the new cruisers from home?" he asked.

"A jump courier from Akaampta arrived in the home system just before the two new Home Fleet cruisers jumped here. The original plan was for the Akaampta squadron to join us at the same time, and then we would have had overwhelming force. This delay complicates everything. With our two remaining operational cruisers and the two from home we do not have the ability to guarantee a victory at K'tok and retain sufficient strength to later defeat the balance of the enemy fleet.

"Fortunately, we will soon be joined by a new ally—an uKa-Maat squadron of three cruisers is being readied for dispatch and will arrive within the week. Although they are untested in battle, the fact that two of the cruisers are of the new salvo variety helps considerably."

"The Federation of Ka-Maat has declared war?" Nuvaash asked. If so, this was good news indeed. A second Varoki nation joining the fight might indeed open the path for others to follow.

e-Lapeela settled back in his chair and considered his words.

"I expect a formal declaration to come later. For now, the uKa-Maat squadrons is acting . . . on the initiative of its command personnel. To avoid diplomatic complications, the ships will be fitted with uBakai transponders until such time as their government's policy catches up with events.

"But tell me, how have the Humans responded to the attacks? Speak for the enemy."

"Confusion," Nuvaash answered. "We have limited information, most of it from the ground stations on K'tok and the three dark sensor platforms in the asteroid belt. There are four surviving destroyers at K'tok, two cruisers and four destroyers moving from the gas giant Mogo toward K'tok, and the balance of the enemy fleet en route back to Mogo."

The admiral shook his head in disdain.

"They had two cruisers at K'tok and two at Mogo, and are now wasting days switching their places? Confusion is a charitable characterization, Nuvaash. Had our reinforcements arrived as planned, we would make short work of them.

"We must not let them regain their balance."

A mess steward brought lunch to Sam in his cabin and he'd just made a fresh bulb of coffee from his drink dispenser when his commlink vibrated and the ID tag of Moe Rice, the supply officer, came up.

"Yes, Moe. What's up?"

Cap'n, you wanted a heads-up if anything changed on the ground supply front. Well, it hasn't exactly changed, but it's getting pretty bad, especially for the Brits. The uBakai are moving those gunsleds south. We don't have the ability to shift our orbital bombardment munitions around so they're sticking to our blind spots. The troops on the ground are going to have to handle this one on their own. They need heavy weapons for that.

"Still no word from Earth about those fabricators?"

No, sir. The Brits are down to using captured small arms, no heavy stuff. The US and Indian cohorts can loan them a couple launchers and missiles, but they're stretched thin on their own fronts. Without those ammo fabricators cranking out some anti-vehicle missiles, they're in a world of hurt. There was talk of evacuating them up the needle, maybe having to pull the plug on the whole operation. Thing is, with the transports gone that's not even an option any more. There's no way a few destroyers can pack two thousand soldiers in, let alone keep them fed and breathing.

"Okay, Moe, thanks."

Shit!

He was back to Dynamic Paradigms and the cheat code. If he broke his nondisclosure agreement and turned the cheat code over to the supply folks, would his old company make an exception for him? Would they decide the critical situation on K'tok justified the breach of trust? No. The Navy had already been trying to get them to allow cross-access and the firm hadn't budged. If they wouldn't budge for the US government, they weren't going to cut him a break.

Why *hadn't* they turned the cheat code over? They were defense contractors. Sure, this wasn't covered by the original purchase orders, but the company could probably charge the Navy a small fortune to go outside the agreed terms. They were in business, weren't they? What was this about if not money?

He really didn't like the Navy, and the prospect of making it his career by default did not appeal to him. In all likelihood the Navy wouldn't have him anyway when this was all done, he being a scummy reservist and all. Dumped unceremoniously on the beach with no job, no money, and no prospects. Delightful future.

And that wasn't all. Navy regulations explicitly *prohibited* him from breaking the law in pursuit of his duty or in following orders. Corporate proprietary information was covered by law. He'd actually be breaking Navy regs to turn over the cheat code. For all he knew he could end up in jail.

There was only one sensible, legal course of action: keep his mouth shut. It still wasn't too late for Dynamic Paradigms to come through with the master codes to allow cross-programming. *Come on, you bastards. Give them the codes.*

He looked at the unopened containers of his lunch but they had gone cold and no longer looked appetizing.

CHAPTER TWENTY-THREE

2 January 2134
(the next day) ***(twelfth day in K'tok orbit)***

Although Sam did not have a fixed spot in the watch rotation, he tried to spell one of the OODs for a few hours once a day. This afternoon he was covering the second half of Marina Filipenko's watch when the comm came through.

"Captain, incoming request for tight beam holocon from the task force N-2," Signaler Second Rosaria Lincoln said.

"Got it," Sam said. He retrieved his helmet, clipped it on, and triggered the link. Sam looked at the holoimage of Commander Cassandra Atwater-Jones, Royal Navy, and smiled. She was weightless again, just as he was, her face framed in a barely contained cloud of red hair. That tailored dark blue Royal Navy shipsuit really did fit her well. He looked again and noticed her smile lacked its normal jauntiness, seemed tinged with melancholy.

"Commander, are you okay?"

"Yes, Bitka, but the news from K'tok has been unhappy, hasn't it? Especially as we on *Pensacola* are all safe and snug, rocketing away from danger."

"That wasn't your call."

She shrugged with her eyebrows. "A matter of moral consolation, but little else. I rather liked Captain Rivera, you know, despite our verbal sparring. Now I have also received word that a . . . a dear friend has been badly wounded. Things are not going well for Forty-Two ROMAC."

"Forty-Two ROMAC?" Sam repeated.

"Ah. Forty-Second Royal Marine Commando, the British cohort on the ground, defending our perimeter around the needle downstation. Freddie is—*was*—the cohort commander. I believe he's being evacuated up the needle. Of course, the fleet auxiliaries, with their fully kitted-out trauma suites, have all withdrawn with us, so he'll have to make do with whatever medical facilities they have at the Highstation."

Sam closed his eyes and felt dizzy for a moment. Even with his eyes closed, he saw or sensed the flickering shadow appear on the edge of his field of vision, watching him.

"My turn to ask: are you unwell, Bitka?"

Sam opened his eyes.

"No, just experiencing my own moment of shame. Maybe I'll explain someday. I'm very sorry about your friend."

"Thank you for your sympathy," she said and frowned at him, but he thought from concern rather than annoyance. "That sounds rather pro-forma, doesn't it? But I mean it, and Freddie's made of fairly stern stuff, so I expect he will recover. Now, before this becomes completely maudlin, to the business at hand."

Her face cleared and she picked up a data pad and waved it gently at him.

"I read Commodore Bonaventure's summary of your analysis of the thermal tracks we detected. Are you trying to steal my job?"

"No, ma'am. Just following the commodore's orders to look the sighting report over and tell him what I thought. Do I take it you agree with my SWAG?"

"SWAG?" she asked.

"Scientific Wild-Assed Guess."

"Don't be modest, Bitka. I doubt it was a guess and of course I concur with your judgment. There is really no other reasonable interpretation. I have several junior staffers—one of them supposedly a career intelligence officer—who were unable to puzzle it out." She paused and flashed the playful, mischievous smile he remembered from before. "They were quite embarrassed when I told them a line officer, a *reservist* no less, had done so, and who, to make matters even worse, was *an American*. I'm sure you can appreciate their mortification."

"Yeah. Tell 'em to keep a stiff upper lip. So what are we going to do about those extra uBakai ships?"

"Haven't the foggiest. I simply pass the analyses along to Dame Kliendienst, and trust that wiser minds than ours are—even as we speak—crafting a foolproof strategy for victory."

"Well, everyone should have a dream."

"Quite," she said with a smile, and then leaned her head back slightly and examined him as if through imaginary spectacles. "Aside from the worry lines you look well, Bitka. Being a ship's captain must agree with you."

"It's a boat, not a ship."

"Right. Commodore Bonaventure was at pains to remind me of that. He also shared a rather amusing name: *Bow-on Bitka*? Somehow I imagined you as a more cerebral tactician than that suggests."

"Don't get the wrong idea. The bow's where all the armor is. I'm just a guy trying to figure the best way to get home in one piece."

Her face grew serious and she nodded.

"Quite so. As my friend Freddie once observed, the military is not a life assurance venture. Well . . . " She gave one of her rapid eyebrow shrugs and the concern disappeared from her face. "Have to run now, but I wanted to personally tell you 'well done' on that sighting report. Any other insights you have of an intelligence nature, contact me directly. Especially as you are now an intelligence officer in your own right," she added with an ironic smirk.

"Will do," Sam said and her image flickered off, but he left his helmet on and the optics engaged. So far as the bridge crew knew he was still in conference, which gave him a moment with his thoughts. His mind crackled with visions of soldiers fighting to defend the needle downstation, an officer carried to the rear, his combat armor broken open and dripping blood.

Of course, he did not have to imagine. He could look. Video feeds were available of much of the fighting, but Sam had never looked at any of them. For a moment he pretended to wonder why, but of course he knew the answer.

He'd railed against the dark side of the Navy, against officers who put paving the way for their post-Navy career ahead of their their duty—nest featherers, Moe called them. So what the hell was he doing that was any different? He sat quietly for several long seconds, trying not to move, simply breathing slowly and steadily, searching for his soul, his true being, as if it were a cork bobbing somewhere in a storm-swept ocean of fears and desires and uncertainties.

Eleventh Principle of Naval Command: Seek responsibility, and take responsibility for your actions.

Don't act like a captain. Be the captain.

He sighed and then took off his helmet and clipped it to his bridge workstation.

It hadn't been a bad dream—to carve out a career, to have a family, to give his children some economic security so they never experienced the humiliation which had driven his mother mad, never had to make the impossible choices which had destroyed his brother's soul, never had to feel worthless for reasons beyond their control. It hadn't been such a bad dream.

"Lincoln," he said to the duty communication petty officer sitting to his left, "patch me through tight beam to the expeditionary brigade supply company. You'll probably have to bounce the signal off one of our comsats. Supply folks are on the needle highstation and I'm pretty sure K'tok's in the way right now."

Signaller Second Class Rossaria Lincoln turned and looked at him. "Sir, if it's not urgent, we can wait until our orbit track brings us across the horizon and we have line of sight to the Highstation. Should only be about fifteen minutes."

Sam looked at the smart wall ahead of him, now set to show the view forward, the curvature of K'tok blurred by cloud-filled atmosphere to their ventral side, the star-flecked expanse of deep space stretching out ahead of them.

"No, Lincoln, better do it now. Might lose my nerve in fifteen minutes."

As he waited for the circuit to open, he found himself wondering about Freddie, who he was, how seriously he was injured, what he meant to Atwater-Jones. It was a strange thought and it annoyed him. After all, it was her business, and he disliked it when people nosed around in his.

"Captain," Lincoln said, "we have a small problem. The comsat circuits are all tied up, routine admin chatter, looks like. I'm trying to get a data pipe but we may have to wait for that direct line of sight."

"Okay, keep at it."

His commlink vibrated and he saw the ID tag for Senior Chief Navarro.

Have a minute, sir?

"Looks like I have fifteen of them. What's up, COB?"

There was a moment's silence before Navarro answered.

You wanted to talk about the crew again later today but something came up I thought you should know about right away.

"Okay, shoot."

Well, sir, it's partly about your name.

"Bitka? It's Slovenian originally."

No, sir. The 'Bow-On' part. A couple of the chiefs—mostly Gordy Cunningham and whoever will listen to him—are starting to think you're trying to impress the brass, make a name for yourself by taking extra chances.

Damn! There was that name again. "That's nuts, Chief. I'm about the last guy in the fleet likely to do that."

He listened to the sound of his own heart for five or six beats before Navarro spoke again.

Sir, that's just about the last thing I want you to say.

"Yeah, I see what you mean. Okay, COB, point taken. Let me think about it and we'll talk this afternoon."

Sam cut the feed and stretched his arms above his head. He looked around the bridge—everyone at their work stations, everyone absorbed in their work. Sensor Tech Second Ron Ramirez, sitting the Tac One seat beside Sam, was studying for his first class sensor tech qualifications.

"Sir, I've got that channel clear to Highstation," Lincoln said.

Sam picked up his helmet, clipped it on, and opened the link.

Two hours later, back in his own cabin, Sam prepared to take the capsule provided by Medtech Tamblinson which, he now knew from experience, would drive Jules's ghost away and clear his mind with two or three hours of untroubled sleep. Before he did so, he again had Lincoln open a tight beam holochannel, although this time not to Highstation.

"Why it's Captain Bitka again," Atwater-Jones's holo-image said with a broad smile. "To what do I . . . what's wrong?"

Sam looked down for a moment, collecting his thoughts. Although he had had plenty of time to get ready for this, he wasn't ready, not really, and all the time in the world wouldn't be enough.

"There is a manufacturer's cheat code which will allow the US Marine cohort's fabricators to manufacture the munitions the British cohort needs."

"Yes, I know," she said. "We've been trying for a week to get the firm to release it, but without success."

"I know the code."

She looked at him, her expression curious. "You?" Then her eyes narrowed and her expression grew cold. "How long have you known it?"

"All along."

"Did you by any chance think to share this information with anyone?"

Sam sighed.

"Yeah, just this afternoon, with the expeditionary brigade's supply company. They won't take it."

"*Won't take it?*" Anger rose in her voice and her eyes grew wide with outrage and surprise, but then she closed her mouth and looked away. Several long, slow breaths later, she nodded.

"Right. Of course they won't take it. Can't, you know. Frightfully illegal. When the uBakai Star Navy is blowing us to bloody pieces, our first concern must always be to protect the assets of Varoki corporations."

Sam started.

"*Varoki?* No, Commander, it's Dynamic Paradigms, the firm I worked for back on Earth."

She looked him in the eye, her expression full of disdain. "Is it possible, Bitka, that you are really that oblivious to the world around you? Dynamic Paradigms is controlled by AZ Kamdaadik, a Varoki trading house trying to make a move into the fabricator industry."

"Varoki own my company?"

"Over thirty percent of it, which in a large publically traded corporation such as yours, all but guarantees them control over its management and strategic policy. I think it unlikely they will consent to our request."

She looked away, mouth set in a hard line. Sam thought about the ownership of his employer and it started making a little more sense why they were not sharing the code, but he still didn't understand the Navy's position.

"We're fighting the Varoki, so why not just say 'We're using the codes to save our soldiers' lives, and if you don't like it go fuck yourselves?'"

She sighed and shook her head. "No, much as I hate to admit it, they are absolutely right. We are fighting only one Varoki nation out of twenty-seven. Nothing will unite the rest of the Varoki against us as surely as will deliberate and flagrant violation of their precious intellectual property laws. Even two or three more joining the war could overwhelm our forces.

"More to the point, this war can only end with a brokered peace, one which is acceptable to the bulk of the *Cottohazz*. Opinion among its officialdom seems to be running in our favor now, especially among the non-Varoki, but disregard of *Cottohazz* law could sour that support rather quickly. There is no point in making gains on the battlefield and then losing them at the conference table.

"No, our high command will not violate the *Cottohazz* charter on intellectual property, because to do so will lose the war, one way or another. Had you decided to turn the codes over earlier, it would have made no difference. That may be some consolation to you."

"It's not," Sam said.

"Well that's something," she said, still looking away. "What made you keep your secret so long?"

"Fear. Fear of ramifications, of disgrace, of jail, of losing the life I've made for myself, the one I'm trying to go back to. Fear of throwing away my future."

As he said it he felt odd, somehow divorced from the person who had put so high a value on those things. Perhaps it was the revelation that his firm was owned, or at least controlled, by a Varoki trading house. Perhaps it was because he no longer understood what he had found so appealing about that future, aside from its safety—its dependable, predictable security. Now that he had probably lost it, it didn't seem like much to have traded his soul for.

"And what made you finally share the code, or at least attempt to?" she asked, her voice cold and hard.

When he did not answer she finally turned to look at him, mouth a thin straight line, eyes narrow.

"That's my business," he said.

"Then why bother telling me all this? You don't owe me an explanation—not that I've really had one."

Sam looked away now, not because he couldn't meet her eyes, but because he couldn't think while looking into them, and he needed to think about that question. Why had he told her?

"The major commanding the supply company told me the information was so toxic, he didn't even want anyone to know he'd spoken with me. The brigade commander would *not* speak with me—I think the major tipped him off. Maybe what I tried to do will leak out, I don't know. Or maybe nobody will ever know I did anything, violated any confidences, or broke any laws. In case that's what happens, I wanted at least you to know the truth—a sort of confession, I guess."

"Confession? So I could absolve you of your sins? I'm afraid I am not in that line of work, Bitka," she said, her voice clipped and hard.

"Secrets isolate us," he said. "Carrying this secret all to myself will make me alone forever. So I'm dumping it on you too, and you can do whatever you want with it. But wait, there's more. I'm haunted by a woman who was killed in the first attack—Lieutenant Julia Washington. I think we were just falling in love and then she was gone, and now I see her."

"See her?" she asked quietly.

"Well, not really. It's like she's just on the edge of my vision, just out of focus, sort of a flickering sparkle, but I sense her presence. When you told me about your friend getting wounded, she came, watching to see what I'd do. She's still there right now.

"So, I've given you enough ammunition to blow me out of the water. I'm not just a lawbreaker, I'm crazy, I'm hallucinating. Ghosts follow me around. I'm clearly unfit for command. My chief of the boat thinks Larry Goldjune, the XO, would be better in the job anyway."

Atwater-Jones studied him, mouth pursed in concentration.

"What do you think?" she said. "About who would make a better captain, that is."

"Goldjune's a pretty smart guy."

"But . . . ?" Atwater-Jones prompted,

"But I'm afraid he's an empty uniform. When things go south, I don't think he's got anything."

She looked away and said nothing for a while. Then she turned back and squared her shoulders.

"I will have to think about this, but I have to say I am not pleased that you have decided to ease your moral burden by trying to shift some of it onto my shoulders. Fortunately, I am very good at declining that sort of gift. I am also not prepared to be your executioner, much as I suppose that would salve your conscience. When you have come to your senses and gotten past this absurd death wish, perhaps you'll be able to make some sense of it all. Do not be so anxious to go gentle into that good night.

"Beyond that, I decline to tell you my opinion on any of it. As I told you once before, you should not concern yourself with where I stand, so long as you know where you stand. Given the situation we all face, I'd sort that out as quickly as possible."

She cut the connection.

Sam sat looking at the capsule in his hand, trying to ignore the increasingly intense sparkle at the edge of his right field of vision. He began to feel slightly dizzy and nauseous, but he fought back the sensations. His commlink buzzed again and he saw Marina Filipenko's ID tag.

"Yes?"

Captain, I think I've figured out how we can rig a boat to maneuver in low planetary orbit with bombardment munitions onboard. Well, sort of onboard.

"Let's hear it."

Filipenko explained her idea and as she did so Sam closed his hand over the capsule. He had one more thing to do before embracing two hours of oblivion.

"Okay, you're on the bridge, right? Have Lincoln open up a tight beam to ComTaskGroup. Let's talk to Commodore Bonaventure."

CHAPTER TWENTY-FOUR

3 January 2134
(the next day) ***(thirteenth day in K'tok orbit)***

There is a sort of clarity and freedom which comes from having lost your future, and Sam had come to the conclusion he had definitely lost his.

Even if no word of his attempt to reveal his company's trade secrets leaked out, even if there were never any repercussions from it, he knew he could never go back to his old job or any job like it. He knew he could never again promise to keep the sort of secrets they would demand, secrets they thought more important than lives.

There was no going back, and as near as he could tell the road ahead led nowhere, at least for him personally. Strangely, that calmed him. When all roads are certain to lead to disaster, the view ahead is obscured neither by fear of the unknown nor by wishful thinking, and all options are open.

Sam shifted his position and brought his attention back to *Puebla's* bridge. He squinted up the time: 1051, coming up on the watch change in half an hour. He glanced to his left and saw Ensign Jerry Robinette's face, tight with concentration and tension, sweat standing out on his forehead. Jerry sat the command chair on the bridge as OOD, and Sam rode in the Tac One chair beside him, just an observer. He could have taken command but he wanted to see how Robinette handled the maneuver.

Ninth Principle of Naval Leadership: Develop a sense of responsibility among your subordinates.

So far Robinette had handled it well, if a little tentatively, but better to be cautious than end up leaking atmosphere. Of course, it helped Sam's peace of mind that Chief Mohana Bhargava, the senior quartermaster, had the helm at Maneuvering One.

The idea for how to carry orbital bombardment munitions on a destroyer, to increase their coverage, had occurred to Marina Filipenko yesterday, and they had passed it to Commodore Bonaventure immediately. The EVA-qualified A-gang from USS *Oaxaca* had worked through the afternoon and most of the night to fabricate the composite and metal saddle rig which now floated a hundred meters ahead of *Puebla*. The saddle rig's central structure included a socket shaped to fit the docking bolt on *Puebla*'s nose, and the two wings of the framework, which would rest back against *Puebla's* forward hull once they were docked, each held a single orbital bombardment missile. It had been easy to assemble because it was pig-simple.

Ensign Robinette had moved *Puebla* from its own orbit down to *Oaxaca's*, and gotten it to the pennant's retrograde position in the orbit track without too many extra maneuvering burns. He'd then lined the boat up with the newly constructed saddle mount, and had waited for the orbital shuttle to recover the last of the EVA construction crew. Now it was time to dock with the contraption.

"You're lined up with that docking socket pretty well, Ensign," Sam said.

"Thank you, sir."

"From here, I think you can finish docking with a single command."

Robinette looked over at him, eyes suddenly wide with surprise and alarm. Moving forward required acceleration, but acceleration would change their orbit, moving them slightly up as well as forward. In theory, one brief burn from the attitude control thrusters at exactly the right angle, compensating for the upward drift, would send the boat directly ahead. But even with the computer-generated thrust solution showing on Robinette's monitor, hitting that socket exactly with a single burn was beyond his level of training and experience.

Robinette thought about it for several seconds, and then his face suddenly cleared and he nodded in comprehension.

"Helm," he ordered, "dock the boat."

"Aye, aye, sir." Chief Bhargava answered.

There might be hope for *the Jughead* after all.

One burn, and a minute and a half later, Sam felt the gentle bump as *Puebla*'s docking bolt slid into the saddle mount's socket and locked in place.

"Ensign Robinette, Chief Bhargava, well done. Signaler, make to ComTaskGroup: 'Docking Maneuver complete. Commencing bombardment run. Signed, Bitka.'

"Mister Robinette, sound general quarters."

Sam moved over to the command chair and relieved Robinette, who moved aft to his battle station on the auxiliary bridge. In a few minutes Marina Filipenko and Chief Abhay Patel strapped themselves into the Tac One and Two seats to his right. Sam gave the crew time to get to their battle stations and settled in and then went live on the all-boat channel.

"This is the captain speaking. You've probably all noticed the maneuvering we've been doing for the last hour or so and have wondered what's going on. We've dropped down to low planetary orbit, only about three hundred kilometers above the surface, and we just docked with a contraption dreamed up by our own Tac Boss, Lieutenant Filipenko. Before I explain what it does, let's review our mission here.

"We're supposed to hold the orbital space above K'tok and support the ground troops in action on its surface. That last part has had us scratching our heads because the cruisers were the only ships rigged to fire orbital bombardment munitions, and the cruisers pulled out almost a week ago. They left a bunch of their bombardment munitions in orbit but we can't fire them through our coil guns because the munitions are bigger in diameter than our coil gun barrels. We don't have external firing racks so that means the munitions stay where they are in orbit, going round and round.

"We can fire them when we're over a target, and with two clusters of munitions in orbit that means we can cover a fair chunk of the equator at any one time, but there are two big moving blind spots as well. Unless we can move the munitions around in orbit, like the cruisers could, we can't cover those blind spots or anything more than about ten degrees north or south of the equator. The uBakai on the ground have figured that out. They brought in reinforcements a few days ago and are moving them in closer around the ground brigade whenever we don't have Thuds overhead. Thuds are what we call the bombardment munitions. Their official designation is Thunderbolt, which is a pretty good name for them, but it has too many syllables for us tac-heads.

"So the uBakai started creeping in closer in the blind spot periods. *Oaxaca* and *Queretaro* made a couple phony attack runs, as if they carried munitions. At first they kept the uBakai back, but now they've learned better. They know it was a bluff and that we don't carry anything that can reach down through the atmosphere and hurt them. They've learned not to fear our destroyers, and they're closing in again, this time with those heavy armored vehicles they landed.

"Lieutenant Filipenko figured out how to fabricate a real simple framework that fits over the bow of a destroyer and carries two bombardment missiles, one on each side. Each one of those missiles has a retrorocket, guidance system, and fifty independently targeted super-dense spikes. There's no explosive in them, but when they hit the planet surface after a meteoric descent from orbit, they have so much kinetic energy they practically vaporize, and create a heat flash and shock wave that will take out just about anything where it comes down.

"The leatherheads have been having their way with us pretty much since this fight started. That's about to change. Let's go hunt some uBakai gunsleds from orbit."

A nice sharp one-gee burn and thirty-five minutes of coasting, followed by a second correcting burn, moved them almost a quarter-orbit prograde from the cluster of orbital munitions tended by *Oaxaca*, approaching the first dead spot.

Sam squinted up the call sign of the British cohort's orbital bombardment controller and had the signaler open a tight beam link to him or her.

"Fortune One this is Red Stinger Two on station. Do you have a target? Over"

Shite yes! 'ordes o' the bastards. Target bearing two eight five degrees true, range four five zero zero from my location. Ironsides, maneuvering in the open. Estimate twenty targets—wankers could do with a proper stonking. Fortune One, over.

Ironsides—British comm jargon for armored vehicles. That would probably be gunsleds, and twenty of them could cause a lot of damage.

"Acknowledged, Fortune One. We're coming up on our firing window in three minutes. Give us a secondary target as well. We've got a lot of spikes in this one package. Over."

Fortune One, through.

Sam blinked for a moment and then remembered in British communication terminology "through" didn't mean the speaker was done talking, it meant the message had been passed through to someone else to act on.

Sam turned to Filipenko at Tac One.

"Tac, what's the threat situation look like?"

"Intel doesn't show any platform missiles in the area, sir, and that's all the uBakai have down there that could reach up and hurt us. Of course, Intel also didn't see the jump scrambler coming, so I wouldn't rule out someone taking a shot at us, especially once we smack them with a Thud or two."

"Recommendation?"

Filipenko thought for a moment before answering.

"Sir, I'd slave the three ventral point-defense lasers to a single battery and go guns up, just in case. Right now the lasers are set to emit ultraviolet, which gets us plenty of range and hitting power in a vacuum, but UV won't penetrate very far into that atmosphere. I'd recommend tuning those three lasers up into the visible light spectrum, say five thousand angstroms."

And she thought she'd never know anything about tactics. Sam grinned.

"Make it so," he said.

Filipenko turned to her tac crew.

"Chief Patel, dump the sensor feed into your station and manage the battle picture. Don't let anyone sneak up on us. Delacroix, ventral point-defense battery, guns up at five thousand angstroms. Marmont, you're on Thud telemetry."

"Filipenko, you handle comms from the Limeys on the ground," Sam said. "Set up the strike. When it's time I'll give the fire order."

Sam settled back and set his workstation to display the feed from the sensors Patel directed at the target area, and he began zooming. At the same time he keyed his commlink to the tactical traffic. The optic display continued to zoom until the surface of K'tok ceased being undifferentiated swaths of blue and green and acquired recognizable features: jungle, savannah, meandering tree-lined rivers, foothills and mountains, small settlements—it did look a lot like Earth.

Then Sam saw the outskirts of T'tokl-Heem, the colonial capital. The optics panned back, stopped moving, and Sam saw a cluster of small specks gliding across an open plain. The resolution on the optics could not pick out individual Varoki or Humans at this magnification, so those must be the gunsleds.

"Fortune One," Filipenko reported to the ground, "I have visual on Target Alpha. Over."

"Thud One internal guidance sees Target Alpha," Marmont added.

Sam watched the specks, the gunsleds, moving quietly across the open ground northwest of the city. Each one, he knew, had a crew of two, and suddenly this was different than ship icons on abstracted tactical displays, filled with numbers and missile tracks and information tags.

The gunsled command links would already have told them a destroyer was in orbit overhead, but the uBakai had learned not to fear them. Only cruisers bombarded from orbit, cruisers and those two islands of free missiles which appeared and disappeared with a regularity recorded by their ground stations. Sam and Filipenko and the others had worked out how to make them afraid again, but as he saw the specks moving at the direction of living drivers and commanders, he felt more a sense of dread than accomplishment.

Yes, those sleds were moving to overrun the Human ground forces. Yes, they had to be stopped. But wouldn't caution serve that purpose as well as death? What if he dropped the hot spikes of the bombardment munition between them and the city? Wouldn't that be enough to show the destroyers had acquired fangs and talons?

No. They might think the miss showed poor targeting. They might think they should press the attack forward before another bombardment munition could launch, and once those uBakai forces got into the city suburbs, strikes from orbit would no longer be possible. Besides, caution was not enough; the uBakai had to learn fear as well, and only the technological equivalent of fire and brimstone would do for that.

Red Stinger Two, this is Fortune One. I 'ave your Bravo Target. Bearing two six seven degrees true, range seven four zero zero from my location. Assembly area, troops debussing from vehicles. Fortune One, over.

Sam heard Filipenko's acknowledgement, as if to some unimportant routine message. The bridge crew was trained to deal with exactly this sort of situation, deal with it calmly and in a routine and professional manner, and Sam was glad of it. But still, there was something unsettling about how casually they talked about what they were about to do.

"Thud One internal guidance sees Target Bravo, added to the queue," Marmont said. "Tac One, how do you want the ordnance divided?"

"Tac Four, um . . . give me forty spikes in the Alpha packet and ten in Bravo," Filipenko answered. "I want to make sure we take out those gunsleds. Troops in the open should be easier to service."

Service, meaning kill. Infantry in the open would be torn apart by the shock wave of the detonations when the spikes struck, incinerated by the searing flash of all that kinetic energy converted instantly to heat. Each impacting spike had a very good chance of killing every unprotected large organism in a one hectare area.

"Captain, guidance is locked on and we're in the firing window," Filipenko said from beside him.

He'd never deliberately ordered the death of another sentient being before. He gave the firing order back during the uBakai attack but that had been in the heat of battle. Besides, they hadn't hit anything that day. When they fired today, they weren't going to miss. Even if they had hit an uBakai ship back in the battle, that would have been self-defense. This was just a cold-blooded execution. He felt his heart rate accelerate, felt his face flush, fists close, and recognized a growing tide of anger, but it was not at the Varoki on his display.

Sam looked at the slowly moving specks on his display. Half of them had bunched up and appeared to be stopping. He wondered why. Maybe just taking a break.

"Very well. Fire."

Sam felt the slight vibration as the saddle mount fired the explosive bolts releasing Thud One. In a moment its retro rocket would fire and send it hurtling toward the planet surface. Then how long to impact? A few minutes at most.

Two crew per gunsled, forty Varoki in that lift cavalry unit down there. Who knew how many at the infantry assembly area? At least a company, if there were enough for the ground forces to notice. A hundred infantry? Two hundred? Plus vehicles, so possibly a logistical support unit as well.

Run away. Disperse. Go back to your families. Touch them, feel their warmth, watch the sunset. Run, you stupid bastards!

"Dispenser release looks good," Marmont reported. "We have fifty free spikes in the atmosphere."

Now the superheated spikes would show up on the ground station tracking sensors. Now the uBakai command posts would understand this was no bluff, but now it was too late. Sam watched the small specks and he tried to imagine what the Varoki inside the gunsleds were thinking, what they were talking about, but he couldn't. They were just specks, but he could not take his eyes off of them. Several hundred unique, sentient individuals neared the end of their existence and probably did not even know it. But he knew it, and he felt that someone should witness the last moments of their lives. Well, maybe not the very last one.

"Ground impact in five, four, three . . . "

Sam turned off his display.

"Impact!" Marmont cried. "Wow! Look at that!"

Chief Patel moved the ground view to the main smart wall display. Sam saw a solid, roiling cloud of dust and smoke, with flashes and flickers of flame deep beneath it, and when the bridge crew saw what they had done, they cheered.

"Fuckin' aye!"

"Take that, leatherhead!"

"*Now* who's in the shit?"

So far all they had done was take damage, suffer casualties, and watch the uBakai inflict losses with apparent impunity. Now they had washed their own spears, and Sam suspected their thoughts were not with the dead Varoki down on K'tok, but with their own dead shipmates up here still orbiting in the cold blackness of space. His own thoughts turned to Jules, and Captain Chelanga, and Juanita Rivera, and he wondered if what he had just done would make them sleep easier. He didn't think so, but if the crew did, let them. They had little enough else to sustain them.

"Well done, crew," Sam said. "Helm, take us up to twelve hundred klicks. No one's taken a shot at us yet, but let's not press our luck."

"Aye aye, sir. Calculating burn for orbit at twelve hundred kilometers," Chief Bhargava answered.

It *was* well done: professionally executed and clearly successful. They'd have to wait for the FDA—Fire Damage Assessment—before they knew for sure, but it looked as if they had removed the threat.

Removed, as in killed.

That meant the ground brigade could hold out at least another few days. That was something, wasn't it? Yes it was. The wolf had been at the door, but they had driven him away . . . for now. For how long, though? Well, he had no control over that. All he could deal with was today and the next day and the next. Someone once described civilization as the art of putting off the inevitable indefinitely—not that what they had just done had much to do with civilization.

Off to the side of his vision he saw a now-familiar fluttering sparkle, come to see what he had done, watch what he would do next.

He didn't like this. The thrill of the hunt was one thing, but this had as much to do with a real hunt as those staged safaris that ended with the shooting of an elderly lion driven into some rich guy's gyro-stabilized rifle sights. This had simply been murder.

Okay, this was his job. It was stupid to romanticize it as some ancient and noble contest where people died but everyone's honor somehow remained intact. What happened was, people died—and that's about all there was to it of any importance. Better their people than his; he got that, and he'd do his job, but it had better be worth it.

Something changed in him. Like his crew, he now wanted to know, *needed* to know, why they were fighting, and what they were fighting for. There was one difference, though. His crew's need to know had been driven by anxiety over their own possible deaths. Anger at having been made a murderer drove his.

CHAPTER TWENTY-FIVE

3 January 2134
(later the same day) ***(thirteenth day in K'tok orbit)***

Once the evening meal had been served, Sam had the mess attendant clear away and secure the table which normally dominated the center of the wardroom. He needed the extra space. Red Watch had just taken over the boat, so Lieutenants Filipenko and Hennessey were on duty, but he'd made sure the other seven officers were present, along with all four senior chiefs: Navarro, Cunningham from Ops, Burns from Tac, and Montoya from engineering. This was as large a leadership meeting as they'd had since the uBakai attack that had crippled the task force. Had that only been a little more than a week ago? It seemed longer.

Sam tethered himself to a bulkhead stanchion and looked at the officers and chiefs, their faces mostly curious or carefully noncommittal.

"Attendant, can we change the smart wall background?" Sam called over to her.

"Yes, sir," she answered. "What do you want?"

"Direct feed from flat-vid tight beam. Bridge will send you the feed."

"Aye, aye, sir."

"Okay, let me start by saying that Commodore Bonaventure sent a well-done to the entire crew for our bombardment run earlier today, and the ground brigade commander sent the same along with his personal thanks. Taking out those gunsleds hurt the uBakai, hurt them bad enough the ground troops have some breathing space. More than that, those two uBakai cruisers the other day killed *Champion Hill* delivering those sleds. We just evened the score. But that's not the main reason we're here.

"Admiral Kayumati received a recorded message by jump courier missile earlier today with orders to share it with the entire task force at 1830 hours. I don't know what the content is, but we're coming up on 1830 now. It will pipe through to the entire boat but I thought it might be good for the boat's leadership to watch this together, whatever it is."

The truth was he was frightened at what the message might contain, frightened enough he had barely eaten during dinner. Whatever the news was, its method of distribution made it hard to think it was going to be good.

A few minutes later the smart wall came alive and the low murmur of conversation fell away. A large seal filled the screen for several seconds, a stylized picture of Earth with "Outworld Coallition" displayed above it and "Chief of Naval Operations (CNO)" below it. Sam had never heard of the Outworld Coalition before, but he supposed the four-nation alliance which had so unexpectedly found itself at war with the uBakai had to have a name. The seal vanished and an enormous image of a Human admiral sitting behind a desk filled the smartwall. The glowing nameplate on the front of the desk identified him as Admiral Cedric Goldjune.

Well, Sam thought, Larry's uncle finally made CNO. It wasn't CNO of the US Navy, but maybe something bigger.

Admiral Goldjune seemed like an older, leaner, and more mentally focused version of Larry Goldjune. He wore a bandage wrapped around his forehead so he must have been in the headquarters compound when it got hit. After seeing what orbital bombardment munitions could do, Sam wondered how he was alive at all. The admiral's hands rested on the bare desk, folded, and he looked directly at the camera.

"Men and women of Combined Task Force One of the Outworld Coalition," he began. "We are in the midst of a war which will determine the destiny of our species, and you are on the very front lines of that war. You didn't ask for that. None of us did. You were sent to the K'tok system as peacekeepers, not war-bringers. The enemy forced this unwelcome role on you with a cowardly sneak attack, launched when all our nations were still at peace. Now they have widened the war with an illegal attack on the neutral Human colony on Bronstein's World.

"Two things you can be sure of.

"First, we're behind you one hundred percent and we're doing everything we can to get reinforcements to you. But the attack on Bronstein's World complicated that and several vessels getting ready to jump out to you were put out of action. It's going to take time to get help to you, and until it arrives it's up to you to hold on. We need the K'tok system, especially close orbital space around K'tok and our foothold on the planet surface. It's going to be tough, but I know I can count on you."

How does he know that? Sam wondered. He hadn't met any of the crew, at least as far as he knew, except for his nephew Larry.

"Second, you can be sure we aren't just going to sit and take this. We're on the defensive now, but everyone in the military knows the best defense is a good offense. If the uBakai want to bring this fight to us, we can take it to them as well, and we will. I promise you we will."

Sam thought that sounded more like a pledge to avenge their deaths than a promise to get them back alive.

"Right now the eyes of the entire Human race are on you, and I know you won't let them down. I am deeply proud of every one of you, and honored to serve as your commander. And I promise I will lead you to the victory you deserve."

And then the screen went blank.

Well, Sam thought, at least he knew how to give a short speech. The news also wasn't as bad as he'd expected. Actually, it was plenty bad, it just wasn't news.

He heard a buzz of subdued conversation, mostly positive he thought. He looked around the wardroom and realized they were waiting for him to say something. Of course they were.

The captain is the navy.

Not some admiral over sixty light-years away, the captain—him.

The youngsters, like Jerry Robinette, Barb Lee, and Rishanda Lipinski, were fired up. Most of the others seemed pleased by the speech, but waiting to see what their captain thought. A couple looked completely unmoved, among them Moe Rice. Sam figured Moe didn't have much use for anyone named Goldjune.

"Okay, the admiral didn't tell us anything we didn't already know, but it's nice to know we aren't the only ones who know it."

That got some smiles and he saw most of them start to relax.

"There are a couple things the admiral probably didn't know when he recorded this. Three days ago the uBakai ran two cruisers right through our picket line to drop off a swarm of lift cavalry. This morning we blew those gunsleds off the face of K'tok. It doesn't take a genius to figure we're due for another visit from the uBakai Express to drop more troops. Well, the admiral says hold this rock and we're going to. Ensign Robinette."

"Sir!" he nearly shouted, coming to attention.

"Get together with your boss, Lieutenant Filipenko, and look at the attack profile they've been using. Make some recommendations to maneuvering as to where our bow ought to point at different positions in our orbit track so we can get missiles off quicker."

"Aye aye, sir."

"Anyone else have any good ideas, write 'em down and send 'em in, or talk to your department heads. You chiefs, get with your acey-deucies, pick their brains. Everybody on this boat has a head on their shoulders and it's time to start using them. This fight coming up, we're going to need every edge we can get.

"Okay, so back to work."

He watched them glide out through the hatchway and as they did he felt a flush course through his body. *They were coming together*, he realized. They really were. They were turning into a team. They were becoming a real crew.

Sam yawned broadly and then slid the visor on his helmet down. It had been a long day and it wasn't over yet. In a moment the comm chair on the bridge triggered the link to the holoconference. At least this was a small one: just himself, Commodore Bonaventure, and Commander Atwater-Jones. Bonaventure nodded a somber greeting to him but Cassandra's image was frozen with a frown on her face. The task force was far enough away that the round-trip communication lag to them was over a minute, and so participants at each end froze their images after speaking and waited for the response. After almost two minutes she unfroze.

"Ah, everyone's here, including your newly appointed intelligence officer," she said. "You may come to regret accepting Commodore Bonaventure's invitation to serve as his smart boss, Bitka."

Her image froze.

"Wasn't aware it was an invitation," Sam said. He thought her voice sounded professional and courteous but not as warm as it once had.

"Commander Atwater-Jones and I were just discussing Admiral Goldjune's address to the task force," Bonaventure said, "but now we should get down to business."

He triggered their image freeze and after a long pause Cassandra spoke again.

"By all means. Admiral Kayumati has ordered me to give Commodore Bonaventure as detailed a brief on fleet policy and enemy capabilities as I can, and the commodore asked you be present, Captain Bitka. You have a dormant Most Secret security clearance—you say Top Secret, don't you?—which was activated when you took command of *Puebla*. That makes things easier."

"First, fleet policy. When the coalition formed and agreed to dispatch this task force, the possibility that hostilities might ensue was certainly considered in detail. Our obvious opponent was the Commonwealth of Bakaa—the uBakai. They had been among the most powerful—in economic, military, and diplomatic terms—of the Varoki nations, possibly *the* most powerful. The abortive coup and brief civil war a year ago changed all that. Bakaa's navy was disgraced and demoralized. The capital suffered considerable physical damage from which it will take a decade or more to recover. In one month, Bakaa went from a leader among the Varoki to an outcast, virtually a pariah state.

"Some in our own intelligence and strategic communities then came to believe that this development presented us with a unique opportunity. A weakened and demoralized Bakaa, if pushed with sufficient force and determination, would have no alternative but to back down. Others believed it was as likely they would lash out in desperation. Is that clear so far?"

Her image froze.

"I think so," Bonaventure said. "Which side did you favor, Commander?"

Her mouth turned down into a frown when she unfroze,

"In my considered opinion those arguing for a hard push against the uBakai, and expecting an easy win, were reckless nearly to the point of insanity. Not that I predicted the opposite, mind you. I always believed it was impossible to predict their actions at all, and so basing a hazardous policy on the imagined ability to do so was . . . well, I believe I already said insane, but it *is* a form of insanity you know, this stubborn, willful self-deception.

"Of course they had intelligence reports and learned political science essays and all sorts of anecdotal twaddle you can string together any way that suits you. But here is the nub of the problem: Varoki politics work *in fact* the way Human politics are *thought* to work by delusional conspiracy theorists. There really *are* secret cabals which stand behind their public figures of power. There really are. Whatever a politician's public position on an issue, you can almost guarantee it was taken in large measure to confuse the opposition as to his real intent. I know I am overusing the word, but it borders on insanity as well, although of a different sort."

She froze.

"Yeah, paranoia," Sam said. "Everyone must be conspiring against you so you better get in there and do the same out of self-defense. So, to push or not to push, that is the question. Just out of curiosity, which side did Admiral Goldjune come down on?"

Bonaventure made a disgusted face but turned away, freezing their image to wait for Cassandra to answer.

"Sorry, Bitka," she said at last. "Need to know only, I'm afraid. Not that it's any more sensitive than what I am about to tell you. It's just good policy to limit information to those with a legitimate interest, as opposed to curiosity.

"So, to return to our subject, there is no consensus. Clearly there was an aggressive contingency plan in place or we would not have had been able to launch the attack on K'tok. That said, there is no agreed-upon strategic policy for moving forward from here. Unless and until there is, I am afraid our mission remains to hold orbital space above K'tok and support the landed troops to the best of our ability. The needle and the city of T'tokl-Heem have enormous strategic and political value, although for the moment the only operational value of holding them seems to be to divert uBakai ground forces from their attacks on the Human settlements.

"Once the war is over we'll give them back, of course. The question is what we'll get in return." She turned and looked at Sam. "You look rather pensive, Captain Bitka, although I may be one reaction cycle behind. It's hard to judge given this delay."

She froze.

"I'm just wondering if the uBakai are fighting the same war we are," he answered.

"What do you mean?" Bonaventure asked.

"Well, they had ten cruisers available, right? Our principle objective is K'tok. If that was their objective too, why not throw all ten cruisers at us? That would have given them overwhelming force at the decisive point. Instead they split them: five cruisers to K'tok, five to Bronstein's World. That doesn't make sense unless these guys are either a lot dumber than they look, or K'tok is not their main objective."

"Then what is?" the commodore asked.

Sam shrugged and nodded toward Cassandra's image. They waited.

"Spot-on analysis, Bitka, ," she said after the pause, "but I haven't the foggiest what they're really after. I anticipate spending a number of sleepless nights grappling with that very question.

"Now on to part two, enemy capabilities. You have an extensive database of their entire fleet roster and their most recent known dispositions. I have little to add to it but would draw your attention to the fact that of their thirty-seven cruisers, fifteen were reported as in low-energy low-manning mode in high orbit around Hazz'Akatu, the Varoki homeworld. They can of course be reactivated, but it will take time. And in passing, one of the principle arguments that the uBakai were not prepared to make a serious fight of it was they made no effort to begin reactivating those ships. That still puzzles me.

"But all of this data, aside from its intrinsic utility, is by way of showing we have a fair amount of prewar intelligence amassed on the size and specifications of the uBakai Star Navy. As a result, it came as something of a shock when analysis of the observed weapons and energy output profiles of the five uBakai ships which attacked Bronstein's World showed that two of them did not match any ship previously identified."

Sam felt his heart rate increase. Beside him Bonaventure's image leaned forward and he muttered, "*Jesús Cristo!*"

"Of course our first thought was secret new construction," she continued. "We rejected that in short order. It is very difficult to imagine how we would not have noticed something like that. There are only so many orbital shipyards, after all.

"But analysis of the decrypts of their transponder codes revealed the two ships in question are identified KBk-Zero Three B and KBk-Zero Four B. As you know, Varoki warships are never named; they instead carry an alphanumeric identifier which is uniform across the *Cottohazz*. Even our own vessels have assigned hull codes for use when we operate as part of a combined *Cottohazz* task force. The first letter K indicates a cruiser-class vessel. The next letters, Bk, indicate the nationality, in this case Bakaa. The hull number follows. But the 'B' at the end is quite interesting. It indicates the hull number assignment is provisional.

"More telling is the fact these energy signatures match exactly with a new class of cruisers employed by the uKa-Maat, another Varoki nation, although one of lesser resources than the uBakai ."

She froze.

"Provisional hull numbers?" Bonaventure asked. "As in temporary?"

"Or as in a cover," Sam said.

"Meaning we might not be fighting just the uBakai?"

Sam nodded. "Either these guys—what are they called? uKa-Maat?—are selling ships to the uBakai or they're sending fully crewed ships to help, but don't want it to look that way. And it means there are probably at least two other ghost cruisers out there." When Bonaventure looked at him questioningly, he explained, "If they've got numbers oh-three and oh-four, as anal-retentive as the Varoki are they've probably got numbers oh-one and oh-two. What I don't get is why the subterfuge. If these uKa-Maat are in this with the uBakai, why don't they just say so?"

"Yes, good question, Bitka. Commander?"

When Cassandra unfroze she shrugged elegantly, with both her shoulders and eyebrows. "I am certain there is an answer for that, but I have no idea what it is. We have intelligence-gathering assets on Hazz'Akatu, but I imagine they have just begun exploring the issue. How long before—or even if—they will have an answer, and how long before it reaches us, is unknowable.

"In the mean time, we do know the uBakai have been reinforced and you should expect to see even more of them before help arrives for you. I am very sorry I can't be more encouraging."

CHAPTER TWENTY-SIX

4 January 2134
(the next day) *(fourteenth day in K'tok orbit)*

Good morning, Bitka, Commodore Bonaventure greeted him by tight beam commlink. *I hope to God you have better news this morning than the Red Duchess did yesterday.*

"Well, if you count a brilliant idea coming from a hygenist's mate third class as good news, then yes I do."

Your boat's barber? Okay, what's his great idea?

"*Her* great idea, sir, and I think she prefers the term *stylist.* Since the orbital bombardment took out those uBakai gunsleds there's a good chance they'll try to land some more, or at least land something new to keep the ground fight going. Her idea is to put a bunch of Block Four missiles just above low orbit and in low-energy mode. They'll look like normal satellite junk on a quick scan and that's all the uBakai will have time for. This way no matter where they come from we've got a good chance of having a missile or two within firing range, and they won't be ready for them."

Didn't Mike Wu on Petersburg *recommend something like that? But the problem is our Block Fours can't maneuver once we dump them out there.*

"That's right, sir, and that makes it a bad investment in a general action that could be forty thousand klicks or more out. But here we're talking about an attack profile that requires them to come in close in order to drop their cargo into the atmosphere. They have to come *to* the missiles."

Well . . . that might work, but where are we going to find those extra missiles? I don't want to strip our magazines.

"She's got that covered, too, sir: *Champion Hill*. The explosion and damage was all forward. The missile rooms aft should still be intact."

Champion Hill? *You know, that's a very good idea. How does your stylist know about missiles?*

"She reads ***Navy Times***, sir. I guess there was a big article about deep space missiles a couple months back. We're still pretty close to the wreck. You want me to get an EVA party ready and shift orbit?"

No. It's a good idea and I'm going to cut your stylist a commendation, but Puebla *still has the bombardment saddle pack so you stay put. I'll put out a call in the task group for salvage volunteers. We have a lot of survivors from the* Hill. *They might want to be part of this. Give her a "well done" from me, Bitka.*

Sam turned the bridge over to Barb Lee and headed back toward officer country but decided it was time he looked in on engineering to see how the radiator patches were holding up. On his way he stuck his head through the hatch of the port-side missile room. Chief Joyce Menzies and another petty officer were at work on a dismantled Block Four missile, and Sam pulled himself through the hatch to glide over to them.

"How's it going, Chief?" he asked.

She looked up and smiled.

"I think we got this *bâtard* sorted out, sir," she said and gestured toward the missile housing.

"Good. I want some fangs to redden when the time comes. How soon will they be ready?"

"This one'll be good to go in an hour and we already have nine others finished. Problem is we have to do all the fine interior work by hand with microdrills, one laser pointer at a time. Takes fuckin 'forever—beggin' your pardon, sir. But the leatherheads are going to howl when we fire these. That is the *de crisse* truth."

"I believe you, Chief. Next time I shoot at an uBakai cruiser, I want to at least see it spilling atmosphere."

She looked down at the gutted missile for a moment.

"We can do better than that, sir."

She looked up and Sam expected to see a smile, but instead faced intense concentration, almost obsession.

"Captain Wu—you know, from USS *Petersburg*, an old tac head like you. Anyway, we get talking, we work out a variant on the multiple-targeting option. We call it *tournesol*—sunflower. How would you like, you shoot one missile with the sunflower program loaded, you take out fifteen incoming enemy missiles?"

Fifteen? Sam thought about that. Most threat situations didn't have to deal with more than a half dozen incoming missiles at a time. Taking out fifteen at once . . .

"If you can really do that, Menzies, it changes the game. I'll have to think about it, but I mean that: it changes the whole game. Well done, Chief."

Menzies actually blushed. She picked up a torque wrench from its magnetic gripper, moved it from one hand to another, then put it back in the holder.

At least they could still turn out technicians like Menzies: just a chief petty officer, bumped up from ace machinist mate, but she wasn't a robot going through the motions by rote. She understood what she was doing, understood the underlying logic of the device, and knew how to tweak it, make it work better than its designers had imagined.

"I don't know if you've thought about what you're going to do after the war, Menzies, whether you're going to stay in the service or move to the private sector, but either way you should go back to school. Navy will pay for it and you've good a good brain in that skull."

She smiled and blushed again.

"Oh, I go to school, sure-sure. I was already accepted and everything, but. . . " she paused and shrugged, then held up her hand and rubbed her thumb against her first two fingers. "*Pas d'argent.* But like you say, Navy will pay now, especially since I made chief."

"Where were you accepted?"

She looked embarrassed.

"Julliard, the ensemble music department. They like my compositions and the arrangements I do for my band . . . I mean, I love this stuff," she said, resting her hand on the missile casing, "but 'Lise and I want a family, and who hires a missile monkey?" She again held up her hand and rubbed her thumb and fingers together. *"Pas d'argent."*

No money. Sam remembered Kayumati's speech, his rambling

complaint about Humans not training enough engineers and scientists. Maybe he had a point. The Varoki had a lock on all the science research, so the real money was in entertainment. Hard to compete with that.

Several hours later the chime on Sam's cabin door sounded and when he turned it transparent he was surprised to see Larry Goldjune floating outside.

"Good afternoon, sir," Goldjune said as soon as Sam released the hatch. "Do you have a minute?"

Sam motioned him in and toward his workstation/desk.

"Come in, Mr. Goldjune, I was just drafting a lessons learned report. Hard to know where to start."

Sam clipped himself to the padded frame behind the desk. "What can I do for you?"

Goldjune hooked his feet through a deck stanchion. "That was a good talk after the admiral's speech," he said. "Short and to the point. I think it will help the crew, too. Did you know Chief Navarro has taken your speech from the wardroom holorecord and is having the crew view it in shifts, by watch?"

Sam shifted uncomfortably. He hadn't known that and he'd expected the chiefs to pass the word themselves. He wasn't sure it was that good a speech.

"Didn't know that. I guess Navarro is exercising her initiative."

"Yes, sir. You mentioned we need to use our heads, come up with all the ideas we can. The reason I came is I think I've figured out the solution to that mapping problem you gave Ensign Lee. Well, not a solution so much as a way around it."

Sam leaned forward, suddenly alert. "A way around it? What do you mean?"

"Well, I had her working on a classic solution. I got the idea from radio astronomy—it's called very long baseline interferometry. They use widely separated radio telescope discs looking at the same object to construct a virtual massive array. I thought, why can't we do something like that to link the observational data from all the ships we've got scattered through the system? If we have their timestamps, we can collate everything and get multiangle views of the asteroid belt and what they're occluding."

That sounded like a reasonable idea to Sam, but he noticed Goldjune had used the past tense. "You came up with something different?"

"Yes, sir. The asteroids only clutter our detection-by-occlusion because we're in the plane of the ecliptic with them. We need to send a sensor drone up, above the plane, and look down on it. That way there's no clutter—well, hardly any—to fox the sensors."

Sam felt the hair on his neck stand up, his scalp tingle, and his face flush, but with excitement rather than embarrassment. "God, am I stupid! Why didn't I think of that?"

"Not stupid, sir. You're just not an astrogator."

"Well, maybe there's something to this whole astrogation business after all." Sam squinted up the watch codes and pinged the duty comm technician.

This is Chief Gambara. What can I do for you, Captain?

"Chief, get me an audio tight beam to the pennant. I need to talk to the commodore."

Aye aye, sir.

"While we're waiting, you want something to drink?" Sam asked.

"I wouldn't say no to a swallow of that bourbon you served the other night," Goldjune answered and smiled—the first time Sam could remember him doing so.

Sam smiled as well and pointed to the wall cabinet. "Pour me a short one, too. This calls for a celebration."

As Sam took the drinking bulb Goldjune handed to him, his commlink vibrated and came alive.

Que pedo? Commodore Bonaventure grumbled. *This better be real good, Bitka. My supper's getting cold.*

"Oh, it's real good, sir. Lieutenant Goldjune, my XO, has figured out how to see past the asteroid clutter. We're going to find out where those bastards are hiding."

Once his conversation with Commodore Bonaventure and his drink with Larry Goldjune were finished, and he was alone, he sat quietly for several minutes. Then he took a deep breath and pinged Chief Gambara in the communications chair again.

Yes, sir?

"Chief, see if you can get a tight beam voice link to the task force N-2, on USS *Pensacola*."

Aye aye, sir.

Was he imagining things or did he hear a bit of a smirk in Gambara's voice? If she thought there was something hot and heavy going on between him and Cassandra Atwater-Jones, it just meant she hadn't been listening in on their conversations.

It took a few minutes to set up the tight beam, and before Gambara patched him in she let him know the round-trip time lag was now about two minutes.

"Commander, this is Captain Bitka on USS *Puebla*. You told me to tight beam you if I had anything of interest for task force intelligence," he began. He outlined the drone idea, being careful to credit it to a subordinate officer, and then went on.

"I alerted Commodore Bonaventure already and he is having USS *Petersburg* launch a sensor drone this evening. Because of the limitations on coil gun payloads, our drones don't have the range and versatility of the drones some of the cruisers carry, so you may want to augment our efforts. Over."

It wasn't standard procedure to use the "over" tag on routine ship-to-ship audio communications, but with time delays this long it helped to let folks know when you were done talking. He sipped water as he waited for the reply. He saw his hand tremble slightly. He wasn't sure where he stood with Atwater-Jones after the business for the cheat code, but he was surprised it seemed to matter to him this much.

Good afternoon, Captain Bitka. Would you please wait a moment? I have to check on something.

Again her voice sounded professional and courteous, but without that impression of a half-suppressed smile he'd grown used to. The time stretched out to over ten minutes and he was beginning to think she had forgotten when her voice returned.

Well, let me start by saying this is an excellent insight, so much so I could not imagine why no one else had thought of it. I expected to discover there was some complicated astrogation reason it would not work. Instead I encountered a very tangled tale. You might want to get comfortable, as this is somewhat long and involved.

Asteroid clutter is not normally a problem because our astrogators have complete data maps of the asteroids in the systems where we operate. We have made maps of our home system and Bronstein's World. Other races or agencies have compiled data maps of most other explored systems. When Human ships have served as part of a combined Cottohazz *peacekeeping force, they have had access to its military-grade data sets, but only while serving on* Cottohazz *duty. They surrender them upon returning to national service.*

Human colonists only began arriving at K'tok within the last thirty months. It took some time to recognize that, in the event of war, we would not have access to the same Cottohazz *data maps as before and would need to compile our own. Then it took time to decide who would do it, who would pay for it, and who would have access to the data once it was compiled.*

In the end, the United Nations Joint Astrographic Consortium—UNJAC—undertook the survey and we—that is to say the Western European Union—loaned the German survey ship FGS Windischgrätz *to UNJAC for that purpose.* Windischgrätz *arrived here about five months ago and began its survey, and five months was the estimated completion time of the project.*

It seems our astrogators and electronic warfare types have simply been waiting for UNJAC to make the new data set available, which should be any time now, right? The problem is Windischgrätz *has gone missing. No one here noticed that until I began asking these awkward questions. Why didn't they notice?* Windischgrätz *was not subordinated to the task force; it reported directly and exclusively to UNJAC back on Earth.*

She paused and Sam imagined her shaking her head and probably shrugging with her eyebrows.

You know, for a number of years we all lectured wisely and quite persuasively about how very hard it would be to break free of peacetime patterns of thought should war—this sort of war—ever come. Yet here we are, repeatedly surprised when we do in fact find ourselves letting go too late of one peacetime habit or another. Then we are surprised that we are surprised.

Well. This is an excellent idea, and long overdue. Please extend my congratulations to your subordinate. I will see to launching a proper remote sensor platform before the next watch is out. Over.

That was it, then, wasn't it? This wasn't a personal call, just fleet business, but there was one more item under that heading.

"Commander, two days ago you said better minds than ours were hard at work figuring out how to deal with those uBakai reinforcements we spotted. A lot's happened since then but the thing is, it *has* been two days and although we got a nice briefing about the enemy and all, I think Commodore Bonaventure is sort of waiting for some more definite orders. The two cruisers from Mogo just did their fly-by today and slingshot back out to follow you folks. After the loss of USS *Champion Hill* we're down to four boats. I know DesDiv Five is coming to join us late tomorrow, and that'll double our strength. But Admiral Goldjune said something about the best defense being a good offense. Is somebody thinking about how to reach out and smack those guys instead of just sitting here waiting for the axe to fall? Over."

Sam sipped his water, and pretended it was a rum and fruit drink with a little umbrella on top, as he watched the wind rustle the leaves of the palm tree on the small island just a few meters beyond the other side of his cabin wall. He should find out where this holo-image had been recorded, go there someday when he got back to Earth, maybe lie down and hug the sand, and thank it for keeping him sane in the middle of all this madness.

Captain Bitka, please tell Commodore Bonaventure I will try to get some sort of coherent command decision articulated concerning your force. Rather, I will continue *to do so. You should know that certain members of the task force staff are sick to death of hearing me harp on this subject—so sick the very mention of it angers them. Fortunately, I rather enjoy angering them, so that's not as much of a disincentive for pressing the case as they might imagine.*

But do not expect much from here. As far as your task group is concerned, the current plan, if you care to dignify it as such, is: 'Do whatever you can, as long as you can, and God bless you.'

If it were up to me, and if the decision was made to pull the main fleet elements back, I would have evacuated the ground troops up the needle, loaded them on the transports, and left with the entire marching band. Failing that, I would have left the transports in orbit so evacuation remained at least an option. Or I would have left USS Queretaro *to strengthen the destroyers. Why we are all in train to Mogo is beyond me. Originally it was to deny the uBakai access to scoop refueling there, but that seems rather a low-priority at the moment. But what do I know? I am merely an intelligence officer.*

Sam listened to several seconds of silence and started to think

Atwater-Jones was done and had forgotten to say "over," but then he heard her draw a deep, shuddering breath and go on.

Sorry for the rant, she said quietly, *but it is disgraceful. It is utterly disgraceful, and I am ashamed to be any part of it. Tell Commodore Bonaventure to look to his own resources. Make whatever plans you can. The uBakai have been reinforced and they can be expected to attack at any time. The task force will do nothing to help you. Nothing.*

It sounds rather hollow, I suppose, but sincere best of luck to you, Bitka. End transmission.

CHAPTER TWENTY-SEVEN

5 January 2134
(the next day) ***(fifteenth day in K'tok orbit)***

Bitka, your hygenist's brilliant idea has presented me with an interesting situation, Bonaventure said as soon as the tighbeam commlink was open. *I need your advice.*

Not even a good morning? Sam thought as he sipped his first coffee of the day.

"What can I do for you, sir?"

I put out the call for volunteers to salvage the missiles and whatever else we might be able to use from the hulk of Champion Hill. Got a good response, including most of her uninjured former crew and a few of those still in sickbay. I also got a half dozen more, including someone on your boat.

"Someone from my crew?"

Not exactly. Lieutenant Commander Huhn volunteered to join the salvage party. I checked. He's EVA-qualified, and we're pretty shorthanded there.

Del Huhn volunteering for a salvage job? Why? Sam though about that as he sipped his coffee again. "What do you need from me, sir?"

What do I need? Jesús Cristo! *He's there on your boat. Is he* loco *or isn't he?*

"I'm not a psychiatrist, sir, and neither are you. We can't answer that. The task force should have taken him with them for evaluation by the fleet surgeon. Admiral Kayumati told me he intended to but I guess it fell through the cracks. There was a lot going on right before they pulled out.

"I'll tell you what, though, Kayumati said he planned to put Huhn to work doing 'light duty.' I assume he meant lower stress. Huhn's currently certified medically unfit to serve in his previous job, but handling a vacuum torch without cutting a hole in your own pressure suit isn't the same thing as running a destroyer."

So you're saying I should give him a chance. I don't know whether you've gone soft, Bitka, or if you'll just do anything to get him off your boat.

"Neither, sir. We just really need every pair of hands we can get."

True enough. Okay, I'm going out on a limb but I'll only approve his request provided he understands he'll be reporting to Gloria Reynolds. She's senior surviving officer from the Hill and I'm putting her in charge of the salvage party. He's got two pay grades on her and almost ten years. If he can swallow his pride enough to take that deal, I'll give him a chance.

"Sounds like a good decision to me, sir."

Okay, Bitka. Oaxaca *out.*

Bonaventure broke the connection. Sam settled back with his coffee and tried to relax, but he couldn't quite manage. Del Huhn still troubled him, probably because he'd never felt like he understood the man. He wasn't sure Del Huhn understood himself, and when you got right down to it how many people did? But that bottle of bourbon had meant something to him. Giving it to Sam wasn't an apology, he didn't think. Not a peace offering or a bribe, either. He thought now that maybe it was a sort of personal change of command, passing along not just the boat but his hopes.

The bottle's label was faded on one side and a little worn. Huhn had probably carried that bottle of bourbon with him for years, intending that some day as captain of his own boat or ship he would drink it with his department heads in celebration of a triumph. Giving it away must have been acknowledgement that that day would never come. Letting go of that must have taken something.

Sam made it to the wardroom in time for a late breakfast and found Larry Goldjune waiting for him, already drinking a bulb of coffee.

"Captain, I've got a couple things for you to sign if you don't mind."

Sam clipped his tether to the table, punched in his breakfast order, and took the data pad Goldjune offered.

"Okay, what have you got?"

"Action summary of your captain's mast of Mariner Jorgenson, Ralph K., showing fine as pay stoppage and loss of one week of liberty, next time we actually get that."

Captain's mast was nonjudicial punishment for offenses not serious enough to send before a court martial. Jorgenson had gotten into an argument with a shipmate and it turned violent. There had been no serious injuries and Jorgenson had looked suitably repentant at the hearing. Sam thumbed the report and started to hand it back.

"Couple more, sir. Page forward, I put together an after-action report for the orbital bombardment on 3 January. It's all straight from the tapes and I appended the fire damage assessment we got from the Brits last evening. If you concur, I added a request for a commendation for *Oaxaca's* EVA crew for getting the saddle rig built on schedule and it holding together."

Sam thumbed the after-action report's signature block and paged ahead.

"Draft plan of the day for tomorrow," Larry explained. "I figured you'd want to add some drills, but wasn't sure which ones. I also wasn't sure if you wanted to go to Readiness Two instead of Three."

"Yeah, Larry, let's go to Readiness Two, half the crew on duty at all times, at least until we get your high probe into position and can get a look at them. That should give us a little warning and we can go back to Readiness Three. Let's do firing drills, one per watch from general quarters and then when we stand down we'll do it again but just with watch personnel."

"Very good, sir. I'll write it up. That's all I need. Enjoy your breakfast."

Goldjune unhooked and kicked away from the table toward the hatch as the ready light glowed from the food portal. Sam drifted over and retrieved his western omelet, kicked back to the table, and enjoyed a delicious breakfast made more satisfying by the added luxury of having an executive officer who was doing his job instead of just going through the motions.

Sam floated tethered to the desk in the cabin and examined the picture on his workstation's smart surface: Atwater-Jones's friend Freddie. Lieutenant Colonel Frederick Matthew Barncastle, MC, Royal

Marines. Sam had looked him up. "MC" stood for Military Cross, a decoration he'd earned seven years earlier, then only a major, when a peacekeeping assignment to the Spratley Islands had turned suddenly ugly and violent. As near as Sam could tell, the MC was the British equivalent of the US Silver Star.

He was handsome, Sam supposed, in a British sort of long-faced and big-toothed way. He was grinning in the official Defense Ministry picture, laugh lines cutting deep at the corners of his eyes. Most officers chose a more serious expression for their official pictures, but Sam had an idea he knew what Freddie Barncastle was grinning about. He was married, and not to Cassandra Atwater-Jones, not that that was any of Sam's business.

Why this interest in Freddie? Well, Sam had almost gotten him killed, and the mutual connection to Atwater-Jones made him a real person, not just a name. No, that wasn't right. He *hadn't* almost gotten him killed. His actions had had no effect one way or another on him, but Sam hadn't known that when he chose not to act. He had the nagging feeling he owed Freddie an apology for not having tried. One of Freddie's Marine enlisted men had been killed the same day he had been wounded. That blood was on his hands as well. No, not his hands exactly; just his conscience.

Freddie was over at the needle highstation, in the infirmary, apparently doing well. His condition had been upgraded from critical to stable, but that was all the information available other than to family and chain of command, neither of which included Sam. Right now the Highstation was probably the safest place in the whole star system, the one place both sides wanted to keep intact no matter what. Needles were just too expensive and delicate to go messing around with.

Twenty minutes later he heard the chime at his cabin door. He turned the hatch transparent and saw Moe Rice, his burly supply officer, in the corridor. Sam released the hatch lock and motioned him in. As he coasted across the intervening space to the desk, Moe's expression was grim and had more than a trace of anger.

"Moe, what's the problem?"

Rice anchored his feet and took a deep breath to calm himself.

"Cap'n, Larry Goldjune didn't come up with the idea of the high probe. Ensign Jerry Robinette did. That son of a bitch Goldjune stole the credit."

★ ★ ★

Moe laid out the ugly details of the story and as he listened, Sam wanted to throw up. He fought back an irrational and unjust irritation with Moe and with young Robinette, as if their revelation of this gross injustice somehow had conjured it into being, as if they rather than Larry Goldjune were the guilty parties. Why? Why would he even feel such a thing?

Perhaps the answer was he had equated Goldjune's acceptance of Sam as captain, and his enthusiastic assumption of the duties of executive officer, as a vindication. Here was a highly respected officer, a regular, an astrogator, and the son of an admiral—in short, as "Navy" an officer as you were likely to find—whose approval could be seen as a well-credentialed endorsement of Sam's captaincy. As he examined that feeling more closely, he came slowly to the understanding that his anger was directed at himself—for attaching so much significance to the judgment of another, of a subordinate at that, and, as it now appeared, an unworthy one.

The facts were simple enough. Robinette had come up with the idea of sending the sensor probe above the plain of the ecliptic. But given his inexperience and lack of self-confidence, he could not believe an idea he came up with would not already have occurred to others, if indeed it would work at all. He took the notion to Larry Goldjune, the senior astrogator on the boat. Goldjune told him the idea wouldn't work as stated but he'd see if he could work out the problems.

The "problems" ended up being nothing more than a recommendation that the DDR's probe be supplemented by more capable sensors from the cruisers, and some minor details concerning the angle of launch of the sensors to get optimal coverage. Goldjune had not mentioned Robinette when he presented the idea to Sam.

When Robinette confronted Goldjune about taking credit for his idea, the executive officer had lectured the ensign about how things worked in the Navy. A junior officer gave his idea to his superior, who cleaned up, presented, and championed the idea to higher command, gained credit and influence from its adoption, and in turn looked out for the junior officer with good recommendations and, where possible, a choice assignment. He said he was disappointed Robinette did not understand an aspect of U.S. Navy culture as fundamental as this.

"He really said that?" Sam interrupted Moe to ask. "That *he* was disappointed in Robinette?"

"Yes, sir, he sure as hell did."

That's how things worked in the corporate sector. Sam knew that from years of experience. It wasn't how they were supposed to work in the Navy. Sam gestured for Moe to continue.

The entire incident might have gone unnoticed except Robinette—disappointed and disillusioned—had gone to Moe Rice, as senior administrative officer, with his resignation, effective upon end of hostilities. Sensing that something rotten was going on, Rice refused to accept the resignation without an explanation of cause. That was beyond his actual authority but Robinette didn't know that, and the entire vile story had tumbled out. Robinette had broken down and wept as he told Rice, and he had been more ashamed of his tears than he had been outraged at Larry Goldjune and the culture he thought he represented.

Sam floated wordlessly for a while, tethered to his desk, staring at the holographic tropical palm trees seemingly beyond his cabin walls. Then he turned the island scene off and returned his cabin walls to neutral gray. His tropical paradise had lost its curative magic for him.

"How did Robinette come up with the idea?" Sam asked.

"He said he got the idea from you. That when the uBakai left K'tok and we were looking after them at a steep angle to the plain, you told him they couldn't hide: no background clutter, just stars and hard vacuum."

Sam remembered the conversation and any lingering doubt he had vanished. *Imagine that . . . the Jughead.*

"Is there any proof?'

Rice looked at the surface of Sam's workstation for a moment and then shook his head.

Of course not. That would be too easy. So what was he going to do about this? What *could* he do? He wasn't the only one interested. Off to his right he saw the flickering shadow of Jules, watching, waiting.

Eighth Principle of Naval Leadership: Make sound and timely decisions.

CHAPTER TWENTY-EIGHT

5 January 2134
(later the same day) *(fifteenth day in K'tok orbit)*

"Larry, come on in," Sam said after triggering the hatch lock from his work station. Goldjune coasted over and hooked one foot through the deck stanchion in front of Sam's desk.

"What's up, Skipper?"

Sam leaned forward and turned off the cabin recorder. No witness except the shadow of Jules's ghost, now stronger than before, more insistent.

"We're off the record. Jerry Robinette is turning in his resignation from the service, effective end of hostilities, but we haven't accepted it yet so it's not in the database. I thought maybe you and I could put our heads together and come up with a way to save a promising officer's career."

Larry colored slightly and shifted his anchor from one foot to the other. "It's too bad he decided he can't take it, sir. But Robinette *is* our weakest line officer."

"I wasn't talking about his career, Larry. I was talking about yours."

Goldjune jerked back slightly and his foot slipped out of the stanchion. He scrambled in midair for a moment as he drifted back and away, but then grabbed a handhold on the wall to his right. He turned to Sam, his face now red with anger or embarrassment or shame—Sam couldn't tell which and he wondered if Goldjune could either.

"*My* career? Look, I don't know what Robinette told you, but I haven't done anything wrong."

"What would he have told me, Larry?"

Larry fumbled with his tether, trying to clip it to the stanchion with trembling hand.

"I . . . I don't know, but—"

"Jerry Robinette didn't tell me anything. But an officer resigns, flags go up, people start asking questions. Somebody else came to me. What made you think Robinette didn't tell anyone else his idea *before* he came to you?"

"He *told* me . . . " Goldjune started, and then his voice faltered and some of the color drained from his face.

"Yeah," Sam said and blew out a long huff of air. "Okay, Lieutenant Goldjune, here's what I think maybe happened. I think you got hold of his idea and you couldn't believe some ensign could come up with anything good, and right away you saw problems with it, real problems. You promised to think it over. Lots of people give you screwy ideas, most of which don't pan out. This one did, after you worked out all the kinks, but along the way you got a little carried away, forgot where it came from. Understandable, and no harm done, provided you recognize Robinette's idea *now*."

Sam watched Goldjune's expression, which changed from moment to moment: panic, bravado, shame, anger, confusion. Sam wasn't sure he had him yet.

"Commodore Bonaventure is talking commendation. If we make sure that commendation goes to Jerry Robinette, all this goes away. I give you my word on it."

Goldjune hesitated, torn between hope and despair and the instinct to fight back.

"Come on, Larry. I can't afford to lose you as my exec. The Navy can't afford to lose you over something this . . . trivial."

Larry ran his hand through his hair and swallowed, and Sam could see the fight go out of his body.

"Yeah, I just forgot, that's all. I had no idea Robinette would take it so hard. He should have . . . What should we do?"

Sam picked up a data pad clipped to his desk and sailed it lightly across the room. "I already drafted a letter of commendation for Robinette's service jacket. We both sign it and then forward a copy to Commodore Bonaventure with a recommendation for a further citation. My ID is already on the commendation. Put yours on it and we're done."

Goldjune caught the data pad and studied the letter of commendation, read it carefully. Sam had the feeling he was doing it to use up time while he got used to the idea, maybe tried to come up with another way out. It was a good deal for him, though, and Sam knew the longer he thought about it, the closer he was to agreeing. He wasn't a fool. Finally Goldjune nodded, pressed his thumb on the data pad, and tossed it gently back across the cabin to Sam.

Sam retrieved it, checked the signature block, entered the commendation letter, and then forwarded the text letter and attachment to Bonaventure. Then he clipped the pad to his desk and looked up at Larry.

"Who did he tell?" Larry asked.

"Nobody."

Anger clouded Goldjune's face as he realized he'd been tricked.

"Then *you* lied when you said he told someone else before me."

"Think back. I never said that. I just asked you why you thought he *hadn't*. Nobody lied to you. And Goldjune, if you try to make yourself out to be the victim in this, I swear I will push you out a fucking airlock with no helmet. If Robinette had told anyone, if we could have proved this without you, your career would be over right now. Instead, you've got a second chance. I gave you my word on it. Make the most of it, or piss it away—your choice. But either way, get your ass out of my cabin."

He left and Sam floated behind his workstation, trying to sort out his feelings. Anger, sure, but also disappointment and a sense of loss. No feeling of triumph at all. For a very brief time he had thought he might not have to do this entirely by himself, and that had been a good feeling. Jules had not visited him, then, but now she was back and he looked at the capsule in his hand from MedTech Tamblinson.

How much longer was this going to go on? Forever? Or would something put her ghost to rest?

"Jerry, I want you to reconsider your decision to resign," Sam said once Ensign Robinette had tethered himself into one of the two zero-gee chairs in Sam's cabin. Sam looked at him and realized there was something different in his appearance. He had shaved off his scraggly moustache.

"Lieutenant Goldjune has admitted the sensor probe idea was yours and there will be a letter of commendation coming from Commodore

Bonaventure for your personnel jacket. I'm very sorry about what happened, sorry particularly for my part in it."

"What's going to happen to him?" Robinette asked.

"Nothing. Only way I could figure out how to get him on board with your commendation was to give him my word there would be no repercussions. Maybe somebody smarter than me could have gotten everything."

Robinette shook his head. "No, sir, I understand. I'm very grateful for what you did, you and Lieutenant Rice. If you were typical of the officers in the Navy, maybe it would be different."

Sam sipped his coffee and looked at the bare gray walls of his cabin. He'd have to find something else for the smart walls to display before people started thinking he was turning into Del Huhn.

"I don't believe in 'typical' anymore," Sam said. "It's lazy thinking, trying to find an easy way to understand hard things. Who *is* typical? You think Goldjune is? Then what about Filipenko? Hennessey. Lieutenant Commander Huhn. You. Me. None of us are typical of anything. We just are who we are."

"Maybe so, sir, but there's a lot more of the Navy lined up behind who Larry Goljune is than is lined up behind me. But I'd already reconsidered. I'd like to withdraw my resignation and just concentrate on doing my job."

"Good. What changed your mind, if you don't mind me asking?"

"I guess I had a lot of illusions about what being a Navy officer meant. In a way Lieutenant Goldjune did me a favor—although I don't feel one gram of gratitude. But all those illusions were about me, my pride, my ego. Once they were gone, I had to look at what was left."

He looked at Sam and he shrugged.

"Duty."

CHAPTER TWENTY-NINE

6 January 2134
(one day later) ***(fifteenth day in K'tok orbit)***

Sam unlatched and removed his helmet as soon as he finished the morning holoconference with Bonaventure and the other destroyer captains. The conference had firmed up plans for the arrival of the four destroyers of DesDiv Five, due to enter orbit in about seventeen hours. The uBakai had good enough sensor platforms squirreled around the system they obviously could see the destroyers coming all the way from the gas giant Mogo so they knew when they were due to arrive as well. If the uBakai Express was going to make another run, it made sense they'd do it before the reinforcements arrived, but so far they hadn't. Sam had put *Puebla* on readiness condition two last evening, which meant half the crew on duty and half resting at all times. He didn't want to go to general quarters yet—no sense in doing it too soon and then just tiring the crew out waiting. They'd keep their edge better if they were rested.

He pinged Chied Joyce Menzies and she answered almost immediately.

"Where are you, Chief?"

Portside missile room, sir, her voice with its coarse *Quebecois* twang answered in his head.

"Jesus Christ, Menzies, do you *live* there?"

Seems like it lately, sir. But I'm just four birds away from having every missile in our magazines refitted.

"Good job. We may need them pretty soon. Look, how many do you have configured as sunflowers?"

Three, sir, but I can make more. It's a quick softward load.

"I think three sounds like enough. But I want a sunflower loaded in the coil tunnel as our hot round, and one more in the ready rack of one of your two missile rooms."

Can do, sir. That's . . . that's a lot of enemy missiles to take out. You think they'll hit us with that many all at once?

"Nope. Call it insurance. You know—it never rains when you bring an umbrella, but if you don't, watch out."

Sure-sure. I'll get my monkies right on it, sir.

Red Watch took over at 1130 hours, with Robinette as officer of the deck and Sung as duty engineering officer, which left all four of Sam's department heads free for a sitdown in the wardroom. Larry Goldjune sat quietly, not making eye contact with Sam or the others. Earlier this morning Sam had made the announcement all-boat that Robinette had been commended by the commodore for "his idea for the high sensor probe." For most of the crew that was all "officer stuff," and they hadn't paid much attention. The officers and senior chiefs had understood that something ugly had happened, but no one had spoken to him about it, and what they thought privately was none of his business.

"We're getting some good thermal imagery from the probe the task force launched yesterday," Sam started once they had all settled with coffee or tea around the wardroom table. "It will get better the higher the probe gets about the ecliptic. The thing is, where the uBakai ships seem to be is about two hundred and fifty million miles away, the other side of the system's primary and almost out into the asteroid belt. That means it takes about fifteen minutes for the light to get to us."

"So fifteen minutes after they get here, we'll see that they're coming?" Filipenko said and shook her head. "That's useful."

"What we're getting isn't timely enough for *tactical* decision making," Sam agreed, "but as operational intelligence it's invaluable. Hennessey, tell them what you were telling me about reaction mass."

Rose Hennessey, the ship's engineer, took a long drink of her coffee and then held up her drink bulb in her right hand and took Moe Rice's in her left.

"'Scuse me, Moe but I need this for just a sec'. This is Mogo," she said, twisting Moe's drink bulb, "and this is the primary," she said, twisting her own, "and my head's where K'tok is, between them. So we're here orbiting my head, the task force is outbound between us and Mogo, and the uBakai are way the hell over to the right on the far side of the primary, and have been pretty much since we entered K'tok orbit.

"Both times they jumped in and hit us they had a pretty big vector on, and they had to get that by firing their drives before they jumped. That takes reaction mass and their cruisers don't have magic fuel tanks. Only place in the system to get more—at least that we've figured out—is to scoop it out of the atmosphere of Mogo." She twisted Moe's drink bulb for emphasis. "But they're not doing that.

"Now, from going over the first data sets we got from Robinette's high probe, it looks like they have a couple big auxiliaries out there in addition to the cruisers. At least one has to be a transport. Cruisers don't carry around a shitload of gunsleds, so that lift cavalry they dropped had to come from somewhere, and I'm betting a transport or two. But they could also have a fleet tanker out there. Even so, a tanker can only carry so much hydrogen and they've got a lot of thirsty ships.

"So if you need to crank up your vector, but you also need to be real serious about how much reaction mass you're burning through, what do you do?"

"Easy," Goldjune said. "Basic astrogation. Low thrust for a long time gets as much total delta vee as high thrust for a short time, and it burns less reaction mass—provided you can do it at higher exhaust velocity, which any military drive can."

"Right," Hennessy said. "And that means we'll have a lot more than fifteen minutes to see them making that kind of burn. Hours, more like."

"Huh!" Filipenko said and sat her drink bulb down in its holder. The others looked at her. "I just came off watch," she explained, "and I went over the data sets that came in while I was on duty. There are two uBakai contacts in formation leaving the main ship cluster at low acceleration."

Sam nodded. "That's right, and it confirms Commodore Bonaventure's assessment. DesDiv Five is due to enter orbit in eleven hours. The best time for the uBakai to run the express again is before we're reinforced. That's not a guarantee, but everything seems to point to it and we'd be stupid not to be ready.

"The commodore has reset our defenses. We figure the uBakai ground stations can see everything we do up here, but a last-minute change still might throw the thinking of an express run commander off a little bit. That's why we dropped Filipenko's saddle rig a couple hours ago, turned it over to *Cha-Cha*, and shifted up-orbit.

"The *Champion Hill* salvage crew just got to work a few hours ago and they confirm most of the Block Fours in its magazine are usable, but we don't have any deployed yet. Most of them haven't had the warhead fix installed."

"That's going to be impossible to do in vac suits, sir," Filipenko said. "It's hard enough as it is, all that fine detail work and close tolerances."

"Yeah, I know. Turns out there's still juice in *Champion Hill's* aft power ring and Lieutenant Reynolds has a plan to seal off the aft section and get atmosphere and power in there, at least get the fabricators running so they can finish the parts they need and do the modifications in a decent work environment. I guess Lieutenant Commander Huhn came up with the idea."

He saw some surprise on their faces at that news.

"It's too bad we won't have those extra Block Fours for the dance coming up, but that's the way it is. Today we'll fight with what we've got, and in a few days we'll have a little more—more missiles, more boats."

The tone for his embedded commlink sounded and he saw the ID tag for Ensign Robinette, the OOD.

"Heads up," he told the others. "This may be it." He opened the link. "Yes, Mister Robinette."

"Um . . . Captain Bitka, we just got word . . . " His voice trembled and then failed him for a moment. "Sir, the uBakai hit Earth. And another Varoki fleet was with them."

Vice Captain Takaar Nuvaash, Speaker for the Enemy, stared in mounting disbelief at the report on the screen.

"Earth?" he finally managed to say. "They struck *Earth*?"

"Not *they*, Nuvaash," Admiral e-Lapeela answered. "We. *We* struck Earth. And the attack was entirely legal under the *Cottohazz* Charter on Limited War. We attacked only legitimate military targets and installations of the four Human nations with which we are at war, and only targets in orbit."

"Their two largest orbital spacedocks and shipbuilding facilities? The ones administered by their United Nations?"

"Both were servicing ships of one or another of the four hostile powers, which was stupid of them, and very convenient for us," the admiral answered calmly.

"This warship listed as North American was sold to Brazil two years ago. Brazil is neutral."

"Oh? The targeting team must not have been aware of the sale. An honest error, I'm sure."

Nuvaash read further and for a moment felt a chill spread across his shoulders and back.

"We broke a *needle*?"

"A needle was broken. Our forces destroyed a number of satellites capable of supporting military operations—each of them legitimate targets. The debris from one seems to have broken one of their two needles. There is no evidence it was a deliberate act on our part. Besides, they have a second one which remains undamaged . . . for now."

"The reports of civilian ground casualties—"

"Undoubtedly exaggerated, and in any case they were caused by the fall of debris, not strikes against ground targets. You know it is illegal to launch strikes against ground targets on a race's homeworld, so of course we did not do so"

Nuvaash sat back from the desk reader and stared at the admiral. e-Lapeela looked so smug, so pleased with himself, that for the first time in his life Nuvaash felt the urge to kill another sentient being with his own hands. Was he mad? Were they all mad?

"The force which attacked Bronstein's World moved on to strike Earth?" Nuvaash finally asked.

"Yes, after being reinforced by a squadron of uSokan cruisers."

"*Another* Varoki nation—Sokana—has joined the war?"

"A squadron of their cruisers have." e-Lapeela walked around his desk and settled into his chair. Nuvaash watched him and thought through all of these new revelations.

"So . . . the uSokan and the uKa-Maat ships . . . they are acting *contrary* to the wishes of their governments?"

"Contrary to the public orders of their governments, but not necessarily contrary to their private wishes. At least so the commanders of the squadrons believe."

"More deception. And when they find out the truth?" Nuvaash asked.

"By then the truth will have changed. Believe me, Nuvaash, where the warriors lead, the politicians will follow. Be honest. What amazes you more? That our government has acquiesced to the war we started here, or that it did so without even a grumble of protest?"

Nuvaash looked at the admiral and felt as if he saw the real person for the first time.

"Why are you telling me this?"

"Because I want you with us, Nuvaash. I *need* you with us, but it has to be your own choice. I have enough lackeys."

"And so you tell me how this entire war is built on a tissue of lies?" Nuvaash tried to control his voice but could hear it rising in pitch. "Is that how you think to win me over?"

e-Lapeela tilted his head to the side in a shrug. "Lies? You have been lied to all your life. The *Cottohazz* itself is an enormous lie. We are all equal? We are all the same under our skins? Do you still believe *that* lie, Nuvaash?

"The Humans are not our equals; in many ways they are inferior. In a few ways they surpass us—but those ways pose a mortal danger to us all. That is the truth I bring you and the truth you must face. Answer this: are you willing to trust our future, possibly even our survival as a species, to the wisdom, forbearance, and mercy of *Humans*? In your deepest parts can you embrace that? If you seek the truth, first stop lying to yourself."

Nuvaash looked into the admiral's eyes, but then looked away. *Would he make the future of his species hostage to the whim of Humans? Would any sane being?*

"Think on it and think on this: the news of this attack stunned you, and will stun them as well. And now, as they struggle to digest these dread tidings, we launch the strike you conceived and planned."

CHAPTER THIRTY

6 January 2134
(later the same day) ***(fifteenth day in K'tok orbit)***

The general quarters gong still sounded as Sam pulled himself through the hatch to the bridge, fighting the lateral acceleration as the boat turned its alignment. Robinette still sat in the command chair but Filipenko was to his right in Tac One, Lee at Maneuvering one, most of the other stations filled as well.

"Boat's aligned," Lee called.

"Fire," Robinette ordered, and then his eyes looked down and saw Sam. "I mean . . . um. . . " *Puebla* shuddered as its first Block Four left the coil gun.

"Carry on, Mister Robinette. You still have the boat."

"Ms Filipenko, continue firing," Robinette ordered, his voice pitched high with excitement or fear, Sam couldn't tell which. Then he turned back to Sam.

"Captain, the boat is at general quarters, MatCon alpha. The reactor's hot, power ring is at ninety-eight percent, thermal shroud retracted, and sensor suite is active. Iris valves are open, laser heads are extended, and we are guns up. At 1737 *Petersburg* detected two bandits emerging from J-space, polar approach, current range six thousand three hundred from *Petersburg* and closing at sixteen kilometers per second. We are antipodal to contact."

Robinette folded back the command chair's display panel, unbuckled from the chair, and pushed himself out of it as he spoke, and Sam pulled himself up and slid into his place.

"Very well, Mister Robinette. I relieve you. Take your station on the auxiliary bridge."

"Aye aye, sir," he said.

Sam felt *Puebla* shudder again as a second missile left the coil gun.

"Tac, what sort of solution do we have?"

"It's not perfect, sir," Filipenko said, "but if they don't accelerate we'll get a piece of them as they come out from behind K'tok's shadow. As it is, their cargo gliders are going to have to retro very hard to make atmospheric insertion and not burn up."

Sam pulled up his own holographic tactical display. *Cha-cha* was in low equatorial orbit tending the bombardment munitions and close by the wreck of *Champion Hill. Queretaro* was in a higher equatorial orbit and currently about a quarter orbit prograde of *Cha-cha. Petersburg* was almost directly above the north pole and right in the path of the incoming uBakai cruisers, ideally placed to let them have it. Unfortunately, that meant *Puebla*, being in *Petersburg's* same orbit but antipodal to it, was also antipodal to the bandits—that is, on the opposite side of K'tok.

Petersburg and *Puebla* were orbiting at about 4,000 kilometers. The uBakai were about 6,000 from *Petersburg*, so with the 12,000 kilometers of K'tok's diameter between them and all that orbital altitude, the uBakai would be about 26,000 kilometers away from *Puebla*, but closing fast.

Sam looked at the projected course tracks on the hologram but could already tell it would be fifteen minutes before the uBakai cleared the disc of K'tok. But by then *Puebla* would have moved forty-five hundred kilometers prograde along its own orbit track, each kilometer taking it away from the uBakai, moving on opposite sides of the bulk of the planet. By the time they had a clear shot, their missiles would never catch the targets. Only the missiles they dumped out right now had a chance of getting a hit.

Puebla shuddered again.

"We could light the fusion drive, sir," Filipenko said beside him, as if reading his mind.

Sam brought up the engineering status panel and looked at it for a moment, then pointed to a readout.

"Seven thousand six hundred tons of reaction mass," he said.

"A little over seventy percent," she said. "We're not exactly running on fumes. That's six hours of flat-out acceleration."

"Yeah, but the closest gas station's at Mogo, about eight hundred million kilometers from here, and I don't know how many times they're going to pull off these little raids before the big show. Don't want to empty our magazines, either. What have we got—four missiles out there? Secure from firing. Maybe *Petersburg* is having some luck."

"Captain, additional bogie," Chief Burns reported from Tac Two, his voice sounding surprised and angry. "Tagged Bandit Three. Jump emergence signature, bearing five degrees relative, angle on the bow one twelve, range twenty-two thousand, closing speed fifty-four kilometers per second."

"*Fifty-four klicks?* He's not on a cargo run!" Filipenko said.

"Captain," Chief Gambara said from his left, "I have Commodore Bonaventure on tight beam for you."

Sam ignored her for a moment. "Burns, stay on long-range sensor scan. Keep your eyes open for more bandits showing up. Lee, align the boat on the bandit. Close enough is good enough for a coil gun shot."

"Aye, aye, sir."

Immediately the lateral acceleration klaxon sounded and seconds later the ACTs kicked in, pivoting the boat to face the rapidly closing uBakai ship.

Sam updated his tactical display and saw the course track for the new contact. It would pass on the opposite side of K'tok from the other two cruisers and, due to the happenstance of orbital positions, only *Puebla* would have a shot at it. All the other boats would have the mass of K'tok between them and the target until it was probably too late to fire. At that speed, once it was past K'tok, no missile they had could catch it.

Sam glanced to his right and saw Filipenko staring intently at him, the way she so often stared at others, and he finally understood. She had grown up on a world which reached out and snatched people away without warning, for the flimsiest of reasons, and so whenever she saw someone, she could never be certain it was not the last time she ever would. She was memorizing how he looked, just in case. Then she looked back at her workstation display.

"Captain, I have a standard block four in the tube and one in each of the two ready racks."

"Sir, Commodore Bonaventure is insistent," Gambara said.

"Okay, patch him through."

Bitka, what's going on over there? We just got the relay feed.

"We have a single bandit closing rapidly. I am engaging."

Another one? That's what Wu on Petersburg *said but—*"

"Sir, can't talk now, he's right on top of us. *Puebla* out."

Sam cut the connection.

"Multiple contacts!" Burns reported.

"More ships?" Sam looked at his display but the contacts had appeared around the original uBakai ship.

"No, sir. He's firing but . . . damn, how many missiles did he just unload? Let me . . . *twenty* missiles, all at once! How did he do that?"

Sam pinged Menzies.

Yes, sir.

"Menzies. Are you still in the missile room?"

Yes, sir.

"Still got a sunflower ready?"

Yes sir. Standard Block Four's in the tube. You want me to swap one out?

"Affirmative. And get ready to load another sunflower right behind it."

Sam cut the connection and looked back at his holodisplay. The uBakai missiles showed hot—still accelerating. As near as Sam could tell they had under three minutes before they were within detonation range.

The bridge hatch opened and Sensor Tech Second Elise Delacroix glided in and quickly strapped herself into Tac Four and Chief Mohana Barghava slid into Maneuvering Two beside Lee.

"Burns, stay on sensors," Filipenko ordered. "Delacroix, take point defense."

"Boat aligned on target," Lee called out.

"I show a sunflower ready in the tube," Filipenko said.

"Fire."

Filipenko hit the firing button and Sam again felt the slight shudder as the missile left the coil gun's muzzle.

"Now we'll see if this thing works as advertized." Sam brought up his weapon system summary. They were down to six operational point defense laser mounts, but at least all four forward mounts were active.

"Delacroix, heads up," he said. "Sunflower will only take out some of those missiles, fifteen if everything works right."

Delacroix looked back over her shoulder at him and Sam could tell what she was thinking: *It better work*. No kidding. Twenty missiles coming at one target was nuts.

Sam checked the display again. The bandit was still coming. If this was some ship that only carried twenty missiles and fired them all at once, Sam figured he'd be breaking off by now. He'd want to get as far away from retaliation as possible, since he couldn't accomplish anything more by hanging around. But he *was* hanging around, so he had more missiles.

"Sunflower just shed its nosecone," Filipenko reported. "It's looking for targets . . . seeing *lots* of targets . . . locked on fifteen targets. We're coming up on twenty seconds to the bandit missiles being within detonation range of us."

Sam took a deep breath but resisted the temptation to cross his fingers.

"Ms Filipenko, light 'em up."

His display immediately turned white in the space ahead of them, and all data behind that white flare disappeared from his screen. The sunflower's nuclear warhead had detonated and the burst of radiation, superheated plasma, and fine debris temporarily blocked the sensor view ahead. They had no way of knowing how many, if any, of the uBakai missiles had been neutralized and wouldn't until the remainder came through that wall of dissipating interference.

Nor could the uBakai missiles "see" *Puebla*. They couldn't even ditch their nosecones and start seeking a target until they were through the debris cloud, not without risking high velocity debris damaging their target acquisition gear. The uBakai cruiser was probably still coming on, but he couldn't see *Puebla* or know what it was doing. The uBakai captain might assume *Puebla* would behave the way an uBakai cruiser would, because that was what they would be used to exercising against.

But *Puebla* had different capabilities than uBakai cruisers: more missiles, lower launch rate, better multitargeting capabilities, and a point defense laser suite with much more punch.

Tenth Principle of Naval Leadership: Employ your command in accordance with its capabilities.

"Maneuvering: sound the acceleration klaxon and then give me a full burn on both the direct fusion and MPD thrusters."

Lee turned and looked at him, eyebrows high in surprise, but her hand already was reaching for the acceleration warning.

"Filipenko, fire that second sunflower, then load a conventional block four."

Sam felt *Puebla* shudder as the sunflower fired, then the klaxon sounded and a few seconds later the main drives kicked in followed by the MPD thrusters. The acceleration quickly built to two gees, pushing Sam and the others back into their acceleration rigs, pressing their eyeballs back into their sockets. It hurt but they could take this; all of them had taken much more in training.

"Lee, cut the MPDs after one minute," Sam said through clenched teeth. They only had about two minutes worth of full power for the MPD thrusters in the power ring, and they had to save some to juice the lasers and coil gun.

"Aye, aye, sir."

Beside him, Filipenko grunted.

"Good plan, sir," she said.

Sam wondered if she'd figured it out or was just being sarcastic. Or maybe both.

The math was simple, except Sam had to do it in his head, fast, and under two gee acceleration. The sunflower had exploded after only about a ninety-second flight time. At six kilometers per second, that put it about five hundred klicks out from *Puebla* at detonation. The uBakai missiles had been right at five thousand kilometer range when the sunflower fired. They were coming in at a closing velocity between sixty and seventy kilometers a second.

That meant seventy seconds from detonation to when any surviving missiles crossed the debris cloud. Maybe another couple seconds to clear their nosecones off and then another couple seconds to acquire *Puebla* and point their laser rods. Seventy-five seconds total, but they should have five seconds after the missiles broke through the debris cloud, but before the missiles could fire, for *Puebla's* point defense lasers to take them out. They'd be firing at under five hundred klicks, so there would be effectively no beam dispersion. Every hit would be a kill. Unless the sunflower hadn't dented the missile package, this should work. Then there was the next step.

Sam had wasted at least ten seconds before the drives kicked in. As he thought this, he felt the acceleration drop to about a gee and a half as Lee cut the MPDs. One minute gone, ten seconds left. Concentrate.

One minute at two gees put their velocity up a kilometer a second. They'd add another half-kilometer per second to their velocity for every minute of one-gee acceleration. Assuming they survived the missiles, they'd hit the debris cloud at about the five-minute mark from when they started accelerating, and their velocity would be about three kilometers per second. But before then that uBakai cruiser would come barreling through in the other direction at over fifty kilometers a second.

"Getting target echoes from the cloud," Burns reported. "Here come their missiles!"

Sam stopped thinking and watched his display: six intact targets. Sunflower had actually taken out fourteen out of fifteen of its targets. ATITEP engaged and fired, fired again as insurance, fired at large fragments of the original targets and some of the larger debris chunks emerging with them. Then it ceased firing and went back into standby.

"I'll be damned," Joe Burns said quietly, "it worked. It really worked!"

"We're not done yet, Chief. We're about four minutes from crossing the debris cloud, little less. Filipenko, our second sunflower is about to penetrate the field and we'll lose direct control. Put it on auto-seek, with a one-second delay after it loses radio contact with us. Then poop out as many regular block fours as you can in the next minute. That cruiser's going to come through that field before we get to it, and we are going to mess him up.

"Gambara, burst transmit our bridge log to *Cha-cha* and get me a tight bean to the Commodore."

"Already open, sir. He's been waiting."

Bitka, what's going on?

"I've got maybe a minute, sir, so just listen. If we get splashed, you'll be able to figure out what I've done so far from the bridge recordings. But I've figured out how to beat these sons of bitches. We use the sunflowers to keep their missiles off us and blind them with the hot debris cloud. We use our regular Block Fours to do whatever damage they can, but also to distract their point defense batteries. But we get our boats in as close as we can and gut them with our own point-defense lasers."

Jesús, Bitka, you're loco, but it's the kind of crazy I think I like. We've got our hands full here, but if we're still alive ten minutes from now, we'll back you up. Give 'em hell, 'Bow-on!'

CHAPTER THIRTY-ONE

6 January 2134
(later the same day) *(sixteenth day in K'tok orbit)*

The fight had been short and violent. A fire lance hit aft of frame seventy-four cut power and communication between engineering and the rest of *Puebla*, plunging the forward hull spaces into darkness. Emergency lighting came up quickly, damage control had been able to route energy from the forward power coil to the sensors and bow point-defense lasers, and with almost the last of their stored power they blew the enemy cruiser open and turned its power systems into rapidly cooling twisted metal.

"Confirm enemy status," Sam said.

"He's dead," Chief Burns answered. "Outgassing, no active sensors or comms, engineering spaces are slagged."

"Boat status, what happened aft?"

"I have pressure in the boat forward of frame seventy-nine, sir," the engineering tech answered, "I don't show anything on my panel aft of there."

For a moment Sam's heart fluttered. Had they lost the entire engineering section? But then the tech put his hand to his ear and nodded.

"Sir, Lieutenant Hennessey's on commlink. She confirms engineering is operational. There's just a bad data and power break between seventy-seven and seventy-nine. Damage control is working on it."

"Filipenko, you have the boat," Sam said. "I'm going aft to find out how bad it is."

Minutes later Sam stood aside as a damage-control party, led by Lieutenant Carlos Sung, pushed three large tool containers ahead of them.

"I thought the damage was aft, Mister Sung."

Sung grabbed a stanchion to arrest his glide and waved the detail to keep going.

"Yes, sir. Main damage appears to be just forward of frame seventy-nine. I left a party there under Ensign Robinette to re-rig the power and data feeds. I'm going to make sure the forward power ring's nominal and see why number four laser has gone off line."

"Okay, get to it. I'll check on Robinette."

Sam pushed back toward engineering, wondering why Robinette was there instead of his battle station in the auxiliary bridge. He slipped though the open hatch at frame seventy-seven and took in the scene with a glance: bulkhead sealed at seventy-nine, glaring work lamps secured to the passage walls, three A-gangers floating near the dorsal corner of the access tunnel with two access plates already removed and fibre circuitry exposed, sparks flying from the line fuser, Ensign Robinette floating a yard back and watching the work.

"What's the situation, Ensign?"

He turned and surprise showed on his face.

"Captain! Um . . . it looks like that fire lance hit tore right through the starboard hull and out the port side, but off center. It blew out a lot of hydrogen tankage and cut the main power and data feeds in the armored conduit that runs just dorsal of the transit tube. But we *really* ducked a bullet, sir. I mean, fifteen meters forward it would have taken out both missile rooms and the aft power ring. Fifteen meters aft it would have taken out the whole forward engineering spaces. Ten meters ventral and we wouldn't have a coil gun. As it is, all we have to do—"

Sam didn't hear the explosion, didn't feel it slam him against the forward bulkhead, didn't fee the brief searing flames before his helmet faceplate automatically snapped shut. He saw the fire around him, felt someone pulling him, then pushing him, felt himself float and the fire fade away, and then everything faded away.

He came to in the the wardroom and found himself restrained in a zero gee harness. As soon as he called out, the medtech Tamblinson pushed over, released the restraints, and ran him through the short form concussion protocol. As he answered the questions, he saw four grey composite body bags tethered and floating at the far end of the compartment.

"How many fingers am I holding up?"

"Two. Who are those?"

"What's the square root of nineteen?"

"I have no idea. Something between four and five. *Who's in those body bags*?"

Tamblinson drifted back slightly and watched Sam for a reaction. "Herrera, Norquist, Simms, and Robinette. Do you remember what happened?"

Robinette. For a moment the lights seemed to dim in the wardroom.

"Not really. Little bit. There was an explosion, right?"

"Captain, are you okay?" he heard, and he saw Lieutenant Carlos Sung at the open hatch. He waved him over.

"Tell me what happened, Lieutenant."

Sung glanced at the floating body bags and then pushed gently off toward Sam. Sung was a big man, big-handed with broad fingers and rough knuckles, flat-faced with broad, coarse features and right then terribly sad eyes. He stopped and then sighed.

"Secondary explosion—an undetected O2 leak contaminating the hydrogen tank right overhead. It blew you forward through the open hatch. Everyone else in the compartment died."

Sam looked at the body bags and he swallowed hot spit two or three times, fighting back the urge to vomit.

"Why?" It came out harsher than he intended.

"Mister Robinette used to be A-gang, sir," Sung said quickly, "and he was always good with electronics. We didn't know what else was broke-dick up forward so I figured—"

Sam held up his hand to cut him off.

"Not why did you turn the party over to him. Why was he even there?"

"He said the XO sent him back to help. Tell you the truth, sir, I think he volunteered. He doesn't . . . didn't like hanging around Mister Goldjune very much."

Sam closed his eyes and felt the competing waves of anger and sorrow wash through him.

"Okay, explain what happened."

"Well, sir, at first it looked like all the damage was external to the access tunnel, so we got to work fixing the power and data breaks. Like I said, there must have been an undetected O2 leak into the hydrogen tanks. Pressure was nominal in the boat so it must have been from a compressed oxygen storage tank. Even that should have shown up on our boards but a lot of our low-level system monitors were still off-line. Anyway, they got cutting and all of a sudden that tank above you blew. It must have been like a blow torch into the compartment, all that oxygen."

"Their shipsuits couldn't take it?" Sam asked.

"The shrapnel from the explosion compromised their suits. We think the three ratings died pretty much instantly. Mister Robinette got his helmet closed, but like I said his suit was compromised too. Don't know why yours wasn't."

"Robinette was in the way, must have stopped most of the fragments himself. Go on."

"We found him by the emergency bulkhead. All the power was out forward so the automatic bulkheads didn't close, but there was still pressure in the access tunnel. That fire could have kept going all the way forward. He hit the manual hydraulic backup and got the bulkhead at frame seventy-seven sealed before he died. Maybe saved the boat, sir."

The Jughead saved the boat.

Sam closed his eyes for a moment. "He saved me too. I didn't get blown through the hatch. I hit the bulkhead, stunned me. Somebody pushed me through. Must have been him."

Sung nodded.

"Sung, why the hell do we store all this hydrogen right next to the pressurized crew spaces? Every time we get poked, we have to worry about O2 contamination, hydrogen and oxygen getting mixed up and turning us into the fucking Hindenburg in space. Now Robinette . . . " He broke off and shook his head.

Sung squinted and looked away for a moment, trying to come up with an answer. Sam realized the question he'd asked must have been stupid. Stupid questions from superiors always require that sort of thought.

"Lieutenant, I'm just a dumb tac-head. Don't worry about offending me with a grade school answer. I just want to know."

Sung nodded. "Well, sir, it's not so much a question of where to put the hydrogen as where to put us. Liquid hydrogen ain't very dense, so even though it's just a little more than half our loaded mass, it takes up over two thirds of our enclosed volume. *Puebla's* mostly a big hydrogen tank with a little bit of other stuff tucked inside. Any place you put something, it's going to be next to hydrogen. That's why any time we get a puncture of a crew compartment, first thing we do is pump it down to vacuum, to keep the O2 from leaking into the hydrogen tanks. Here, there wasn't a puncture, least not that we could detect."

Sam's commlink tone sounded.

"Captain here."

Sir, Signaler Lincoln. I have the commodore on tight beam commlink for you.

"Wait one, Lincoln." Sam closed his eyes again and took a steadying breath.

Robinette wasn't dead because the boat's designers had screwed up and he wasn't dead because Carlos Sung made a bad call. Much as he wanted there to be someone to blame, Sam wasn't even sure Larry Goldjune had sent him to his death. That might have been the right call as well. Jerry Robinette was just dead, and that's all there was to it. He opened his eyes.

"Sung, what shape are we in other than this hit?"

"We can do a workaround on the data feed, get you maneuvering control in probably a half-hour, sir. The power feed'll take longer, hour at least, maybe two. After that she'll be a hundred percent operational. Didn't even shake that radiator patch-job loose."

Sam nodded and dismissed him with a wave.

"Go ahead, Lincoln. Patch the commodore through."

Bitka! I was worried about you, Bonaventure said as soon as Sam opened the connection. *You sure did a job on that cruiser, Amigo. How bad is your damage?*

Sam moved through the hatch to the forward access tunnel and pushed himself toward his quarters.

"We lost an officer and three ratings. Everything else is repairable, sir, and we'll have maneuvering control in thirty minutes. I'll start reversing vector then, but I want to do it at low thrust, keep our reaction mass expenditure down. We're still not sure how much hydrogen we lost this time, but it's starting to add up. How did you do against the raiding force?"

Both the uBakai cruisers dropped their cargo into the atmosphere and escaped under full acceleration, but one traded hits with Petersburg. *The uBakai cruiser ceased firing after that but kept accelerating. Petersburg lost two lasers aft and half its radiators, but they're working on fixing the radiators at least.*

I think the two uBakai will jump away as soon as they're clear, but the wreck of that cruiser you killed is passing close by K'tok. The only boat with a chance of matching course with it and getting back here in less than a day or two is Queretaro, *so I'm going to have them check for survivors.*

You've probably been pretty busy over there, Bitka, too busy to realize what just happened. That cruiser you took out was the first hostile spacecraft ever destroyed in combat by the United States Navy while at war.

Sam thought about that for a moment and then shook his head.

"What about Captain Gasiri in *Kennedy* three years ago? She took out two uZmatanki cruisers, didn't she?"

That was while serving as part of a combined Cottohazz *peacekeeping force. We weren't technically at war. This is different. Until today we've just been taking it from the uBakai. It's about time we started paying some of that back. So you give your crew a hearty well-done from me,* comprende?

"Aye aye, sir."

Sam signed off and slipped through the hatch to his quarters. He pulled off his scorched shipsuit and put on a fresh one and then glanced in the mirror. His face was bright red and glistened from the burn spray Tamblinson had applied. He'd lost his eyebrows and all the hair on the front part of his skull. He took a few minutes to shave the rest of it off; at least it would grow back evenly.

He tethered himself to his desk but did not bring up any files. Instead he spent a moment thinking about the deteriorating condition of the task group. Every one of these encounters left them diminished in some regard, and the damage mounted steadily. *Petersburg*: down two lasers and at least some of its radiators. *Puebla*: down two lasers. *Oaxaca*: no coil gun. *Queretaro*: only half its power ring.

They really needed the four boats in DesDiv Five. Sam checked the chronometer. Seven more hours and they'd be here. He pinged Lincoln in the comm seat.

"Get me all-boat."

You're live, sir.

"All hands, this is the captain. I have some sad news. Four of our shipmates died from that fire lance hit. We will hold a memorial service later today. Otherwise the damage is repairable and engineering will have us up and running in a couple hours.

"I also just spoke with the commodore and he informed me the uBakai cruiser we splashed is the first official kill of a United States Navy vessel in this war, so we're in the record books. He sent, in his own words, a hearty well-done, and I concur. It couldn't come at a better time than the day after those bastards hit Earth. So far no other ship or boat has done what we just did, and we did it because everyone did their job the way we've trained. The first beer's on me tonight. Toast our fallen shipmates and remember the folks back home. I'm sure they could use good news right now and we just gave them some."

As the afternoon wore on and turned to evening, Sam presided over the memorial service for the dead and went over all the repairs with Rose Hennessey. He also stopped back in the wardroom and had Tamblinson give him another shot of burn spray on his face. Then it was back to work. He met with Marina Filipenko and her three chiefs to refine the tactics he'd improvised earlier in the day, and put Chief Joyce Menzies to work converting more of their remaining missiles to the sunflower configuration.

Their missile supply was becoming a concern. They fired nine in the First Battle of K'tok, as that disaster had come to be called, but had resupplied from *Hornet* before it passed on its way to Mogo. That topped their magazine off at thirty, but they shot eight more off today. Twenty-two left, with four to be rigged as sunflowers and eighteen as standard ship-killers. Was that a good mix? It was as good as he could come up with for now.

If it hadn't been for the casualties, Robinette in particular, Sam would have been glad the uBakai hit them when they did. Everyone had still been in shock over the news about the attack on Earth. There was nothing like the threat of imminent death to snap your mind back to the here and now. They needed that, he supposed, but every time he thought about Ensign Robinette he felt a weight on his chest, a pain in his heart. How could someone start off so wrong-footed and end up so good? Maybe because he had all the bullshit stripped away and found something worthwhile in himself: duty. And it hadn't been just a word for Robinette, had it? It sure hadn't.

As they re-entered K'tok orbit they saw the sensor echoes from five new lethal satellites in orbit, the first fruits of the salvage teams on *Champion Hill*. Sam wondered how Huhn was working out and, as if in answer to his thoughts, Commodore Bonaventure tight beamed him not long after.

Huhn and Reynolds had come up with a plan to make *Champion Hill* operational again.

The reactor and drives were undamaged, as was the aft power ring and the four aft point defense lasers. Their plan consisted of permanently sealing the bulkhead at frame forty-seven and cutting away everything forward of there. Removing all that twisted wreckage would balance the boat and they could use the maneuvering drive, although they'd have to do some fine tuning of the exhaust angle. They'd have to con the boat from the auxiliary bridge, and they didn't have many sensors working, but the communication suite was in excellent shape and they could use sensor feed from the satellite network around K'tok.

If all they ever wanted to use *Champion Hill* for was an orbital gunboat, it might work. Bonaventure was reluctant, however.

"Well, sir, you don't have to make a decision right now, do you? I mean, they're going to be busy for a while just recovering and placing those missiles in orbit. Let them refine the plan. Make your decision later."

Bonaventure agreed and signed off, but within an hour was back on tight beam.

I just got some bad news, Bitka. I'm telling you first as task group N-2. We weren't the only ones the uBakai paid a visit to today. DesDiv Five got jumped, too.

Sam felt a surge of adrenaline. He'd been counting on those reinforcements.

"How bad, sir?"

Amiens *bought it—fire lance hit in engineering apparently took down the fusion reactor bottle while they were under full thrust. No survivors, but at least they went quick. The other three boats got beat up, too, but Rocky says they'll all be under power in time to decelerate and enter orbit*

"Rocky?"

Sadie Rockaway. She runs the division. You'd remember her if you'd met her. Anyway, that pretty much decided me on Champion Hill. *I'm going to let Huhn and Reynolds patch her up and use it for the low orbit boat. We can weld the saddle rig to it or something.*

"How long will that take, sir?"

I don't know, but we need the extra boat. We're just spread too thin.

Sam didn't have an answer for that; it was true.

Also, I think I'm going to give the boat to Huhn. Reynolds gave me a pretty good report on him and she says she'd be more comfortable backing him up than trying to run the boat herself. What do you think?

Sam spent a moment listening to the soft conversations between his own bridge crew, watching the data feeds scroll across his work station as K'tok grew larger on the smartwall forward.

"Sir, I think . . . I'm glad I don't have your job."

Bonaventure chuckled.

You're a pretty smart hombre, *Bitka. Okay, I'm giving* Champion Hill *to Huhn, assuming they can actually get it working. I'm also sending over the initial tac recordings from DesDiv Five's fight with the uBakai. Take a look as a tac-head, see if there's anything in there we can use.*

"Aye aye, sir."

One more thing, Queretaro *is getting close to matching velocities with that cruiser you wrecked. The Varoki apparently have an emergency transmitter running off of stored power or something. The Varoki captain's still alive. He says he's not uBakai, he surrenders to us unconditionally, and he needs to talk to us about something big.*

"That sounds interesting, sir. He must be one of those uKa-Maat guys, huh?"

We'll see. Since you're acting N-2, you do the interrogation. Set it up by holoconference with Queretaro.

"Me? I've got a damaged boat to nurse back into orbit, sir."

I read your damage report, Bitka. You're fine. Talk to this hombre *once he's on board* Queretaro. *See what this big thing is he has to tell us.*

CHAPTER THIRTY-TWO

7 January 2134
(the next day) ***(eighteenth day in K'tok orbit)***

The uBakai cruiser KBk Five One Seven was not as badly damaged this time as it had been at K'tok, but smoke and the smell of compromised electronics still drifted through the passageway, and damage control parties still had priority of movement. Once several of them had passed, Vice-Captain Takaar Nuvaash, Speaker For the Enemy, made his way down the corridor and to the infirmary where Admiral e-Lapeela's wound was being dressed. The wound was not serious, and Nuvaash was unsure how he felt about that. In a sense he had already made his choice when he shared the details of the conspiracy with the uKa-Maat Captain Lorppo. He was simply not sure he had chosen wisely.

He entered and saw the admiral in an undignified position, bent over and holding an examination table. The lower half of his pressure suit had been cut away, and a medtech was laser-cauterizing the open gash across the . . . *back of his hip*, Nuvaash decided, was the polite way to describe the location of the wound.

"Another scar earned in the service of our race," e-Lapeela said when he saw Nuvaash.

"No one who views it will deny the admiral's courage. I bear new intelligence on the battle at K'tok yesterday."

"Does it tell us anything about the new destroyer missiles? The ones that did not work and now do?"

"Unfortunately no, Admiral. Although we received no

communications from KBk Zero Two B—the uKa-Maat salvo cruiser which was lost—ground stations there partially monitored the battle in orbit."

e-Lapeela rolled onto his side to face Nuvaash and momentarily winced with pain.

"So, now you believe my decision to send just three ships against K'tok was in error?"

Nuvaash looked to the medtech, who had finished his work and was now simply listening. The technician hastily gathered his equipment and left. As he did, Nuvaash activated his commlink and pinged the admiral's orderly.

"Bring a pressure suit for the admiral to the medical bay, procedure room three."

At once, Vice-Captain.

That done, he turned back to the admiral. To his surprise, e-Lapeela stared at the blank wall of the treatment room, eyes empty, mouth slack, ears sagging.

"Admiral, are you unwell?"

e-Lapeela gave a start and his façade of tough determination returned immediately.

"A moment of weakness, thinking of the warriors who died with us yesterday, and at K'tok. I sent them to their death, Nuvaash. But that is what a leader does in wartime: sends warriors to their deaths. I cannot flinch from that, will not flinch from it. But it is not a task which lifts my heart. The Humans we slew at Ktok and here seem a poor payment for the good lives I spent. I am sure you agree with that, especially now, with the unsuccessful attack against K'tok by three ships."

Nuvaash studied the admiral and again saw depression or remorse hiding behind his war mask. Did e-Lapeela now regret his part in the rash conspiracy which ignited this war? If so, did his regret change anything important? Did it even change how Nuvaash felt about him?

"Your decision did not produce its desired results, but was worth the risk, which I believe was well-calculated. Dispatch of a single salvo cruiser, coming on the heels of a two-ship raid, gave those three ships their greatest chance of success. Detachment of enough ships to guarantee success at K'tok would most likely have resulted in defeat against the reinforcing destroyer force we attacked here, and that action was equally important."

e-Lapeela studied him for a moment, perhaps trying to decide if Nuvaash meant what he had said. For a change, Nuvaash did mean exactly that. The admiral's death in battle might have given Nuvaash some satisfaction, but the loss of a fine uKa-Maat cruiser at K'tok gave him none at all, even if its loss might reflect poorly on e-Lapeela.

"*Kunka suurilaa yus haluaat?*" Lieutenant Moe Rice said.

"You're kidding, right? How the hell do you speak aGavoosh?" Sam asked. Heading forward to his cabin, he banked softly off the wall of the central transit tube to avoid the next half-bulkhead.

"Cap'n, I'm a logistics specialist," Moe answered, gliding along beside him, "here in the Navy and back in my civilian job. As in interstellar logistics? Ship stuff from here to there, sooner or later you got to deal with leatherheads. You speak their lingo, they treat you with a little more respect. Saves a lot of time and money."

Although the Varoki had as many different languages as Humans did, each race had one language used in interstellar commerce, government, and diplomacy, a sort of off-world *lingua franca*. For Humans it was English and for the Varoki it was aGavoosh.

"Yeah, but what's wrong with using auto-trans? It does a good enough job, doesn't it?"

Moe shook his head. "It's okay for meaning, not so much for inflection. When you're doing business, inflection counts. Might not hurt when you're interrogating a prisoner, neither."

He had a point there. Sam opened the hatch to his quarters and they floated in and attached their tethers to his desk. He brought up the flat-vid feed and for a moment the two of them looked at the Varoki naval officer tethered in a secure compartment on *Queretaro*, his helmet on and ready for the holo-con interrogation.

"What I don't get is why you're s'posed to grill this feller," Moe said. "*Queretaro* picked him and his boys up. Why not have them do it?"

"I'm the task group smart boss, remember? Commodore wants me to handle it. So here's how this works. It's a standard three-way holocon except he only gets the feed from my helmet, not yours. He won't be able to see or hear you. He'll hear the autotrans version of my questions. You feed me the translation as he answers. If I want to consult with you, I'll freeze the conference feed and we'll talk by commlink. Okay?"

"Let's do it," Moe answered,

They helmeted up and Sam opened the connection to the conference. The Varoki officer looked up, his face grew animated, and his ears immediately stood out to the side, or as far as his now-invisible helmet allowed.

"Ah wonderful, you are here. But you are only a lieutenant? I must speak with your admiral as soon as possible. I have vital information about the war he must know."

Sam realized he'd heard the direct audio feed, not the machine-generated translation. He stared wordlessly for a moment.

"Surely you speak English," the Varoki officer said impatiently.

Sam had a hard time finishing the interrogation. He wanted to contact Bonaventure after about ten minutes but he knew he should do a thorough job, try to get as many answers as he could to the questions he knew his commodore would ask. After three quarters of an hour the uKa-Maat officer—Captain Lorppo—also began to get impatient. Well, they could always quiz him again if any new questions came up. He wasn't going anywhere.

Half an hour later Sam was live with Bonaventure, but the commodore had included Cassandra Atwater-Jones as well and the time lag to and from the task force was over two minutes. Her image—very serious and frozen in mid-frown—looked on from the third virtual chair.

"*Jesús*, Bitka, you look like hell!" Bonaventure said as soon as the link opened.

"Yeah, getting some blisters from my burns, but Tamblinson say it looks a lot worse than it is."

Bonaventure shook his head and turned back to the frozen image of Cassandra Atwater-Jones.

"Captain Bitka, serving as my acting N-2, has developed some sensitive intelligence which, from what little he has told me, I believe to be critical to my operational decision-making. I have asked Commander Atwater-Jones to join the conference as well. As I will be making several decisions based on this intelligence, and as those decisions may prove controversial and will be my responsibility alone, I am treating this conference as 'privileged advice by staff,' and so there will be no record of its content. Nothing either of you say can be used to shift any responsibility for my decisions to you. Is that understood?"

Sam felt a surge of excitement. He'd heard of "privileged advice by staff" conferences but had never been anywhere near one before.

"Understood, sir."

The two-minute turnaround time seemed much longer.

"Quite clear, Commodore Bonaventure," Cassandra answered at last. She looked at Bitka, her eyes wide. "Good lord, Bitka!"

"Worse than it looks," Sam repeated.

"I am now blocking the data capture for this conference." Bonaventure said. "There. We are off the record. Now, let's talk some treason."

That took Sam by surprise. *Treason?* What the hell was Bonaventure talking about? Was it some sort of euphemism? A joke? If it was meant to cut the tension, it hadn't worked. One glance at the commodore's unusually hard expression disabused Sam of that theory.

"Sam, let's hear what your uKa-Maat captain had to say."

"Yes, sir. As we suspected, a squadron of four uKa-Maat cruisers are working with the uBakai. All four of them are of a new class which we had some background on but it appears we incorrectly assessed. The aGavoosh word for their subtype translates roughly as 'salvo cruiser.' They spit out a lot of missiles all at once to overwhelm the point-defense systems of a target. It probably would have plowed us under if it hadn't been for the sunflower-modified missiles we had.

"That much is interesting but fairly routine. The really radioactive information is all tied up in the politics of the war. He was still shaken up from his ship getting torn apart and half his crew dead, so he was a little disorganized and rambling, but very anxious to make us understand how much of a threat we're under."

"I'm going to interrupt here for a second, Bitka," Bonaventure said. "Why is he anxious to warn *us?* We're the enemy."

"I wondered the same thing, sir. He doesn't see it that way. His government's not at war with us, so he figures maybe he's not at war with us either."

"So what are those four uKa-Maat salvo cruisers doing if they're not at war with us?" Bonaventure demanded.

"Just getting to that, sir. The admiral running the uKa-Maat cruiser squadron told the captains and crews it was a secret mission authorized by their government, but the government couldn't support it in public until they had drummed up domestic support for the war. But Captain Lorppo found out that was all bullshit. His own admiral is part of some secret society that's staged the whole war. Even the uBakai home government didn't know it was coming; it was cooked up out here by the fleet and the colonial government. Bakaa's going along with it, although Lorppo doesn't know why. That part sounds really odd, but all I can tell you is what he said. I can't say that it's true, but I'm pretty sure he believes it is. He's taking a big chance telling us so much, but I think he's more afraid of where this war may go than he is of the consequences for him. He struck me as a pretty honorable fellow."

"How does he know all this about his own admiral and the plan for the war?" Bonaventure asked.

"A high-ranking member of the uBakai admiral's staff told him. Lorppo wouldn't tell me who, but he clearly trusts the guy. Apparently there's some dissention in the ranks over there. But here's where it gets really interesting. They're deliberately doing things that will provoke a reaction. They *want* us to hit them back, *hard*. Right now it's a group of fanatics led by a few rogue admirals, but if they can get us to hit back hard against their homeworld, they figure a lot more Varoki nations will pile on. A lot of them are just looking for an excuse.

"He's not sure how far they want to go but he thinks the long-term plan is genocide. If they can't get enough Varoki nations on board for that, they'll settle for bombing us back to the stone age, as we used to say."

Bonaventure didn't say anything for a few seconds as he chewed that over. Sam was surprised he didn't look more shocked—Sam sure had been. Instead the commodore had the look of a man who already had a few pieces of a puzzle and just got the extra ones that made it all make sense. He nodded after a few moments and turned to the frozen image of Atwater-Jones.

"Your turn, Commander, although I'll tell you, it sounds a lot like Operation Shangri-La to me."

Operation Shangri-La? Sam had never heard anything about an operation with that code name.

"I would rather we had not brought that up, Commodore," Cassandra said as soon as her image un-froze, "but I suppose it is the quarter-ton primate in the parlor. Before we wrestle with it, however, let me add some information from a report I just received via jump courier, which unfortunately seems to back up Captain Bitka's analysis.

"As the last intelligence update reported, six uSokan cruisers were part of the uBakai fleet which attacked Earth. Unlike the four uKa-Maat cruisers, they did not have altered transponder codes, which is to say they openly flew their national colors. Officially both the uKa-Maat and uSokan governments have affirmed they do not consider a state of war to exist with any Earth nation, and they have issued orders for the rogue squadrons to return to Hazz'Akatu, the Varoki home world. That much we already knew.

"However, in the last two days a series of increasingly enthusiastic public demonstrations have taken place in the major uKa-Maat cities, particularly the capital, most of which are in favor of supporting the rogue squadron and joining the war alongside the uBakai. These are, of course, planned and orchestrated. There are very few spontaneous public displays in Varoki society. These, however, have at least the appearance of striking a genuinely popular note. A great many Varoki are not very fond of us, and some are using this opportunity to express their feelings in that regard.

"More alarmingly, similar demonstrations have taken place in seven other Varoki nations that we are aware of, including the Republic of Sokana. This is all developing as we speak, of course, and our intelligence-gathering resources on Hazz'Akatu are quite overwhelmed. At the moment they are reduced to little more than watching news feeds, so I cannot offer any assessment of whether this new fire will burn out quickly or continue to grow and spread, but we must be prepared for the more dangerous possibility.

"Which unfortunately brings us to Operation Shangri-La. There is an old joke, something of a tradition in British military intelligence, which all but requires me to begin this section of the brief with, 'M'Lords, I have a cunning plan.' To be precise, it is your Admiral Goldjune who is so blessed. He has championed a scheme to launch a counterstrike against Hazz'Akatu, the Varoki homeworld, originally limited to uBakai targets but now tentatively to include the uSokan. I imagine a number of uKa-Maat targets have been surveyed as well. It's all rather vague, but the purpose seems to be to let the Varoki know how it feels for their home planet to be hit from orbit."

"Shit!" Sam said, although Cassandra would not hear that since

they weren't transmitting down the long-distance tight beam during her speech. He frowned and it hurt his forehead where the burned skin bunched and wrinkled.

"You can say that again, Bitka," the commodore said, his expression grim.

"Admiral Goldjune seems to appreciate large gestures," Cassandra went on. "It's always dangerous to think we understand people too well, but he does strike me as the sort of admiral who prefers large, decisive battles which settle everything in an afternoon. His sealed orders to Admiral Kayumati—which you are not privy to, Captain Bitka, but which the commodore and I have both read—are another example of that. Suffice it to say he was a member of the 'push hard' school.

"Were he Royal Navy, loyalty to the service would demand I say no more. But as he's one of yours—and we *are* off the record—I will confess this fascination with big, quick solutions strikes me as the mark of a lazy and superficial mind, not willing to do the hard and often boring work necessary to earn success over the long haul. In short, I suspect he is a dilettante, and one whose hunger for simple answers may prove the undoing of our civilization, and perhaps even our species.

"I will now pause in the event you feel the need to offer a defense of your countryman, or perhaps a more nuanced view."

Bonaventure shook his head. "No, that's pretty much the way I see him, although I only met him once, very briefly, at a reception on the BW. He does have that reputation, though—charge ahead and sort the details out later. Bitka, you may feel differently. You're by far the most tactically aggressive officer I know. Maybe you see something in the admiral I'm missing."

Bonaventure's words took Sam by surprise. *The most tactically aggressive officer he knew?* The description did not seem to fit him very well. He certainly hadn't charged the uKa-Maat salvo cruiser just to feel the wind in his face. Of course, it had been . . . exhilarating.

"Why is it called Operation Shangri-La, do you know, sir?" he asked.

"Somebody on the combined staff must be a history buff. Right at the start of World War II the US launched a bomber strike against the Japanese home islands, the Doolittle Raid—sent from the carrier

Hornet, coincidentally. When President Roosevelt was asked where the bombers came from, he said, 'From Shangri-La.' You know, the mythical place in the Himalayas."

Sam nodded.

"So if Admiral Goldjune and the combined coalition command get this information, won't they abort Shangri-La?"

Bonaventure turned to Cassandra's frozen image. "Commander, you're closer to the brass than we are. What do you think?"

After her image unfroze she shook her head. "It is of course a possibility, but Admiral Kayumati has been lobbying quite hard to get the operation cancelled and the fleet assets dedicated to it shifted here instead. Admiral Goldjune has rebuffed all such recomendations, and appears to have substantial political support from several of the Coalition governments. The testimony of one rogue Varoki captain, itself based on hearsay testimony from an unnamed uBakai staff officer, and all of it produced by officers under Kayumati's command, will probably not carry much weight. Honestly, were I back on Earth I would have a hard time giving it much credence myself.

"So the question is: What is to be done?"

Cassandra's image froze again.

What is to be done? What *could* they do, all the way out here, to alter fleet policy crafted back on Earth and Bronstein's World. Not much, probably. But fleet policy was government policy, and government policy wasn't made in a vacuum, was it? What had Cassandra said about the sealed orders to Admiral Kayumati being a product of the 'push the uBakai hard' school? Maybe there was something they could do after all.

"Sir, ever since I heard about the strike against Earth, I've had this feeling we're all misreading this whole war. What Captain Lorppo said sort of brought it into focus. I don't think the uBakai—or at least the guys behind this war—give a rat's ass about K'tok. It's just their excuse."

"Excuse for what?"

"Putting us under the dirt. Not us personally. *Humans*. All of us. They aren't trying to kill us over a rock. They're trying to kill us because they just want us all dead. Admiral Goldjune may be too pigheaded to see it, but that doesn't mean we all have to go gentle into that good night."

He glanced at Cassandra's frozen image, remembering the last time he had heard those words.

"Commodore, if we're really here to talk some treason, hadn't we better get down to it?"

Five hours later his commlink vibrated, waking Sam from a deep sleep, and he saw the ID code for Marina Filipenko, the OOD. He checked the time: 0147

He raised the light level in the cabin and made sure there were no urgent message alerts flashing on his work station before answering her.

"Yeah, Filipenko, what's up?"

I think it's trouble, sir. It just came in broad band from a comsat. Not sure who bounced it to begin with.

"The uBakai task force show up?" he asked. It was only a matter of time before they did.

No, sir. It's weirder than that. Someone has leaked Admiral Kayumati's sealed orders, the ones we've been acting under, and broadcast it to everyone: us, the uBakai, everyone.

Well, that was quick, Sam thought.

"What do they say?" he asked, because that's what she would expect him to.

They're just coming in, sir. I haven't had time to read them. I'll dump a copy to your personal folder.

"Okay. If it's broadband, I suppose everyone will read it pretty soon. May as well get out ahead of it. Don't distribute copies to anyone else, though. Not until you have my okay."

Sir, as you said, everyone will be able to get copies from every open database, including a couple dozen personal e-nexus cores on board.

"Yeah, but not from us. We still have a responsibility to safeguard whatever restricted information is under our control. This is probably sensitive, so I'll have a read first. Thanks for the heads up."

He cut the connection, put on a pair of viewer glasses, and accessed the new file. He read for five minutes, long enough to make sure this was the same version he had read earlier, and then took his glasses off. He floated in the middle of his stateroom for a few minutes, staring at the gray bulkhead. Then he nodded.

"Well, now we'll see what happens."

CHAPTER THIRTY-THREE

8 January 2134
(the next day) ***(eighteenth day in K'tok orbit)***

Sam put his viewer glasses back on and spent the better part of an hour reading and rereading Kayumati's sealed orders. After ten minutes he was interrupted by an urgent tight beam from Commodore Bonaventure, who thought they should call an immediate holoconference of the captains to discuss the leaked orders. Sam convinced him to hold off long enough to at least let the other captains read through them. Sam then got back to his own reading. He tried to read them with the clear mind of someone who had not read them before, tried to gauge the emotional effect they would have. He thought there were many interesting things about the orders.

One was that the orders included a cover memo from Captain Marietta Kleindienst, the task force chief of staff. The purpose of the limited and eyes-only distribution was so senior officers commanding ship divisions and squadrons could answer "potentially awkward questions" from junior officers. The date on the distribution note was 8 December, the day after the holoconference where Marina Filipenko had asked Kleindienst just such an awkward question concerning the task force orders. Filipenko would be interested to know that she had had a hand in getting these orders distributed to a wider audience, one of whom had leaked them.

The second interesting thing was the specificity with which the orders directed Kayumati to respond to the uBaka fleet during peacetime.

"You are under no circumstances to allow any act of provocation to go unanswered. You are to respond to any potential act of violence with commensurate actual violence. Every act you take must leave the uBakai with the unambiguous certainty that we are prepared to go to war over access to K'tok and in defense of all Human colonists currently on the planet, regardless of their nationality. If additional colony vessels arrive, you are to prevent any interference with their approach to and landing on K'tok by any and all means at your disposal."

The kicker was this line: "Any act of violence against your command, or against any colonists once you are on station with your task force, is to be treated as an act of war against the member states of the Outward Coalition. You will then respond as outlined in Annex Three."

Any colonists? That was a guarantee of war right there, given the constant muttering violence along the borders. Sam stopped for a moment and took a few deep, slow breaths to keep his heart rate down.

Sam checked Annex Three; he hadn't bothered to before, during the holoconference. It was essentially the invasion plan they had executed, but with some additional instructions.

"BuShips directs Commander, Combined Task Force One, to use the new Battle-class destroyers aggressively and in as many varied combat roles as their design allows. Operations staff, Combined Task Force One, will prepare a detailed evaluation of the performance of the destroyers deployed, with recommendations as to whether additional examples should be acquired and with respect to design enhancements. This priority is sufficiently high that Commander, Combined Task Force One is directed to consider the destroyers under his command expendable in pursuit of this information, provided their loss does not jeopardize the success of the mission."

So, as long as there was going to be a war anyway—and there clearly was—be sure to run these experiments we've been curious about, and don't worry about losses. We'd like to see what happens when a destroyer breaks. For a moment Sam thought he was going to be sick.

The distribution list—division commanders and above—pretty much limited the culprit to someone on Commodore Bonaventur's *Oaxaca* or Captain Rockaway's *Vimy Ridge,* the only two surviving division lead boats. Bonaventure had already told him at the holoconference that, once the orders became public, as task group smart boss he would be tagged to "ferret out the leak." He had already sketched out in his own mind the detailed investigation and collection of data records he would assemble for his report. They would leave no data file concerning the orders or any use of communication equipment in either *Oaxaca* or *Vimy Ridge* unexamined or uncopied. They would also turn up no evidence of either copying or leaking the orders because, Sam already knew, there was no evidence to discover.

Readers of the sealed orders would also find the signature interesting: Admiral Cedrick J. Goldjune, Commander, US 11th Fleet—the same Admiral Goldjune who was now CNO for the Outworld Coalition, the same one who had looked the task force in the eye four days ago and said it was never his intention to send them in harm's way. Utter bullshit.

Sam also remembered that the head of BuShips—who had directed Kayumati to use the destroyers "aggressively" and to consider them expendable—was Larry's father, and both the father and the uncle knew Larry was serving on a destroyer when these orders were drafted.

What did that say about Goldjune's family? Perhaps that they subordinated family ties to duty, but everything he'd ever heard about their family influence, and willingness to use it, made that hard to credit. It seemed more likely they were willing to subordinated family loyalty to personal ambition.

Or maybe they just didn't like Larry, or didn't think he would measure up. Maybe they had another golden boy waiting in the wings, a better heir apparent. Maybe that's what Larry was so afraid of.

Vice-Captain Takaar Nuvaash, Speaker for the Enemy, found Admiral e-Lapeela in the cruiser's tactical command center, in the main hull section where there was no spin-induced gravity. He steadied himself by a handhold and waited for the admiral to finish his conversation with the cruiser's captain. When the captain pushed away, e-Lapeela turned to Nuvaash and gestured for him to speak.

"I bear new intelligence on the enemy. For reasons uncertain, a member of the enemy fleet broadcast a copy of the enemy admiral's sealed orders from his high command."

"Probably forgeries intended to mislead us," e-Lapeela said.

Nuvaash cocked his head to one side.

"I am less certain of that than is the admiral. There is really nothing of immediate tactical use, nothing which, were we to believe it, might lead us into a misstep."

e-Lapeela shifted impatiently. "Then why is this worth my time?"

"It suggests some level of disaffection among the enemy, or the document would not have been shared. The political department is ecstatic. If authentic, and I believe it to be so, it appears to prove the Earth fleet came here with the intention of beginning a war."

"Ha!" e-Lapeela exclaimed. "We were right all along."

"It seems so, Admiral. How sad that Governor e-Rauhaan did not survive. Even he would have been an enthusiastic supporter of war with the Humans once they provoked the conflict."

e-Lapeela's eyes narrowed and his ears folded back against his head. "Tread carefully, Speaker."

Nuvaash bowed.

"I live to obey."

e-Lappla grunted. "I wonder sometimes. But there is nothing wrong with your brain, I cannot deny that. So let it work for you now. Were you the Humans, where would you most fear an attack? Speak for the enemy."

Nuvaash paused, not considering the question so much as his answer to it. He had already thought through that very issue, knew exactly what conclusion he had reached, but he hesitated. This war created by e-Lapeela's ambition, or perhaps his political fanaticism, or his nearly psychotic fear of Humans, was criminal. But regardless of its genesis, the nation was now at war. Was Nuvaash's obligation to wage that war as successfully as possible or to try to derail it? Although his countrymen might not be well-served by this war, would they be any better served by a defeat? And was that his decision to make? His feelings for e-Lapeela were, he found, a mix of grudging respect and mounting repulsion, but what did his feelings for the admiral really matter? He could not bring disaster on all the blameless others in this fleet just to humble the one monster, particularly a monster who might be right about the Humans.

"Admiral, I cannot look into the soul of the one unique individual guiding their decisions, but I can tell you what my two greatest fears would be.

"The results of the last raid on K'tok clearly show that the enemy destroyers have overcome the problem with their missiles. Nevertheless, K'tok remains the key to this part of our campaign. If we sweep the remaining destroyers away, we win the campaign in a single day. The Human ground forces will be forced to surrender once their bombardment support and all possibility of additional supplies and reinforcements getting to them are cut off. "

"Yes, that would do nicely," e-Lapeela said, sitting back in his chair and smiling.. "Imagine how the Humans will respond to that humiliation!"

"Yes, Admiral, provided we can best them given the limited number of ships currently at our command. But the force in transit to Mogo is the weakest in combat power and has the most valuable assets—the support echelon for the enemy fleet, as well as its commander and staff. If we destroy the force entirely, the remaining Human elements will be widely separated and without a unified command."

e-Lapeela looked away for a moment and shifted uncomfortably in his chair.

"Nuvaash, your choice torments me. I wonder, do you mean it to?"

Two hours later all of *Puebla*'s off-watch commissioned officers were assembled in the wardroom and all had read the sealed orders for the task force. They, along with three of the four senior chiefs, now shifted uncomfortably, casting furtive glances toward Sam who had tethered himself to the main mess table in the center of the room.

"Three things," he said, "one about home, one about the enemy, one about those leaked orders. Home first.

"The strike against Earth was bad, but it mostly hit military targets. Our orbital repair facilities are wrecked and they broke the Quito Needle."

He saw an uneasy stir run through the men and women.

"Civilian casualties were in the thousands, repeat, *thousands*. Not millions. I don't take that as good news, but it could have been a lot worse. But if they're going after Earth, it means they're after Humans, *all* Humans, and just because we *are* Humans. I want you to think about that.

"Second, the enemy.

"We've been interrogating the Varoki prisoners from the last fight, and we've gotten some intelligence about what's going on back on the Varoki home world. This is big, bigger than we thought. It's still just the uBakai formally at war with us, along with some renegade ships from two other Varoki navies, but a lot of Varoki countries are on the fence and ready to fall either way. If we pull back from K'tok, or let the uBakai take it from us, it'll signal all those fence-sitters that we're easy to push around and it's safe for them to join the war. In other words, if we back down or buckle here, the war gets bigger, not smaller. The next strike against Earth will be a lot worse. Not one step back, understood?

"The folks who put us here didn't know that's the situation we'd find ourselves in. They probably should have, it was their job to, but they didn't and here we are. Feeling bad about it isn't going to change anything. All we can do is deal with it. Our people are trying to get us some reinforcements, but until they do it's up to us to hold K'tok with what we've got here right now."

He looked around and saw grudging agreement. He didn't blame them for their reluctance. They'd have to be stupid or crazy to like the situation they were in. They needed to accept it, though, and the necessity for what they were doing. They needed to focus on the how, not the why. But the why wasn't just going to go away on its own.

"Okay, third thing. Has everyone read through the sealed orders, which apparently some idiot on *Cha-Cha* or *Vimy Ridge* leaked?"

Sam saw some nods and awkward looks. Senior Chief Pete Montoya, floating next to Rose Hennessey, his department boss, spat out, "Yes, sir," in an angry voice. Pete had a talent for anger. Well, anger wasn't necessarily a liability, provided it was pointed in the right direction.

"Good," Sam said. "So now you know what one admiral really thinks. I don't know how you felt, but reading it wasn't the proudest day of my career, especially thinking back to what that admiral said a few days earlier about why he sent us here and why we're fighting this war.

"Maybe sometimes they forget this, but admirals aren't the whole Navy. They're our bosses and when they give us an order we follow it. They get to do that. That's how the chain of command works. What they *don't* get to do is tell us why each one of us is fighting a war, especially when they aren't even here fighting it with us."

That got a reaction. Some of the younger officers grinned after their look of surprise disappeared. Rose Hennessey and Moe Rice exchanged a worried look. Sam knew this was dangerous ground, but he didn't care. The danger all around them, the nightmare they were headed into, made pissing off an admiral or two seem pretty tame by comparison.

"I don't get to do that either—tell you why you're fighting, I mean—even though I'm right here with you. All I can do is tell you why I'm fighting.

"I'm fighting for my life, because there's a bunch of Varoki who want to kill me and every other Human they can, just because we're human. What is it about being Human that would do that? What does it even *mean* to be Human? What do we have in common that makes us who we are?

He paused and held up his open hand for them to see. "Look at this. No claws, just these weak little fingernails that come off and hurt like hell if you scratch something too hard."

He opened his mouth wide and showed his teeth. "No fangs, either. We're not fast enough to catch anything small enough to kill and eat, and also not fast enough to get away from most animals big enough to kill and eat us. We are piss-poor predators and not even very good survivors—on our own.

"What have we got?" He patted his forehead with his palm. "We got this, a brain, and you know what this great big Human brain we've got mostly does? It figures out how to communicate with other Humans.

"That's our edge—other Humans. You drop a naked Human in the middle of a jungle, he ends up something's lunch. You drop *twenty* naked Humans in a jungle together, in a month or two they come out wearing animal skins, and a couple of them are probably pregnant."

That got some chuckles.

"The way we survive—the way we've *always* survived—is together. This lone wolf everyone-for-themselves fantasy you hear sometimes—how that's what we *really* are deep down inside—it's all crap. We live in families, in clans, in tribes. We divide ourselves up dozens of ways, but always into tribes. The tribe of the tac-heads, tribe of the snipes, the officers, the chiefs, the acey-deucies.

"One thing the Navy gets right is it puts the most important tribe front and center. The single most important unit in the US Navy, and probably every other Human navy, isn't the individual mariner or the division or the department or the task force or the fleet. It is the crew of a single vessel. Everything revolves around that and builds on it. I didn't always get that, but I do now."

He saw some nods following that.

"So what am I fighting for? The most important thing for me now is this crew I'm part of. I'm fighting for us. But that's not my only tribe. I have family back home—father, mother and younger brother—and I'm fighting for them.

"The US of NA is a tribe we all share, too. As countries go, ours isn't very old, just turned seventy last October 10th, but it's got a lot of history going back further than that. It's put together from three countries that got put together and almost taken apart themselves a few times. But we did get put together, and we've stuck so far. Some of our parents were born citizens of Mexico or Canada or the old USA. Most of our grandparents were, and can still remember those days, but for us that's just history. Our national motto says it all: *E Pluribus Unum*. It's Latin, means *from many, one.*

"The names of our boats in DesRon Two are like a history of where we come from.

Our division, DesDiv Three, had *Oaxaca, Tacambaro, Queretaro*, and *Puebla*. Those are the four decisive battles where Benito Juarez drove Maximilian and the Europeans out of Mexico permanently. I didn't know that until a few days ago, had to look it up. Mexico came together as an independent nation at those four battles.

"DesDiv Four had *Vicksburg, Champion Hill, Petersburg*, and *Shiloh*. They're named for four battles in a war fought to decide the future of the USA—not just its physical boundaries, but its soul, who we are, what we value most.

"DesDiv Five had *Vimy Ridge, Amiens, Arleux*, and *Canal du Nord*, four battles in World War I where Canadian soldiers went over the top for the first time as Canadians, instead of guys from a bunch of different provinces that happened to be next door to each other. *E pluribus unum.*

"We have four Earth nations in the fight, but I think it's about everyone back home. In a way, that's our tribe, too: Humanity. And I think that's where this fight is going, the Human race pulling together for a change, because—and make no mistake about this—we are *deep* in the jungle right now. But every instinct and racial memory we share trumpets to us how we get out of it: we get out *together*."

He saw a lot of nods now.

"All of our family histories are road maps of where we've been, and I think of where we're going. Who better to blaze this trail than the US Navy? *E pluribus unum*."

Sam paused and took a breath, knew he about to cross a line, but knew if he didn't it would be an act of cowardice.

"And I'll tell you something else: what some admiral sitting in some office on Bronstein's World says doesn't change one damned bit of that."

He dismissed them and sent them off to the crew to spread his message of determination mixed with quiet contempt for Admiral Cedrick Goldjune.

What he hadn't told them was that, by withdrawing the transports from K'tok and moving them out toward Mogo, the gas giant, Admiral Kayumati had deliberately "pulled a Cortez," as Atwater-Jones had described it to him yesterday.

Hernán Cortés had burned his ships when his small army arrived in the New World, so that retreat was no longer an option, and victory was their only way home. Kayumati had as much as burned the ships of the Combined Expeditionary Brigade down on K'tok, or at least moved those ships to where it would now take a couple weeks to turn them around and bring them back. Admiral Goldjune had ordered the brigade withdrawn, but too late. Withdrawing the brigade was no longer an option. Two thousand men and women of the Combined Expeditionary Brigade were stuck on K'tok, with no immediate way to get them off-planet.

Kayumati had made Admiral Goldjune and the Coalition hostage to those soldiers.

The leak of Goldjune's orders had probably sealed the deal. Sam hoped it had. No one's career would survive the loss of a full expeditionary brigade, especially Goldjune's since he'd dispatched the task force with such little apparent concern for its survival. That was now widely known. Only success could save him, and not a success which included two thousand ground troops in POW cages. Whatever forces the Coalition could scrape together wouldn't be launched on some glorious but disastrous Doolittle-style raid on the Varoki home world; they would have to concentrate on saving the Combined Expeditionary Brigade.

Sam knew there was no way he could have made the decision Kayumati had. He couldn't think of any other way Kayumati could have derailed Goldjune's plan, but he wasn't even sure it was Kayumati's place to do that. Of course, it might not have been Sam's and Bonaventure's and Cassandra's place to decide to leak the secret orders, but they had. That decision only put Admiral Goldjune on the spot, though. Kayumati's decision put the lives of two thousand men and women on the line.

Sam wasn't sure it was the right decision—right as in moral and honorable. But Kayumati had done it. Talk about taking initiative and responsibility! And as a reward, Kayumati would be branded a coward, or at best an incompetent fool. Sam shook his head. The guy had a lot more guts than Sam had credited him with, and was a lot more ruthless than his grandfatherly image suggested.

But none of that meant squat if the task group couldn't maintain its hold on K'tok orbital space until help arrived from Earth. If the time came when there was no Combined Expeditionary Brigade left on K'tok to rescue, Sam was pretty sure Admiral Goldjune's next order would be to avenge them. And then things would really go to hell.

CHAPTER THIRTY-FOUR

9 January 2134
(The next day) ***(nineteenth day in K'tok orbit)***

Nice speech, Bitka, Commodore Bonaventure told him early the next morning via tight beam commlink. They weren't holoconferencing, but Sam spoke with his helmet on and sealed anyway for privacy as he sat in the bridge command chair.

"Thank you, sir."

No, really. I mean, Admiral Godjune's going to shit bricks, but I'm playing it for every crew in the task group. Now we just wait and see what fish that grenade brings to the surface of the pond.

"Yes, sir. Just between you and me, what the hell was Admiral Goldjune thinking when he cut those orders?"

No clue, Bitka. Maybe they vacuum your soul out your ear right before they pin those stars on your collar.

Listen, this leak really is going to cause a shitstorm and I need to find out where it came from. Since my boat is one of the suspects, and since you're acting smart boss, it's your assignment. Find the leak and arrest whoever is responsible. Clear?

This was an order, and so there would be a permanent record of their exchange. It would be part of any subsequent investigation, which made Bonaventure's comment about the souls of admirals particularly interesting. Knowing he spoke on the record, Sam pretended to think for a moment before answering.

"I'll need your authorization to access the data files and comm logs on both *Oaxaca* and *Vimy Ridge.*

You have it.

"I'll do my best, sir. When do you want a report?"

An hour ago. Ops is sending over our whole log and data index now and I'll make sure Rocky does the same. Expedite. Hey, good speech.

The "investigation" took most of the rest of the morning. He pulled in Chief Adalina Gambara, acting head of the communication division, to help with sorting through the comm logs and interpreting the user tags on them. After three hours of painstaking and mind-dulling work, they had found exactly nothing. Sam had known all along they would not find anything, because they were looking in the wrong place. He did not say that to Gambara, however.

"Well, I'm stumped, sir," she said. "As near as I can tell, none of the transmitters on either boat sent a communication of any sort at the time the message packet showed up on the first comsat's log, nor was either data file copied at any time within days of the leak."

Sam looked at the smart surface of his desk and nodded.

"I don't see any other possible conclusion from this data, Chief. So how do you think it got sent? A private transmitter?"

"No way, sir! Both those boats had their full-spectrum passives on. They'd have detected any radiation passing through the hull, going in or out. Maybe we should be looking someplace else."

"Orders were only distributed to division commanders and above and those are the only two division leaders left here. No, I think we just bundle this up and submit it to the Commodore along with a report of our findings. You want to draft that? I'll sign it. At least we cleared him and Captain Rockaway."

Gambara looked doubtful, but Sam knew she had other work to do and so she nodded.

"Aye, aye, sir. I'll bang out a one-page summary report and send it for your signature."

"Thanks, Chief," he said and triggered the door for her. Once she left he pushed away from his desk and floated to the cabinet where he kept the bottle of bourbon Del Huhn had given him about a week earlier, although it now seemed like a month, maybe longer. The bottle was almost empty, about enough for one more drink. It wasn't quite lunch time yet but he siphoned the bourbon into a drinking bulb and headed back to his desk.

There were only two division lead boats surviving in the system, but there was also the wreck of *Champion Hill*, which had very briefly served as the lead boat of DesDiv Four after the First Battle of K'tok, when Juanita Rivera had been advanced in rank and command. The order was posted to her as a matter of course, since she had been added to the division commander distribution list. *Champion Hill* was now partially powered up, enough for life-support and control, and that included the communication and data retrieval systems.

Maybe when this was all over, someone else would be assigned to figure out where the leak came from, but only if the task group managed to hold out here. If they lost, everyone would have far bigger problems to deal with, and the evidence would probably be swept away in the defeat. If they looked hard enough, maybe they would find the record of a brief private (and unrecorded) audio conversation between Captain Bitka of *Puebla* and Captain Huhn of *Champion Hill*. And then maybe they would figure it out.

Maybe. Probably not.

Sam raised his drink bulb in a toast to his former captain and then drank the last of Del Huhn's bourbon.

Every afternoon Larry Goldjune met with several engineers, including Rose Hennessey, to try to solve the riddle of the uBakai jump scrambler. After lunch Sam decided to sit in on the meeting and found Goldjune and the engineers stumped, as they had been from the start.

"We've gone over it and over it," Goldjune said. "There's nothing there."

"So go over it again for me," Sam said. "Start with the ship profiles but let's talk about the drive manufacturers, too. I've got a feeling that might be important, but I can't put my finger on why."

Goldjune looked at Sam, his eyes full of defeat and regret. Sam knew he wanted to solve this last problem, get at least one thing right, but he couldn't. Goldjune shrugged and started.

"We lost six starships: two US cruisers, one Indian cruiser, one British transport, one Indian auxiliary, one French auxiliary. Eight starships survived the attack: six US, one Indian, one Nigerian. Surviving ship types were two cruisers, one command vessel, two transports, three auxiliaries. There's no pattern by nationality or ship type.

"Of the six starships that blew up, four had AZ Kagataan drives. But the British transport had AZ Techtragaan drives and *Bully Big Dick* had AZ Simki-Traak drives."

"Nope."

All the members of the working group turned to Moe Rice, drifting past with a clear-wrapped pita sandwich in one hand.

"We've got the tech readouts right here," Goldjune snapped. "As usual, you don't know what you're talking about."

Rice grabbed a bracket with his free hand, spun slowly around, and pushed himself back toward the table, his face dark. Goldjune started to unclip his tether but before Sam could say anything, Rice drawled.

"Sit down, bus driver."

Goldjune bristled but Sam put a restraining hand on his arm.

"Settle down, both of you. Moe, what makes you think *Bully* didn't have Simki-Traak drives?"

Without taking his eyes off of Goldjune's he spoke.

"'Cause I was on her when she went in for her final refit before we shipped out. You were too, Cap'n. We both transferred over to *Puebla* right after."

Sam nodded. They had.

"No offense, Moe, but you're a supply officer," Rose Hennessey said. "How would you know a Simki-Traak drive from any other?"

Moe finally broke eye contact with Goldjune and looked at Hennessey, his expression much less murderous. "Wouldn't know the difference if one bit me, but I can read a work order. All the work orders passed through my office, and I remember they didn't have enough Simki-Traak jump actuators at the orbital spacedock to give *Bully* a full set and backups. They did some quick control system modifications and fitted her with a drive set they had enough modules on hand for."

Sam felt a strange prickling sensation in his shoulders and up the back of his neck. He took a quick breath and let it out.

"AZ Kagataaan?" he said, already knowing the answer.

"Yup."

Sam's mind raced during the short glide through the central transit tube to his cabin: too much information, too soon, with too many implications to think through, and no time.

The common link was manufacturer—that much he was almost certain of. But that meant something else entirely. It meant Sam knew how the ECM missiles could remotely access a powered-down jump drive: a manufacturer's cheat code, just like his company used to open locked-up systems. But that meant something else. At least one jump drive manufacturer actually *had* cheat codes. If they all did, every jump drive in the *Cottohazz* was potentially a remotely triggered bomb.

It also meant that either one of the largest Varoki trading houses in the *Cottohazz* had decided to pick sides in a war, or its second-most-tightly-guarded secret—its cheat codes—had been compromised. Sam wasn't sure which was worse.

But, most tantalizing of all, if AZ Kagataan's *second*-most-tightly-guarded secret had been compromised, perhaps its *most*-tightly-guarded one could be as well: *how the jump drive worked.*

He sealed the door on his cabin and pinged the duty commtech.

Signaler Lincoln, sir.

"Lincoln, I need a tight beam holocon to the task force smart boss."

Very good, sir. Turn-around on that is going to run about three minutes.

Sam put his helmet on, opened the channel, and waited. It took almost five minutes before Cassandra appeared. She must have gone to one of *Pensacola*'s holosuites because he could tell from the way the neck ring of her shipsuit rested on her shoulders that she was not helmeted.

"Bitka. I wasn't expecting you so soon. Has something happened?"

Her holoimage froze as a still picture, as it did when long time delays were involved.

"You said to comm you if I came up with anything useful for fleet intelligence. Well, we figured out something important about how the jump drive scrambler works, or we're about ninety-five percent certain we did.

"We were stumped when the drives were from three different manufacturers, but it appears our common ship database is not up to date. I have found out that USS *Theodore Roosevelt* refitted with AZ Kagataan drives shortly before the deployment, which means every ship we lost had Kagataan drives with the single possible exception of HMS *Furious*. If our data base was wrong once, it can be wrong a second time. I thought you might be in a better position to track down a last-minute refit on a British vessel than I am."

Sam stopped and licked his lips, thinking through his next sentence carefully.

"Another thing. I know how it works. They're using the cheat code from the manufacturer, have to be. It's the only way into a powered-down system. I've got a feeling that's more of a political hot potato than I can handle, but it's probably right down your alley."

Sam triggered the image freeze and waited for the reply. The notion of Kagataan being in on this was too big for Sam to feel comfortable keeping to himself, but now that it was out there, what came next?. There'd be congressional hearings and God only knew what else, and that would just be the start. Cassandra was smart, though. If anyone could manage the information, she could.

Two minutes went by, then three, then four. After eleven minutes Atwater Jones's image unfroze, her face glowing with excitement and triumph.

"Brilliant! Bloody Brilliant, Bitka! Oh, I normally abhor alliteration. Ha! Well, I'll make an exception just this once. Your suspicion about HMS *Furious* was correct. Fortunately, none of our remaining cruisers have Kagataan drives, so we can start acting offensively again. I believe this has altered the operational battlescape, perhaps decisively. Oh, well done!

"And yes, I see what you mean about the cheat codes. It's the only way to break in, but I shudder to think what this will mean. You will be happy to know that I just sent off a jump courier missile with this intelligence in it, so they will know at fleet headquarters on Bronstein's World within hours."

She looked at his image and did not move, but he realized she had not frozen the image. She was instead simply regarding him. Knowing she couldn't see him, he smiled at her. Interestingly, she smiled at the same time and then froze the image. He laughed.

Sam unfroze his image and began transmitting, still smiling. "Understood and much appreciated. *Puebla* out."

He froze it again and waited for her sign-off. This time it came sooner, after no more than three minutes.

"Do take care of yourself Bitka, and if you have any other flashes of insight, I hope you can again—"

Sam heard the gong of general quarters in the background at her end and saw Cassandra react to it, eyes open wide in surprise.

"I don't . . . " she started, and then looked back at the holo-image of Sam, her face again composed. She picked up her helmet and made ready to clip it on. "We appear to be under attack. Best of luck to us as well, I suppose. And whatever happens, Bitka, remember: *Not one step back.*

"*Pensacola* out."

CHAPTER THIRTY-FIVE

10 January 2134
(the next day) ***(twentieth day in K'tok orbit)***

"Any news on the task force, sir?"

His commlink remained silent for a moment.

Total loss, Bonaventure answered. *All ID transponders dark.*

"*Pensacola* too?" Sam asked after swallowing hard.

Pensacola *too. Looks like the admiral bought it. That puts him in a pretty select group: Callahan, Scott, and now Kayumati, only three US admirals ever killed in ship-to-ship action. There may be some crew survivors, either in escape capsules or an airtight compartment in some of the wrecks, but they won't last long without a ship there to rescue them. Freeze to death within a day or two.*

There were a lot of people in the main body of the task force, over a thousand in the crews of all those ships. Sam had known a fair number on *Hornet*, including its skipper, Captain Albright, although none of them well. But when he thought about Cassandra Atwater-Jones—whom he had never actually met face-to-face—he felt a hollow feeling in his chest so sudden and so sharp he took a breath and checked his bio-monitor to make sure he was not having a heart attack. He wasn't, not in the medical sense.

He closed his eyes and took a deep breath.

"Enemy losses?"

uBakai hit them with eight cruisers and it looks like the task force took four down with them. Four jumped away about an hour ago. There are four cold hulks and a debris cloud still on their original course. They must have had more of those missile-packers with them. We're still going through what log recordings we got before everything went dark, but the task force got hit with mucho *missiles.*

"Four enemy cruisers left? I think we can handle four, sir, so they'll have to wait for reinforcements before they come here. Who's in charge, with the admiral dead?"

Some Nigerian rear admiral lower half—they call him a brigadier general—name of Irekanmi, flying his flag in NNS Aradu. *Next in line after him is British, Captain Ranjha in HMS* Exeter. *Irekanmi texted half an hour ago, said he'll get his cruisers here as soon as he can. They're outbound, about halfway between here and where the task force was destroyed. Between you and me, they're not likely to get here within much less than a week.*

"I'm suspicious of navies run by generals," Sam said.

Me too, but that's just between us, amigo.

Bonaventure broke the connection. Sam raised his helmet visor and turned to his left.

"Chief Gambara, get me all-boat."

"You're live, sir," she answered.

"All hands, this is the Captain. I just spoke with the commodore and I've got some bad news. The main body of the task force was hit by eight uBakai cruisers and every vessel was lost, including our sister-boat *Tacambaro*. Our folks took four cruisers down with them, but we still lost a lot of shipmates today.

"One thing's for sure: they'll be coming here next and looking for a fight. We're going to give 'em one. Carry on."

"Have you studied the damage assessment from our battle here?" the admiral asked.

Nuvaash gestured with the data pad in his hand.

"Yes, Admiral. More friendly losses than we anticipated—two of our cruisers destroyed and two with crippled jump drives—but still an overwhelming victory. Every enemy ship destroyed and we still have our flagship, and three other cruisers fully operational. I am uncertain that is sufficient force to crush the enemy at K'tok, but our object was decapitation, and in that we have succeeded."

The admiral nodded.

"Now we strike and finish this business. I have received word by jump courier that the Forward Striking Force, in transit back from Earth, will join us in two days.

"We will jump with the remaining ships to the rendezvous point and finish our repairs while we await them. The troop transports will accompany us on this next attack, which will be the final one.

"Meanwhile, the two cruisers with disabled jump drives will continue on their current course while shrouded. The debris cloud of our two destroyed cruisers will provide them with cover and they will appear to be derelicts from the battle. One additional day of preparation, once the Forward Striking Force joins us, will allow the two damaged cruisers to close on K'tok undetected. We will catch the enemy in a pincer and destroy them.

"In three days this phase of the campaign will be over, and the Humans will take care of the rest."

CHAPTER THIRTY-SIX

11 January 2134
(the next day) ***(twenty-first day in K'tok orbit)***

"Okay, sir, what are we looking at?" Sam asked.

"That's the debris cloud of the Varoki task force," Commodore Bonaventure said, "the wreckage left after their four operational cruisers jumped away."

Sam looked across at the other holoconference participant—Captain Sadie Rockaway, commanding USS *Vimy Ridge* as well as the battered DesDiv Five. This was really a conference between her and the commodore; Sam was here as the N-2 to provide staff support as necessary, although he also had the feeling Bonaventure had started thinking of Sam as his tactical advisor.

Sam knew Rockaway in the sense that he knew who she was and that she had a reputation as a solid boat skipper and division commander. Bonaventure was right; he'd have remembered her if he'd seen her before. She wasn't pretty so much as striking, or maybe impressive was the right word—an intelligent face now frowning in intense concentration, her brown hair pulled back severely completing the effect—definitely no nonsense. Her nickname was "Rocky," and Sam didn't think it was meant ironically.

The three sat in a shallow U-shape, the commodore between them. In the middle floated the virtual image of a circular flat sensor display, greatly enlarged to make it easier to study.

"What are those glowing dots?" Rockaway asked. Sam looked back at the screen display. There *were* four faintly glowing dots in the midst of the tangle of wreckage.

"Radiators," the commodore answered. "Somebody deciding to trickle charge their power rings, probably getting ready for a fight in a couple days. Those derelicts are still coasting on their original course, the one they were on when they hit the task force. Since it was almost an exactly reciprocal to the task force's course, they'll end up passing very close to K'tok."

"But they aren't derelicts, are they?" Sam said.

"Two of them are, two aren't. I'm pretty sure you're looking at the glow of the dorsal radiators of two active uBakai cruisers, two radiators per ship. They're at very low power and have their shrouds deployed so we can't pick them up from here. We'd never have seen them at all except for Robinette's sensor probes. They don't just avoid the back-clutter, they're looking down past the occluding angle of the thermal shrouds."

Sam leaned back in his bridge command chair and just thought for a while.

"Bitka, you got something going on upstairs," the commodore said. "I can practically hear the gears grinding. Spill it."

"Well, sir, everyone does things for a reason. I'm just thinking what theirs was. Might be because those two cruisers have banged-up jump drives. Or it might be they're just being extra-cagey. You know, jump away with four ships and we assume those are the only ones left operational, which is exactly what we did."

Clever boots, these uBakai.

"Either way, two ships drifting into our area of operations undetected could give us a hell of a surprise, but we could probably deal with it. Now, if they hit us with their other force at the exact same time as these guys show up . . . "

"Yeah," Sadie Rockaway said, "all our eyes are on the attack force. Then these guys playing dead hit us from behind."

Bonaventure nodded. "Makes good sense. What do we do about it?"

"Our boats end up pointing about the right direction for a shot at them a couple times a day," Sam said, "once per orbit. It won't take much of an adjustment to make it a straight shot. Next orbit have a boat pump out . . . oh, four missiles. The uBakai ground stations won't pick up something that small. The missiles will be cool all the way, so the uBakai will never see them coming unless they go active—which would kind of defeat the purpose of the whole playing dead thing. But we need to time the arrival of those missiles so it's just when the uBakai are getting into attack range themselves."

"Sure-sure," Bonaventure said, nodding vigorously. "Because they'll time their main attack to match that."

"Yes, sir, I think they will. Let's not give them any chance to call off the attack. We hit their main force with every boat."

"I don't know about that," Sadie Rockaway said. "If they're going to coordinate two attacks, why not three?"

"What do you mean, Rocky?" the commodore asked.

"From what I understand, the leatherheads on the ground have been real quiet ever since *Puebla* gave 'em their come-to-Jesus moment last week, and that's even after they got more reinforcements. If I were going to make a push on the ground, I'd do it when I figured the deep space fight would pull the orbital bombardment boats away."

Sam nodded to himself. Rockaway was right—the uBakai would be stupid to let that chance go by, and so far they hadn't been stupid. Even if the Human task group took out every uBakai ship hitting them, if the ground brigade got overrun in the process, the uBakai won.

"Boss, you need to let me take them on with the five coil-gun boats," Rockaway said. "You run the bombardment division and keep the leatherheads on the ground honest."

Bonaventure frowned in thought, studying the virtual display of the two uBakai wrecks and two Trojan horses coasting silently through deep space toward them. Finally he shook his head.

"Rocky, I think your read of the situation is right on the money, but I'm going to lead the attack force, not you. You send *Arleux* down and take over my low orbit slot."

"Boss, don't do this. *Cha-cha* doesn't have a coil gun. At least *Arlo* has that much going. You know we need every coil gun we can get when the uBakai show up."

Arlo, Sam knew, was the nickname for USS *Arleux*.

Bonaventure squinted at her holo-image and cocked his head a bit to the side as if in curiosity.

"Did *Arlo* get those three radiators repaired and maybe discover four point-defense lasers in their parts locker?"

Rockaway leaned back and the intense look of determination on her face gave way to surprise.

"They've got one of the radiators lashed back together."

"*One.* Rocky, you know Bitka's attack plan: balls to the wall with all drives to get in close, and then laser them to death. *Arlo* can't go balls-to-anything, and half its lasers are wrecked.

"Your own boat, *Vimy Ridge*, is down half its power ring, isn't it? You've only got half as much stored power as the other boats, which means you can either get a one-minute burn from your MPD thrusters *or* you can fire your lasers and coil gun. So what's it going to be? You going to fall out of formation, or are you going to run your power ring dry and not have any laser juice?"

"I . . . sir, I can still accelerate for thirty seconds on MPD and have a good power reserve," she answered. "I don't think we'll need any more than that."

"What if you do? *Cha-cha* doesn't have a coil gun, but it's got a full power ring, all its radiators, and all eight point defense lasers. Here's what I want to do; you tell me if I'm crazy when I'm finished.

"When the main uBakai attack force shows up, we're going after it in two divisions of three boats each. I'll lead DesDiv Three and you follow with DesDiv Five, although we'll do a little bit of boat swapping to make things work. I'm taking *Petersburg* with me and turning *Toro* over to you.

"That gives me *Cha-cha*, *Puebla*, and *Petersburg*. I'll have three boats with full power rings and a full set of radiators, so we'll be able to run faster and harder than you will. Two of them will have coil guns, which will be enough. We'll go in first, plow the road, cut them up as much as we can, and maybe break up their formation.

"You'll follow with *Vimy Ridge, Can-can* and *Toro*. *Can-can* is missing her coil gun but she's your powerhouse boat other than that—all her radiators, power rings, and lasers. You'll still have two coil guns, but they're both in boats down to half their power ring, so don't use your MPD drives for that last sprint. You'll drop back a little but that's okay. You come in behind us and slam them hard while they're still reeling from our attack. We cut them up, you put them on the canvas.

"Like I said, move *Arlo* down here to take over low orbit along with the wreck of *Champion Hill*. The *Hill* can take the saddle rig and handle bombardment. *Arlo's* coil gun is our last line of defense in case anything gets through us.

"So what do you think?"

Rockaway sat motionless for a while and then nodded her head.

"I think I wish I had both my power rings operational. Then maybe you'd let me ride up front with the adults."

"Nope. You're senior after me. It makes sense to keep us separated. Bitka, it's your tactics so I guess you're on board?"

"Yes sir. We'll need to convert a bunch more block fours to sunflowers if they have many more of those salvo cruisers. Also, Lieutenant Filipenko, my Tac Boss, made a real good recommendation. Since the salvo cruisers flood our zone with missiles, we need to reprogram the sunflowers to engage thirty targets each, not double-tap fifteen of them like the original program did. Statistically we'll get better results."

"Can we swing that in the time we've got?"

"Yes, sir. Chief Menzies, my resident missile genius, is working out the programming now."

Bonaventure looked from one to the other.

"Okay, it's settled then. It looks like we have a couple days to get ready, given the closing rate of those two supposedly dead cruisers. Sadie, have *Can-can* off-load most of its missiles to you and *Petersburg*, as many as they can handle. Anything left pass to *Puebla*.

"We've got a good plan based on what we think they can do, but you know what they say: the enemy gets a vote. In this case I don't thing they've stopped voting, so stay alert, ready for anything.

"We'll stand maneuvering watches today. Try to get as much sack time for your crews as you can. Tomorrow we'll go to Readiness Two. *Vaya con Dios, compañeros.*"

For perhaps the tenth time Vice-Captain Takaar Nuvaash, Speaker for the enemy, contemplated the enemy. In this case "the enemy" was a single craft of the variety the Humans called a destroyer rider, pitted in a hopeless struggle against the salvo cruiser KBk Zero Two B, but a struggle which had, inexplicably, ended with the destruction of the uKa-Maat warship. The ground station which had recorded the battle had—because of the rotation of K'tok and the courses of the two vessels—been unable to view the final act of the fight, but they had this recording of the minutes leading up to it. Transmission of the report had then been delayed for almost an entire day due to a mechanical failure in the long-range tight beam transmitter. Now it was here.

The Human ship made no change in course until KBk Zero Two B had closed to well less than thirty thousand kilometers. When KBk Zero Two B launched its first spread of missiles, the enemy vessel turned its bow and fired a missile of its own. One missile. The detonation of that missile obscured the sensor picture and little was clear after that. The one thing which the thermal imagery confirmed, however, was that the Human ship had accelerated *toward* KBk Zero Two B.

Why would the Human captain accelerate *toward* the missile cruiser? If he accelerated away, it would give his point defense lasers more time to engage the swarm of missiles targeted on him, while accelerating toward them gave him less time. It materially reduced his chance of survival.

Did he think the missiles were decoys? Did he think the uKa-Maat ship had expended all of its missiles and was now vulnerable to a counterstrike? Was he simply suicidal?

Unfortunately, the combination of the warhead detonation and the rotation of K'tok deprived Nuvaash of a clear record of how the Human ship destroyed the Varoki cruiser, and how it managed to survive the encounter. Survive it certainly had, as it was later positively identified in orbit. KBk Zero Two B had apparently inflicted no damage on the Human squadron at K'tok, which Nuvaash had difficulty understanding. By rights it should have overwhelmed them, one ship after another.

Nuvaash! Where are you? he heard the admiral's voice sound in his head. He looked at the chronometer on the wall—ten minutes late for his briefing!

"My apologies, Admiral. I was reviewing the new record of the battle over K'tok. I will join you immediately."

Nuvaash walked briskly toward the admiral's office but knew the briefing was a waste of both their times. The report from the K'tok ground station added nothing substantive to their understanding of how the battle had played out. The timing of their own attack was fixed: two days hence, because that was when the hidden ships would drift into attack range.

The four fully operational cruisers of the original attack force, as well as the eight new cruisers of the Forward Attack Force—two of which were uKaMaat salvo cruisers and three of which were their new uSokan allies—would constitute the main striking force. Twelve cruisers, including three salvo cruisers, was the most powerful force they had yet managed to assemble. The Human ships at K'tok were outnumbered, outclassed, and probably damaged from previous battles. The two ambush ships, coasting in as part of the debris cloud from the previous fight, were not necessary, but would certainly clinch the issue.

The only tactical modification Nuvaash would recommend was a longer, more careful approach run. They needed range to take advantage of their superior missile throw-weight. Furthermore, several of the Forward Strike Force cruisers had sustained damage in the fighting around Earth—none of it crippling, but some caution was warranted. But beyond that, they did not know enough to make more elaborate planning sessions productive.

No, there was nothing to be accomplished in meetings and briefings between now and then, but the admiral insisted. Nuvaash would give his empty intelligence briefing and then listen to e-Lapeela's increasingly lengthy and strident harangues about how the Human morale must have been broken by the destruction of their main fleet. It must have been. Everything the admiral knew about the weak, easily excited, and easily cowed Humans told him so. They could not stand up against the sort of losses the uBakai had inflicted on them, battle after battle. They could not.

Nuvaash would nod.

Captain, I've got a tight beam from Commodore Bonaventure.

"Okay, Krammer, patch it through."

Sam sat back in the zero-gee chair in his cabin and stretched.

"I'm on, sir."

Bitka, got some news from General Irekanmi. His two cruisers were on almost the same vector as the task force so yesterday they tried that uBakai trick of an in-system jump and got close enough to rendezvous with the wreckage. They went in and found survivors, fair number of them. It looks as if they can get one of the transports repaired, or at least air-tight and powered up.

Sam felt some of the blood drain from his face. He swallowed.

"Any word on . . . the admiral?"

Admiral's confirmed dead, but some of his staff survived. We'll have a list later, but I asked: the Red Duchess made it. Figured you'd like to know.

Sam laughed.

"Thank you, sir. You might contact a Limey colonel named Freddy Barncastle in the infirmary at the needle highstation. I think he'd probably appreciate the news as well."

Sam cut the connection and smiled, shook his head in wonder, and wiped his eyes.

CHAPTER THIRTY-SEVEN

13 January 2134
(two days later) ***(twenty-third day in K'tok orbit)***

"Sir, the boat is at readiness condition two, MatCon alpha, in formation with the Lead Division. No orbit change since the last watch change. Reactor on standby, power ring fully charged, shroud retracted, sensors active."

"Very good, Lieutenant Filipenko, I relieve you. Why don't you just slide over into the Tac One chair?"

Filipenko did so as Sam strapped himself into the command chair on Puebla's main bridge. To make way for Filipenko, Chief Patel moved from Tac One down to the Tac Two chair, but Sam stopped him from strapping in.

"Chief, may as well take a break, get a coffee or something. Use the officers' wardroom. Tell the steward I said it was okay,"

"But what if something happens, sir?"

"Well, your new battle station is at Tac One on the auxiliary bridge, right down the corridor from the wardroom. Something happens, Lieutenant Goldjune will need you there right away."

Patel's expression soured at the mention of Goldjune, but then a different look came over his face as he realized Sam was telling him something *would* happen, and soon. He looked around the bridge: Marina Filipenko's battle station was Tac One and he saw other crew who were supposed to be off duty but had drifted idly to their battle stations. He nodded in understanding.

"Okay, sir. I guess a cup of officer coffee would hit the spot." He started for the hatch.

Sam sat quietly after Patel left. He watched the bridge crew going over their checklists, making sure instruments were calibrated, or in some cases just reading from their monitors or viewer glasses. Ensign Barb Lee at Maneuvering One, Mohana Bargava at Two, Chief Gambara in the communication chair, Ron Ramirez at Tac Three and Elise Delacroix down in the starboard pit, at Tac Four. Only Tac Two and the Boat Status chair in the port pit sat empty. Jerry Robinette would have been back in the auxiliary bridge even if he had survived, but Sam felt his absence anyway.

"Robinette turned out pretty well," Sam said to Filipenko. "You did a good job bringing him along. Too bad."

She nodded but didn't say anything and the bridge became silent for a while except for the occasional hum of a servo motor as someone repositioned their workstation. Chief Joe Burns came through the hatch and strapped himself into Tac Two.

"Wish I had a cigar," Marina Filipenko said after a minute or so. Several of the bridge crew turned and looked at her.

"What?" she said.

"Never figured you for a cigar girl, that's all," Barb Lee said and smiled her nervous bird smile.

Sam noticed Delacroix's eyes were closed and her head moved rhythmically forward and back as she listened to music, apparently through her commlink.

"What are you listening to, Delacroix?" Sam asked.

She turned to him, surprised.

"Oh, it's a demo collection by Joyce's . . . by Chief Menzies' band."

"She's got a band?" Barb Lee asked. "That's *thanda!*"

"Oh, yes, ma'am, and they're really good! They're on hold now, because of the deployment, you know. The rest of the band's back on Earth. But she does most of the writing and scoring."

"What kind of music?" Sam asked.

Delacroix hesitated, maybe looking for words to describe it, words Sam would understand.

"It's sort of a fusion of post-lyric-Dadaism and *carnaval noir*, sir, with some retro-*mechnod* themes down underneath."

"Oh," Sam said. "Um . . . I was really into *mechnod* when I was in college."

She smiled politely and respectfully. "Yes, sir."

"Well, carry on Delacroix."

She turned back to her workstation and Sam saw Marina Filipenko smiling beside him.

"Did I get really old and somehow not notice?" Sam asked her softly.

"Captain, I've got a hail from the pennant," Gambara called out, her voice suddenly businesslike. "Tight beam for all captains."

Show time!

Sam gestured for Gambara to open the channel. "This is Bitka. I'm on."

The other captains reported in rapid succession.

We're getting close, Bonaventure said. *The cruiser-launched sensor probe above the plane just picked up the thermal signature of a formation of hostile ships out past the asteroids. The system primary blocks our line of sight to them but the sensor probe is far enough off-axis from us to have a view of them.*

The good news is we can calculate their vector and if they're planning on doing a close pass-by of K'tok, we can figure at least the corridor they've got to come along when they jump. It looks like they'll break J-space almost straight above the north pole of K'tok and come right down, same way as usual. Since our two bombardment boats are in equatorial orbits, this overhead approach will give the uBakai a clear shot at both of them for most of their run in. I'm sending the numbers for their approach corridor now.

Bitka, Wu, we're going to revector the Lead Division to run right up that corridor, and as soon as we're in the pipe and up to our intercept velocity I want you to poop out two missiles each right back up their expected course line. I don't know how close those will be when they exit J space, or even if they'll keep the same vector, but I'm willing to invest four of our missiles in maybe screwing them up right out of the gate.

Rocky, you follow with your division, but give us some room, about a thousand klicks.

You said that was the good news, sir, Sadie Rockaway said. *Is there some bad news?*

Bonaventure paused for a moment before answering.

Well, yes. First thing is they're far enough away, all the way across the star system, there's a fifteen-minute lag from the time what we're looking at happens to when we see it here. So they could alter their vector, accelerate for fifteen minutes, and then jump, and they'd be on top of us before we saw them light off their thrusters.

Second thing is, there aren't four cruisers in their strike package. We knew they'd get reinforcements, but it looks like there are twelve cruiser-sized thermal signatures, and a couple great big ships accompanying them. I think they're bringing their transports along this time.

Oh my God!

That was someone else whose voice he didn't recognize, one of Rockaway's skippers. Twelve cruisers against six beat-up destroyers. Sam felt his face flush and he felt slightly dizzy.

An hour later, most of it spent under acceleration, the Lead Division's orbital vector had been bent to line up with the incoming uBakai fleet and in the process had increased to fifteen kilometers per second. Now the three boats accelerated under a continuous one gee. All acceleration had been by their direct fusion drives. Detection was not a problem and each boat had to keep its power ring at full charge as long as possible. After another twenty minutes Bonaventure ordered them to cut their drives and coast at a respectable twenty-seven kilometers per second. *Puebla* and *Petersburg* then each fired two missiles.

"Sir, the missiles we launched two days ago, the ones out looking for those uBakai Trojan horses, just went active," Chief Burns reported.

"Make sure *Cha-cha* knows," Sam ordered. Then he loaded the missile telemetry and the live feed from the high sensor platform onto his own display and watched the first two missiles engage and hit the two uBakai ships. Twenty seconds later the second pair of missiles hit the wrecks again, but the high sensor platform made it clear both uBakai ships had been gutted the first time.

Poor bastards, Sam thought. There'd be survivors in some of the compartments of those ships, or in escape capsules, but nobody was coming to save them. Well, actually their odds weren't that bad, come to think of it. Their course would make a close pass-by to K'tok in a day or so, and once those twelve uBakai cruisers coming in dealt with *Puebla* and the other destroyers—which was the odds-on favorite outcome—they could go looking for survivors of their other cruisers.

"Won't the uBakai call off the attacks?" Gambara asked. "They'll know their ships are dead when they stop reporting,"

"They'll know in about fifteen minutes," Sam answered. "Or as soon as they emerge from J-space, at which point it will be too late. The sword of light-speed delay cuts both ways."

Privately, he wished they *would* call off the attack. In a few more days their own two cruisers would be here. That would make the odds a little better. He didn't think the uBakai would blink, though, even if they knew they'd lost their big surprise. Whoever was running this show didn't seem to care much about losses. He just kept throwing ships at them, and then more ships.

"Multiple contacts!" Burns shouted.

Sam turned his display to long range and saw the cluster of contacts, straight ahead. The uBakai hadn't changed their vector! They were coming out right where Bonaventure wanted them.

CHAPTER THIRTY-EIGHT

13 January 2134
(minutes later) ***(twenty-third day in K'tok orbit)***

"Fifteen distinct contacts," Burns said, his voice now under control. "Bearing forty-seven degrees relative, angle on the bow five degrees, range twenty-four thousand seven hundred, closing at forty-seven klicks a second."

Sam punched the general quarters alarm, although he imagined that every key position was already manned. Every bridge position was.

"Where are our missiles?"

"Seventeen thousand from target and closing," Burns answered. "They will hit the detonation envelope in two hundred seconds."

"Incoming text from *Cha-cha*, sir," Chief Gambara said, her voice tense. "Text reads, 'Launch sunflowers at mark plus twenty seconds . . . Mark.'"

Sam started his countdown timer.

"Captain, Sunflower One is hot," Filipenko reported. "Sunflower Two is in the ready rack."

"Very well, fire when the time expires. Then follow with a second sunflower and switch to standard Block Fours, four missiles in succession as fast as we can load them. Then check firing."

"Two sunflowers followed by Four Block fours. Aye aye, sir. "

Sam's commlink vibrated and he heard the ID tag for Larry Goldjune.

Captain, all battle stations are manned and ready.

"Thank you, Mister Goldjune."

Sam cut the connection and then felt the shudder as *Puebla* fired its first sunflower. He looked at his hand and was surprised it did not tremble. He felt calm, almost detached, but his mind was fully engaged. He worked through the numbers of the closing problem in his head and then turned to Gambara.

"Give me all-boat."

When she gave him the thumbs up he took a breath and then started.

"All hands, this is the captain. You just felt us firing our first sunflower and you'll feel more pretty soon. Here's the situation.

"The uBakai decided to emerge from J-space further from K'tok than they have before and at a lower velocity, so they'd have an hour or so of gliding in to get ready. The commodore figured out what they were up to, and he has us on a reciprocal course. We're about a quarter as far away from them as they planned and are closing two and a half times as fast as they anticipated, so there are probably some pretty excited leatherheads over there right now.

"We have four birds out there in the lead and we're coming up on the two-minute mark before they get to detonation range. We're not counting on a lot from them, but we might get lucky.

"We're about three to five minutes from our first sunflowers being in range of their missiles. It depends on when they actually fire them, which they haven't done yet. They may still be trying to man their battle stations—"

"New contacts," Burns called from Tac Two. "Small, hot, and lots of them, accelerating from the bandits."

Finally the uBakai were reacting. Sam felt the shudder as their second Block Four left the coil gun. With *Petersburg* firing as well, that made four sunflowers and Four Block fours on the way. He muted the all-boat channel.

"Lieutenant Filipenko, iris valves open and guns up. Chief Burns, what's the count?"

"It's a raggedy-ass salvo, sir. Some of their ships are still firing, but I've got forty-three birds so far."

Forty-three and more coming! That meant at least two salvo cruisers, possibly more. He triggered all-boat again.

"Okay, the uBakai are awake: over forty missiles coming our way.

Things are going to get pretty busy up here, and everything will happen very fast, but we all knew this was coming. This is what we planned for, and what we trained for.

"I know two things for certain. First, we're all going to die some day and no power in the universe can prevent that. But second, no power in the universe says we have to die *today*.

"So everyone do your jobs and remember the wrecks still orbiting K'tok. This is where we even the score. I'll talk to you again in about ten minutes. Good luck to us all. Captain out."

Yeah, he thought, *I'll talk to you in ten minutes if we're still alive.* At this closing velocity, ten minutes would decide everything.

Sam cut the connection and looked at the swarm of tiny luminous dots on his display gaining clarity as the active sensors formed a better picture of their sizes and trajectories. He was again surprised at how calm he felt—alert, concentrated, but without any sensation of anxiety.

"Captain, they've got so many point defense lasers out there, our four initial missiles aren't going to do anything," Marina Filipenko said from the seat to his right. "We're about one minute from our missiles being in detonation range, so the uBakai will open up on them any second. Let me fire one of them now, use the heat flare and radiation to shield the others until maybe they can get in closer."

"Do it," Sam ordered. He saw the flare on his display instantly. The signatures of the uBakai cruisers blurred and the three other leading block four missiles disappeared into the cloud.

"Incoming text from Commodore Bonaventure," Gambara said. "'Interogatory what happened.'"

"Send: Tac Boss had brilliant idea will explain later."

If there is a later.

"What else, Filipenko? What else have you been thinking but were too shy to say?"

She threw him a quick look, eyes wide with surprise.

"Well . . . I think we should let our first pair of sunflowers coast past the firing point and take out their first wave of missiles with our second pair. Set the first pair to auto-engage but after a time delay."

"Why?"

"So when they fire, they'll be further along and their debris cloud will get us that much closer before the uBakai can engage."

"Gambara, comm the commodore and patch him through to Filipenko. Marina, you've got about twenty seconds to sell your idea."

As Filipenko frantically explained her idea to the commodore, Sam saw the flare of one of their leading missiles firing after passing through the debris cloud. The uBakai must have taken out the other two with lasers before they detonated, but one made it.

"That had to hit somebody," Burns said. "Coming up on the firing threshold for the first sunflowers."

"Filipenko?" Sam asked. She held up one finger for a moment, clearly listening to her commlink, and then grinned and nodded.

"Aye aye, Commodore!" She began typing new instructions into her workstation and spoke to Sam without taking her eyes from her display. "We're going to try it."

We have to go for every edge we can find, Sam thought. *There are too many of them to play it safe. There is no safe.*

Things began happening very quickly. The second pair of sunflowers fired, blanking everyone's sensors, which was the signal for all three lead boats to go to full acceleration with both drives. Rockaway's Trailing Division just used its fusion thrusters, which meant the other three started pulling ahead, adding an extra five meters per second per second to their velocities. For thirty seconds all conversation stopped as every crewperson on all three lead boats was forced back into their acceleration racks with a force of two gees. Then the MPD thrusters cut out to save juice for the lasers, but the direct fusion drives maintained a steady one and a half gee acceleration.

"Guns up, small targets. Coil gun, commence firing block fours, cyclic rate," Sam ordered.

"Small targets, breaking through debris field!" Burns reported, and then the bridge became a bedlam of voices.

"ATITEP engaging. That's a kill!"

"Who's got the one at three thirty?

"Lead sunflowers fired, plowing the road."

"*Cha-cha's* been hit!"

"Penetrating first debris field," Sam added to the cacophony. "Switch ATITEP to large target profile."

"There's a cruiser! Burn him!"

Sam saw a larger image take shape on his display, emerging from the background clutter and heat, and then it grew suddenly bright—a heat spike from some sort of explosion.

"Hit!

"Another hit. Another! Take that, you sons of bitches!"

"Incoming laser fire. Mount five is off-line."

"Hit on *Petersburg*. Lost her tag!"

The tactical display on his workstation, even at one more zoom of resolution, made little sense. There were too many nuclear weapons detonating in too small a space, too many metallic objects reflecting radar beams, too much electromagnetic noise. *Puebla's* deadly lasers blowing holes in uBakai ships, as the range dropped to less than four thousand kilometers, showed as bright thin lines with targeting tags floating nearby, but none of the enemy laser shots, or those from the other friendly boats, showed. Even without them, it was hard for Sam to imagine any boat or ship passing through this region of fire and surviving unscathed. As he watched, one of the uBakai ships flared and then became two smaller targets, drifting slowly apart.

"We cut that bastard in two!" someone yelled.

Puebla lurched hard to the side and the bridge suddenly went dark. He felt his heart race and panic close his throat, choking off his breath. Someone screamed.

This is it! Sam thought. *This is how I die, terrified and in the dark.*

Then the dim blue emergency lighting came on and the tactical displays began rebooting. Sam looked around at the men and women on the bridge, some trying to regain their composure and reassume their battle mask of blank unemotional concentration which had vanished in the darkness, others already focused on their work stations. Sam took a deep, shuddering breath and triggered his commlink.

"Goldjune, have you still got power in aux?"

Yes, sir. We have control. You want to take it back?

"Not ready yet. Carry on for now. Continue engaging the enemy," Sam said and cut the commlink. He scanned the bridge. "Everyone, get your stations up and running. What's the damage?"

"Sir, multiple small laser hits and one major hit aft of frame seventy," the engineering petty officer at the boat status chair said. "Aft power coil is dead. MatCon Alpha-Zulu: we're leaking lots of hydrogen and atmosphere. Starboard missile room is MatCon Victor. PDL mounts three and five not responding. Active radar and HRVS optics down. Oh shit! We lost radiators two and three."

That was bad news. The boat had two emergency sodium heat sinks which could absorb some of the excess, but Sam would have to cut back to half power shortly or convert the stern half of the boat to glowing, molten metal.

Sam looked at his tactical display as it came back online. *Puebla's* marker stood clear in the center of it but everything around it was blurred and indistinct, reduced almost entirely to passive infrared detection in an environment choked with hot wreckage, accelerating ships, and cooling plasma.

"Have we got a coil gun?"

"Affirmative."

"Sir we are passing the enemy squadron," Burns reported. "Range one thousand one hundred, now opening. Look there! Three large contacts, bearing two-eight-four, angle on the bow one five six and dropping fast."

Sam pinged Goldjune.

"Lieutenant, kill our thrust. Turn the boat one-eighty and give them one last Block Four missile. I think we're about to pass their transports. Rake them with the lasers until they pass out of range and hit them with whatever block fours you can. You've got about a minute to get it off before they're down the road and see you later. And get us a sensor probe out there with an active radar on it as soon as the Block Fours detonates."

Aye aye, sir.

Sam drew another long breath. He heard the single klaxon for lateral acceleration and in moments the boat started rotating. Most of the bridge stations were back up and running but he decided to let Goldjune run the boat, at least for the moment. With the two forces having passed in opposite directions, there was little they could do to each other until they had modified their vectors. For a few minutes Sam could take stock and find out the condition of his boat and the task group.

"Trailing Division is engaging sir," Chief Burns reported. "Can't make out—damn! Somebody just blew up."

Sam saw the flare on his own screen, even through the clutter of hot wreckage and detonating nuclear warheads.

"Gambara, make to pennant: We are operational. Advise next maneuver. Signed Bitka.

"Engineering, get me as detailed a damage report as you can manage. Weapons, power, maneuvering, and life support, in that order. Somebody get me a crew casualty count.

"Burns, who's still alive out there? Can you tell?"

"*Cha-Cha*, and us, and a shitload of leatherheads, plus whoeveer's still alive from the Trailing Division.Can't tell yet. *Petersburg* is gone. At least one of the leatherheads is too."

"Ought to be," Sam said. "Somebody cut him in half."

"Captain," Gambara broke in, "*Cha-cha* text signals to us and *Vimy Ridge*: Commodore Bonaventure killed in action. Interrogatory who in command. Signed, Chen, Lieutenant Commander."

Shit! Bonaventure dead?

"Trailing Division's emerging from the clutter, sir," Burns reported. "I've got transponder tags for *Vimy Ridge* and *Canal du Nord*. Looks like *Toro* didn't make it."

"Gambara, give me a tight beam to Commander Rockaway on *Vimy Ridge*."

When she nodded he opened the channel.

That you, Bitka?

"Affirmative, ma'am. Looks like you're in charge. I'm down two radiators, so I can't make much acceleration, but I've got power, atmosphere, and at least some weapons. What shape are you in?"

A power spike pushed the reactor to standby and we don't have enough juice left in our one power ring to restart the reaction. We're floating cold, living off the LENR generators and whatever we've got in the ring. Lost our coil gun and some other things, but power's our big problem right now. Chen, Swanson, are you on?

This is Chen, Ma'am. I'm on.

Swanson here.

Chen, what shape's your boat?

Still assessing, ma'am, but for sure we lost the bridge and shroud, our forward power ring, five laser mounts, and three of our four radiators.

Swanson, how about you?

We are coasting dark, ma'am. We took a major hit aft and I have no contact with engineering and no power aside from nine percent banked in my power ring. I am still trying to assess the extent of the damage, but it doesn't look good.

Okay, Rockaway said. *My sensor suite's mostly broke-dick-no-workee. Anybody have a read on the bad guys?*

"I've got a sensor probe live," Sam said. "Looks as if we got at least one of them—two if that was a ship blowing up back when you cut through them—and damaged the rest. We also took a bite out of a couple transports there at the end. Nine of the cruisers and two transports are still generating power, but we haven't got a handle on how banged up they are. What are your orders, ma'am?"

Sam listened to the soft crackle of static for several seconds as Rockaway thought that through.

Sam slid down the faceplate of his helmet so the crew couldn't hear his conversation. No telling where this could end up.

Huh. I just got an encrypted broad beam text from some admiral named Crutchley, commanding the forward squadron of a relief force from Earth. They broke J-space about fifteen minutes ago but the broad beam just got here.

Sam did some quick mental calculations. "That puts them about three hundred million kilometers out, huh? Their astrogators sure weren't taking any unnecessary risks, were they?"

Peacetime habits die hard, Bitka, much harder than flesh and blood mortals. They haven't learned that yet but they will, soon enough. At least they're not being stingy with reaction mass. They're giving us a one gee continuous acceleration for twenty-four hours, with a mid-course flip and deceleration at the end, so they'll be here in about five days.

"One gee? Well, I wouldn't want anyone to be uncomfortable."

Reaction mass, Bitka. They aren't going to find any around here, so they'll have to revector to Mogo. I figure it's nice of them to stop off here first. I sent a sitrep to General Irekanmi earlier. Just got his reply. Quote: Reinforcements on the way. Act at your discretion. Unquote.

My discretion. Goddamn, I love my job, she said, her voice heavy with sarcasm.

"Yeah, I can't believe they're paying us," Sam answered with a laugh. "Who wouldn't do this for free?"

What kind of guy laughs at a time like this? he wondered. Maybe somebody half-crazy with relief and surprise that he was still alive.

Chen and Swanson said nothing.

Okay, I really hate to say this, Rockaway said, *but I’m supposed to act at my discretion, and my discretion tells me we’ve done everything here we can. Our main priority now is saving the boats and crews we’ve got left. I’ll tight beam Kropotkin on* Arlo *to recover the orbital EVA crews and prepare to pull out. Can* Champion Hill *maneuver, Bitka?*

“They claimed they can. As beat up as *Arlo* is, I imagine they can keep up.”

Okay. Chen, you match course and dock with the wreck of Petersburg, *take aboard any survivors. Then dock with us. We’ll run a power link and jump our reactor from your power ring.*

Swanson, see what you can do with your damage, but if necessary we’ll take your crew off as well.

Bitka, it looks as if Puebla *is closest to mission-capable, so you’re our rearguard. You’re already pointed the right direction so give me about ten gee-seconds of acceleration to drop back a way, and keep your eyes on the uBakai.*

Sam ran the numbers in his head. They were headed away from K’tok, and with the hard burn they’d made during combat their departing speed was over thirty kilometers per second. As banged up as their radiators were, they could only manage partial power. *Puebla* could kick out nine thousand tons of thrust, *Cha-Cha* probably half that, and who knew if *Vimy Ridge* or *Canal du Nord* were even salvageable? It would take a long time to just get stopped and then turned around to head back toward K’tok too long. Unless the uBakai came after them, they were out of the fight. Rockaway was right. All they had left was to live to fight another day.

“Aye aye, ma’am.” Sam answered. “*Puebla* out.”

So this was what defeat felt like. Not just getting jumped, or taking more damage than you inflicted, but major defeat, as in end of the road, end of the campaign, everything gone for nothing. Still, you had to be alive to know you’d taken a beating, and being alive was better than the alternative. *Live to fight another day.* But what odds would they face next time?

The new task force commander with all those reinforcements would decide where to rendezvous. Sam hoped it was close; as many radiators as they’d lost, none of the boats was going to be able to manage much acceleration for a while, and reaction mass was getting to be a big problem. There’s been so many holes punched through

Puebla, Sam's instruments said he was down to less than three thousand tons of hydrogen, and he didn't really trust the instruments any more.

The ground troops were the ones who had no way out. Once *Arlo* and *Champion Hill* pulled out, once it was clear the orbital bombardment threat was gone, the ground brigade would have to surrender. It was a lousy way for the campaign to wind down for them, and all because the Navy couldn't figure out how to do their job.

"Helm, give me whatever acceleration engineering can manage without melting the boat. Cut it after ten gee-seconds of delta vee."

"Aye, aye, sir," Ensign Barb Lee answered, and hit the acceleration klaxon. In another few seconds the main drive fired, kicking out perhaps a tenth of a gee. At that rate Sam figured the burn would take about two minutes.

"Gambara, get me a broadcast frequency the uBakai Star Navy monitors."

"Sir?" she asked, but when she saw his expression she hastened to bring up a standard frequency listing on her workstation. "Uh . . . got one, sir. You want an open channel?"

"Yup, and no encryption," When she signaled him the circuit was live he spoke.

"This is Captain Sam Bitka of USS *Puebla*. I know you can hear me. Go ahead and run, you cowardly fucking leatherheads. Slither away into your nests. Who'll blame you? Of course you're afraid of us; you only outnumber us two to one.

"It sure didn't take much of a beating for you to show the color of your souls, did it? So I guess you'll live, but I don't know how you'll look yourselves in the face. Maybe uBakai warships aren't equipped with mirrors."

Sam cut the channel. He looked down and realized everyone on the bridge had turned and was watching him.

"Back to work," he said and they all turned away, but not before Ensign Lee at the helm grinned and gave him a thumbs-up.

"Well, we'll see if that gets a reaction," Marina Filipenko said softly.

"This may be one," Gambara said. "Incoming tight beam voice from *Vimy Ridge* for you, Captain,"

As soon as Sam opened the commlink channel, Commander Sadie Rockaway barked, *Why the hell didn't I think of that?*

CHAPTER THIRTY-NINE

13 January 2134
(minutes later) ***(twenty-third day in K'tok orbit)***

Vice-Captain Takaar Nuvaash, Speaker For The Enemy, stood in the admiral's tactical center and waited patiently as e-Lappela vented his anger and incredulity.

"We *defeated* them! Don't they understand that? They are beaten, but they pursue us. They pursue *us!* I don't believe it!" he roared. "And these insulting taunts!"

His voice rose as he spoke and Nuvaash saw the half-dozen members of the admiral's personal staff trade uncomfortable glances, ears folded back and skin beginning to flush. Nuvaash kept his own ears relaxed and open by sheer force of will, and he made himself speak calmly.

"Only one ship pursues us and it would have taken them almost twenty hours to reach K'tok at their initial rate of acceleration. In fact, it has already stopped accelerating and has not come close to reversing its vector. We will arrive at K'tok long before they possibly can, and we will have dealt with their orbital bombardment assets. Then let them come. The ground campaign will be—"

"Let them come?" the admiral shouted, cutting him off. "Would you have our crews think their leaders fear three Human ships? Will our crews think the Humans have good reason for their confidence? That we are facing some secret weapon?"

"The crews will follow your orders, Admiral. Tell them this is a trick to lure us away from the objective. Tell them—"

"I will tell them to tear open the hulls of those ships, to spill their atmospheres and crews into the void like an animal's guts."

Nuvaash felt the blood run to his face.

"Admiral, our sensor platforms have detected jump signatures, ships arriving above the plane of the ecliptic, and they are not uBakai. The Humans have sent reinforcements. They will be here in a matter of days. We have very little time."

"We have sufficient time. To take out the three Human ships and then return to K'tok will take less than a day. All the pieces are on the game table, Nuvaash. Now we will take them one by one, and the first will be the Human captain who thinks he can insult the uBakai Star Navy."

e-Lapeela seized Nuvaash by the shoulder, pulled him roughly into his private office, and closed the hatch. Nuvaash had never been manhandled by a superior officer before, had never seen it done to another officer. It came to him it was a remarkably *Human* reaction. eLapeela was responding as he had hoped the Humans would respond to the attack on Earth—he was *over*-reacting, and Nuvaash wondered if, as it was sometimes claimed, we eventually become the thing we hate. He expected a rebuke, but instead heard a question.

"What is wrong with our missiles, Nuvaash? The Humans cannot have survived the barrage we launched."

Nuvaash stared at him for a moment, unsure if he was serious. Everyone saw what the Humans had done.

"Admiral, they used their missiles to kill ours, and used the warhead detonations to cover their ships as they closed the range to attack with their high-powered ship lasers. It is proving an effective combination."

"You are the Speaker for the Enemy. Why did you not anticipate this?"

Nuvaash considered his answer. Why indeed? The situation was beyond the need for nuanced answers, so what was the core truth?

"I believe the Human admiral is more clever than I," he answered.

"That may very well be, but he is not smarter than me," e-Lapeela shot back. "He will soon find that out and the discovery will be the insight he takes with him to The Beyond."

He turned his head to the side and spoke, clearly into his embedded commlink.

"Senior battle staff. My cabin. Now."

Since they had all been standing outside in the admiral's tactical center, within seconds the three others had filed in and stood at anxious attention.

"Force status, report" the admiral ordered.

"Three cruisers destroyed," the asset chief replied, "including an uKa-Maat salvo cruiser by catastrophic explosion of its reactor. Two of our operational ships have matched course with the others and are trying to recover survivors. Of our nine remaining warships, four have disabled jump drives, including the flagship."

"We do not need jump drives," e-Lapeela answered. "We are where we need to be. Weapons and maneuvability?"

"One cruiser has lost its power ring, Admiral. Two have lost sufficient radiators they cannot operate their reactors except at low power, All ships have lost some point defense lasers and sensor capability, although we still have an intact battle-net and so can pool our sensor readings."

"Missile supply?" the admiral asked.

The asset chief shifted uncomfortably.

"Very low, sir. By your command, we made a maximum effort in the first pass. The two surviving salvo cruisers have only forty-two missiles left between them. The other seven cruisers have barely thirty missiles total remaining. The flagship has none."

The admiral turned to his tactical advisor, the Master of the Lance.

"What course do you advise?" he demanded, although Nuvaash had already learned that e-Lapeela never seemed to follow Lance's advice.

"We should continue to K'tok, eliminate the orbital bombardment force, and clear the way for the ground forces to recapture the needle downstation. This renders the enemy fleet irrelevant, until they can bring more troops. In any case, we will have time to prepare the defenses of the downstation and the surrounding city. It will need more than two or three cohorts of *Azza-kaat* for them to take it back."

Azza-kaat were the troops dropped in meteoric assaults from orbit, which Nuvaash knew the Humans called Mike Troopers.

e-Lapeela turned to his senior advisor. "Speaker for the Future, what do you counsel?"

Although he was senior, Nuvaash considered the Future's Speaker the weakest and least-self-confident of the admiral's advisors. His only talent, so far as Nuvaash could determine, was an uncanny ability to understand in advance what advice the admiral most wanted to hear.

"Attack the Human ships now. Wipe away the insult with their screams. K'tok will still be there when we are finished."

Finally e-Lapeela turned to Nuvaash. "Speaker for the Enemy, what do you counsel?"

Nuvaash looked at him and could tell this was as much challenge as question. He was not asking what Nuvaash thought so much as where he stood. He thought only for a moment before answering.

"The transports cannot easily decelerate and one has suffered critical damage. Send them on to K'tok as planned. There is one Human ship in orbit there. Send the two cruisers with heavy damage to their radiators as escorts, as they can hardly match the acceleration the fleet will need to turn on the enemy. They should be able to finish that destroyer. Turn and fight with the other cruisers."

Admiral e-Lapeela nodded.

When it became clear the uBakai were decelerating and intended to turn back on them, Sam felt a sense of dread wash over him. Yes, he had pulled them away from K'tok for a few hours, bought the ground troops, *Arlo*, and *Champion Hill* perhaps another day of life. But he might have purchased it with the lives of his crew and that of the other two boats in the task group.

Then it got worse. As the sensor echoes made increasing clear, there were now two groups of enemy ships, drawing away from each other. The transpirts were still heading for K'tok. He had gained nothing.

Although it had seemed as if it took hours, the initial engagement, from the time the uBakai fleet emerged from J-space to the time the surviving boats of the task group had passed far enough beyond them to be out of effective laser range, was only slightly over ten minutes. Twenty minutes later the uBakai had begun decelerating, by which time the distance between the two forces had grown to over fifty thousand kilometers. Seven uBakai cruisers turned to face two damaged destroyers and two more without power, trying to save as many lives and repair as much damage as possible.

"Gambara, tight beam to *Vimy Ridge*."

Rockaway, here. How's it look back there. Bitka?

"Well, ma'am, they took the bait, but they're sending five ships on to K'tok. Looks like two transports for sure, maybe two cruisers, and can't make out what the fifth one is."

Well, it was a good try. I'll tell Kropotkin to get ready to pull the plug.

"Begging your pardon, ma'am, but I think that may be premature. They are only sending two or maybe three cruisers, and we know we banged them up. I don't think they realize we have *Champion Hill* operational. I think they figure to face only one destroyer, probably damaged. I know they don't know about the block fours we seeded in orbit."

What's your idea, Bitka?

"Have *Arlo* stay in low orbit, engage with missile fire, but have the *Hill* stay dark, play dead. Make those cruisers come to them and trip the orbital missiles. Then have the *Hill* join in. It may be the edge they need—at least psychologically. If either of those boats of ours survive, we still hold orbital space, and as long as we do the leatherheads can't move against the grunts, right?"

Well, it's sounds a lot better than just running away. Okay, we'll try it.

The math of their situation was both simple and stark. It took the uBakai forty minutes to cancel their residual vector and begin accelerating back toward what was left of the Human task group, and it would take another hour to match the velocity of the destroyers hurtling away from K'tok. By that time the distance between the two forces would have opened to almost two hundred thirty thousand kilometers, but from then on the distance would steadily close.

One comfort Sam took from these numbers was that they showed a steady acceleration of about three-quarters of a gee. The uBakai ships were capable of better than that, but they must have taken a beating as well in the confused melee. At least some of them couldn't manage more than that, and the uBakai admiral had not decided to surge ahead with his less-damaged ships.

He was afraid to.

The other comfort—although a very mixed one—came a little over an hour after the initial battle, when the uBakai transports and escorts reached K'tok. It was a short, sharp engagement which Sam and the other survivors were able to follow by a live voice report from the Combined Expeditionary Brigade's rear service unit on the needle highstation. The supply personnel had a ringside seat, about twenty thousand kilometers above the main action, which was mostly fought in low and middle orbit.

Okay, I think Arlo *is firing again. There goes another nuke. Not sure if it was ours or theirs. Oh!* Arlo *just got hit. I don't have its tag any more. Dex, does that mean it's knocked out? Shit. We're going to . . . wow! Another nuke, and this was one of ours. The laser hit that one cruiser hard. He's free-floating. I can see atmosphere and a lot of wreckage and—wait!* Champion Hill's *tag just came up and it's accelerating up-orbit. What the hell do they think they can do? That other leather-head cruiser—looks like he's rotating to fire. There's a missile off but, Jesus they're close! The* Hill's *firing, maybe at the missile, hard to see what . . . Aw, man. The* Hill's *hit. Hit again. There goes its bottle! Jesus, it just blew up! It's gone! We're fucked. We're—wait,* Arlo's *tag is back on. They must have power up. There's so much shit down there, I can't see shit. Dex, can you tell what's going on? I think . . . is that another hit on the leather-head? Yeah, his tag's flashing. He's down.* Arlo's *accelerating up-orbit, going for the transports. Go get em,* Arlo!

There wasn't much of a fight after that. It sounded to Sam as if, in all the confusion, the uBakai cruisers never realized there were orbital mines attacking them. Within another fifteen minutes two of the transports had been damaged and surrendered while the third one accelerated away.

By any standard it was a remarkable victory: two damaged destroyers had broken the ground invasion component. Two uBakai cruisers were destroyed, two transports and all their troops captured, and all at the cost of "only" one destroyer, already crippled and manned by a skeleton crew of volunteers.

Only.

What did the uBakai admiral think about that, Sam wondered? Well, one transport had escaped. Perhaps after the balance of their fleet crushed the remaining destroyers here, they would return to K'tok and swat USS *Arleux*. Even without the other transport, just removing the orbital bombardment munitions would probably be enough. But whatever the admiral's plans for K'tok, he did not turn away from the destroyers.

The two hours had given *Puebla's* crew time to assess their damage and put the least serious of it right. Casualties had been heavy: twelve dead including Lieutenant Carlos Sung and over half of his damage control parties from the auxiliary division—the A-gang. Chief Tanaka had taken over the survivors, and had gotten the worst atmosphere and fuel leaks under control. They'd also lost all three crewpeople from the starboard missile room. Seven more were seriously injured, several from low temperature frost burns when liquid hydrogen had poured into several work spaces. They'd lost a lot of reaction mass. Well, that would make them more nimble, he supposed.

The lull had also given time to receive the routine data dump from the newly arrived Earth task force and for the surviving boats to update their data nets. Much of it was admin chatter, but it included the latest round of mail from home.

"Crew has a lot of work to handle, sir," Larry Goldjune had said when Sam pinged him about distributing it. "I'm not sure they need the distraction right now."

"Maybe not, but I've got the feeling that for a lot of us—maybe all of us—this might be our last words from home. Distribute the mail, Mr. Goldjune."

Almost immediately Sam's own commlink vibrated. He slipped on a pair of viewer glasses and scanned the list of mail, and he was ready to blink them back into storage when one return address caught his eye. He opened the document.

Hey Sam Bitka!

As part of Dynamic Paradigms LLC's "We Value Our Deployed Service Personnel" program, we are happy to inform you that your time in uniform will count as time and a quarter toward employment seniority and vesting in the RewardShareTM program. In addition, after reviewing your employment service and qualification folder, the Advancement Selection Panel has chosen you *for transfer from the Line Management to Executive Service employment track, effective upon your return from service, and successful completion of your Doctor of Financial Management (DFM) degree.*

Sam Bitka, I am delighted *to be the first to welcome you to the executive family of Dynamic Paradigms LLC.*

Nora Kawaguchi, Junior Vice President of Communications

Personnel Enhancement Department, Dynamic Paradigms LLC

"Huh," Sam said.

"What's that, sir?" Filipenko asked from the Tac One chair beside him.

He hesitated for a moment, looking at the letter, and then squinted to delete it.

"Just junk mail."

"Tight beam from *Vimy Ridge*, voice for you, sir," Kramer reported.

"Bitka here," he said as soon as he opened the channel. "Are you up and running?"

It took a bit more fiddling than we figured, Sadie Rockaway answered through his commlink, *but we've got the reactor back on line.* Canal du Nord's *finished, though. Most of the stern of the boat's just gone. It's a wonder their reactor shut down instead of just torching them. We're splitting the survivors up between* Oaxaca *and us. How are our friends back there doing?*

"They've turned around and are starting to close the vector. They're making about three quarters of a gee so if they keep it up I figure three more hours. They're going to need reaction mass to get turned around again and headed back to K'tok, though, so I bet they're looking at their fuel numbers and starting to think hard. If they're coming up on bingo fuel, they'll cut the acceleration and coast. That'd give us a couple more hours."

We can start accelerating, she answered, *but with* Oaxaca *down to one radiator they can't make much more than two or three tenths of a gee. That'll at least make the uBakai burn more reaction mass coming after us, and take them that much further from K'tok. What do you think?*

"Beats the hell out of my plan. All I've come up with is find a hill, shoot the horses, and save the last bullet for yourself. What does Lieutenant Commander Chen on *Oaxaca* say?"

Not much. Between you and me, I think he's overwhelmed by the situation. He's following orders, but he's having a hard time contributing to the solution. I'll order him to conform to whatever we decide and I don't think he'll object; I think he just wants someone to tell him what to do.

"I hear that. So tell me what to do."

Oaxaca *is our lame duck. They've got fifty-six survivors from* Petersburg *and* Canal du Nord *onboard as well. I'm going to have them start accelerating now. You and I will stick around here for a while, see what happens.*

"Okay."

We can catch up with Oaxaca *later.*

"Sure."

She didn't say anything for a while.

You know, if it makes sense to.

"I understand."

Three-Twenty-One has experienced a radiator failure. Two-Ninety has a reactor shutdown," the asset chief reported to Admiral e-Lapeela and the rest of his staff. "Both are falling out of formation."

e-Lapeela turned from the sensor display and took several quick steps away, then stood studying the smart wall which showed the star display forward. Nuvaash and the other members of the staff exchanged apprehensive glances.

"All ships terminate acceleration," e-Lapeela said at last, and Nuvaash felt a surge of hope. Perhaps the admiral had come to his senses and would turn back to K'tok.

"We will coast while the two damaged ships conduct repairs. The fleet must remain concentrated. Speaker For The Enemy, has the Human fleet altered its status?"

"No, Admiral," Nuvaash said, and he sighed. "One continues to accelerate away at low energy. The other two coast."

"The two cover the retreat of the damaged ship," e-Lapeela said. "They will fight to protect it."

Nuvaash wondered why they would do so, given the admiral's previous conviction that Human morale could not withstand the sort of losses they had already inflicted on them, but he did not ask that question. Instead he turned to the Master of the Lance, which Humans called the Tactical Boss.

"How long to overtake them at our current speed?"

The Lance spoke directly to the admiral instead of to Nuvaash.

"Two and one half hours."

e-Lapeela nodded.

"How are we to deal with the new Human tactics? There is no question of our victory, but we must also minimize damage to our forces."

Nuvaash exchanged a look with the Speaker for the Future, but the Lance spoke.

"Admiral, the Human missile-killing missiles can engage and destroy up to thirty missile-sized targets at a time. They are clearly adapted to deal with our salvo cruisers, although we received no report that they were even aware of that class of ships."

At that he paused and looked down but glanced in the direction of Nuvaash, the Speaker for the Enemy, his meaning clear.

What a low creature, Nuvaash thought. *What low creatures surround me.* Only the Lance had a first-rate mind, but he had no character. Asset had character, but a head only for lists and sums. Speaker for the Future had neither.

"Our mistake was delivering dense salvos of missiles," Lance continued, "which maximized the effectiveness of their tactics. I propose we modify the missiles in our lead cruisers to engage small targets—the targeting parameters are easy to adjust. We will launch these singly, well in advance, and then fire them one at a time, taking out the enemy missiles they have launched and also providing sensor cover for the main missile salvo which follows.

"But our main anti-ship salvo must not come in a single wave. It must be staggered, many waves, each of only four missiles. As they emerge from the interference, the Humans must either expend one of their remaining missile killers to take out those four, or attempt to do so with their point-defense lasers.

"With the waves following in quick succession, and any actual detonations providing an additional layer of sensor interference, the computer model predicts over an eighty percent chance of success by the third wave."

e-Lapeela nodded, his expression grim. "Yes. Make the modifications to the missiles in the lead cruisers. Brief the ship captains on the tactics. Rest the tactical crews while engineering continues repair work. If the enemy does not accelerate, we will be within thirty thousand kilometers of them in one hour. Then we will call the tactical crews to their stations and accelerate with every ship capable of doing so. We will close the gap and execute our attack plan. Triumph or perish!"

CHAPTER FORTY

13 January 2134
(thirty minutes later) (*twenty-third day in K'tok orbit*)

The range between the uBakai and *Puebla* had dropped to slightly under forty thousand kilometers when Sam ordered the boat to Readiness Condition Two, which enabled them to rotate half the crew at a time for a meal, sanitary break, and a little private time. Sam turned the boat over to Larry Goldjune in the auxiliary bridge and went back to the wardroom, now serving as the boat's medical recovery area, to check on the wounded. He talked with each of the seven, ending with Chief Joyce Menzies, both of whose hands were encased in thick protective mittens with tubes connected to an autodoc unit.

"What happened to you, Chief?"

Menzies held her hands up. "Liquid hydrogen, sir. Tried to open a frozen exhaust duct manually. Fucked me up pretty good."

"You're still going to be able to play in your band, though, right?"

"Unless they mess up the reconstructive surgery I'll be okay for the stuff we play. Tamblinson says I gotta stay hooked up to this gizmo or I'll lose some mobility. That'd make the third movement in Prokofiev's Seventh Piano Sonata pretty tough. Course, it always was, but I was finally getting the hang of the *crisse de calice* thing."

"I didn't know that was your kind of music."

"It's *all* my kind of music, sir. Well, maybe not Gregorian chants or that Tuvan throat singing stuff. And I'm not big on hillbilly music, neither, 'less you count zydeco." After she said this she looked away and sighed.

"We're going to have another fight, aren't we?"

"Looks that way."

She turned and faced him. "You gotta get Tamblinson to unplug me, sir. Let me head back up to my missile room. I gotta be with my monkies."

Sam looked and he was surprised to see a tears detach from the corner of her eyes and float lightly away.

"But you said it'll mess your hands up. And besides, what can you do with them all wrapped up, anyway?"

"I can tell them what to do next, be there with them. I mean, what's a chief supposed to do if not that? Let me worry about my hands."

She stopped and rubbed her eyes awkwardly with her mittens.

"Sir, everybody took losses, but nobody's had it worse than Weapons Division. We started with eight people. Jules—I mean Lieutenant Washington—she got killed in that first attack."

For a moment Sam had a flash of memory, seven grey body bags floating in this same compartment. He blinked and the ghostly image disappeared.

"Chief Burns got moved up to Bull Tac," Menzies went on, "and we had three of my people killed when they took out the starboard missile room. There's only Joe Guerrero—a Machinist Third—and Mariner Cheri Wilcox left up there in the port missile room. Without me, that's your whole fuckin' Weapons Division, sir!"

She paused and wiped her eyes again, and Sam had to stop himself from taking her in his arms and holding her. But he did stop himself. She wasn't a little girl; she was a chief petty officer with a great big heart.

"You're right, we need you up there, Chief. You want me to have Rose Hennessey send you one of her techs to help? Maybe another mariner/striker, too?"

She shook her head. "We've only got six missiles left. We can handle it, sir. Ms Hennessey is shorthanded too. Sorry I got all girly on you there. Can you unplug me from the autodoc? And help unclip my tether? I can't really manage it the way my hands are."

Sam got her unplugged and unclipped just as his embedded commlink sounded the urgent tone.

"Captain here."

Captain, it's Chief Gambara. You better get back to the bridge quick. Something's happening!

Sam yelled to Tamblinson to help Menzies aft to the missile room, and then he kicked through the hatch into the central communication trunk and pushed himself forward.

"I'm coming," he told Gambara through his commlink. "Put the OOD on."

That would be Ensign Lee back in the auxiliary bridge. Patching you through now.

"Lee, what's happening?"

Sir, we've got jump emergence signatures, two of them, bearing two eight five degrees relative, angle on the bow seventeen degrees, range forty-eight thousand and closing fast.

"Punch general quarters!"

The gongs began sounding instantly. Sam had intended to return to the bridge, but the auxiliary bridge was right forward of the wardroom. He grabbed a handhold, arrested his forward motion, and scrambled through the hatch and into the slightly smaller version of the main bridge.

"Where's Goldjune? I left him in command."

"Sir, Lieutenant Goldjune ordered me to come aft and take the watch. I'm qualified."

"Not the point, Barb, but that'll wait." Sam nodded to Chief Patel in the Tac One chair as he pulled himself into the command chair, turned on the tactical display, and began strapping himself into the harness. Lee had already moved to Maneuvering One.

"Barb, I've got the boat. Alert engineering: any minute now I may need as much thrust as they can give me without killing us."

"Aye aye, sir."

"Captain, I've got multiple drive flares ahead of us," Patel said. "The uBakai are accelerating again!"

Sam checked the tactical display. The two new contacts were crossing at a slant, intersecting the uBakai course, and they were coming fast: forty kilometers a second at least. If they were more hostiles, *Puebla* was going to have a hard time outrunning them with two busted radiators.

"Bogeys are squawking, sir," Patel said. "Hey . . . is that some kind of uBakai trick?"

No, it wasn't a trick. The two new contacts had just lit up with identity tags: HMS *Exeter* and NNS *Aradu*, coming in from behind the uBakai, and fast. The uBakai had rotated to accelerate toward the new threat, turning their sterns to *Puebla*.

Captain, I'm getting a broad beam transmission from one of the two new contacts, Gambara told him by commlink. *I think it's from HMS Exeter.*

"What's the message?"

Not exactly a message, sir. It's just . . . some weird music.

"Weird music? Pipe it back so I can hear."

The auxiliary bridge suddenly filled with the sound of a lively, exuberant song.

A hunting we will go!
A hunting we will go!
Heigh ho the dairy-o,
A hunting we will go!

Sam laughed. "Okay. Helm, sound the acceleration warning, and then give me every ton of thrust you can wring out of this tub—MPDs too, *everything*. Who's got their nuts in a vice now?"

In less than twenty minutes it was all over, and Nuvaash had been well-positioned to watch the disaster unfold.

At first the admiral had turned the fleet to face the new enemy ships, but when the Human destroyers began to accelerate toward the fleet's rear, e-Lapeela ordered three ships to turn back and face them. The complicated maneuver orders following one after another, combined with the different procedures of three different nationalities, had produced confusion at first, and then something which might look, to the unsympathctic eye, very much like panic.

e-Lapeela intended to take the three other ships with the flagship to face the new, more powerful threat. After less than a minute of acceleration, one of the uSokan cruisers experienced a massive power failure and not only stopped accelerating, it broadcast its surrender code. The uKa-Maat salvo cruiser—in concert with the flagship and the one other ship—had continued to accelerate for a minute or two after that but had then initiated jump and blinked away. Less than a minute later the one cruiser remaining with the flag, another uSokan ship, had done the same. The flagship, however, did not have a functioning jump drive, nor did it have any missiles remaining, and so was left to face the two Human cruisers by itself, with nothing but low-powered point-defense lasers. The outcome was a foregone conclusion, but e-Lapeela refused the ship captain's request to broadcast the surrender code.

Victory or death.

The three-cruiser force sent to deal with the Human destroyers had done little better, although Nuvaash's attention had been mostly absorbed by their own forlorn and solitary fight. Before the bridge power failed, and took the sensor feed with it, he saw one more flashing surrender tag of another uSokan cruiser and no sign of a coherent uBakai formation.

When the admiral's tactical center lost atmosphere and was evacuated, the staff had scattered. Nuvaash made his way by the illumination of his helmet light through the strangely silent mass of struggling crew. A few who had not managed to don their helmets in time no longer struggled. Although no sound travelled through the vacuum of the breached and now-stationary habitat wheel, Nuvaash felt several thunderous hits to the cruiser transmitted through the structure of the vessel itself and into his hands wrapped around stanchions.

Nuvaash pulled himself to the closest access shaft between the habitat wheel and the main ship hull. If any part of the ship retained power, it would be the main hull. The power lift was inoperable but he joined the crowd of crew free-floating down the shaft, occasionally colliding with crewmen coming the other direction, trying to escape from whatever disaster they had experienced there.

Nuvaash found a handful of compartments which still had power and atmosphere, and many more where there was at least evidence of power. He had powered down his commlink when leaving the bridge but now powered it up again and pinged the admiral.

Nuvaash! Where in the name of the Hereafter are you? Where is the rest of the staff?

"Admiral, power down your commlink at once! There is a plot to kill you. You can be traced by your commlink signature. Meet me at the number three power ring maintenance access bay."

Nuvaash heard no more and so he waited inside the maintenance bay hatch. There was power here, of a sort. A broken power router at the far end of the bay, six or seven meters from the hatch, arced and made flickering, shimmering spider webs of high voltage power, and lit the room, if irregularly. Nuvaash hooked his tether to a stanchion near the hatch and made his simple preparations.

Ten minutes later he saw the admiral move into the corridor outside. He was alone and carried a neuro-pistol. Good. Nuvaash had made him suspicious of everyone. He showed himself at the hatchway and waved the admiral in. As he came through the door Nuvaash motioned for him to touch helmets, the only way they could communicate without using their commlinks.

"Tether yourself to a stanchion," Nuvaash told him. "It is dangerous here." He pointed at the naked, arcing electricity at the end of the bay and e-Lapeela nodded. He turned to clip his tether to a stanchion and as he did so Nuvaash reached back behind himself, took hold of the neuro-wand he had left floating there, and lightly tapped the admiral on his hand.

All of the admiral's muscles contracted instantly, and the neuro-pistol flew from his hand, bouncing off of a bulkhead and tumbling toward the other end of the bay. Nuvaash had set the charge deliberately low so it would temporarily incapacitate the admiral but not render him unconscious. There were things Nuvaash still needed to understand.

First he closed the hatch and secured it. He took the small magnetic jammer from the utility pocket of his shipsuit, the pocket which earlier had concealed the collapsible neuro-wand. He clipped the jammer to the back of the admiral's helmet. Once e-Lapeela regained his senses he would try to power up his commlink, but now that would do him no good. Nuvaash turned the admiral's still-trembling body and looked at the faceplate of the helmet. E-Lapeela's eyes were open and they tracked Nuvaash, so the Speaker for the Enemy touched helmets again with his admiral.

"How did you learn the secret access codes for the Kagataan jump drives? Of all the great mercantile families, none feel more hostility toward the uBakai than do the e-Kagataan. Why would they share their greatest trade secret with you?"

"Y-y-you are a f-f-fool, N-Nuvaash."

"Speak," Nuvaash said, and held the glowing tip of the neuro-wand up for e-Lapeela to see.

"S-s-secret brotherhood. D-Dazzling New Dawn Brothers, passed codes to us. Use as w-weapon, then b-b-blame Kagataan. One b-b-blow . . . strike two t-targets."

He smiled broadly, if jerkily, in triumph, as if his revelation proved his brilliance, as opposed to demonstrating his stupidity and the stupidity of everyone who had been party to this disastrous scheme.

Nuvaash drew back, made sure he was not touching the admiral, and applied the neuro-wand, incapacitating e-Lapeela again. A second shock this close after the first would give Nuvaash at least a minute before the admiral could control his movements, more than enough time. He touched helmets.

"When you entagled the Great Houses in your scheme, you compromised the entire edifice of the *Cottohazz*. Three hundred years of carefully built trust—now shattered. I am uBakai, but that is not my only loyalty."

Nuvaash reached into his utility pocket and drew out the third object he carried there, the shining metallic shield of the *Cottohazz-Gozhakampta Sugkat Jitobonaan,* the *Co-Gozhak* Provost Corps. He held the shield against the faceplate of e-Lapeela's helmet so he could see it clearly and understand its meaning. Then he touched helmets a last time.

"My fellow provosts—and I as well, should I somehow manage to survive—will do everything we can to undo the damage you have wrought. You once said that governments must be careful how they deal with their heroes, and you were right. Take some satisfaction in knowing your heroic reputation, however undeserved, has shielded your family from your disgrace."

"K-k-kill me," e-Lapeela said, "b-but not for what I attempted, only for f-failing. And ask yourself this, Nuvaash: c-could a conspiracy this broad, touching this many n-nations, have advanced without the knowledge of your superiors? Without the tacit approval of the Provost Corps?"

"I have wondered that myself," Nuvaash said. "Should I survive, I intend to find out. Now, die a hero's death."

Nuvaash removed the portable jammer from e-Lapeela's helmet, unclipped the admiral's tether, and then used his foot to give him a soft, carefully aimed push out into the maintenance bay. The admiral floated back and back, slowly tumbling, until his body exploded into the shimmering web of raw electricity.

For two hours after the brief but violent fight, USS *Puebla* coasted, running off the remaining power in its forward energy coil and the trickle of power from its LENR generators. All four radiators were out, as well as seven of its eight lasers. Its coil gun was still operational, but it had fired off the last of its missiles. Miraculously, *Puebla* had suffered no additional serious crew casualties. Sometimes the randomness of battle cuts in your favor. Sam supposed that it had to once in a while or it wouldn't really be random.

Rose Hennessey's EVA crew worked, cutting plumbing from the number four radiator and fusing it into the remnant of the number three mount. After two hours, they had a lash-up that had about ten percent the heat dispersing power of the original radiator suite, but it was enough to light the fusion reactor, recharge the power ring, and kick out about a tenth of a gee in acceleration.

Vimy Ridge had taken a worse pounding than *Puebla*. Gambara had been unable to get any sort of response from them. As Hennessey's crew finished their work on the radiator, the cruiser NNS *Aradu*, after a long burn to reverse course, docked with the wreck of *Vimy Ridge* and began taking off survivors. Sam hoped that Sadie Rockaway had made it, but he tried not to hope too hard. Not long afterwards, the other cruiser, HMS *Exeter*, matched course with *Puebla*. By then Sam had moved forward to the main bridge and taken command there.

"Captain, I have incoming text," Gambara reported. "Message reads: *Exeter* to *Puebla*. We are matching course and are prepared to evacuate survivors. Signed, Ranjha, Captain."

Sam sat silently for a moment, at first unsure what the message meant.

"Survivors?" Marina Fillipenko beside him in Tac One said. "What does that British asshole think? That we're a bunch of shipwrecked mariners?"

Sam laughed.

"We probably look that way. Gambara, make the following reply: *Puebla* to *Exeter*. Negative. We are operational. Signed, Bitka, Captain. PS Hunting music appreciated."

Gambara transmitted the message and after a moment spoke again.

"Captain, incoming text: '*Exeter* to *Puebla*. In my judgment your craft not salvageable. Recommend in strongest terms you set scuttling charges and transfer personnel to this ship.'"

The routine activity stopped and several of the bridge crew exchanged somber looks. He heard the hum of servos as Chief Barghava, and then Ensign Lee turned their chairs to look up at him. To his lower right Burns and Ramirez did the same, and Sam saw Delacroix beyond them craning her neck to see his reaction.

"Kramer, send: *Puebla* to *Exeter*. Noted."

For a moment the bridge was silent, and then it filled with the sound of relieved laughter and the hum of servos as the bridge crew reset their stations.

"Helm, are our docking and maneuvering lights still working?"

"Captain, it looks like about a third of them might be," Ensign Lee answered.

"Well turn them on. Turn on every exterior light we've got. Let 'em see us. USS *Puebla* has power, thrust, atmosphere, and one laser, and by God we are a boat to be reckoned with."

CHAPTER FORTY-ONE

16 January 2134
(three days later) ***(twenty-sixth day in K'tok orbit)***

It took nine hours at one tenth of a gee to get *Puebla's* vector away from K'tok cancelled, and then they were low enough on reaction mass they just gave her a gentle nudge back toward K'tok. By then Sam had gotten the final tally: *Vimy Ridge* was a total loss, but the uBakai had lost six cruisers to concentrated missile and laser fire, including their flagship. Two cruisers and two transports had surrendered. Three cruisers had jumped away, and one cruiser and one transport had escaped under high acceleration. Where they thought they were going was anybody's guess.

He also found out Sadie Rockaway from *Vimy Ridge* was alive but injured, which meant Lieutenant Commander Chen in *Oaxaca* was technically the commander of the division. In reality, there was no task group, just two broken boats trying to limp back to K'tok, and *Arleux*, damaged and undermanned, in low orbit, all of which Brigadier General Irekanmi had taken under his direct control. His commanding hand so far had rested lightly on the destroyers. He asked what the cruisers could do to assist them, and beyond that left things up to the captains. Well before *Puebla* got back to K'tok, the two heavy cruisers had taken over the bombardment duty and given *Arleux* a well-earned rest.

It took three days of coasting for *Puebla* to make orbit. Somewhere along the way he found out that rescued Varoki crewmembers from the uBakai flagship said tht it had also been the ship which fired the opening shot of the war, the one which had killed Jules. It was just a machine and turning it into twisted junk did nothing to bring Jules or any of the others back. Still, it brought Sam a small measure of satisfaction knowing it was gone. The enemy admiral was also dead; that was better.

The big, new Human task force was on its way, and Sam would later learn that was why Brigadier General Irekanmi had taken the chance of making an in-system jump. He figured if he lost his gamble, there would still be fleet elements to fight for system control, but if he didn't do something the Coalition was going to lose K'tok before the cavalry even got there. Of course, he had also waited until the uBakai had followed the task group over a hundred thousand kilometers above the densest part of the plane of the ecliptic. The risk was well-calculated and nicely timed. Sam was forced to rethink his opinion of naval officers with army-sounding ranks.

He couldn't remember when exactly he'd found out all that, because those three days became a blur of activity without much rest. *Puebla* needed a lot of fixing, just to keep its core systems up and running. Sam spent a lot of time in engineering, trying to smooth the road for Chief Miko Tanaka's A-Gang, pitching in whenever one of their two undamaged fabricators started acting up, but otherwise trying to stay out of their way.

By the time *Puebla* made its final correcting burn to enter K'tok orbit, the crew had settled down into the routine of watch-standing and repairs. The boat now had two operational lasers, both on the port side, and could radiate active radar from enough panels on its port side to get a decent picture of one tactical hemisphere. They had to roll the boat to get a complete picture. In some ways it was as if *Puebla* had suffered a stroke.

The active crew had been reduced from its original complement of ninety-five to just forty-six fit for duty: eight officers, eight chief petty officers, and thirty other ranks. One chief and six other ranks were still in sick bay while one officer, one chief, and eight others were critically injured and in cold sleep. Half of the crew still active had suffered some form of injury, most of them serious enough to qualify for a Purple Heart. If people thought *Puebla* looked sad from the outside, they should come inside and look.

The crew went about their duties differently than they had. At first there was an enormous burst of relief that they had survived when so many other had not. There was a bit of swagger as well, at first, which Sam put down to pride in part, but more than that to whistling past the graveyard, a graveyard which had for the moment closed its gates but which was nevertheless still there, still open for business.

But Sam noticed something else, first in Tanaka's A-gang and then the rest of the crew. Once the immediate reactions cooled, they went about their duties quietly, without haste, and with a careful deliberation, as if the circuit boards and hull panels and antenna arrays they worked on were made of spun sugar instead of composite alloy, as if they would crumble at the touch if you weren't careful. They treated their fellow crewmates with the same deliberate, careful attention. It wasn't just fear of breaking them, Sam thought, but also a sort of wonder that somehow *Puebla* was still here, that their crewmates were still here, that *they* were still here, and if they weren't still here, if this was just a dream, they did not want to do anything that would wake them from it. One word came to Sam over and over, even though he knew it wasn't exactly the right word, but maybe there was no exactly right word, and maybe this was as close as he could ever come: reverent.

The last day before entering orbit he gave himself three hours off to get some sleep, but once in his cubby he found himself wide awake, thinking about those who hadn't come through to this side, all of them, but three in particular who had died most recently. Three people gone from the world, three people in the tidal wave of death which would flow from this war, three drops in an ocean: Ensign Jerry Robinette, the Varoki Admiral named e-Lapeela, and Lieutenant Commander Delmar Huhn.

What to make of this, of these lives, or these deaths? Was there some sort of lesson to be learned here, in these lives lived so differently but which had all ended the same? Sam had, in a sense, lived with them, even though he had never met his Varoki adversary. It made him feel something for them, even for the uBakai who had killed so many others—a sense of loss. They'd been here in the world with him, had left a mark on his life, and now were gone. Before them, Jules, connected to him in different ways than these three, but connected nevertheless, and all the connections now severed.

He wasn't sure the feeling was just loss. Maybe also fear? Sure, fear too. Live your life however you choose, but whether you are hero or villain or fool, the reaper's long blade topples you all with the same single sweep. *The military is not a life assurance venture,* Cassandra had said. Well, neither is life itself, is it? Bargain away everything you hold dear, your pride and self-respect and the lives of everyone you ever cared for, to get an extra month, or day, or hour of life, or a bit more comfort or power or acclaim, and death can *still* cheat you out of it. No matter how you live, there is no bargaining with death, and Sam decided only fools think they can. So how you live is just . . . who you choose to be, minute by minute, until the clock stops.

These thoughts did not gladden him but neither did they oppress him. He remembered, days earlier, realizing there was a sort of freedom which came from being completely screwed. And they were all completely screwed, weren't they? Screwed at birth, screwed good and proper.

And so they were all free . . . gloriously, terminally free.

Two hours after entering K'tok orbit, the chime on Sam's cabin door sounded and he saw Larry Goldjune waiting in the corridor. They had not exchanged a single word since the battle, beyond the minimum communication necessary to their jobs. Sam had forgotten to reprimand him for turning over the watch to Barb Lee before the last battle, and then had decided to let it slide. For now he was done with battles of all sorts, or at least he thought so.

"Lieutenant Bitka," Goldjune addressed him as soon as he entered the cabin, "I have just received orders from the acting task force commander to relieve you, and assume command of USS *Puebla* immediately, and further to inform you that you are to consider yourself under house arrest pending transportation to the task force flagship, there to stand trial by court martial. I believe the principal charges will be gross insubordination and conduct injurious to order."

Sam felt blood drain from his face, felt momentarily dizzy. After all they had gone through during the last week, this was the last way he'd expected it to end. After a moment's thought, though, it made at least a glimmer of sense: *his speech*. His ridicule of Larry's uncle, the admiral. He looked back at Goldjune, whose face now bore the faintest evidence of a smirk.

"Try kicking admirals around. See what happens," the executive officer said. "You're going to get a big chicken dinner, Bitka—six months to eat it and six months to pay for it."

Sam looked at him and felt the contempt rise in his throat like something physical, like bile bubbling up from his gut.

"That's interesting," he said keeping his voice under control. "I actually know every word you just said and I still have no idea what you're talking about."

"No, you wouldn't. It's an expression we have in the real navy. Big Chicken Dinner—BCD—it stands for Bad Conduct Discharge."

"Okay. And the rest of it?"

"BCD usually comes with six months confinement and six months pay forfeiture."

There had been times when Sam thought Larry might turn out alright, but whatever fear ate at his soul and drove him to turn away from his better angels, it never slept, it never stopped whispering to him, nagging at him, drowning out the voice of his conscience.

What was Goldjune really afraid of? It wasn't failure. He had too many people making sure he never stumbled, too many people making sure he *couldn*'t fail. No, the problem was, with all those thumbs on his side of the scale, it wasn't enough to just not fail. No one would admire him for just average success. With all those legs up, if he didn't make it to the top faster than anyone else, people would nod to themselves when they saw him, and think, "There goes another no talent hack who just made it by politics and family connections."

He really only had two choices: brightest star in the heavens, or no-talent hack. It didn't look like brightest star was working out, so what does a person do when confronted by that? Sam suddenly understood something important.

"Poor, sad Del Huhn," he said. "Del Huhn, another no-talent hack like you who never really succeeded at much of anything except rescuing a teenage girl from a jammed airlock. As the years drifted by he kept scaling back his dreams, didn't he? Kept making them smaller and smaller, trying to make them attainable, so in the end he could point to having achieved something. He couldn't even manage that, except right at the very end. But I'll tell you something, Larry, he turned out to be twice the man you are."

"What the devil are you talking about?"

"Twice the man. He stepped up. He stepped up twice, did something you've never had the courage to do."

"Courage to do what? *Quit?* Quit being captain? Quit living?"

"He came to where, if he kept his dreams, he'd end up destroying lives and maybe disgracing himself. Or possibly not disgrace. Maybe he could cover up his failures, get well-connected people like you to help, in return for some dirty service further down the road. But he'd know. He'd always know. He threw his future away rather than become that guy."

"And he regretted it," Goldjune said.

"Yeah, he had some second thoughts. Life's never simple. But when the time came, he did it, and that's what counts. And then he stepped up again, ended up giving his life, and I don't think you even understand why."

Goldjune glanced away, his mouth twisted in contempt, but also fear.

"What did he have to live for, anyway?" he asked.

"Exact same thing you and I have, Larry: the possibility of tomorrow."

Goldjune looked at him, the anger trying to drive the fear away but not succeeding.

"Now, if you don't mind, Mister Goldjune, I'd appreciate you getting the hell out of my cabin. Just one more thing: don't screw up my boat."

"It's not your boat anymore."

"The hell it's not."

Larry pushed himself off and back through the hatch, perhaps with more force than he intended because his shoulder caught the hatch frame as he passed through, and he cursed.

An hour later Sam's door buzzed again and he saw Moe Rice in the hallway holding two drink bulbs. Sam triggered the hatch and waved him in.

"Hemlock?" he asked, nodding at the drink bulbs.

"Almost as bad: Navy beer. Besides, if it was hemlock, wouldn't be two of 'em. No disrespect, cap'n, but you ain't *that* good a friend."

Sam grinned, took the offered beer, and drew a mouthful—cold and bitter and cleansing. He nodded his gratitude as Moe attached his tether to the other zero-gee chair.

"So . . . is stupid up to ninety bucks a barrel yet?" Sam asked. Moe looked blank for a moment and then remembered the conversation and laughed, a deep, booming rumble.

"When was that, cap'n? Twenty years ago? Seems like two different guys."

"No need to call me captain any more. I'm just a passenger these days. Sam will do."

"Thanks. I appreciate that, cap'n." Moe looked at the open file windows on Sam's desktop. "Writin' your memoirs?"

"Recommendations for design improvements on DDRs based on our combat experience."

"Does it start with, 'Find the designer and string his sorry ass up'?"

Sam laughed. "No, I think the original designers did a pretty good job. The battlescape's changed, though. If we're going to make destroyers work, we need smaller and more survivable carriers, maybe just lift one division per carrier instead of a full squadron. We need armor, couple layers of composite plates with expansion voids between them. We could use a better coil gun, too. A muzzle velocity of six kilometers a second isn't getting the job done. More redundancy on the radiators. More close-in lasers and as big as we can make them. That's a start."

"Whew!" Moe said. "A *start?* Shit, son, where you going to find space for all that gear?"

"Reaction mass. We don't need near as much as we had, given the situation we're actually facing. Only reason we ran so low was how much we lost from battle damage. Armor will help fix that. For all the good it did us, we could ditch the thermal shroud, too."

"You think those pinheads in BuShips will buy it?"

Sam shrugged and took another long draw of beer. "That's their call. But I'm not the only one who can see this. I mean, it's right there in front of you if you look. After what we did to them with our lasers, I bet we start seeing armor show up on Varoki warships. Bigger lasers, too."

They drank in silence for a while. For the last several days Sam's mind had been absorbed by the simple physical requirements of keeping his boat running and his crew alive. Now his thoughts seemed released to contemplate broader concerns.

"I haven't spoken to Filipenko about much of anything but the job since the last battle. She took Bronstein's World getting hit pretty hard. She okay?"

"Depends on what you mean," Rice answered.

"I mean is she any happier than she was."

"Happy," Moe repeated thoughtfully, as if the word was unfamiliar. "Cap'n, all respect—and I mean that—but you're gonna have a lot of disappointment going forward if you don't get one thing straight. You can't make everyone happy. Some folks just ain't wired for it."

"You're saying she'll never be happy."

"Well, never's a mighty big word. I don't think she has been, not so long as I've known her. Don't think she's likely to until she gets square with her own self. Tell you what, though. She's turned into a damned fine tactical officer. In the middle of a shootin' war, I reckon that counts for something."

Was Moe right? That Sam wanted to fix everyone, make everyone happy and see them get that way on his watch, as if their happiness was an accomplishable task, like writing an after action report? Devote X amount of time, see the task accomplished, move on.

Put that way, it didn't sound like a virtue.

"How about you?" Moe asked. "You square with yourself?"

Sam took another swallow of beer and thought that over. He'd burned his bridges to his civilian past. He was under arrest and charged with offenses that would probably end his naval career and possibly end in incarceration. But he was alive, unlike so many others who had walked this road with him. And he hadn't done anything *he* thought disgraceful.

"I am."

His commlink vibrated and he heard Chief Gambara's voice.

Captain, I'm sorry to disturb you. I want you to know the crew thinks this is a shitty deal you're getting.

"Gambara, don't you ever sleep? Why don't you turn the comm chair over to one of your petty officers and get some rack time?"

I plan to do that, sir, but in the mean time I have a request from Commander Atwater-Jones on board HMS Exeter *for a holoconference with you. I've got the line open if you can helmet up.*

"Give me one minute and then open the channel." Sam finished his beer in one long chug.

"Moe, thanks for the drink, but I got a call from Commander Atwater-Jones. I think I need to take it."

Moe's eyebrows went up a bit as he collected Sam's beer bulb and unclipped his tether. "She's a thoroughbred, that one is."

"Just a professional relationship."

Moe grinned. "Yup, and I'm the king of Sweden. Shalom, pardner."

As soon as Moe cleared the hatch, Sam clicked on his helmet and slid his faceplate down. He found himself sitting in a neutral gray background facing Cassandra, who sat behind a narrow table or desk facing him. It appeared to be some sort of crew-access holocon cubicle on HMS *Exeter*. Sam smiled but said nothing for a moment, waiting for the lump in his throat to go down.

"I see the condemned man is at least allowed virtual visitors," she said after a moment.

"How are you? I . . . I thought you were dead."

"For a while I thought so as well," she answered and smiled, but a bit too brightly to be believable. "Rather unsettling, being in an escape pod with the power running down and no prospect of anyone else surviving to rescue me." She turned away and looked at something he could not see, or perhaps at nothing at all. After a moment she turned to him again.

"My joy at being so unexpectedly rescued by HMS *Exeter* was mitigated only by the fact that your Commander Holloway Boynton was rescued by *Exeter* as well. Not that I would wish a fellow shipwrecked mariner ill, but he might have been rescued by *Aradu* instead. He really is quite unpleasant to be around. He is the one behind your arrest, you know."

"The task force ops boss? No, I didn't know. I hardly know him. I think we only spoke one time, in that first task force holocon. He ended up looking a little stupid, but it wasn't that big a deal. Maybe he's pals with Admiral Goldjune, or wants to be. Did Captain Kleindienst survive?"

She shook her head and looked away again. After a moment she seemed to shiver, and then took a breath, sat up straighter, and turned back to him again.

"Now, aside from expressing my happiness at your survival, and offering my heartfelt good wishes for dealing with this absurd court martial Boynton has dreamt up, I had one other important reason for contacting you. I want to ask you about these visions you have of the deceased young lady."

Sam felt himself shiver, as if the room had turned cooler.

"Jules," he said. "Lieutenant Julia Washington."

"Yes. You say you always see her to one side, out of the corner of your eye, as a sort of flickering shadow. If you close your eyes, is it still there?"

"Yes, *she* still is."

"Only to one side and, I imagine, only in the eye on that side."

Sam thought for a moment.

"Yes," he said, but he felt suddenly apprehensive. Why would he feel that way? He had nothing to hide.

"This flickering, would you describe it as almost sparkling?"

"Yes, that's right, a sort of long, dark sparkling shadow. What are you getting at?"

Cassandra pushed on, ignoring his question.

"How do you feel when you see it?"

"How do I *feel?* I feel . . . sort of sick a bit. How would you feel if you realized you were seeing a ghost?"

"I imagine I should feel apprehensive," she answered, "and the sense of unreality of the whole business would leave me somewhat detached, dissociated."

How did she know that? Was she haunted by someone as well? Her face lacked any clearly defined expression other than concentration.

"That's exactly how it feels."

"And these . . . visitations often occur after you have felt considerable stress or . . . "

"Or guilt," Sam finished for her. "Yeah, that's usually when she shows up."

"And what do you do after this experience, as a general rule?"

"Tamblinson, our medtech, gave me a sedative that cleared my mind and let me sleep. I generally took it to calm down and catch a couple hours of rest."

She nodded to herself as if confirming what she had suspected from the start.

"You aren't seeing ghosts, Bitka, nor are you insane. You are experiencing ocular migraine, brought on by a combination of stress and prolonged weightlessness."

"No. I had migraine headaches when I was a kid. Outgrew them, but I know what they're like. The pain's a killer, like the top and back of your head's coming off, like your eyeball's about to cave in. There's no pain when I . . . when this happens."

"My doctor friend—the fleet surgeon, by the way—informs me there isn't invariably pain with ocular migraine. A full-blown migraine headache often follows within an hour or two of the onset, but not invariably so. It appears you short-circuited that with the sedative. It must have been quite powerful. Still, migraine is nothing to toy around with, especially as this is almost certainly an early symptom of intracranial hypertension. Untreated, you may begin to suffer permanent vision loss and possibly a stroke. You were weightless for nearly two months. There are medicines you can take which are better suited to address this condition. I'll have the fleet surgeon send your medtech the prescription."

Was that really all it had been? Just migraine? Had his mind filled everything else in? Added Jules's ghost? Why?

Sam looked at Cassandra. After a moment she flushed and looked away, and he realized his face was wet with tears, could see them float away from his face inside his helmet, where he could do nothing to wipe them away, nothing except turn on his helmet exhaust and suck them out, like old trash swept off a floor.

It was true. He really had lost Jules, lost every bit of her, now even her ghost, forever.

Cassandra looked back and her face stiffened with anger. What would make her angry?

"You never made love to her, did you? No, not the very proper *Leftenent* Bitka. Wouldn't do, would it—intimacy with a fellow-officer?"

"She was in my chain of command."

"Of course. Against the rules and all that. Well, I suppose you're right, it *wouldn't* do, but there's still the rub."

Where did she get off poking a finger in his pain? She could at least let him grieve for five goddamned minutes.

"It reminds me of something de Laclos said in *Les Liaisons Dangerouses*," she said. "Have you read it?"

"You know, it's right at the top of my list of things to read once I learn French."

For a moment she looked tired. "It's available in translation. Don't play the ass, Bitka. You're not very convincing."

"Okay, what does he or she say?"

"'Didn't you know that it's not until *after* enjoying its delights that Love can stop being blind?' That's your problem, Bitka. You were never intimate with her, and so she will forever be this chaste angelic memory, perfect in every way."

Sam felt a denial rise to his lips, but it tasted stilted and childish. It tasted like a lie. Why bother lying to her? Who cared what she thought about Jules?

"Is that so terrible?"

"Actually, yes it is," she answered, and to Bitka's surprise her voice broke and tears shone in her eyese. "It is an insult to *her*, you bloody idiot. It reduces her from a human being—as glorious in her failures as in her triumphs—to a character in a bad romance novel."

He saw her fighting back her own tears and wondered who they were for. Jules? Sam? Herself? As if to drive her sadness back, he saw her expression harden and her next words came out harsh.

"*Love* her, did you? So what? What's the trick in loving someone who's perfect? What's love like that worth?"

"She was in my chair!" Sam blurted out, without ever having thought the words but now hearing them from his own mouth, understanding them, and then his own voiced cracked and the reservoir of grief and guilt he had bottled up inside so long finally broke through his defenses in a torrent and once free would not stop until it ran its course. He lowered his head, covered his helmet's faceplate with his hands, and sobbed, unable to find his voice for what seemed like a very long time.

Finally he breathed deeply and lowered his hands.

"In the very first attack, I couldn't get forward to my battle station because of hull damage. So she took over, manned my station, and died there."

He looked up at Atwater-Jones who sat rigidly upright, cheeks still stained with tears but eyes wide with surprise.

"Don't you get it? She was in *my* chair. It should have been *me*."

She openened her mouth to speak but he pushed up his helmet faceplate, cutting the connection. He sat there for a long time, panting for air, face hot, blood pounding in his ears, as hurt and confused and angry as he could ever remember being.

And as alone.

CHAPTER FORTY-TWO

19 January 2134
(three days later) ***(twenty-ninth day in K'tok orbit)***

"Stand easy, Captain Bitka. Would you care to sit?"

"Thank you, ma'am." Sam sat, trying not to grunt as he collapsed into the armchair at his side. After more than fifty days in zero gee he was unused to carrying a hundred kilos around on his legs. His balance wasn't very good yet, either.

Rear Admiral Victoria Crutchley, Royal Navy, was a tall, distinguished-looking woman. Sam guessed she was in her late fifties. She wore her reddish-brown hair long and gathered in a fairly elaborate bun-and-braid arrangement—the sort of hairdo unseen in the US Navy and not that common even in European service. It gave her an old-fashioned look, as if a relic of an era long gone.

Sam sat in front of the admiral's desk in her day cabin on the habitat wheel of FGS *Thüringer*, the heavy cruiser flagship of the newly formed Outworld Coalition Combined Fleet. With more reinforcements on the way, the word was she would soon be superseded by a US Navy vice admiral, but for now she was the boss. The admiral examined him with curiosity.

"Any word on the peace talks, ma'am?" he asked. It wasn't proper for a junior officer to speak to an admiral without being invited to, but with as much trouble as he was in he figured that was the least of his worries

"I understand the uBakai and uKa-Maat are balking at the demand for reparations. They don't want to rebuild our orbital spacedocks or repair the Quito Needle, which may derail everything before it's properly started. I suppose we'll see what happens next."

If the admiral had an opinion on that, Sam couldn't make it out. He wasn't sure what he thought, either. Yes, end this absurd, pointless, nightmarishly dangerous war as soon as possible. On the other hand, if people could just take a swing at Earth, kill thousands of people, screw up its spacefaring infrastructure for maybe a decade, and then step back and say, "Sorry, we quit," with no price to pay, what was to keep the next guy from trying the same thing?

"I suppose you are aware Commander Boynton recommended you be court martialed?" she said.

"Yes, ma'am. I found out when I was placed under arrest. Under the circumstances I don't see that you have many options."

"Humm," she said, and studied the smart surface of her desk, spending a moment arranging display windows on it. "Well, that's up to me, of course, as I would be the convening authority for such a court. Your Vice Admiral Stevens is due to arrive and take overall command within two weeks, but I see no need to put off resolving this.

"We have recordings of your address to your officers and senior chiefs on 8 January concerning Admiral Goldjune's sealed orders to the task force. Commander Boynton charges those remarks constitute insubordination, and furthermore undermined the authority of superiors in your chain of command."

"Understood, ma'am."

Crutchley frowned and glanced back down at the document on her desk but Sam had the feeling she wasn't really reading it, or at least not for the first time. The admiral raised her face, looked him in the eye.

"You were only to serve as acting captain until relieved, isn't that so?"

"Yes, ma'am, but my scheduled relieving officer was killed in the First Battle of K'tok."

"Yes, that would be this Lieutenant Commander Barger. And they didn't replace him because the task force was short of line officers. Also, you appear to have performed well in that action."

She slid another display document from the side of her desk to the center.

"Humm," she said, which Sam began to suspect was her favorite expression. "I have a recommendation for a commendation for you here, from Commander Atwater-Jones, the former task force N-2."

"Former, ma'am?"

Crutchley looked up. "Yes. The task force has of course been disbanded and replaced by the combined fleet, and I have my own smart boss. I'm used to working with him, but Aye-Jay has agreed to stay on as deputy N-2 once she's had a bit of convalescent leave. Probably all academic, as I imagine your Admiral Stevens will have his own staff."

Cassandra's nickname was Aye-Jay?

"Convalescent leave? Was she injured, ma'am?"

"Oh, nothing serious, a bit of hypothermia and some frostbite on her feet. Besides, having a ship blown out from under you always rates a spell of shore leave. You are . . . acquainted with her?"

She asked this question with her head cocked slightly to the side.

"Only in an official capacity, ma'am. We have holoconferenced a few times, half dozen. Aside from that we've never met."

Crutchley nodded and settled back in her chair. "She's an interesting officer, if rather unconventional. I suspect she would be a full captain by now but she doesn't seem to know when to keep her mouth closed."

"Oh, I can attest to that, ma'am," Sam said, but he regretted it as soon as he said it. Yes, there were times he wished she'd kept silent, that last time in particular. Still, everything she'd said had been true, hadn't it?

"She was sent out here as a form of Coventry, you know," Crutchley continued. "Exile, I suppose you would say. She needed one really brilliant intelligence coup to get back in good odor with the CDI—that's Chief of Defense Intelligence."

Crutchley paused and looked with particular intensity at Sam as she continued.

"Ironic how close she came."

"Close?" Sam said. "What would you call figuring out the jump drive scrambler and the Varoki plot behind this war?"

Crutchley leaned forward and squinted at Sam as if trying to tell if he were being disingenuous. "Perhaps I should read you the pertinent passage of her recommendation. I quote:

"*Captain Bitka organized the working group which discovered the error in our drive specification data base and correctly identified AZ Kagataan as the manufacturer of the drives on both USS* Theodore Roosevelt *and HMS* Furious. *Further, drawing upon his experience in his civilian occupation, he identified the manufacturer's so-called "cheat code" as the likely avenue for remote activation and reprogramming of the jump drives by ECM missile. While serving as acting N-2 of Task Group 1.2, his interrogation of the captured uKa-Maat Captain Lorppo gave us our first genuine insight into the nature of the forces arrayed against us."*

Crutchley looked up from her desk. "In other words, Captain Bitka, *you* are solely responsible for uncovering every important aspect of these intelligence coups, and before your sense of modesty prompts you to say anything, let me point out that to deny any detail of this would be to charge a serving officer of the Royal Navy with willfully falsifying an official report."

Sam had been about to do just that, but he shut his mouth. She had been in trouble with her bosses, which explained why she'd always told him he had a direct line to her for intelligence matters. She must have decided he was a source worth cultivating, someone who might deliver the intelligence gem she needed. In a sense, he had.

But it wasn't his working group, it was Moe Rice who had figured out the truth about *Bully*. Cassandra had followed up with *Furious*. Yes, he'd come up with the cheat code idea, but all he'd done with Captain Lorppo was show up. Lorppo had been ready to spill his guts as soon as his ship was disabled. Cassandra had won the lottery that would take her back home in triumph, and then she'd thrown her winning ticket away. Why would she do that?

"Do you have anything to add to Commander Atwater-Jones's report?"

Sam sighed. "No, ma'am. Nothing to add."

Crutchley sat back and pulled absent-mindedly at her right earlobe.

"Of course, given the sensitive nature of this information, her report is marked Most Secret, and we could not enter it in the official record of a court martial unless it were heavily redacted, perhaps to the point of incomprehensibility. But I also have a recommendation from the late Commodore Bonaventure concerning incorporation in training circulars of what he called 'The Bow-on Bitka Attack Profile.' Do people really call you that?"

Sam felt his face flush.

"Some . . . Unfortunately . . . Yes, ma'am. Not my idea."

"I'm glad to hear that. I also have a report from Brigadier General Irekanmi stating that without the confirmation that his two cruisers were not vulnerable to the jump scrambler, he could not in good conscience have ordered the attack which settled the battle in our favor. Your doing as well, I suppose, but also classified as secret.

"Well, stack the tactical innovation and your performance under fire on one side of the scale, and the unquestionably inflammatory remarks about a superior officer on the other, and I'm not sure what a court martial would say. Now, with Atwater-Jones's unredacted recommendation and Irekanmi's report . . . well. Nevertheless, these are serious issues raised by Commander Boynton, and they must be addressed—officially."

"I understand, ma'am. I offer no excuse."

Her lips pursed in irritation and for the first time she gestured impatiently, dismissively.

"*No excuse!* Junior officers and their automatic replies. God, I am so heartily tired of it. Heartily tired. Why is it so important to impale yourself on these tired formulae? Just once I would like to hear, 'Yes, mum, everything went tits up but 'ere's why.' Can you not bring yourself to give me one sensible excuse?"

Sam sat quietly for several long seconds thinking about Crutchley's question. He understood the intelligence and compassion from which it grew, but finally he shook his head.

"Sorry, ma'am, it's hard to explain . . . no, maybe it isn't. You see, I have an officer who turned out to be a liar and a cheat, and who abandoned his responsibility to his subordinates. If I asked him I'm sure he could give me plenty of excuses, and a few of them would actually be pretty good, but so what? What would they change?

"A couple months ago I was a different guy in a different world. But here in orbit around K'tok, when ships were coming apart around me and people I loved were dying, excuses stopped meaning anything. All my brain has room for now is solutions. If that's not enough . . . well, I don't know what to tell you. Sorry, ma'am."

She shook her head and turned away, eyes thoughtful but distant. For a while she said nothing, but then spoke.

"Someone once observed that an army is as brave as its privates and as skillful as its generals." She turned back to him. "I imagine that's true, but you know it's just the opposite for us. A navy is as skillful as its mariners and as brave as its admirals. Or I suppose its captains, when there are no admirals handy.

"Why did you reverse course at the final Battle of K'tok?"

"Ma'am?"

"When Brigadier General Irekanmi's cruiser division jumped to your proximity, the uBakai fleet turned away from you and toward it. Your force had already suffered casualties and considerable damage." She paused and glanced down at her desk for a moment, then directly back at him. "There were repairs to conduct, assistance to render to the other two surviving ships—I beg your pardon, *boats*—and yet you immediately ordered a course reversal to overtake and reengage the enemy."

"Lieutenant Commander Rockaway—" Sam started but Crutchley cut him off.

"No, Captain Bitka, the logs are quite clear. You issued your order to accelerate toward the enemy prior to any communication with Lieutenant Commander Rockaway. Why did you do so?"

Sam thought back to those moments on the bridge, trying to reconstruct the waves of conflicting emotions which had washed over him, which had struggled for control of his consciousness, his will, and as he did so he felt a rising flush of anger.

"Why? I'll tell you why, ma'am. To hit them, hit them again, and keep hitting them. All those tactical theories we studied in peacetime, all the intricate problems of long-range missile intercept solutions, it's all bullshit. What matters is getting in and hitting them, as quickly and as hard as you can, over and over until one of you dies or he gives up.

"The cruisers came and distracted the leatherheads, so I hit them from behind. I hit them because I needed them thinking about how badly we were hurting *them*. I couldn't let them have the time to think about how badly they'd hurt *us*. I hit them because we had them surrounded and off-balance. I hit them because *that's what we do*."

He realized he was leaning forward and almost shouting. He sat back in his chair and took a deep, unsteady breath.

"Humm," she said and then for several long seconds she sat staring at him, unmoving, her face unreadable. Finally she spoke again.

"This may surprise you, Captain Bitka—it certainly did me, but the facts are indisputable. There are only six surviving Human captains who have commanded a vessel in combat in this war. Ranjha of *Exeter* and Irekanmi of *Aradu* fought only at the Fourth Battle of K'tok. Rockaway, Swanson, and Kropotkin of the Fifth Destroyer Division fought at the Third and Fourth Battles. You commanded *Puebla* at First, Second, Third and Fourth K'tok. Captain Bitka, whether due to skill or extraordinary luck—and I rather expect it is both of those—you are currently the most combat-experienced captain in any Human space navy, and by a substantial margin. So when I ask you why you conducted particular tactical maneuvers, I assure you my interest is professional.

"As to this other business, you have two options: accept summary judgment by admiral's mast—which is to say by me—or trial by court martial. Which will it be?"

It took Sam a moment to realize what the admiral was asking. Either go before a court martial and take his chances, or put his entire future in the hands of a stranger—a Limey, at that.

"Before you decide, let me remind you that by accepting the judgment of an admiral's mast you would waive your right to trial by court martial *and* to any appeal of the judgment rendered. If you would like advice of legal counsel, I have a US Navy judge advocate officer waiting in an adjoining office with whom you can speak."

A court martial could turn . . . ugly, especially when it came time for Larry Goldjune to testify. Of course he'd known that all along, but now . . .

Sam looked at the three rows of ribbons on the admiral's uniform. He wasn't familiar with European decorations, or what the ribbons stood for, but he saw that two of them had battle stars—or at least on US ribbons they would be battle stars.

"Understood, ma'am. I don't need to talk to a lawyer. I'll take the admiral's mast."

CHAPTER FORTY-THREE

22 January 2134
(three days later) (thirty-second day since entering K'tok orbit)

Sam fidgeted as he stood in the badly worn VIP lounge at T'tokl-Heem Downstation, in the heart of the administrative capital on K'tok. He and his crew, apart from a small anchor watch he had left under the command of Lieutenant Goldjune, had come down the needle the previous day to begin their "medical liberty." They'd been in zero gee long enough they needed recovery time in plus-gee, and K'tok was the only liberty port available. A day had given him more time to regain his "dirt legs." They were still unaccustomed to carrying his weight and he tired quickly, but his balance was coming back. He just had to be careful not to stand too quickly. Now he was back at the downstation terminal, waiting for the next passenger capsule to arrive down the needle.

Two weeks earlier the street surrounding the downstation had been swept by small arms fire, and the terminal's interior still showed its effects: torn and oil-stained carpet, light composite sheets replacing the glass in half the exterior windows, temporary workstations standing in for the permanent stations which for some reason were still off-line. A lot had happened in the intervening time. In the face of the now-overwhelming forces in orbit over K'tok, the uBakai had declared T'tokl-Heem an open city and instructed the civilian municipal authorities to cooperate with the Coalition military government. Peace talks had restarted.

Troops and equipment had been pouring down the needle and had also landed by one-way shuttle gliders. What had been a desperate bridgehead held by a single understrength brigade was now a bustling military headquarters and logistical complex. In addition to fresh ground troops, crews of the other destroyers of DesRon Two, as well as rescued crews of the destroyed warships and auxiliaries, were getting their shot at convalescence liberty as well.

The next capsule down, due in five minutes, included one of the last contingents of naval liberty personnel, many of them just released from hospital. Cassandra Atwater-Jones would be in that capsule. Sam knew this because he had bribed a newly arrived and souvenir-hungry yeoman at the downstation transit office with a small piece of debris from the uKa-Maat salvo cruiser destroyed in the Third Battle of K'Tok, the first spacecraft ever destroyed by a US Navy vessel in wartime.

Actually, it was part of a plasma flux regulator from *Puebla*, mangled by uBakai buckshot much earlier, but who could tell?

Sam wasn't sure if he owed Cassandra an apology or the other way around, but he knew he owed her a thank you. He hoped the liter of scotch he'd paid a small fortune for, in cash as well as additional souvenirs, would do, at least as a down payment. He didn't know what he could do to patch things up between her and her former boss on Earth, though.

For that matter, he wasn't even sure why he was here. What did he expect from this encounter? As carefully as he searched his mind, though, he could not find any clearly-defined expectation, only an ill-defined feeling of anticipation.

He rose when the warning gong announced the car's arrival. He waited to the side by the offloading gate and felt an odd flush when he saw her in the crowd. He realized he had never seen her "in the flesh" before, never seen her as anything but a hologram. He'd thought of her as tall but was still surprised to see her head came up level with his. She wore a dark blue Royal Navy shipsuit, but not the custom-tailored one he had seen earlier. This one looked a size too large—probably what they had on the fleet auxiliary where she'd gotten her medical care. She carried a black musette bag over one shoulder but otherwise was unencumbered.

"Commander," he called out.

Several officers turned but Cassandra saw him, her eyes opened wide in surprise for a moment, and then she smiled—a little sheepishly, he thought—and waved. Limping slightly, she walked over to him,

"Ah, Bitka. How unexpected. I'm a bit startled you're even speaking to me after our last conversation. Well, you're not in irons, I see."

"Thanks to you, no," Sam said. "It's a pleasure to finally meet you face-to-face."

He realized he wasn't sure what to call her: Commander? Aye-Jay? Cassandra? He mentally shrugged and held out his hand. She hesitated, surprised at the gesture, he thought, but shook his hand, tentatively and then warmly.

He handed her the box.

"Welcome to K'tok."

"What's all this, then?" she said.

"Combined thank you and apology."

She glanced up at him quickly and then opened the gift box and saw the bottle, slipped it part-way out and held it up in the light to admire.

"Oh, *spendid!* I know exactly what to do with this, but you didn't owe me anything. Oh, you mean that letter to the admiral? I just told the truth."

Sam shook his head.

"*You* found out HMS *Furious* had Kagataan drives."

"Oh, rubbish. I *confirmed* the information about *Furious*, but you knew it was true as well as I did, and well before. And I am ashamed I did not think of the cheat code myself, especially after you'd made me so bloody angry about it."

"Yeah," Sam said, and felt himself color. "Sorry about that."

She shook her head and held up the bottle of scotch. "Paid in full, Bitka."

She took a step back and examined him with more care, squinting slightly in concentration.

"There's something different about your uniform—more stripy, somehow."

Sam laughed and held up his cuff. "Added a half-stripe between the two full ones. When it came time to decide what to do with me, Admiral Crutchley picked 'all of the above.' She gave me one letter of reprimand, two letters of commendation, and a field bump to lieutenant commander. It'll have to be confirmed whenever I rotate back home—and I don't have a lot of faith it will be—but until them I'm drawing O-4 pay."

"Well, better call me Cassandra then, since we're both commanders now, of a sort."

They paused as a party of tall Varoki in uBakai naval uniforms was led past under Marine guard. Several of the uBakai officers turned and looked curiously at Sam and Cassandra, and one nodded. Cassandra nodded in return and gestured to Sam, as if introducing him. The uBakai officer's ears spread wide in interest, but a Marine guard prodded him on his way with the business end of an assault rifle.

"Prisoners from the last battle," Cassandra explained. "We rode down the needle together. Several of them spoke English, and that one was actually a fellow intelligence officer."

"Bet that was an interesting conversation," Sam said and Cassandra laughed.

"As a matter of fact, it was. He was quite impressed that I actually *knew* the chap who baited his admiral into turning away from K'tok and pursuing your destroyers. Now he's gotten to see the officer in question."

Still smiling, she stuffed the scotch in her musette bag, shouldered the strap, and began walking toward the exit. Sam fell in beside her.

"Where's your luggage?" he said.

She held out the strap of her musette bag. "This is it, for the moment. Toiletries and a change of hospital-issue unmentionables. Everything else went with *Pensacola*. I don't imagine the shopping prospects are very good down here, but they must at least have some uniforms in stock somewhere. Do you know where to find the billeting office?"

"Sure, but won't you be spending your leave with Freddie? Colonel Barncastle? Or is he still laid up?"

Cassandra looked at him questioningly, and then realization came to her face, a mixture of surprise and amusement, and she stopped walking.

"What? *Freddie and I?* I don't think my cousin Maude would like that very much. Married, you know."

"Oh. Well . . . I suppose I just assumed . . . you know, when you said he was your friend."

"He *is* my friend. Really, Bitka, do you have a sexual relationship with every one of *your* female friends? It must be exhausting!"

"No, of course not. I . . . *no!*"

Sam felt his face flush again—*getting to be a habit*, he thought.

"Then why would you assume that, simply because I described Freddie as my friend, we were rolling about with each other?"

Good question. The truth was, as much as he had thought he ignored all the gossip about Cassandra's alleged promiscuity, it must have left some sort of tint on the lens through which he viewed her.

"Because I'm a bloody idiot?" he ventured.

"Well, there is that." She looked at him a moment and he thought he saw some disappointment back behind her carefully maintained facade. She turned and started walking away.

Sam felt suddenly off-balance. Reality was, it seemed, different than he had been imagining it for weeks, and for those weeks he'd had nothing much to go on *but* imagination. Now he had to strip away the gossamer web of fantasy from what was real, from what mattered, and he had to do it fast.

Why had he come here? Why did he find himself drawn to her company? Was it her intelligence and curiosity? Her sense of humor? The way she was completely unintimidated by anyone, especially her superiors? Was it the way she would sometimes look at him without turning her head, just moving her eyes, sharing a secret moment?

"Wait," he heard himself say.

She stopped and turned, her expression a mixture of caution and interest. *Interest.* That's something she'd taught him: the difference between idle curiosity and genuine interest.

"What is it, Bitka?"

He caught up and stopped beside her and his mind momentarily went blank. Yeah, what was it?

"Uh . . . I just wanted to say . . . about Lieutenant Washington—"

"I deeply regret that," Cassandra said, cutting him off, and he saw some of the color drain from her face. "It was no business of mine to judge you and what I said was unnecessarily cruel, especially given your circumstances."

Sam shook his head. "No, you don't understand. You were right. Yeah, maybe your timing could have been better, but you were right. I was idealizing her, not really remembering the person she was."

Cassandra nodded, her expression fixed, noncommittal. She turned away and resumed walking, out the wide portal of the downstation terminal and into the open air of the broad plaza filled with men and women in the uniforms of the different armed services of a half-dozen nations.

He caught up next to her and fell into step. The late afternoon air was cool as the day prepared to give way to evening, with long shadows tangled and snaky at their feet, and thin clouds in the west just beginning to turn pink.

"I mean," Sam said, "it's not the first time I've done something like that, put a woman up on some kind of pedestal. I've been thinking I'm in danger of making the same mistake again, so it's good to know there's a solution."

"Solution? Oh yes, *sex*," she said and nodded. "But what of your professional scruples? Doesn't that put you in a bit of a bind?"

"Oh, she's not in my chain of command."

Cassandra stopped and looked around the bustling plaza, studied the unbroken sea of uniforms, and shook her head.

"Here? I hardly see how that's possible."

"Well, the thing is . . . I don't take orders from Limeys."

She frowned thoughtfully and turned to look at his torso. She picked an imaginary speck of lint from his uniform, smoothed a wrinkle on his chest with the palm of her hand, let it rest there, and looked up at his face.

"We'll see about that."

HISTORICAL NOTE

The inspiration for this novel grew from James D. Hornfischer's stirring and detailed account of the naval campaign in the Solomon Islands (including Guadalcanal) in the second half of 1942—*Neptune's Inferno*, but I never intended to shift the events of that campaign wholesale to deep space. A few incidents may be familiar to students of the historical battles, but my main interest was in how officers and sailors—as well as the admirals who led them into battle with varying degrees of success—responded to a war which took them unawares and psychologically unprepared.

My reading concentrated on what it was like to live and work and fight in the smaller ships (and boats) of the Pacific fleet, and that included both memoirs and some novels written by veterans based on their experiences. The most useful were (in no particular order) Russell Sydnor Crenshaw Jr's *South Pacific Destroyer: The Battle for the Solomons from Savo Island to Vella Gulf*, and the same author's *The Battle of Tassafaranga*, Capt. Frederick J. Bell's *Condition Red: Destroyer Action in the South Pacific*, Forest J. Sterling's *Wake of the Wahoo*, William Tuohy's *The Bravest Man: Richard O'Kane and the Amazing Submarine Adventures of the USS Tang*, and of course Herman Wouk's *The Caine Mutiny*. Although it covers a different theater and a different set of naval traditions, I also found Nicholas Monsarrat's *The Cruel Sea* useful. People do not change so very much, and studying how they reacted and responded once will tell you much about how they will do so again.

A final reason for examining past events is they contain the seeds of future traditions. On February 27, 1942, the cruiser HMS *Exeter*—which two years earlier had successfully traded salvoes with the German pocket battleship *Graf Spee*—steamed out of Surabaya in the Dutch East Indies, bound for the Battle of the Java Sea which would be her final action. As she cleared the harbor mouth the crews of the accompanying US destroyers could clearly hear, blaring from her loudspeakers, the song *A* "Hunting We Will Go."

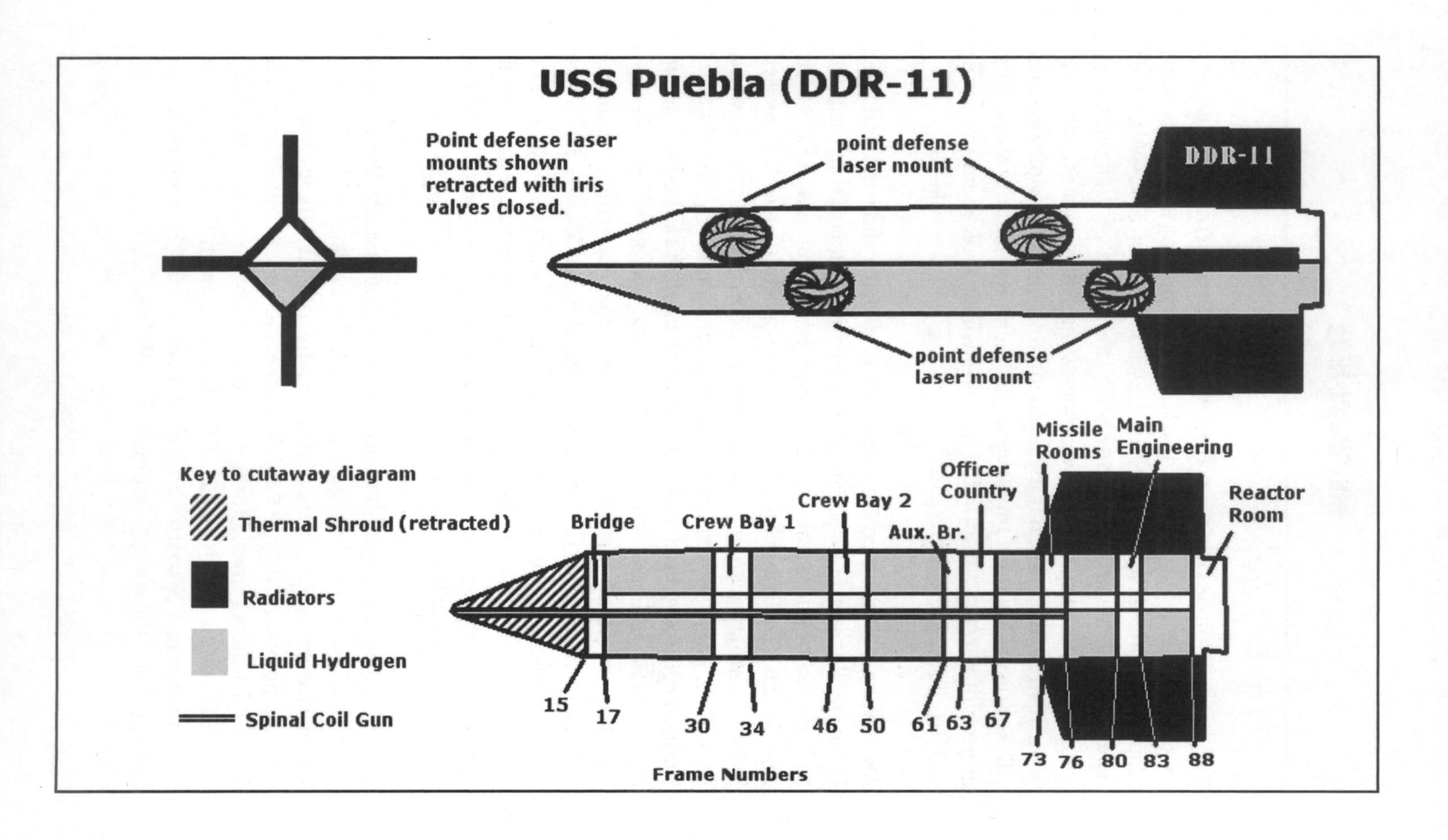
USS Puebla (DDR-11)
Point defense laser mounts shown retracted with iris valves closed.
point defense laser mount
DDR-11
point defense laser mount
Key to cutaway diagram
Thermal Shroud (retracted)
Radiators
Liquid Hydrogen
Spinal Coil Gun
Bridge
Crew Bay 1
Crew Bay 2
Aux. Br.
Officer Country
Missile Rooms
Main Engineering
Reactor Room
15
17
30
34
46
50
61
63
67
73
76
80
83
88
Frame Numbers

USS *Puebla* Described

USS *Puebla* (DDR-11) was constructed at the IOS (International Orbital Space-dock) facility from January 2130-July 2131. It was commissioned on September 17, 2131 and, following its shakedown cruise, joined Destroyer Division 3, Destroyer Squadron 2, assigned to the destroyer carrier USS *Hornet* (CDS-2).

As a destroyer rider (DDR), Puebla does not have an interstellar drive and is transported from one star system to another by its carrier, along with the other eleven DDRs of DesRon 2, nor does it have its own artificial gravity spin habitat. On long-term deployments the crews of the twelve destroyer riders are birthed in the habitat wheels of USS *Hornet*. The DDRs can operate autonomously within a star system for protracted periods, but after two to five months crews begin to experience adverse health effects from prolonged weightlessness.

Physical Description

Length: 140m

Average Beam: 18m (square cross-section, 15 meters narrowest, 21 meters broadest)

Mass (empty): 5,700 tons

Mass (loaded, excluding reaction mass): 8,400 tons

Mass (loaded, including reaction mass): 18,000 tons

Interior Volume: approximately 32,000 cubic meters

- 3000 cubic meters crew habitation and work space
- 1500 cubic meters storage
- 4500 cubic meters machinery and access space
- 23,000 cubic meters liquid hydrogen reaction mass (9,600 tons)

Crew: 95

- 14 Officers
- 12 Chief Petty Officers
- 50 Petty Officers
- 19 Mariner strikers

Machinery

1 x magnetized target fusion (MTF) reactor and direct thruster, 2.25-GW output

- Drive exhaust velocity at maximum thrust: 500,000 m/s (500 km/s)
- Energy input per ton/second of thrust: 83 Kj
- Reaction mass expended per ton/second of thrust: 0.02kg
- Maximum thrust: 27,000 tons
- Reaction mass expended per second at max thrust: 540kg (32.4 tons/min)
- Reaction mass endurance at maximum thrust: 296.3 minutes (4.9 hours)
- Acceleration at maximum mass: 1.5G

"Average" acceleration of 2.05G at average mass, (i.e. with half of total reaction mass remaining)

1 x 375-MW thermoelectric multi-cycle Seebeck generator for converting thermal output of fusion reactor, stellar radiation, and internal waste heat, to electricity for ship power and recharging SMESS. (9-min recharge time at full power)

4 x thermal radiator panels (12m x 30m) mounted aft, for discharging unrecoverable waste heat.

6 x low-signature magneto-plasmadynamic (MPD) maneuver drives with a combined thrust of 8,500 tons (83.356525 Mn).

- Drive exhaust velocity at maximum thrust: 100,000 m/s (100 km/s)
- Reaction mass expended per ton/second of thrust: 0.1 kg
- Energy input per ton/second of thrust: 200 Kj
- Maximum thrust: 8,500 tons
- Full thrust endurance on fully-charged SMESS: 117 seconds
- Reaction mass expended per second at max thrust: 0.85tons
- Theoretical acceleration of 0.64G at average mass

2 x superconducting magnetic energy storage systems (SMESS) with combined rated capacity of 200 Gj (sufficient to power the MPD thrusters at full power for 117 seconds, or to generate 100 pulses from point defense lasers or 50 discharges from the spinal coil gun).

Performance

Provides up to 480 Mt/sec of thrust, or approximately 36,266 G/seconds of thrust at average mass, (604 G/minutes, 10.1 G/hours) on direct fusion thrusters.

MPD thrust using fully-charged SMESS: 8,500 tons for 117 seconds (average acceleration of 0.64G).

Combined sprint thrust at average mass: 2.69G

Armament

1 x Mark 19 coil gun, spinally mounted, 32cm bore, 2.8-Gj peak muzzle energy, for launching torpedoes and inert munitions.

38 x DSIM-5B, block four "Fire Lance" torpedoes, each with thirty composite laser rods pumped (once, very briefly) by the 180-kt warhead. Each laser rod generates a single pulse for 2-4 nanoseconds with a total energy of approximately one gigajoule.

- Warhead: 180kt thermonuclear
- 30 composite laser rods, independently targetable
- Each laser rod generates a single 1 GJ pulse for 2-4 nanoseconds

(Virtual) focal array: 0.26 meters
Wavelength: 15 Å (X-ray)
Effective range: 4,000-6,000 km
8 x 1.5 Gj point defense pulse lasers
(Virtual) Focal array: 20 meters
(10 meters actual focal diameter)
Wavelength: 1000 Å (ultraviolet)
Effective range: 7,000-10,000 km

8 x 1.5 Gj point defense pulse lasers

(Virtual) Focal array: 20 meters
(10 meters actual focal diameter)
Wavelength: 1000 Å (ultraviolet)
Effective range: 7,000-10,000 km